Crossed Bones

Crossed Bones

JANE JOHNSON

VIKING
an imprint of
PENGUIN BOOKS

VIKING

Published by the Penguin Group

Penguin Books Ltd, 80 Strand, London WC2R ORL, England

Penguin Group (USA) Inc., 375 Hudson Street, New York, New York 10014, USA

Penguin Group (Canada), 90 Eglinton Avenue East, Suite 700, Toronto, Ontario, Canada M4P 2Y3
(a division of Pearson Penguin Canada Inc.)

Penguin Ireland, 25 St Stephen's Green, Dublin 2, Ireland (a division of Penguin Books Ltd)

Penguin Group (Australia), 250 Camberwell Road, Camberwell, Victoria 3124, Australia
(a division of Pearson Australia Group Pty Ltd)

Penguin Books India Pvt Ltd, 11 Community Centre, Panchsheel Park, New Delhi – 110 017, India

Penguin Group (NZ), 67 Apollo Drive, Rosedale, North Shore 0632, New Zealand
(a division of Pearson New Zealand Ltd)

Penguin Books (South Africa) (Pty) Ltd, 24 Sturdee Avenue, Rosebank, Johannesburg 2196, South Africa

Penguin Books Ltd, Registered Offices: 80 Strand, London WC2R ORL, England

www.penguin.com

Published in 2008

I

Copyright © Jane Johnson, 2008

The moral right of the author has been asserted

Set in 12/14.75pt Monotype Dante
Typeset by Rowland Phototypesetting Ltd, Bury St Edmunds, Suffolk
Printed in Great Britain by Clays Ltd, St Ives plc

A CIP catalogue record for this book is available from the British Library

HARDBACK ISBN: 978–0–670–91731–0
TRADE PAPERBACK ISBN: 978–0–670–91732–7

www.greenpenguin.co.uk

To Abdel: *tanmirt*

To the Right Honorable Lords of his Majestie's most
honorable Privy Council
Haste, haste, posthaste
Plymouth, the eighteenth of april, eight in the eve
– Thomas Ceely, Mayor

May it please yr honors to bee advertized that this daie I have heard
of certaine Turks, Moores, & Dutchmen of Sallee in Barbary, which lie
on our coasts spoilyng divers such as they are able to master, as by the
examination of one William Knight may appeare, whose report I am
induced the rather to believe, because two fisherboats mentioned in hys
examination were very lately found flotyng on the seas, having neither
man nor tackle in them . . .

    I am also credibly informed that there are some thirtie saile of
shippes at Sallee now preparing to come for the coasts of England in
the begynnyng of the summer, & if there bee not speedy course taken to
prevent it, they would do much mischeef.

    Hereof I thought it my dutie to inform yr honors.

        And so I rest,
        Yr honors in all dutie bounden,
        Thos. Ceely, Mayor
        Plymouth, the 18th daie of april 1625

I

'There are only two or three human stories, and they go on repeating themselves as fiercely as if they have never happened before, like larks that have been singing the same five notes for thousands of years.'

I had scribbled this down in a notebook after reading it in a novel the night before I was due to meet Michael and was looking forward to slipping it into our conversation at dinner, despite knowing his likely reaction (negative, dismissive – he was always sceptical about anything that could even vaguely be termed 'romantic'). He was a lecturer in European literature, on which he took an uncompromising post-structuralist stance, as if books were just meat for the butcher's block, mere muscle and tendon, bone and cartilage, which required flensing and separating and scrutiny. For his part, Michael found my thinking on the subject of fiction both emotional and unrigorous; this meant that at the start of our relationship we had the most furious arguments, which hurt me so personally that I was brought to the edge of tears; but now, seven years in, we were able to bait one another cheerfully. Anyway, it made a change from discussing, or avoiding, the subject of Anna, or the future.

To begin with it had been hard to live like this, on snatched moments, the future always in abeyance, but I had got used to it little by little, so that now my life had a recognizable pattern to it. It was a bit pared down and lacking in what others might consider crucial areas, but it suited me. Or so I told myself, time and time again.

I dressed with particular care for dinner: a devoré silk blouse, a tailored black skirt that skimmed the knees, stockings (Michael was predictably male in his preferences), a pair of suede ankle-strap

3

shoes in which I could just about manage the half-mile to the restaurant and back. And my favourite hand-embroidered shawl: bursts of bright pansies worked on a ground of fine black cashmere.

I've always said you have to be an optimist to be a good embroiderer. A large piece (like the shawl) can take six months to a year of inspired and dedicated work. Determination too: a dogged spirit like that of a mountaineer, taking one measured step at a time rather than panicking at the thought of the whole immense task, the crevasse field and the headwall of ice. You may think I exaggerate the difficulties: a bit of cloth, a needle and thread – how hard can it be? But once you've laid out a small fortune on cashmere and another on the silks, or you're under a tight deadline for some nervous girl's wedding, or an exhibition, and you must not only design and plan but also complete a million stitches, I can tell you the pressure is palpable.

We were meeting at Enoteca Turi, near the southern end of Putney Bridge, a smart Tuscan restaurant which we usually reserved for celebrations. There were no birthdays looming, no publications or promotions, that I knew of. The last would, in any case, have been hard for me to achieve, since I ran my own business and even the word 'business' was something of a stretch for my one-woman enterprise: a tiny craft shop in the Seven Dials. This was more of an indulgence than a money-making concern. An aunt had died five years ago, leaving me a decent legacy; my mother had followed two years later, and I was the only child. The lease on the shop had fallen into my lap; it had less than a year to run, and I hadn't decided what to do with it at the end of that time. I made more money from commissions than from the so-called business, and even those were more of a way of passing time, stitching away the minutes while awaiting my next tryst with Michael.

I arrived early. They do say relationships are usually weighted in favour of one party, and I reckoned I was carrying seventy per cent of ours. This was partly due to circumstances, partly to temperament, both mine and Michael's. He reserved himself from the world most of the time; I was the emotional profligate.

4

I took my seat with my back to the wall, gazing out at the other diners like a spectator at a zoo. Mostly couples in their thirties, as we were: well off, well dressed, well spoken, if a bit loud. Snippets of conversation drifted to me:

'What is *fagioli occhiata di Colfiorito*, do you know?'

'So sad about Justin and Alice . . . lovely couple . . . what will they do with the house?'

'What do you think of Marrakech next month, or would you prefer Florence again?'

Nice, normal, happy people with sensible jobs, plenty of money and solid marriages; with ordered, comfortable, conforming lives. Rather unlike mine. I looked at them all embalmed in the golden light and wondered what they would make of me, sitting here in my best underwear, new stockings and high heels, waiting for my one-time best friend's husband to arrive.

Probably be as envious as hell, suggested a wicked voice in my head.

Probably not.

Where was Michael? It was twenty past eight, and he'd have to be home by eleven, as he was always at pains to point out. A quick dinner, a swift fuck: it was the most I could hope for; and maybe not even that. Feeling the precious moments ticking away, I began to get anxious. I hadn't allowed myself to dwell on the special reason he had suggested Enoteca. It was an expensive place, not somewhere you would choose on a whim; not on the salary of a part-time lecturer, supplemented by desultory, amateurish book-dealing, not if you were – like Michael – careful with your money. I took my mind off this conundrum by ordering a bottle of Rocca Rubia from the sommelier and sat there with my hands clasped around the vast bowl of the glass as if holding the Grail itself, waiting for my deeply flawed Sir Lancelot to arrive. In the candlelight, the contents sparkled like fresh blood.

At last he burst through the revolving door with his hair in disarray and his cheeks pink as if he'd run all the way from Putney Station. He shrugged his coat off impatiently, transferring briefcase and black carrier bag from hand to hand as he wrestled his way out of the sleeves, and at last bounded over, grinning manically, though not quite meeting my eye, kissed me swiftly on the cheek and sat down into the chair the waiter pushed forward for him.

'Sorry I'm late. Let's order, shall we? I have to be home . . .'

'. . . by eleven, yes, I know.' I suppressed a sigh. 'Tough day?'

It would be nice to know why we were here, to get to the nub of the evening, but Michael was focused on the menu now, intently considering the specials and which one was most likely to offer value for money.

'Not especially,' he said at last. 'Usual idiot students, sitting there like empty-headed sheep waiting for me to fill them up with knowledge – except the usual know-it-all big mouth showing off to the girls by picking a fight with the tutor. Soon sorted that one out.'

I could imagine Michael fixing some uppity twenty-year-old with a gimlet stare before cutting him mercilessly down to size in a manner guaranteed to get a laugh from the female students. Women loved Michael. We couldn't help ourselves. Whether it was his saturnine features (and habits, to boot), the louche manner or the look in those glittering black eyes, the cruelly carved mouth or the restless hands, I didn't know. I had lost perspective on such matters long ago.

The waiter took our order, and we were left without further excuse for equivocation. Michael reached across the table and rested his hand on mine, imprisoning it against the white linen. At once the familiar burst of sexual electricity charged up my arm, sending shockwaves through me. His gaze was solemn: so solemn that I wanted to laugh. He looked like an impish Puck about to confess to some heinous crime.

'I think', he said carefully, his gaze resting on a point about two inches to the left of me, 'we should stop seeing each other. For a while, at least.'

So much for discussing larks. The laugh that had been building up burst out of me, discordant and crazy-sounding. I was aware of people staring.

'What?'

'You're still young,' he said. 'If we stop this now, you can find someone else. Settle down. Have a family.'

Michael hated the very idea of children: that he would wish them on me was confirmation of the distance he wanted to put between us.

'None of us are young any more,' I retorted. 'Least of all you.' His hand went unconsciously to his forehead. He was losing his hair and was vain enough to care about it. For the past few years I'd told him it was unnoticeable; then, as that became a bit of a lie, that it made him look distinguished, sexy.

The waiter brought food; we ate it in silence. Or rather Michael ate in silence; I mainly pushed my crab and linguini around my plate and drank a lot of wine.

At last our plates were cleared away, leaving a looming space between us. Michael stared at the tablecloth as if the space itself posed a threat, then became strangely animated. 'Actually, I got you something,' he said. He picked up the carrier bag and peered into it. I glimpsed two brown-wrapped objects of almost identical proportions inside, as if he had bought the same farewell gift twice, for two different women. Perhaps he had.

'It's not properly wrapped, I'm afraid: I didn't have time, all been a bit chaotic today.' He pushed one of these items across the table at me. 'But it's the thought that counts. It's sort of a *memento mori*; and an apology,' he said with that crooked, sensual smile that had so caught my heart in the first place. 'I am sorry, you know. For everything.'

There was a lot that he had to be sorry for, but I wasn't feeling strong enough to say so. *Memento mori* – a reminder of death. The phrase ricocheted around my mind. I unwrapped the parcel carefully, feeling the crab and chilli sauce rising in my throat.

It was a book. An antique book, with a cover of buttery-brown calfskin, simple decorative blind lines on the boards and four raised, rounded ridges at even intervals along the spine. My fingers ran over the textures appreciatively, as if over another skin. Closing myself off from the damaging things Michael was saying, I applied myself to opening the cover, careful not to crack the brittle spine.

Inside, the title page was foxed and faded. *The Needle-Woman's Glorie*, it read in bold characters, and then, in a fine italic print, *Here followeth certain fyne patternes to be fitly wroghte in Gold, or Silke, or Crewell as takes your plesure. Published here togyther for the first tyme by Henry Ward of Cathedral Square, Exeter 1624.* And beneath this, in a small, neat hand, *For my cozen Cat, 27th Maie 1625.*

'Oh!' I cried, ambushed by its antiquity and its beauty. An intricate pattern filled the verso page. I tilted it towards the light in a vain attempt to examine it better.

Michael had just said something else, but whatever it was flew harmlessly over my head.

'Oh,' I exclaimed again. 'How extraordinary.'

Michael had stopped talking. I was aware of a heavy silence, one that demanded a reaction.

'Have you heard any of what I've been saying?'

I gazed at him wordlessly, not wanting to answer.

His black eyes were suddenly almost brown. Pity welled in them. 'I'm so sorry, Julia,' he said again. 'Anna and I have reached a crucial point in our lives and have had a proper heart to heart. We're going to give our marriage another go, a fresh start. I can't see you any more. It's over.'

I lay alone in my bed that night, sobbing, curled around the book, the last thing in my life that would carry a connection with Michael. At last, sheer exhaustion overtook me, but sleep was almost worse than being awake: the dreams were terrible. I surfaced at two thirty, at three; at four, retaining fragments of images – blood and shattered bones, someone crying in pain, shouts in a language I could not understand. Most vivid of all was a sequence in which I was stripped naked and paraded before strangers, who laughed and pointed out my shortcomings, which were many. One of them was Michael. He wore a long robe and a hood, but I knew his voice when he said, 'This one has no breasts. Why have you brought me a woman with no breasts?' I awoke, sweating and shamed, a creature of no account who deserved her fate.

Yet, even as I loathed myself, I felt disorientated, detached, as if it were not me suffering the indignity but some other Julia Lovat, far away. I drifted back into sleep, and if I dreamed again, I do not remember it. When I finally woke up, I was lying on the book. It had left a clear impression – four ridges, like scars, on my back.

2

The doorbell rang. Michael crossed to the window and looked down. In the street below a man stood, shifting awkwardly from foot to foot as if in dire need of a visit to the lavatory. He was dressed too warmly for the weather, in an old wool Crombie and cord trousers. From his bird's-eye vantage point Michael could see for the first time that the top of Stephen's head was almost bald, save for a thin covering of comb-over which looked almost as if it had been glued down. He looked comically out of place in this part of Soho, where young men paraded up and down in muscle shirts, ripped denim or leather and knowing smiles, and tourists got vicarious thrills by entering, if only for an hour or so, the cruising scene.

Old Compton Street hadn't been quite so outré or lively when Michael first moved into the flat: he felt now, watching the tide of young life passing by outside, as if he were looking through a window into someone else's party, one to which he was too old and straight to be invited. Especially now that he was back on the narrow path, playing the good husband.

'Stephen!' he called down, and the balding man lifted his head, shading his eyes against the sun. 'Here!' He threw his keys out of the window. 'Top floor.'

Not just his keys either, he thought ruefully as they left his hand, but Julia's too. He supposed he should return them to her now that it was over. But it just seemed so . . . final.

The arrival of Stephen Bywater interrupted his thoughts.

'You could have come down to the shop,' he said accusingly, wiping the sweat off his forehead. Four flights of rickety stairs, and he wasn't a young man. 'It's not as if Bloomsbury's more than ten minutes' walk.' He struggled out of his Crombie as if to emphasize his discomfort.

'I didn't want people interrupting us,' Michael said quickly. 'You'll see why in a moment. Sit down.'

He pushed a pile of newspapers and textbooks off the threadbare sofa to make space for his visitor. Stephen Bywater looked at the stained canvas dubiously, as if he didn't want to risk his trouser seat to it, then balanced himself uncomfortably on the edge, his bony knees and elbows sticking out at all angles like those of a praying mantis.

'It'll be worth your while,' Michael went on excitedly. 'Just wait till you see this. It's quite extraordinary, a real gem, unique. Really, there's no point in my wittering on. Take a look at this and see for yourself.'

From a black carrier bag on the coffee table he extracted a small, brown-paper-wrapped parcel. This he handed to Bywater. His visitor opened it gingerly, removing a little pale, calf-leather-bound book with flecks of gold tooling on the spine. He murmured appreciatively, turning it to examine the back board, the rough paper edges, the binding.

'Very nice. Sixteenth, seventeenth century.' He opened the front cover with infinite care, turned to the title page. '1624. Remarkable. *The Needle-Woman's Glorie*. Heard of it, of course, but never actually laid my hands on a copy. Very pretty. A little light spotting and some old handling marks, but generally very fine condition.' He grinned up at Michael, showing teeth as yellow as a rat's. 'Should fetch a few quid from a specialist collector. Where did you say you got it from?'

Michael hadn't. 'Oh, a friend. Selling it on behalf of a friend.' This wasn't the entire truth, but it wasn't too shy of it. 'Look inside, look properly,' he urged impatiently. 'It's a lot more extraordinary than you might think at first glance.'

He watched avidly as the book-dealer blew on the pages and separated them gently, making faces as he did so. 'Well, it's all there,' he said at last. 'The patterns and slips and all.'

Michael looked deflated. 'Is that all you can say? Come on, man, it's unique, a . . . a palimpsest! Can't you see the secret text, written in the margins and between the patterns? It's not easy to make out, I'll admit, but you can't have missed it!'

Bywater frowned and reapplied himself to the book. Eventually he closed it and looked at his friend oddly. 'Well, there's certainly no palimpsest here, dear boy. This is paper, not vellum: there's no sign of scraping, no scriptio inferior, nothing that I can see. Marginalia, well, that's quite a different matter, as you should know. Now marginalia in the author's own hand, that would add some value, possibly double it –'

'It's not in the author's hand, you idiot: it's written by some girl. It's a unique historical document, and it's probably priceless! You must need glasses –'

Michael snatched the book roughly from the dealer's hand, opening it at random, and flicked through it frantically as if the writing he had seen the previous day might magically reappear.

After a minute, he put it down again, his face like thunder.

Then he ran to the phone.

3

I knew Anna, Michael's wife, from university. There, we had been the Three Amigos, me, Anna and my cousin Alison, as unlike from one another as you could imagine. Where Anna was petite and doll-like, Alison and I were of solid Cornish stock, raised on rich dairy products and pasties. When I let it down, I could sit on my blonde hair, while Anna's was short and black and model-perfect; and Alison's shoulder-length hair was chestnut brown, then red, then black, then scarlet and back to brown again, depending on whether she was teaching English or Drama. Together we made the perfect symbiotic unit for getting through the trials of university and our first post-degree jobs – Anna in a bookshop, Alison teaching, me in an endless series of cafés and bars.

Alison and I messed around, took drugs, got drunk, got laid, had fun, but Anna made shapes with her life: she took the threads of her experiences and wove them into something purposeful. She worked hard, and it showed. She was now a successful fashion-magazine editor, earning a small fortune, although ironically she was the only one of us who never really needed the money. Her family were, from what I could gather – though she was quite secretive about her background, and a bit shy around me and Alison and our noisy and frequent financial crises – really rather posh.

After college it was, I suppose, inevitable that we should drift apart. Alison met and married Andrew, for a start. I have to admit I was never that keen on Andrew. He was one of those ruddy, sweaty, rugby-playing men, hearty and over-confident, with a tendency to grab your knee, or something else, in the middle of a conversation, depending on how drunk he was. But he had a wicked sense of humour and no facility for embarrassment, and he made

Alison happy, for a while at least, and so I did my best to make friends with him. They took me in time after time when I got my heart broken by one unsuitable man after another, poured drink down me, and Alison would look on indulgently as Andrew flirted clumsily with me while I laughed and wept and choked on my wine. When he cheated on my cousin and caused her to come running to me in tears, feeling that her life had come apart and could never be put back together again, I was livid with him and did not speak to him for the best part of two years.

How ironic. For shortly after that I met Michael.

How well I remember it all. Anna, a little breathless, flushed, embarrassed. 'Julia, come and have a drink. There's someone I want you to meet. My fiancé, in fact.'

Well, she'd kept that quiet. I was astonished, and rather hurt, by the secrecy and suddenness of it all. She'd never even had boyfriends at college. When the rest of us were making the most of our newfound freedom, Anna was writing essays, researching, revising. While I was cheerfully experimenting with sex, Anna stayed focused and celibate. She took life a lot more seriously than the rest of us. After college she had ploughed her energies into her career: she had a plan, she said, and it certainly seemed to be working for her. 'I'll marry in my thirties,' I remember her telling me, 'once I'm properly established at the magazine and can take time off to have children.' And I'd scoffed and reminded her that life was what happened to you while you were making plans. So there she was, at thirty, announcing her engagement, the next step in her life-scheme.

'Are you pregnant?' I'd teased her.

She was indignant; but went very pink. 'Of course not,' she said.

I wondered if she had even slept with him.

There had to be a flaw, since there is no such thing as perfection, in life or art or anything else. Perfection tempts fate. I remember reading that ancient Japanese potters always worked a tiny flaw into each pot they created, for fear of angering the gods, and Anna must surely have tempted some impish spirit somewhere in the pantheon, to have been punished for her hubris with Michael. And in having me for a friend.

Unfortunately for all of us, the attraction between me and Michael was instant. We made electric eye-contact, and, at one point during that first evening at a crammed little bar in Covent Garden, he brushed his hand, quite deliberately and with devastating effect, against my bottom. Three weeks later, after a lot of meaningful looks and some furtive touching, we slept together.

'I can't tell Anna,' he said to me that same afternoon, as if it were a foregone conclusion; and I, missing my first and best opportunity to unravel the developing tangle, lay there concussed by sex and guilt, and agreed. After that it became increasingly unthinkable to admit our treachery.

I was a bridesmaid at the wedding.

As we lay together on snatched Wednesday afternoons in Michael's Soho flat when he wasn't teaching, summer sunlight slipping through the louvred blinds, slicing our bodies into lit and shaded slivers, he would confide to me, 'She's not very physical, Anna. I always feel I'm imposing myself on her.' At the time I felt triumph, but my confidence was misplaced. Anna's cool distance intrigued and challenged him: she remained an unseized prize, an elusive country he had only fleetingly glimpsed but never claimed as territory. Whereas I had been staked out, explored, tied down – often literally. Sometimes when we made love, Michael would wind my long, pale hair in his hands, using it like reins. Once he tied me to a hotel bedstead with it. To cut me free, we had to use the pair of miniature sewing scissors I kept in my handbag with my embroidery kit, he had made such a mess of the knots.

I recalled that particular incident now, four years later: it seemed an apt metaphor – an omen perhaps – for how things had turned out. Michael had knotted my life into a vile tangle, and then cut me free. I was angry with him; furious in fact, before admitting to myself that I had to take at least as much of the blame for the situation. Anna was, after all, my friend. I had felt ashamed of the affair, my betrayal of our friendship, from the start. But shame is an uncomfortable emotion, one we don't much like to confront. The pressures of Anna's work made this easier than it might otherwise have been, and I had become a master of excuses in avoiding dreaded *tête-à-têtes* and dinner *à trois*. Racked by the knowledge of how I was betraying her, day by day, hour by hour, I found I could not bear her company. She was so happy; and only I knew the truth that would render that happiness rotten and hollow.

Now that Michael and I had come to an end, I wasn't sure I could ever endure to see her again.

The day after our break-up, exhausted by weeping, I took myself out of London to walk the cliffs of the south coast, feeling much of the time like throwing myself over them, but never summoning the courage. I left my mobile phone behind in the Putney flat, to ensure I did not weaken and call him. Instead, in the time when I was not stalking mechanically along footpaths, impervious to the magnificent scenery, I devoted myself to a new embroidery design I had been meaning to start for some weeks.

It was for a wall hanging, and therefore to be worked on stout linen twill, in coloured wools rather than silks. Ever since the Elizabethan and Jacobean periods this type of work has been known as crewel work, from the old Welsh word for 'wool'. Which seemed fitting. I spent many bitter hours playing on the unfortunate pun in my head as I stitched. Crewel world, crewel fate, crewel to be kind, crewel and unusual . . . I had already marked out on the fabric a coiling monochrome pattern of stylized acanthus leaves, with flares of colour where flowers burst through the foliage. Very traditional in style, after the Flemish Verdure tapestries I'd seen in the Victoria & Albert Museum, the delicate infilling of the leaf design inspired by the filigree of Venetian needlepoint lace. It was a large piece, and would easily cover the space where the beautiful, framed black-and-white photograph of Michael had hung in my bedroom. The photo, I had ceremonially burned in the back garden before leaving the flat; but the wall annoyingly retained its ghostly shape, and it would be a constant reminder of the absence of both man and picture.

Embroidery is an improbable hobby for someone as disordered as me; but it's the very precision of it that attracts me, the illusion of control it offers. When engaged in stitching a new pattern I can't think about anything else. Guilt, misery, longing, all flee away, leaving just the beautiful microcosm of the world in my hands, the flash of the needle, the rainbow colours of the thread, the calming exactitude of the discipline. It was the wall hanging that saved my sanity in the days following our break-up.

I returned to London a week later, somewhat restored to myself, to find my answering machine flashing crazily. *You have twenty-three new messages*, the digital voice informed me. My heart thumped. Perhaps Michael had had second thoughts about finishing the relationship, perhaps he wanted to see me. I pushed this possibility firmly away. He was a bastard, and I was well rid of him. Before I could backslide, I deleted all the messages. If there had been any-thing crucial, the caller would phone again, I reasoned. I knew that if I so much as heard Michael's voice, my resolve would crumble.

I walked into the bedroom, where all was still in the disarray in which I had left it: the bed unmade, discarded clothes scattered across the room. I cleared everything away, filled the washing machine and came back to make the bed.

The book Michael had given me lay in the tangle of sheets. It weighed beautifully in my hand, its soft calfskin cover warm, as if it were still alive. I opened it at random, folding the ancient paper back with care, and was confronted by a pattern for a slip: a deli-cate repeated motif of a twining vine designed to be executed in blackwork, which, the author suggested, *would doe beste in a quaife or a caule, or to edge a handcarcheef.* The rest of his instructions were obscured beneath a defacing cross-hatch of pencilled markings. Annoyed, I carried the book to the bedside lamp and squinted at it under the round of golden light.

Someone had written all over the page in a tiny, archaic hand. Long *f* instead of *s*, and that sort of thing; it was hard to read and in places blotched and faded, but, from the words I could make out, it had nothing to do with embroidery at all; not unless the author had a taste for samplers themed on blood, and death. I retrieved a magnifying glass from the bureau, fetched a notebook and pencil of my own, turned to the frontispiece and began to make a sort of translation of what I had found.

This daie 27th of Maie in the yeare of Our Lord 1625 markes the sad deth of oure kyng James, & the 19th yr of the birth of hys servant Catherine Anne Tregenna & I must give thanks for that & for the gifte of this booke & plumbagoe writing Sticke from my cozen Robert with which he sayes I may record my own slippes & paterns. That shall I doe but like my myStresse Lady Harrys of Kenegy I wille also keep herein my musings, for she tells mee it ys a goodly dutie & taske for the mynd to thus practiss my letters . . .

4
Catherine
June 1625

Matty woke her just after dawn. 'Come down to the parlour,' she said. 'Jack Kellynch is down there, with Thom Samuels and your cousin Rob.'

'Robert?' Cat blinked, still half asleep, and struggled upright. Pale light was forcing its way past the curtains she had made from an old petticoat to hang over the draughty attic window. 'What is Rob doing here with those rogues?'

Matty made a face. 'Don't say that, they're good lads.'

The Kellynch brothers ran a pilchard boat out of Market-Jew, sometimes joining the seiners and coming back in with the tuck-net full of fish, but more often disappearing for weeks on end, no one knew where, and turning up again much richer, with sly grins and winks for the girls, flashing foreign gold. Matty sighed over Jack; Cat thought him a blackguard and a fool, if a handsome one. Thom Samuels had not even that advantage: he boasted but a single eyebrow, black and lowering, right across his forehead. She laughed. 'Smugglers and brigands, the pair of them.'

But Matty was already out of the door. Cat heard her footsteps, heavy on the creaking boards outside, then thundering down the stairs. Sir Arthur and Lady Harris had their quarters in the quiet west wing of the house; the servants were in the east, where the noise from the adjacent farm was loudest: if Matty hadn't woken her, then the dogs and cockerel would. She slipped out of bed. Her stiff dark-green working dress and corset were arranged over the back of the single chair, her linen stockings lying over them like a pair of empty legs. No time for all that lacing and strapping: she straightened her shift and grabbed up her shawl: a vanity, for it was her best, hand-embroidered with a cross-hatch of briar roses in fine wool.

Why was Robert here, and at such an hour? She knew that Margaret Harris had a soft spot for her cousin, and encouraged him to come to the house far more than his duties about the farm might require. With his tangled yellow hair and bright blue eyes, Rob towered over the Mistress by a good fifteen inches. He towered over most folk; Lady Harris teased him that he was descended from the giants of Carn Brea, who had dragged their captives up the hill and sacrificed them on the great flat rocks there, before stripping them of their gold and jewels, which they hid deep in the granite caves beneath. But Cat could never imagine her gentle cousin taking anyone captive, let alone beating their brains out on the stones. It was quite strange enough that he should appear in the company of Kellynch and Samuels, and at a time when the Mistress was still abed.

Curiosity piqued, she slipped her bare feet into her cold boots and headed for the stairs. She found Matty and the dairymaid, Big Grace, peering furtively through the crack in the parlour door. Male voices drifted out into the passageway, along with the sharp smell of small beer and a fug of smoke from the kitchen fire. In low tones, one of the lads said something Cat could not quite catch. The girls listened intently, straining for every word of the hushed conversation within. Grace squeezed Matty's hand, and the two exchanged a horrified glance. Cat grinned and tiptoed across the flagstones, laying a hand on Matty's shoulder for balance so that she too could peer into the parlour. Matty made a high-pitched yelp like a rabbit taken by a fox.

Jack Kellynch wrenched the door open. Small-boned and dark, he had the brown skin and bright eyes of the Spaniard his mother was reputed to be – taken, it was said, off a merchantman wrecked on the Manacles, along with a cargo of fortified wine, a chest of gold and silver plate, and bales of Orient silk bound for the old Queen. The silk and most of the plate had made its way to Her Majesty; but the wine had most mysteriously vanished, along with the Spanish merchant's daughter.

'Well, now, Matty,' he said, giving her a hard look, 'you should know no good comes to those who listen where they shouldn't.'

Matty flushed a powerful red and looked at her feet, unable to frame a sentence. For her part, Big Grace could do no more than grip Matty's arm, her eyes round and awed, her mouth hanging open. She was only thirteen, a touch simple, and tiny despite her familiar name.

Cat strode forward. 'What are you doing here, Jack Kellynch? Matty and Grace have reason, being honestly employed in this house; but you, as far as I know, are honestly employed by no man and have no business in our parlour at break of day.'

Kellynch regarded her sardonically. 'My business is my own and not something that should concern a Danish wench.'

Cat tossed the tawny hair that had earned her this inaccurate insult and stepped past him into the parlour, ready to berate her cousin Robert for allowing such an invasion of ne'er-do-wells. In the smoky, firelit room beyond, however, were three figures: not only Robert Bolitho and Thomas Samuels, as she had expected, who sat at the table; but also a third man standing in the shadowed corner, leaning against the wall. He wore a dusty travelling cloak, and his boots were muddy. It was only when he took a step forward and the lantern's light fell upon him that she realized it was the Master, Sir Arthur Harris himself, his expression grim.

'These men are here at my invitation, Catherine, bringing me information.'

Cat dropped a desperate curtsy, head spinning. 'I beg your pardon, sir, I thought you were at the Mount –'

'And that gives you licence to appear half dressed in company?'

There was nothing she could say to that; so wisely she said nothing, dropping her regard just in time to catch Robert nudging a discarded hat to conceal an object that shone silver against the dark and pitted oak of the table.

When she lifted her puzzled gaze to his face, Robert gave her a fiercely eloquent look. *Go away*, the blue eyes blazed at her. For a moment she stood her ground; then, 'Excuse me, sir,' she muttered and fled the room.

She felt Jack Kellynch's eyes on her back and worse, all the way up the stairs.

'Now, then, Catherine,' Margaret Harris said as firmly as she could, 'my husband tells me you were indecorous this morning, appearing in full view of his companions in little more than a chemise. He has asked me to have a word with you: we want no scandal here at Kenegie; and I promised your mother that I would be as a mother to you in her stead.'

Cat's head came up at the mention of her mother. Her father, John, a militiaman for Sir Arthur in the garrison on St Michael's Mount, had been taken by the plague that had swept through the region two years previously, leaving Jane Tregenna and her daughter without income. It was generally whispered that Mistress Tregenna had been cursed by piskies, for since the birth of Catherine there had been no other children; Cat herself suspected there had been little love lost between her parents. Margaret Harris had offered them both positions at the house, but Jane Tregenna regarded herself as far too much a lady now to be a servant again. Instead she had taken herself off to her brother Edward's well-appointed home in Penzance, leaving Catherine to be taken under the Mistress of Kenegie's wing, whereby she was generously offered not only the income of a bodyservant, but more education and encouragement than any girl of her upbringing had ever been bred for. Cat knew her mother harboured wild ambitions for her; she probably had her eye on one of the Harris boys. If she lost her position at the manor, she knew she would never hear the last of Jane Tregenna's bitter tongue.

'My pardon, my lady. I had not meant to give offence. Matty . . . I heard a disturbance below and was concerned that there might be intruders.'

'Going half naked downstairs to investigate does not seem to me the wisest course of action. Had there been ruffians down there, you would have endangered yourself and placed me, as your guardian, in a most difficult position. Do you understand that?'

Cat nodded slowly. 'But, my lady, I was not "half naked"; I held a shawl over my shift to guard my modesty, I swear.'

The Mistress of Kenegie smiled. 'And would that have been your best shawl, Catherine, bearing the crewel roses?'

Cat had the grace to blush. 'It was.'

Margaret Harris appraised the girl silently. Cat was nineteen now and comely, even though her hair was that unfortunate golden-red. Her mother, Jane Tregenna, was small and dark, worn out by life's disappointments; her dead husband had been a crabbed, brown-haired man with the small, close features of the Lizard villages (where it was well known they had gone on all fours till the crew of a foreign vessel wrecked on the coast had settled among them and improved their stature and physical development). An unlikely marriage that had been, and one that hinted at compromises made under pressure: Jane was a Coode, a proper old Cornish family: reputable, deep rooted, well respected. The Tregennas were farmers from Veryan and Tregeare; John had been a third son without even a land-living to fall back on, which was why he had signed himself up as a militiaman. Not the best prospect for a pretty girl from a decent family; and certainly there was no clue in that parentage to the provenance of Catherine's fox-red hair and long, straight limbs. Nineteen was a dangerous age: the girl herself should be married, and soon. She had seen how her sons William and Thomas watched Catherine as she moved around the house.

'You saw your cousin this morning?'

Cat frowned. 'Yes, my lady.'

Margaret Harris smoothed her skirt. 'He is a good worker, Robert. Sir Arthur has often said as much. It would not surprise me if he were to offer him the position of steward when George Parsons retires.' She watched the girl's face for a reaction. 'Of course, he would be more likely to progress thus were he settled, with a family,' she pressed.

'Oh, Robert has a great many family hereabouts,' Cat said airily. 'There are Bolithos and Johns in every hamlet and farmstead from Gulval and Badger's Cross to Alverton and Paul. He'll never leave the area: he has not that type of ambition.'

'That's not quite what I meant,' the lady said quietly. 'He is a gentle and an able young man: not to put too fine a point on it, quite a catch for a country lass.' She fixed Cat with her lucent grey eyes until her meaning came clear.

'Oh.' Cat stared at the patterned rug that stretched between them: the Turkey rug, her mistress called it. It was brightly woven, with gorgeously dyed motifs in cream and crimson and umber, and it glowed like a living thing among the dull, earth hues of the rest of the room: the wood-panelled walls, the granite floor, the heavy, dark walnut and mahogany furniture. She would give her eye-teeth for wool like that to work with. How beautiful the tapestries and embroideries of the Orient must be; how she would love to see them, but it was likely she would never be closer to such work than she was at this very moment, standing on the Turkey rug. She raised her head and looked the other woman steadily in the eye. 'My cousin is a good man, and I am as fond of him as if he were my brother,' she said firmly.

Lady Harris decided that it was not yet the right moment to pursue the subject; but she was determined that before the summer was out, Catherine Tregenna would be Catherine Bolitho.

Robert came to find her later that day. 'Will you take a walk with me, Cat?' he asked.

It was four in the afternoon; Lady Harris had taken her daughters Margaret and Alice over to Trevaylor to visit the Reverend and Mrs Veale. Smiling, she had made it clear to her servant that she would have no specific duties for her to perform until they returned after dinner that evening.

Cat shaded her eyes, looking past him across the knot garden and the courtyard towards the open country beyond. Sun spangled the waters of the distant bay and made a fairytale castle of the Mount. High up above the hills, towards Lescudjack, a kestrel hovered, drifting lazily on a current of warm air in pursuit of rabbit or vole. Mare's tails were strewn across the summer sky: the weather boded fair for another day, and a soft breeze shimmered in the bright leaves of the sycamores and oaks that clothed Rose-morran's valley. She could find no reason to refuse his offer; nor did she wish to, in truth: she found the house stifling on these hot summer days, and Robert was handsome company: she had no wish to wed him, but it did her pride no harm to be seen walking out with him. Besides, she was keen to discover exactly what it was that had been discussed in so secretive a fashion in the parlour that morning.

She transferred her gaze to her cousin. Robert was watching her much as the kestrel had been watching for its rabbit: hungrily, his keen blue eyes searching her face for every reaction. 'Thank you, Robert,' she said at last, drawing out the moment. 'That would be most kind. Pray wait for me here while I change my shoes.'

There was a small window halfway up the main staircase. Cat glanced out of it as she passed only to see her cousin twisting his hat in his big hands, as if he were wringing a chicken's neck. He jammed it on his head, took it off, stuck it in his pocket, then wiped his forehead with a large coloured kerchief.

Nervous, she thought, satisfied. And well he might be, for she would never say him yea.

In her quarters, she took her time, changing out of her working dress into a pretty, full-skirted petticoat of white cotton decorated with Flemish lace. She had bought it at Penzance market with the little she had left after handing the best part of her wages to her mother. Around an overdress of blue wool, laced up the front, with a wide white linen collar, she wrapped the crewel-work shawl, with its pretty tracery of twining flowers and leaves. It was a pity to spoil the delicate effect of these pastel shades with her heavy leather boots, but even Cat's vanity could not countenance spoiling her only pair of satin slippers on a country walk. Sighing, she laced the boots tightly and dabbed a little rose-water carefully on her neck and bosom, where the sun on her skin would surely waft it to poor Rob's nose.

He was pacing the cobbles when at last she appeared, but he had the wit not to chide her for being tardy. More sensibly, he said, 'You look most becoming, Cat.'

He won a smile for that, but she still corrected him with 'Catherine'.

His face fell: she could almost feel the change in his expression as a tangible thing between her shoulder blades as she walked past him towards the lane that ran by the farm cottages.

'Let's go up to Castle an Dinas,' she called back to him. 'I want to blow the cobwebs out of my head.'

'Are you sure? It's a long way.'

'I do have two legs, in case you hadn't noticed,' she snapped back. She quickened her pace, elbows pumping.

He had noticed, of course. The thought of them made him shiver inside. He fair ran after her. 'I do have to be back by sundown to help Will with the cows.'

'Best not be wasting time in idle chatter, then,' Cat declared. She strode out, her skirts swinging wildly.

They took the footpath across the meadow towards Gariss and Hellangrove. Celandines, scabious and ox-eye daisies studded the grass through which they walked like fallen stars. Cat imagined how she would pick them out in a frieze: little cross stitches of yellow and blue and white against a field of emerald-green.

To their left the land rose gently through brambled coverts to wooded hills loud with birdsong. The creamy heads of cow-parsley and old man's beard laced the hedgerows, and a long day's sunshine had released the hot, peppery scent of herb Robert and the tang of wild garlic into the air. Gulval Downs rose up in front of them, golden with gorse. Invisible overhead, larks poured their hearts out into the azure sky. Cat looked back at her companion, moodily switching the heads off the taller flowers with a willow wand. 'Come on, you laggard! Have you got lead in your boots?' She took off running, feeling like the hoyden her mother would have called her had she seen her.

Forty minutes later they were on the hilltop, in the teeth of a stiff southerly coming in off the sea that flattened the grass on the headland and carved the gorse stands into hawk trees. Cat's hair whipped back and forth as she sat on a granite cairn in the centre of the earthworks. Eroded and grassed over down the centuries, its warlike origins lost in time, the ancient hill fort curled protectively around her, as if she sat cupped in the hand of the past. Something about the scene made Rob's heart swell inside him.

'You might be a warrior queen, sat upon your throne. Stay there . . .'

She turned to watch him running away from her until he disappeared from view. Discomfited, she frowned; then turned her attention to the sheet of shining sea stretching away to the ends of the world, as it seemed. What lay out there, beyond the horizon, she wondered. Surely marvels beyond price and monsters beyond imagining, exotic lands and other ways of life, where women of talent and ambition were not confined to sweeping and darning and feeding the chickens . . .

Robert interrupted her reverie. He held something gingerly in his hands: a circlet of gorse and briar rose and tiny ferns fashioned so that the golden flowers glowed through the spiky foliage like jewels. 'A crown for a queen,' he said, and bent to offer it to her on one knee, sunlight pooled in his blue eyes like liquid sky.

'Well, you'd better crown me, then,' she said peremptorily, though the gesture pleased her.

He stood and set it gently on her head, and, as he did so, the wind took a tress of her hair and set it blowing free like a great red pennant. He caught it and wound it around his hand, wondering at its silky texture and the fiery sparks trapped within its length. 'They built these fortresses in King Arthur's day against the coming of the Danes. Reckon that must make you a prize nabbed from the ships of the sea kings, then,' he said, grinning. 'Not proper Cornish like the rest of us.'

Annoyed by this inference, Cat retrieved her hair from him. 'Why would I want to be Cornish like the rest of you? Cornwall's a poor little county full of brigands and idiots and superstitious old biddies.'

Robert looked pained. 'And which am I – brigand or idiot?'

She shrugged dismissively, avoiding the question. 'What were you discussing with the Master this morning?'

Rob's eyes took on a hooded expression; careful, evasive. 'Nothing important. Jack and Thom had a bit of information for him, is all.'

'Information about what?'

'Oh, shipping and the like.'

'Shipping? What would Sir Arthur care about shipping? You forget: I saw you; and I saw you hide something.'

But he was not to be drawn. 'You can see Carn Galva from here,' he said wonderingly, gazing at the menacing serrations on the distant skyline. 'The Giant's Chair. I never knew that.' He turned, his blond hair blowing around his broad, open face. 'And Trencrom and Tregoning and the Godolphin Hills. No wonder the chieftain who built his fortress here chose this spot.' He shaded his eyes. 'I can even see the Scillies. 'Twould be hard to take the folk here unawares, by land or sea. It's said they lit beacons from the Mount to here and Trencrom, to Carn Brea, then St Agnes Beacon, and on to the Great Stone on St Bellarmine's Tor; and from there Cadbarrow, Rough Tor and Brownwilly, all the way through to Tintagel, to warn the king that the raiders were coming. Arthur and the other nine kings reached Land's End by forced march in two days and gave them battle near Vellan-Druchar. So many were slaughtered, 'tis said, the mill ran on blood rather than water that day, and not a single Dane escaped.'

'Pity he wasn't around to save Mousehole and Newlyn from the Spanish,' Cat replied. Her uncle had been among the men who had followed Sir Francis Godolphin on that fateful day in July 1595 to stand against the Spaniards who had overrun the village of Mousehole and fired the church at Paul. Outnumbered and ill armed, the Cornish had been forced to retreat under the bombardment of the galleons' guns and wait for reinforcements while the invaders burned the better part of four hundred houses in Newlyn and Penzance. Her parents' generation still spoke of the attack in hushed voices: it was an outrage, an insult that foreign invaders should set foot on Cornish soil, after the glorious defeat of the Armada, a defeat dealt out largely by West Country men.

'Anyway,' she said, shooting him a sharp look, 'you still haven't answered my question.'

Robert stared out across the sea, his jaw set. 'Are you using the book I gave you?'

'Yes. It was most kind of you to remember that I admired Lady Harris's copy. It is most gratifying to have one of my own,' she said stiffly. 'Some of the slips are very useful, and I have devised a few variations which the Mistress says are exceeding pretty.'

'Good. I am glad to hear that you are practising your craft.'

'I mean to be a master embroiderer and join the Guild.'

Rob grinned despite himself. 'And how will you do that from the depths of darkest Cornwall, Catherine? I fear geography is against you. And will you change your sex? The Broderers' Guild is for *master* embroiderers, not for little chits, be they ever so clever with a needle.'

'So you gave me the book merely to humiliate me?'

Rob took her fingers between his two huge hands. 'Never, Cat, believe me. I am more than proud that you have your commission from the Countess of Salisbury.'

She pulled her hand away as if burned. 'How do you know about that? It is a secret. I have been told to say nothing of it.'

'Lady Harris mentioned it; she could not contain her delight: to work the altar cloth for the Howard family's own church is a great privilege, and that she played her part in the Countess's decision to give a Cornishwoman such a prestigious task has given her no little satisfaction.'

Cat bit her lip, colouring. 'It is a great responsibility. I have never undertaken anything so large or so ambitious before – I have not even planned it out yet.'

Rob's eyebrows shot up. 'You mean to design it yourself?'

'Of course.' She glared at him, daring him to question her right to do so.

It was unheard of that a woman should take it upon herself to create her own grand design; in the natural order of things this was the place of a man. It was why he had bought her the book: to aid her work and ease her way, to enable her to copy a master's designs. Everyone knew that women had not the capacity for abstract thought; in this, as in so much, men dictated and women followed.

He suspected, rightly, that, even as Lady Harris had recommended her protégée to the Countess for the task of embroidering the altar frontal, the agreement had been that Cat would be a journeywoman, working to the pattern created by one of the master embroiderers who made their living travelling between the great houses selling their designs. Unfortunately, no one had told Cat this. One day, he thought, she will overstep herself and take a great fall. He hoped he would be there to catch her when she did. 'As long as you are sure,' he said quietly.

'Quite sure. But until I know I can do it, I do not want to discuss it. Let us instead talk of the blade that was laid out on our parlour table, the big curved silver knife that you tried to cover with your hat.'

Robert caught his breath, taken by surprise. 'The Master said we were to discuss it with no man.'

Cat laughed. 'Unless it has escaped your notice, Robert Bolitho, I am no man.' She watched him, as unblinking as her namesake.

Rob sighed. 'For the Lord's sake don't tell Matty or the entire county will know by sunrise,' he warned her.

Cat crossed herself, solemn at last. 'On my father's bones, I swear.'

'You know the Newlyn boat – the *Constance* – that went missing last week?'

She nodded. 'Crew of eight, including Nan Simon's cousin Elias? She's come in – they're alive and well? Nan's been half sick with worry.'

Robert shook his head. 'There's no good news. She came drifting in through the fog to Mousehole this morning. Jack and Thom were down there, attending to . . . some business. They caught her bumping against the rocks outlying St Clement's Isle, with not a soul aboard, the sails hanging limp and the nets unused.'

Cat frowned. 'But it's been fair weather this past week, there have been no waves high enough to overturn a boat.'

'And certainly not a well-made vessel like the *Constance*. Thom said the sides were raked, though that might have been the rocks; but Jack swears the gunwale was split by something like a grapple.'

Cat's eyes went wide. 'And the blade?'

'Left between the planking in the bilges.'

'It looks like no blade I've ever seen.'

'Nor I, and I like it not.'

'What does Sir Arthur say?'

'There's been an increase in attacks by privateers on shipping off the south coast. But up to now it's been mainly unaccompanied merchantmen that have been struck and their cargoes taken. Nothing unusual about that, and heaven knows our own boys have been guilty of similar attacks on French and Spanish merchant ships all through the British Sea; but I cannot understand what profit there is to be made in attacking a fishing skiff.'

Cat shuddered. 'Perhaps 'tis sheer mischance?'

Robert made a face. 'Perhaps. But mischance does not explain the presence in the boat of a Turkish blade.'

'Turkish?'

'Truly, Cat, I can say no more without earning the Master's ire. I have already said too much. Rumours spread like wildfire in this region, and Sir Arthur is concerned that there will be widespread panic over something that may prove to be no more than an isolated incident.'

She gripped his arm. 'Rob, are you telling me there are Turkish pirates in these waters?' Her eyes shone. 'How . . . exotic. I would dearly love to see one.'

Robert stared at her in disbelief. 'I am sure you say such things to pain me, Catherine. For myself, I pray to God that I never have the misfortune to encounter such a creature, for they are little more than beasts. Some of the tales I have heard . . .' He shook his head at Cat's avid expression.

'Come now, the day draws on, and I must take you back. I have the excitement of the cows to attend to and no doubt you have some duties to carry out for Mistress Harris's return; and we'll have no more talk of pirates.'

Cat untangled the gorse circlet from her hair. With the next great gust of wind she tossed it seawards, and together they watched it buffeted till it sprang apart and rained its flowers down upon the rocks.

5

13th of June. This daie markes the marriage of oure new kyng Charles with Henrietta, Princesse of France & Navarre; & also the discoverie of the fishing bote Constance off Mousbole rocks, all crewe lost & her gear cut lose. None knoe the fate of these men but a Turkiss sword was found stucke in her woode & Rob has made mee sware to say nothynge of Pyrats or Turks lest rumor spred feare. So I wryte my secret here & this Booke & I alone shall share it. I have heared the Turks are blacke men with shaven heades & crewel wayes. Rob sayes they are no better than wyld beasts, but I woulde trewlye love to see one for my selfe …

I put the book aside, astonished. I don't know what I had been expecting, other than notes on the patterns that the book contained, thoughts about the colours of thread and the type of stitch one might use to execute the design, but this sudden window into the past was like a glimpse of treasure.

I found myself wondering whether Michael had read any of Catherine's cryptic, faded entries, or had merely glimpsed them and seen them as defacements, maybe even beaten down the price with the dealer because they spoiled the edition? I could easily imagine him doing just that, complaining about a small or imagined flaw, always seeking a bargain, a way of saving money. I could not count the number of times I had turned away, embarrassed, as he haggled with some hapless stallholder or car-boot seller. The idea of him trawling through his favourite antiquarian bookshops of Bloomsbury seeking a suitable farewell gift for me made me nauseous. How long had he been preparing for that moment? How long had he and Anna been back on 'good terms' – and just exactly what did that mealy-mouthed little phrase mean? I imagined the pair of them, dark-haired and olive-skinned, similar in build, elegantly intertwined . . . had this rapprochement overlapped with our trysts for days, for weeks or for months? I ran to the bathroom and threw up till my eyes and nose burned with bile.

When I came back to my bed, feeling shaky and void, the book was waiting for me on the lamp table. My notebook lay beside it, filled now with my own scribbled interpretations of Cat Tregenna's journal entries. I had pored over the strange formations of her letters, the bizarre spelling and the unfamiliar sentence structures of another age for over three hours, filling six pages of my notebook, though my handwriting was in no way as neat as that of the young embroiderer, being marred with crossings out, underlinings, question marks where I could not make sense of a word. Hardly a pretty artefact for someone to discover four hundred years hence. And yet, for all the difference between our times, I felt a strong connection with Catherine Anne Tregenna; and not just for our shared love of embroidery. I too had grown up in Cornwall and, like her, had dreamed of escape.

On a new sheet of paper I wrote her name, then idly sketched a curling vine around the capitals: a simple cross-stitch exercise to work on a sampler, the sort of thing with which a young girl might have begun her needlework education in times past. I wondered if Catherine had done this very thing: picking out her name in a simple, plain colour before embellishing it with leaves and flowers. My knowledge of Jacobean needlework told me that it would have been unlikely that she would have been able to work with anything very fine for her first attempts. If she had come from a poor family, even one that had some social aspirations, she would probably have been limited to practising on hessian or sacking and roughly dyed hanks of homespun wool she had had to colour herself with vegetable dyes culled from the herb garden and hedgerows – woad for blue, madder for red and broom or onion skins for yellow. And most certainly she would have had no access to the pretty skeins of coloured silks, like those that as a child I had kept obsessively in their box arranged according to the spectrum, that glided so smoothly through all those squares of perforated binkercloth we used in sewing classes at school.

I finished my sketch and held it at arm's length. It was then that I saw what had been right beneath my nose: Catherine Anne Tregenna, with the capitals thus emphasized: CAT – Cat. I laughed aloud. I had wondered why she was not Kate or Cath; Cat seemed a remarkably modern sort of moniker for a seventeenth-century girl. I felt a sudden warm affection for this long-dead woman who had imposed her own lively chosen familiar name upon the world. Did she live up to her self-appointed totem animal, I wondered. Was she neat and sly, eyes slightly aslant, ever watchful? Did she move soft-footed around the manor house where she worked and smile quietly to herself at the foolishness of others? I could imagine her, small and dark, curled in a big wooden chair on cushions she had made herself, under the light of a narrow window, picking out the tail feathers of a fabulous bird with needle and bright threads on a length of pale linen – a runner for a dressing table, perhaps, the edging for a bedcover, or even the altar cloth so briefly mentioned. That commission intrigued me. What fun it would be to track down such a treasure and know a little of its provenance, maybe even follow the progress of its creation through the pages of the little book.

I passed my hand affectionately across the age-foxed title page. 1625: the best part of four centuries away. At thirty-six and unmarried, in the seventeenth century I would have elicited both pity and ridicule. A spinster; an old maid: of no use to anyone and with no place in society. Pretty much the same as now, which was not particularly cheering; but what did I really know about the early seventeenth century? For me, it occupied a rather hazy space between the glorious Tudors and the Civil War and Restoration. Before continuing with my translation of Catherine's journal, I should surely make an effort to set it in a bit more context.

I went to examine my bookcase to see if there was anything there that might educate me further. From college, some poetry and Shakespeare plays with commentaries, Penguin guides to literature, a little gentle philosophy – nothing of much specific use. On the dusty bottom shelf of the bookcase in the spare room I found a set of children's encyclopedias that probably dated from my grandmother's schooldays. I hefted them out on to the floor. They gave off a whiff of mildew and face powder, the very smells I associated with being a child in the house my grandmother shared with her crabby older sister, and I wondered whether the scent was real or imagined, a memory that had imposed itself on the object by association. I had loved these encyclopedias and spent hours poring over their neatly engineered pull-out sections with dissections of an apple, a frog and a fly; diagrams of a steam engine and a medieval castle. I flicked through one of the volumes, finding in a short space long, detailed and illustrated articles on the history of art, Greek mythology, human anatomy, the Trojan War and the English feudal system. Two volumes further on (past the discovery of penicillin, wildlife on the savannah, Chaucer and Galileo) I found just what I was looking for.

I put the other five volumes back on the shelf and took the sixth to my living room, settled myself into the leather sofa and started to read.

Forty minutes later I felt replete with information. For what purported to be a children's compendium of knowledge, the encyclopedia had proved a challenging and frankly spicy read, full of surprising details. I had known that James I was the son of the executed Mary, Queen of Scots; what I had not known was that he had a Danish wife, and flaunted such a succession of male favourites that when he inherited the English throne it was openly voiced that 'Elizabeth was King; now James is Queen!' Nor had I known that James had come poor and unpopular to the throne, with a seriously extravagant spending habit which drove the country so deeply into debt that he was forced to sell titles and land and had stopped paying the navy – asserting his divine right to do as he pleased and dissolving Parliament rather than risking criticism. He had attempted to marry off his surviving son, Charles, to the rich Spanish Infanta at a time when England was fiercely Protestant; the

Spanish had high-handedly rejected the marriage proposal and a humiliated Charles had eventually married Princess Henrietta Maria of France some months before the death of his father, coming to the English throne in March 1625 at the age of twenty-five. He was just six years older than Catherine Tregenna.

Even more interesting was the fact that King James's chief adviser had been Robert Cecil, Earl of Salisbury. Wasn't the Countess of Salisbury mentioned as the source of Cat's commission? In a sudden fever of excitement, feeling like an amateur detective, I went back to *The Needle-Woman's Glorie*.

10th daie of Juleye. Todaie has been the most vexing daie of my lyf, enow to dryve a sowle to distraction. All the wrath of the Lord has fallen uppon mee, as if I am punished for my temeritee in desiring better for my selfe. I am felynge so encholered I can not think of ony thynge, what with Will Chigwine's wyf Nell callyng mee a Temptress & the Harlot of Babylon & Mistress Harrys takyng her parte, & now my cozen forced uppon mee . . .

6

Catherine

June 1625

Cat smoothed a hand across *The Needle-Woman's Glorie*. Dawn light slanted through the window, illuminating her intent expression and making a bright halo of her red-gold hair. She had woken with an image twining through her mind like a skein of ivy, at once obdurate and fragile: she felt that if she so much as blinked, it might disperse into the air, and she was determined that should not happen. For, even as she surfaced from sleep, she had recognized the image for what it must surely be: the design for the altar cloth, come to her like a divine visitation.

It had been weighing heavy upon her these many weeks, the responsibility for this commission; not just for its aesthetic challenges, but also for the chance of advancement and escape it might represent. Secretly, Cat harboured a dream: that if she created an altar frontal that pleased the Countess of Salisbury sufficiently, then that august personage might decide that Catherine Tregenna was a necessary ornament to her life and home, and bear her away to her grand London house. Given such a possibility, Cat knew that she would leave her position at Kenegie, leave Penwith; leave Cornwall and everyone and everything in it with barely a backward glance. She would gladly exchange the southerly winds and sparkling seas, the gorse-grown hills and lichen-rosetted granite of her homeland, for life in a properly aristocratic house. The gossip and backbiting of Kenegie stifled her; her duties for Lady Harris – no matter how pleasant her mistress might be – bored her; and the likelihood that her cousin Robert might be the best husband she could aspire to made her fair weep with frustration. She was born for greater things: her mother had always told her so, and she believed it with every bone in her body.

She had gone to sleep pondering the altar cloth, its theme, its design, the materials she would use; and a strange alchemy appeared to have taken place during the night, drawing desire and inspiration together into visual form. The vision shimmered in her head: but could she capture that form and set it down before it escaped her? Her whole future might depend on her ability to do so, and the thought of that set her hand to trembling.

She took a deep breath, firmed her resolve and swept the writing stick in a light, curving line from top to bottom of the page. The first mark on the virgin surface broke the spell; and suddenly she was free. The outline of the tree's trunk was quickly achieved, her hand moving swiftly and decisively, marking in branches here and there, twining in graceful counterpoint to one another; a flourish of leaves, a spray of berries, buds, flowers. The design unfurled itself like a young bracken frond – elegant, curvilinear, iconic – its symmetries both powerful and reassuring. From a base of twisted roots out of which peered tiny creatures – a hare, a frog, a snail – the Tree of Knowledge stretched heavenwards. Adam on one side, Eve on the other, the apple hung above them. In the branches near Eve's head, the serpent writhed and smiled.

'Cat, Cat!' came a voice through the crack of the door. 'Why have you not come down? Are you sick?'

Sighing, Cat shut the book and pushed it out of sight underneath the bedclothes. The other girls already thought she had ideas above her station; it would not help the ease of her day to have them sniggering about her unnatural aspirations. 'I am coming,' she called back. 'I will be down directly.'

'Cook won't have you in the kitchen if you don't go now: she's got dinner to prepare for the Master's guests. You'll have nought to break your fast, and we've already been told there'll be no noonmeat today, that we must take now what bread and cheese we need to get us through till supper.' Matty sounded aghast at the idea: she was a chubby girl, and to miss a meal was close to being the worst thing she could imagine.

'What guests are those?' Cat asked, her interest piqued.

There was a moment of puzzled silence from the corridor, then:

'Don't rightly know. Just some men come to see the Governor. Do hurry up, or there'll be nothing left.'

Cat rolled her eyes. Trust Matty not even to inquire. 'In truth, I am not hungry,' she said, pulling on a clean chemise, then hesitated. If Sir Arthur had guests, perhaps she should make a greater effort. She tossed her plain work dress aside and out of her oak chest drew a dress of scarlet wool that had belonged to her mother. 'Come, help me with my corset.' It would do no harm to have two pairs of hands narrow her already small waist.

Matty pushed the door open gingerly. 'You are sure you are not ill?' she said again, looking over the older girl as if searching for signs of pox or plague.

Cat caught her too obvious scrutiny. 'No, you goose. Now hurry, or I will be late waiting on our mistress, and you know how she frets.'

Lady Harris was indeed in a fretful mood, but it had nothing to do with the tardiness of her maidservant that morning.

'I do wish my good husband would give me a little more warning before inviting important guests to the manor,' she declared, as Cat took up the poke stick and began the complex business of plaiting her mistress's ruff. 'I already had my day planned out, and now I must oversee Cook and set the dining room to rights; and the best linen is all packed up and is no doubt the breeding ground of a thousand moths; and Polly is suffering with a cruel cold and cannot serve; and I must dress in a manner befitting my husband's post. Oh, and the box must be trimmed; the garden is in a state of disarray ever since we lost poor Davey, and what will Sir Richard think of us, coming from Lanhydrock to our poor house?'

Out of her mistress's sight, Cat made a face. Sir Richard Robartes lived the best part of a day's ride to the east from tucked-away Kenegie, just outside the county town of Bodmin. She wondered what had brought him so far. She took a keen interest in knowing all she could of the gentry, and she knew that this gentleman had a few years back acquired the much neglected estate of Lanhydrock. With an army of gardeners, he had at once set about redesigning

40

its extensive grounds, spending so much money on the project that it had everyone talking and shaking their heads the length of the county. Cat had heard her mother on the subject, her face twisted into the characteristic sneer she adopted when speaking of anyone of whom she did not approve. 'A self-professed Puritan, and there he is spending his fortune trying to improve on what the Lord has provided in all its rough simplicity! They are hypocrites, the lot of them, with their canting talk and their own private vanities. Give me an honest rogue any day.'

Cat drew the folds of the ruff together with an expert flick, secured the ties and tucked them out of sight inside the rich Italian brocade. 'I truly do not think Sir Richard will be riding all the way over from Bodmin to inspect the state of the knot garden, my lady,' she said gently. 'Nor to pay great attention to the linen, moths or no moths.'

Margaret Harris gave her a quick, nervous smile. 'Of course you are right, Catherine. Be that as it may, we should not shame ourselves. My home may not be the richest in the district, but these men are influential and well travelled: even if they do not remark these details consciously, you may be sure an impression will be formed, and I firmly think they are more likely to hear Sir Arthur out and lend him their support if they see him to be a solid man with a well-run estate.' She wrung her hands and stepped away to survey the results in the long Venetian glass. 'Do I look well enough, Catherine?'

Cat surveyed her mistress silently. There was no denying that Lady Harris looked most proper, but the style of her dress was dull and hideously outmoded to one who set great store by following the latest turns of fashion. The fabric of the mandeville was rich enough, and the bodice was trimmed with seed pearls; but the neck was too high and the skirt was too full. No one was wearing such a stiff, formal style nowadays, and certainly not an old cartwheel ruff, which was such a blessed nuisance to clean and starch: a task she was not looking forward to at all. But she kept these thoughts to herself and nodded approvingly. 'You look very well indeed, my lady: Sir Arthur will be proud of you.'

And that was undoubtedly the case. Despite the fact that his duties as Governor of St Michael's Mount took Sir Arthur from home more often than not, he remained devoted to his family, and whenever in the presence of his wife regarded her out of his hooded blue eyes with far more warmth than such a staid and mousy woman might expect. It must be true, Cat conjectured, what Polly said of the marriage: that it had not lasted as long as it had, nor produced eight healthy children, nor six poor dead ones, out of chilly duty alone.

Margaret Harris crossed to the window and gazed out across the grounds. Through the trees she had a clear view of St Michael's Mount, rising like legendary Avalon out of the still sea, the close waters of the bay gleaming turquoise as the sun struck through to the pale sands beneath. She sighed. 'I wish I had never laid eyes upon that place,' she said with sudden venom.

Cat stared at her, for a moment lost for words. She knew that it had been Margaret Harris's decision to maintain her household here at Kenegie rather than moving into the castle on the Mount, a decision that Cat simply could not understand. Kenegie was well enough in its way: foursquare and granite grey, high on the Gulval hills in its sheltering nest of trees; but, had she been the wife of such a man as Sir Arthur, she would have demanded they leave the family estate at once and take up residence in the castle, holding court there in fine style in its spacious halls, hanging its walls with fabulous tapestries and lading its long table with linen and crystal and silver. Taking ship across Mount's Bay to ascend to the castle in its majestic position atop the isle would surely impress any visitor, no matter how worldly-wise they might be.

She had once been foolish enough as to say so much to her mistress and been sternly admonished. 'My dear, in my eyes it is hard to make any castle a home; and the Mount is a particular case, being rocky, inaccessible and exceeding draughty. Moreover, the Mount is visible for miles around from land and sea, which renders it a natural target for foreign enemies; and, as my husband keeps complaining, it is most insufficiently garrisoned and armed.' At this, she had shivered. 'Believe me, Catherine, I would not trade my small comforts here for all the grandeur of such a castle.'

Lady Harris now turned away from that view, her mouth set in a hard, straight line. 'That place is slowly destroying my husband's health,' she declared. 'It is a burden and a worry, when he should be taking his ease in the late afternoon of his life. He has been a most loyal and faithful servant to the Crown for thirty years, but it has repaid him not one whit. Fine words butter no parsnips, and pretty flags may proclaim a king; but they will never save his kingdom.'

King James had sent his royal union flag to the Governor in reward for his 'good and dutiful service', instructing him to fly it always from the highest point of the Mount as a sign of his sovereign's favour. Cat regarded her mistress in surprise: not just for the unwonted vehemence of her outburst but for its substance. The arrival of the flag had surely been a mark of honour; such words were surely close to treason. It was as well they were not overheard.

'I could take Polly's place serving at table,' she said, filling the awkward silence that followed. 'If it would ease your ladyship's concerns. I am not as practised as she, but I am sure I would not disgrace you.'

Lady Harris shook her head. 'I would not ask it of you, Catherine. It will be long, dull work, and you might spoil your pretty dress.' There was a glint in her eye. For all her apparent mousiness, Margaret Harris was no one's fool, and she had quickly remarked the coincidence of her servant wearing her best red gown with the imminent arrival of wealthy visitors. 'But you may help me set the dining room to rights.'

Thus Cat, swathed in a most unbecoming linen apron, found herself running around at her mistress's beck for the next two hours, sweeping the flagstones, beating the rugs, polishing the chairs, the glasses, the knives, changing the flowers, shaking the inevitable moths out of the linen despite the vile-smelling herbs interleaving the pieces, and then sitting in the brightest light she could find with a fine needle and white silk thread patching and darning the myriad little holes they had left in the best Dutch tablecloth. Matty ran in and out of the kitchen with cloths and brooms and a pressing iron full of hot coals. Margaret Harris took up residence in the parlour so that she could oversee Cook and Nell Chigwine in the roasting of the sheep slaughtered that morning, the making of pastries and fish soup, the preparation of fruits and cheeses. To a huge bread-and-butter pudding studded with candied berries she set her own hand. 'Run to the dairy and ask Grace for a skim of cream,' she called to Nell, who duly wiped her floury hands on her apron and took a short cut through the dining room to the courtyard, beyond which lay the farm buildings.

Seeing Cat on her hands and knees putting the finishing touch to the hearth, Nell stopped on the threshold, smirking. There was no love lost between the two.

Cat straightened from her task and looked Nell full in the eye.

'Have you nothing better to be about than spying on my doings?' she demanded crossly, getting to her feet and removing at last the grimy apron.

Nell's lip curled. She looked Cat up and down in visible disgust. 'I have seen the extreme vanity of this world, Catherine Tregenna: the Lord has showed me the vanity of outward things, that they are the vanity of vanities, a blast, a bubble and things of no consequence. Ecclesiastes 1:14.'

Cat burst out laughing. 'It's no good quoting scripture at me, Nell: it runs off me like rain off a duck and I can make neither nose nor tail of a word of it. Speak plainly or let me alone.'

'Thou should seek the salvation of the Lord afore it is too late for thee; thou art little better than a pagan creature.' Nell stood there, hands on hips, sure in her righteous knowledge. 'I saw thee at church last Sunday casting sheep's eyes at the young men and writing in thy little book rather than praying for the Lord's forgiveness for all thy frivolous thoughts and impious deeds. And just yesterday I saw thee in the orchard reaching up to pick the apple blossom for thy poor innocent cousin so thou might show him thy ankle, like a very Eve.'

Cat shrugged and moved towards the kitchen. 'I was doing no such thing, and my conscience is quite clear,' she said sharply.

Nell drew back as if even to touch the red dress were likely to infect her with sin. 'Thou art a temptress and a Jezebel and the Lord will damn thee for thy vanity.'

Cat swept past, a ship in full sail. 'At least I am not a canting old witch,' she said, barely audible.

Nell stared after her, suspicious but a trifle deaf.

Having worked hard in readying the dining room, Cat was hopeful that she might have won Lady Harris's favour. Instead, she found herself banished to the bedchamber to sew her mistress a new chemise. There was something about the nature and timing of this task that made her hackles rise as high as those of the old foxhound Blind Jack when the farmyard cats sneaked past him to steal his food; but there had been nothing she could do save bob her head in assent and turn away quickly before anyone saw her distress. She flew up the stairs, unearthed the roll of fabric and her sewing basket, and settled herself in the high-backed chair, still seething. She cut the cloth, using an old shift as a pattern, and for a while did her best to immerse herself in the work, stitching and hemming with as much skill as she could bring to bear on the task. Even so, the injustice of the situation revisited her like a dog scratching at a door. It really was infuriating to think of fluff-headed Matty and sour Nell downstairs, scrubbed and spruced and making ready to serve at table instead of her. There would be little use asking Matty what was discussed among the visitors – she had the memory of a gnat – and the idea of having a voluntary conversation on such a subject with Nell Chigwine was simply unthinkable. She bit her lip with frustration, drawing blood that she did not notice until it dropped on to the fine white linen, where it spread like a wound.

'God's teeth!' Cat fumed. She hurled the ruined thing to the floor. All that had been left of the task had been stitching the hem: it had been all but finished. Now she would have to start again, and hope that Lady Harris would not with her customary pecuniary care measure the roll of fabric and find the discrepancy; it was that, or own up to the error and pay the three pennies' worth she had wasted. She sighed mightily, retrieved the spoiled item and took it to the window.

Through the distorted squares of glass she saw five horsemen enter the grounds, rippling across the grass as if through a sea. The first rider was clearly Sir Arthur; she knew the big grey as Kerrier, from their own stables. Behind him came two bay hunters bearing men swathed in dark cloaks, an older gentleman on a stately chestnut mare whom she recognized as their neighbour Sir Francis Godolphin, a regular visitor at Kenegie, and a man all in black with an elaborately plumed hat. Sir Arthur came clattering into the yard and dismounted stiffly, throwing the reins to Jim the stable boy. Cat opened the window for a better view, and, as she did so, perhaps alerted by the sound of the latch, the last man looked up and caught her eye. He held her gaze curiously all the way across the courtyard, a strange half-smile on his face, then swung down from his horse with such a flourish that the hat flew off his head, revealing a tumble of auburn hair and a sharply trimmed red beard. He looked very unlike the type of man Cat would have expected Sir Arthur to consult with on any matter of importance.

Moments later, the visitors had disappeared into the house, leaving Cat in a ferment of curiosity. It took great strength of will to resettle to the matter of the chemise.

At last, all her stitching unpicked, the stain cut out and the seams resewn without losing too much volume, Cat put the garment aside, thanking the Lord that Margaret Harris was a meagrely built woman and unlikely to notice the difference between this shift and the others Cat had sewn for her. She put her needle and thread aside, and stood and stretched till her joints cracked. Outside, she spied her cousin Robert crossing the courtyard. Cat rapped on the window, then ran quietly down the stairs, and, instead of taking the corridor towards the privy that would provide her with a reasonable explanation for this break from her tasks, she crept past the kitchen towards the room in which the guests were gathered. The rumble of their voices filled the air, but the door from the dining

46

room remained firmly closed. For the space of a few heartbeats she listened at the crack, but heard nothing of great import: interspersed with polite comments on the repast, the men appeared to be discussing the merits of different types of cannon. There was a sudden lull in the conversation, and Cat, fearing discovery, fled. Robert was likely to know more than she could glean from a few seconds of eavesdropping; he had a knack for learning of everything that went on at the manor and the Mount. People trusted Rob – with information, with difficult tasks, with their welfare. He was that sort of person: dependable, determined, capable. He would, she was quite sure, make some other girl a fine husband.

'Robert!' She slipped into the courtyard and beckoned him to follow her out of earshot of the main house.

He did so, his face creased by puzzlement. 'What is it, Cat – Catherine?'

'Who are those men, the four who came riding in with Sir Arthur, who are taking dinner with him now?'

Rob regarded her askance. 'Why do you ask?'

'Am I not allowed to have a little curiosity as to the nature of such important guests as to throw the house into turmoil all morning and have her ladyship running our feet off with a thousand chores?'

He grinned. 'Running your feet off, eh? And you in your best red dress?'

'This is by no means my best,' she lied. 'Besides, what would you know about such things, Robert Bolitho?'

'Not a great deal,' he admitted, colouring somewhat.

'So, who are they, and why are they here?' she pressed. 'I know Sir Richard Robartes has come from Lanhydrock,' she added quickly, to show off her little knowledge. 'And of course I recognized Sir Francis. But the other two I did not know.'

'The older of the two is the politician and courtier Sir John Eliot, come all the way from Port Eliot,' he said respectfully. 'He is well known for speaking his mind, even to the King, and holds great sway in London.'

Cat nodded, storing this information away. The touch of London at Kenegie: that was something fine indeed, and that Sir John had ridden the length of the county to see the Master meant that their discussion must be important. 'And the other?' she inquired. 'The gentleman with the red hair and the fine hat?'

'John Killigrew of Arwenack,' Robert said, and did not elaborate.

'The pirate?' Cat cried excitedly.

'The Governor of Pendennis Castle,' Rob corrected her stiffly, though everyone knew that the Killigrews were pirates, thieves and rogues who had climbed high on the social ladder by means of starting halfway up it from a large pile of misappropriated gold. This of course made them heroic figures to many of the Cornish, especially those who still mourned the passing of Queen Bess and the years in which the Crown had so often turned a blind eye to a little nautical initiative.

Cat's mother had worked three years at Arwenack, close by on the Helford River, and had talked of little else, as if that short time had been for her a golden age, and the intervening twenty years had belonged to some other woman's life. Far from displaying any shame at working for folk who sailed too close to the wind, Jane Tregenna revelled in the wild tales that surrounded the Killigrews. She had particularly enjoyed telling her daughter, over and again, each time with a little more embroidered detail, the story of Jane Killigrew, wife of the first Sir John, who had ended his days in the Fleet, London's debtors' prison. He left his widow with great debts and no way of paying them – until that resolute woman determined to make her fortune with her own hands. When two Dutch galleons, disabled by heavy weather and bearing Spanish gold, were brought into the shelter of Pendennis, Jane Killigrew led her retainers – armed with pikes and swords – and stormed the ships, overpowering the crew, killing the two Spanish factors aboard and making away with several hogsheads of gold. It was the killing of the Spanish grandees that had earned many of those involved a hanging at Launceston; but it was rumoured that Elizabeth herself had intervened on behalf of Lady Killigrew; certainly she had issued a royal pardon, and Jane Killigrew had escaped the gibbet. The current Sir John was her son.

'Is he the man who has built the lighthouse on the Lizard Point?' Cat inquired, knowing full well the answer.

'The same,' he replied, tight-lipped.

Rob did not approve of Sir John Killigrew, and Cat was minded to twitch his reins. With a gleam in her eye, she said, ' 'Tis surely a most charitable Christian gesture to construct a lighthouse to warn the shipping about the wicked rocks on that black coast.'

Rob snorted. 'Oh, most charitable. Were it not for the fact that he charges a toll upon each vessel that passes the point.' Or indeed extinguishes the light when strong south-westerlies and a particularly rich prize look as if they might converge, he thought but did not add.

'A man of admirable acumen,' Cat offered, enjoying herself. 'Perhaps Sir Arthur has thought of raising a lighthouse of his own upon the Mount and seeks his counsel.'

'I hardly think our master is likely to take to licensed robbery of his neighbours and countrymen,' Rob returned acidly. 'He seeks, in quite the opposite manner, to protect us all. He has gathered his allies about him to aid him in making overtures to the Privy Council for funds to furnish the Mount with more guns, and somehow Killigrew has managed to gain royal favour sufficiently to acquire such for Pendennis, though he says it is never enough.'

'Will the Spanish attack us again?' Cat asked. 'Or is it the French he wishes to protect us from?'

'Or the Turks, or privateers, or the rogue Dutch – there are many enemies who might be attracted by the sight of an unprotected stretch of coast such as this.'

'But there is nothing here to steal! What are they going to take – our pilchards?' She leaned towards him, laughing. 'Or perhaps Nell Chigwine and her mother? How I would love to see them carried off to some Catholic noblewoman's house – can you imagine their horror at all the terrible papist trappings and Latin Mass?'

'You should not make mock of others' religious beliefs, Cat,' Rob said severely, though a smile was lurking behind his words. 'It is not very Christian of you.'

'Truth be told, I often feel like the wicked little pagan she names me,' Cat told him solemnly.

Horrified, Rob put his hand over her mouth.

'Unhand that lady, sirrah!'

The cousins sprang apart guiltily. The red-haired man stood there, a long clay pipe in one hand, a leather pouch in the other. He tamped a quantity of the contents of the pouch into the bowl of the pipe and surveyed it with interest while Rob and Cat looked on in silence. Then Rob bowed. 'I beg pardon, sir. This is my cousin Catherine.'

'Is she really?' Sir John Killigrew looked Cat slowly up and down in blatant assessment. 'And that gives you the right to affront her, does it?'

'No, sir. But –'

'Don't "but" me, boy!' Killigrew yelled suddenly. 'Get out of here and leave the poor girl alone. I shall report your behaviour to Sir Arthur. Now, go!'

Rob glanced back at Cat in case she might speak up for him, but she was carefully studying her feet, for once uncharacteristically quiet. Then he stalked angrily away across the courtyard.

'Are you all right?' Sir John asked. 'He has not hurt you, your . . . cousin?'

Cat gave him her best smile. 'Thank you, sir, no, not at all. Rob was merely attempting to teach me some manners.'

'You seem to me to be a most mannerly young woman, Catherine – Catherine, what? I must know the name of the lady I have rescued.' He took a step closer and gave her a long, slow grin, fox-like. There were deep crinkles around his bright blue eyes; he was older than she had first thought.

'Tregenna, sir.'

'Catherine Tregenna. A pretty name for a pretty girl.'

Cat bit the inside of her cheek to stop the laughter that threatened to escape. 'Thank you, sir.'

He stowed the pipe away, unsmoked, and took her by the hand. She could feel the hard calluses on his fingers and remembered how they said that as a smuggler he had rowed his own boat. Unwisely, she said as much.

Killigrew roared with laughter. 'Are you fond of smugglers and thieves, then, Mistress Catherine? Do you dream of wild adventures in your narrow maiden's bed?'

Cat tried to withdraw her hand. 'No, sir,' she answered; but her high colour told another tale.

He grasped it tighter. 'I do believe our discussions are likely to take longer than expected and that I shall be staying the night at Kenegie,' he said smoothly. 'I hope I may have the chance to become better acquainted with you, Catherine Tregenna. Here is a little promissory note for you that I shall make good on later.' And before she could begin to protest, he caught her to him and pressed his full red mouth upon hers. The fume of wine engulfed her as his tongue tried to force a passage between her lips. Cat squirmed and struggled, to no avail. His right arm imprisoned her, twisting her arms behind her back; his left hand clasped itself around her breast and squeezed hard. No one had ever touched her in such a way before, and for a moment she thought she might faint. She kicked out, but he was wearing sturdy leather boots, and her assault on his ankles had no effect other than to make him clasp her closer still. She felt his laugh rumble through the bones of her chest; her resistance seemed to add savour to the situation.

Salvation came in a most unlikely form.

A harsh voice broke the spell. 'He carried me away in the Spirit into the wilderness. And I saw a woman riding a scarlet beast which was full of names of blasphemy, having seven heads and ten horns!'

Nell Chigwine stood at the threshold of the courtyard door, pitcher under her arm, her other hand outstretched, finger pointing in accusation at the sinning pair before her.

Surprised by this bizarre interruption, Sir John Killigrew stepped away from his prey. 'Away with you, you whey-faced creature! Go share your mad words with the pigs and hens, who will certainly appreciate them more than I!' And away he strode, without even a glance back at Catherine, who now crumpled to her knees in the courtyard, heedless of the dirt and dust.

But Nell had no interest in the nobleman: all her scorn was directed at Cat. She put the pitcher down, took a pace forward and stood over her, hands on hips, declaiming her words at full volume like one of the tub-thumpers who now so regularly toured the region.

'The woman was arrayed in purple and scarlet, and adorned with gold and precious stones and pearls, having in her hand a golden cup full of abominations and the filthiness of her fornication.

'And on her forehead a name was written: "Mystery, Babylon the Great, the mother of harlots and of the abominations of the earth."

'Shame on you, Catherine Anne Tregenna, in your scarlet dress and your fornicating ways, for thou art truly Babylon!'

'Whatever is going on here?'

The Mistress of Kenegie stood framed in the doorway, her hands balled into tight white fists. She took in the scene at a glance: John Killigrew striding away towards the stable yard, his pipe in his hand; Catherine in the dust with her hair rumpled and her face as red as her dress; Nell Chigwine a figure of righteous triumph. 'Such an unholy row,' she scolded the pair of them, 'when Sir Arthur is trying to hold a civilized conversation.'

'Unholy is thy servant,' Nell sniffed. 'That dress the temptress wears is enough to provoke the very Devil.'

'My husband's guests are not all angels, that is true,' Margaret Harris said quietly, 'but I think none of them are quite as bad as all that. You had best speak plainly, Eleanor, and explain to me why you were shrieking so stridently.'

Nell Chigwine's eyes went as small and black as sloes. 'I came out to fetch a pitcher of water and found Catherine fornicating with a man, as brazen as you please in full view of all and sundry.'

Cat leaped to her feet. 'You did no such thing!' she cried hotly.

'By all that is sacred,' Nell returned primly, her hand laid upon her heart, 'I know what I saw. And all know she would do anything to land herself a rich husband.' She smiled slyly. 'Even one who has run himself into debt gaining an unholy divorce.'

'Go about your duties, Eleanor,' Lady Harris said sharply, 'and speak of this to no one. If any gossip of what has passed here reaches my ears, I shall know immediately whence it came.'

Nell shot Cat a malicious parting glance, took up the pitcher, carried it to the pump, filled it with insolent slowness and stalked back into the house. No one said a word in the two long minutes this took.

When the door was firmly shut behind her, Margaret Harris turned back, pale and drawn. 'I shall not ask you exactly what passed here, Catherine. But what I will say is that that man has a very bad reputation.' Her eyes indicated the retreating back of John Killigrew, his red hair glowing through a cloud of smoke in the next enclosure. 'For very many reasons it were best you kept out of his way.'

'I did not invite his attentions, my lady, whatever Nell Chigwine says,' Cat said in a low voice.

'You are young, Catherine, and not as worldly-wise as you like to think. Not every gentleman by name is a gentleman by nature; and Killigrew is no gentleman. I can only imagine he does not know your identity –'

'I told him my name was Catherine Tregenna.'

Mistress Harris's eyes glinted. 'Had you told him Coode, he would have turned on his heel on you and good riddance. Now go back upstairs and change out of that dress. Scarlet has no place in an honest woman's wardrobe.'

'It was my mother's dress,' Cat said sullenly.

'I fear that is no great surprise to me. It may not be fair that the sins of the parent be visited on the child, but in your mother's case personal sin was added to original sin, and it weighs heavily upon you, Catherine, though you know it not. For your own best sake I tell you now that there are men with no title, no estate and no riches who are worth a hundred of men like John Killigrew. Your cousin Robert is one, and you should look to him while you may, before your reputation is sullied beyond repair.'

Cat had little time to think on this strange speech; after supper that night, Polly the footmaid came to fetch Cat from her room. Her eyes were as big as saucers; her nose red from sneezing. 'My lady says you are to come at once to her sitting room. Sir Arthur is there too; he has left his guests.'

But when Cat presented herself in the little low-beamed room the lady of the house used as her own, she found not only Lady Harris and her husband present, but Robert too in his best doublet, with his wild blond hair slicked down. He would not meet her eye when she gazed upon him, questioning.

Ten minutes later she was out again in the long dark corridor, trembling in outrage and with Sir Arthur's words ringing in her ears.

'We will call the banns next Sunday. You and Robert shall have the cottage behind the byre. Tomorrow, Matty will start to help you in putting it to rights.'

So that was to be her life: stuck here at Kenegie for ever, married to her dull cousin, living in a hovel behind the cowshed. That night, Cat prayed for the Lord to take her in her sleep. She never wanted to wake up again.

After tossing and turning for hours, she lit a candle, turned to her pattern for the altar frontal in her book, sharpened her plumbago stick with the little knife she kept for the purpose, and by the guttering light added a clear caricature of Nell Chigwine's sly face to the serpent.

7

So that ys to be my lyf, trappd for ever here at Kenegy wed to my dull cozen Robert living in a hovel behynd the cow-sheds, large with childe year after year, rasyng a pack of brattes & dying in obscuritee. I must away from heere. The Countess of Salysbury ys to visit Lady Harrys in Agost. If I can compleat the Altar Frontal before then & thus perswade her to take mee away with her, may bee there ys a chaunce of escape . . .

The harsh ringing of the telephone jolted me out of the seventeenth century.

I went into the kitchen and stared at it as if it might suddenly manifest Michael out of its din. But the voice that started to leave a message was not Michael's, or any other man's.

'Julia?'

It was my cousin Alison.

'Alison, it's brilliant to hear from you. How are you? I've been meaning to call you. Life's not been too great –'

'Julia, for God's sake, shut up and let me speak.'

I stared at the phone, shocked. Alison was usually such a gentle soul. I applied my ear to the receiver again, only to hear her breathing heavily, as if she had run a mile.

'It's . . . it's Andrew –' and she broke down into great racking sobs.

I waited, not knowing what to say. Had he left her again? Andrew Hoskin had always had a roving eye; they'd moved down to Cornwall in part because of some work affair he'd had, but that had been a while ago. Had she left him? She'd been threatening to for years, but never had, and I could not imagine that she ever really would . . .

'He's . . . he's dead.'

'Oh, Alison, no. I'm so sorry. Are you OK – sorry, of course you're not OK. My God, what happened?'

There was a long pause as Alison gathered herself. 'He . . . ah . . . he hanged himself. In the attic. I –' The explanation became the wail of an animal in unbearable pain. It shivered in my bones.

'Oh, God, Alison, that's terrible. Stop, stop, please. I'm sure it was nothing to do with you.'

Why had I said that? I had no idea. Of course it had something to do with her: he was her husband. At the other end there was a sudden ominous silence.

'Alison? I really don't know why I said that. Alison?'

She had put the phone down. I tried to call her back at intervals throughout the day but only succeeded in getting the answering machine. At last I left a message of abject apology and gave up.

That night I did not read Catherine Tregenna's little book, but resolutely put it away from me and thought instead not about that distant girl, almost four hundred years dead, nor for once about my own sad life, but about my poor cousin. What must it feel like to share your life with someone who suddenly and with no explanation or warning removes himself not just from your relationship but from the whole world, irretrievably and for ever? However bad their marriage had become, what would have driven the usually buoyant and thick-skinned Andrew to take his own life, in such a brutal manner, and in the very house the two had resurrected from the shamble of dust and mildew and rotting timber they had bought so long ago?

But when at last I turned the light out and went to sleep, it was not Alison I dreamed of, nor of Andrew swinging from a beam, but of Cat Tregenna. Something was happening to her: something terrible, but I could not quite grasp the nature of the threat or see the menace that had come for her. The words 'Lord save us!' echoed over and over in my head, and when I awoke it was in a state of some alarm. Usually I woke slowly, like a diver coming up to the surface from deep water, but that morning something was different. My skin felt prickly and alert, as if someone had been watching me as I slept. Suddenly fixated by this thought, I hurled the bedclothes from me and leaped out of bed, staring wildly around as if I might surprise an intruder. There was, of course, no one there. Cursing myself for such pointless and neurotic behaviour, I made a cup of coffee and called Alison's number again.

This time, she picked up.

'Hello?' Her voice was thready and faint as if coming from a very long way away down a very poor line.

'Alison, it's me, Julia. Look, I'm so sorry about my gaffe yesterday, I wasn't thinking . . .' I tailed off, unable to think of anything useful to say.

'That's all right. I just couldn't talk to you – to anyone – any more. I had to get away from it, from him; from the house.'

'But you're back now,' I observed, stupidly.

'Yes,' she said, sounding unsure.

'Look,' I said quickly and without any real thought, 'why don't I come down to help you with the arrangements and stuff? Give you a break, or a shoulder to cry on: anything, really. It's no problem, there's nothing keeping me here.'

There was a long pause. Then, 'Could you? I can't bear it here. Will you come? Today?'

'Of course,' I said. After a few minutes of practical arrangements, I put the phone down, my heart sinking. Why had I offered? I really did not want to go all that way – to the end of the world, as it seemed. There were ghosts waiting for me down in Cornwall; and I did not count Andrew's among them.

Nevertheless, two hours later I found myself at Paddington buying an open return to Penzance.

It had been nearly three years since I had visited my home county, commuting back and forth to visit my mother, a particularly dark time in my life. My mother, who had right up to that last year been a remarkably hale and energetic woman, still running marathons at sixty, still swimming at seventy, had suffered a sudden stroke and in a moment lost not only the use of one side of her body but her independence and her entire personality, and had ended up in a care home which stank of urine and antiseptic.

It was guilt that drove me to my frequent visits, guilt and fear: a barely suppressed terror at the realization that this was what we all came to in the end. And at least my mother had some moments of comfort in having friends and family around her as she failed. Being a single woman with no children made the prospect of old age and physical and mental decline cut me particularly deeply, even at thirty-three. As a result, I clung to Michael out of a yawning need that soon had him avoiding late-night phone calls and making more trips away from town than he had before, anything, I suspect, to avoid hearing my woes and sensing my pain. It took me some months to realize that my behaviour and his more frequent absences – geographical and emotional – had a direct correlation, but even then I had not had the wit to see the relationship for what it really was.

As the train passed through Liskeard Station, with its pretty little branch line that followed the twisting river valley through rolling wooded hills to the sea at Looe, I remembered how Michael had given in to my badgering and gone down with me for a weekend. His family had moved from St Austell long ago; there was nothing left in Cornwall for him except bad memories of school and camping on the moor, as he told me in no uncertain terms. I remembered how, unable to deal with my tears after I returned alone from visiting my mother at the home, he had abruptly gone for a long walk and left me sitting in the hotel garden, wondering whether he was ever coming back. Surely, I reasoned with myself now, I was better off on my own than with such a weak and selfish man? For a long while my thoughts were as bleak as the moors through which we passed, and I could not concentrate on embroidering my wall hanging to pass the time.

But, as the train approached Camborne and I saw the ruined mine workings on the skyline, my heart leaped up in a most disconcerting way. Swathes of bracken and gorse on windswept hills and lonely heaths punctuated by standing stones and tumuli gradually gave way to rolling farmland, beyond whose boundaries

I sensed a huge and empty space. Something about the quality of the light – bright and numinous – suggested the imminent presence of the sea. Just over that horizon lay the end of the line; indeed, the end of the land.

This was where our family, a fiercely Cornish clan, had originated: West Penwith, the most westerly toe of England. My mother always referred to it as 'real Cornwall', as if the south-east was only for incomers and county traitors, folk whose affiliations lay more closely with (heaven forbid) Devon and the modern world than with Cornwall's ancient past as an independent nation with its own language, king and laws. Our ancestors had been tinners before the industry had disastrously failed, and along with it the family fortunes, and many had dispersed far and wide across the globe – to the Argentine and Australia, to Canada and Chile – wherever mining expertise was still a tradeable asset.

I had not had much contact with my few remaining relatives in this toe of land. Some of them, cousins at third and fourth remove, had attended my mother's funeral, but we had not had much to say to one another beyond the stock exchange of condolences. Alison knew them better than I did. They had properly Cornish names – Pengelly and Bolitho, Rowse and Tucker – and lives that seemed fifty years and a continent removed from my own. Why Alison and Andrew had removed themselves quite so far from London I had never really understood, beyond the small scandal of Andrew's affair; but, as the train neared its destination, I began to understand. Alison had needed the comfort of her family; but she had also said when she had first moved down to this part of Cornwall that it was a magical place, full of powerful energies. I had suspected her of seeking solace in her new surroundings, glossing the landscape with a much needed mystique. Now, across the wide bay before me, St Michael's Mount rose out of the sea like a castle from the Age of Legends, wreathed around by low cloud and hazy rain, and the hairs stood up on the back of my neck.

The Mount. How many times had that name appeared in Catherine's book in her tiny, exquisite hand? I gazed at it, feeling the presence of the past. I shivered. Goodness, here we were pulling into Penzance Station, and I was feeling shaky and not a little haunted; not the best state in which to greet my poor bereaved cousin.

I was quickly brought back to earth. As the train pulled in, a great, ugly Victorian rail shed greeted me, grey and forbidding, that and a penetrating Cornish mizzle which misted my exposed skin and got into the roots of my hair in the few seconds it took to walk along the platform into shelter. Alison was waiting for me beside the station buffet, the garish light making her pale face ghastly.

We lurched into an awkward embrace, and I could feel her slender frame trembling. As I held her, I thought sadly how that bold, bright, brazen girl of my twenties – the one who had streaked round the local park, high on E; who had crawled through the churchyard of St Nicholas, Deptford, at two in the morning, having lost the power to walk after three too many tequila slammers, still determined that I should see the memorials to Kit Marlowe and to the great seventeenth-century shipwright John Addey; who had danced at raves and partied till dawn and sworn she would never get old – had been rendered frail and uncertain, her hair showing streaks of grey and her face etched with lines.

During the time Alison and Andrew had lived in Cornwall, my cousin and I had maintained our friendship through long phone calls and periodic visits by her to London, when she would escape her married state as we pretended to flirt with younger men in pubs along the river. She had never encouraged me to visit the Cornish house: this would be my first sight of it, except in a thousand before-and-after photos.

Alison and Andrew's home was a short drive from the station: a rambling converted farmhouse in the hills to the north and east of Penzance. She had loved it from the start, even though it was neglected and abandoned: no one had lived in it for years. She had practically bullied Andrew into buying the place, having seen its potential from the outset, and Andrew, with so much to make up for, had eventually given in and let her have her way with it, and his money. They had lavished a great deal of effort, imagination and time on their home: you could see that at soon as you entered the driveway. A formal garden had been planted: concentric circles of box enclosing bay trees and beds of lavender and hand-laid pebble paths which ran between the beds. A fountain occupied the centre of a sunray patio made of smooth white pebbles against a dark ground, but the water was still and silent, pocked by the rain.

Inside, the house was fresh and bright – walls painted in old white, soft pale-green carpets, ethnic rugs in cool colours, modern paintings of seascapes and fish which looked to be originals, solid furniture in heavy dark wood, but absolutely no clutter. Instead there was a sense of space, simplicity and serenity. I did not feel Andrew's presence in any of it. The ambience was that of studied order and balance. It was hard to believe a man had so violently, and so recently, ended his life under this roof.

'I've put you in our room. I hope you don't mind – I just can't face sleeping there at the moment. It's got its own bathroom, and a lovely view,' she added apologetically.

'That's fine,' I lied, though the idea of it made my skin crawl.

On the landing, I watched as she inevitably fixed her gaze on the stairs to the attic, then looked away sharply, remembering.

She made us a pot of tea, and we took it out into the back garden. There, amid fragrant beds of peppermint and thyme, she told me how the two had renovated the farmhouse together room by room as the money came in, right the way up to the attic, which they had converted only this year. They had dug up the old cobbles and concrete of the yard and replaced them with flowers and trees and herbs. And for a time that had been enough: hard physical work that exhausted them and devoured their time, throwing them together in a shared project in which they both took pride, and in which they buried their troubled past. But it was as if converting the attic had been the last straw. Ever since they'd finished that, Andrew had withdrawn into himself, becoming gradually more taciturn and short-tempered – very different from the convivial, rumbustious Andrew I had always known – started drinking heavily, neglected first his family, then his work. He was an internet trader, and it had not taken long for his business to fall apart and the debts to mount up.

'I never saw it coming,' Alison said at last. 'I knew he was depressed; I kept trying to persuade him to go to the doctor, but he just wouldn't go. He wouldn't talk to me, wouldn't talk to his sister, his friends, anyone. Kept saying there was no point, that what had happened had happened, and no one could change it. I had no idea what he was talking about, still don't. But suicide . . . how could I have been so blind?'

I threw my arms around her, and she wept loudly for a good long while.

'I miss him!' she wailed. 'I miss the smell of him in the house. I even miss his cold feet in bed.'

Eventually she broke away from me to blow her cracked, red nose.

'Al, darling, I'm quite sure there was nothing you could have done to stop him,' I said. 'How could you possibly have foreseen such a thing? I mean, Andrew never struck me as someone who took life that seriously.'

She shot me a look. 'Neither did I. Even when he proposed to me, I thought he was joking.' She grinned weakly. 'In fact, I think he was. We were both pissed; and then suddenly everyone was talking about it, and we just sort of went with the flow. And then I got pregnant and, well . . .'

She'd been four months pregnant when she walked down the aisle; but she had told only me, Andrew, her mother and her best friend, Susie. The dress had been Empire line, the bouquet carefully positioned, and no one made any awkward little jokes. Which was just as well, since two weeks later she miscarried and almost died and had never been able to get pregnant again.

'The thing is . . .' she started, looking away as if making an uncomfortable confession. 'The night he . . . died . . . I was trying to persuade him to have a go at IVF. I never saw him so furious. I honestly thought he was going to hit me. "Don't you ever try to trap me like that!" he screamed at me. "Isn't it enough that you've got me caged up in this godforsaken corner of the world, in this bloody house, without passing the whole fucking disaster on through our genes?" And then he stormed out of the room and went up to his den. It was the last thing he said to me. So when he didn't come down for supper I wasn't surprised – to be honest, I was relieved. I couldn't face having another row with him. I picked at a salad, went up to bed early, fell asleep. I woke up at three in the morning, suddenly, in that way that you do sometimes. My heart was knocking so hard I could hardly breathe. And then I knew.' She turned to me. 'I just knew. And still I couldn't go up there. Not till it was light.' She gulped, mastering herself. 'The police surgeon said he'd been dead since before midnight, so there was nothing I could have done. But I feel terrible that I didn't try to patch things up, didn't take him up his usual glass of brandy. Something. Anything . . .' Her words ran out.

I gazed at her, not knowing what to say. She dug in her pocket and pulled out a crumpled sheet of A4.

'It's just a photocopy,' she explained as I stared at it. 'The police took the original, though they've said I can have it back. Not that I need it; I know it all by heart.'

'Are you sure?' I knew as I took it from her that I didn't want to read it. As if on cue my stomach rumbled loudly, breaking the sombre mood. I looked down at it as if at a badly behaved pet. 'God, I'm sorry.'

She looked at her watch. 'Have you not eaten anything? I didn't think –'

'The buffet car pretty much ran out of supplies before Plymouth,' I said, relieved to change the subject. 'I ended up ordering one of their microwaved hamburgers, but when it came out of its wrapping all damp and wrinkled-looking, I just couldn't face it.'

Alison made a face. 'That sounds disgusting.' She thought about it for a moment, then added, straight-faced, 'Reminds me of a couple of men I've known. Good job it wasn't hairy as well.'

I stared at her, then we were both roaring with laughter, and didn't stop for the next ten minutes as humour gave way to a huge release of tension and made the world a better place again.

Even so, by the time it came to go up to bed that night, I was feeling apprehensive. Paper-thin, paper-light, the letter lay in my pocket like a lead weight. I put all the lights on in the master bedroom and stretched out on the bed, staring at the ceiling. Was the attic beam from which Andrew had hanged himself directly overhead now, I wondered, and had to push the thought out of my mind.

I ran a bath and settled back with a book I'd picked up at the Smith's at Paddington Station, but after three pages I just didn't feel like reading it.

I got out, dripping, wrapped myself in a towel and sat down on the bed. Andrew's letter lay there, folded in quarters: a silent rebuke. Gingerly, I opened the sheet of paper and smoothed out the creases. Andrew's handwriting was small and neat and rather old-fashioned-looking, not what I had been expecting at all.

Dear Alison, it read, formal, formulaic.

My death will, I know, come as a terrible shock to you, even though you have, in part, been responsible for driving me to this point of no return. I cannot go on. This house has taken everything from me. It has sapped my will to live. When you started again to talk about children, I knew I couldn't do this any more. Why bother to pretend there's a future – for me, let alone a child of mine? History repeats itself, again and again: there is nothing we can do to change our fates, and it is madness to think we can shape our lives. I am sorry that our marriage has been a sham. I am sorry for the pain I have given. Most of all, I am sorry that I did not see the course my life would take in time for me to follow the path alone, rather than dragging you down it with me. At least now you have a chance to make a new future for yourself. Sell this house and get out of here. It is a stifling place, full of despair and failure. Get out while you can: save yourself. Go back to London, find someone else and do not tie yourself to the lead weight of my life, or my death.

Go, if not with my love, then with my care.

Andrew

I sat there with the photocopied note in my trembling hands for twenty minutes. At last I got up and went over to the window, looking out across the lawn to the ocean beyond. This lovely light-filled house that he and Alison had made, with its pretty garden and its wide, open views, gave me no sense of a prison or cage. It was hard to hear Andrew's voice in the phrasing or in the sentiments expressed, but I had never known Andrew in extremis, only in the grip of alcohol and/or lust, full of bonhomie and testosterone. Even so, something about his words rang true in a part of me I could not quite access.

Up above, a slender crescent moon shone like a glimpse through night into another world. An owl hooted in the distant trees. My mother had always averred that owls called with the voices of the dead. She, with the deeply ingrained superstitions of a long Cornish ancestry, had touched wood (but only without legs, for fear your luck would walk away from you); and, if she spilled salt, had tossed some over her left shoulder to ward off the Devil, even though she said she didn't believe in him. She believed that there was a transitional state between life and death, and that spirits walked till they were at peace – something that she thought certain spirits never found.

I shivered, despite the warmth of the night; yet I suddenly felt compelled to throw open the windows, as if to cleanse the atmosphere, to allow myself to breathe more easily; or to let out Andrew's spirit.

8

Some days later, in order to divert Alison from her misery, which pressed harder upon her now that the adrenalin of the initial shock had run out and the distractions of the funeral and practical arrangements had passed, I told her some of my more entertaining Michael stories.

My affair with Michael had driven a bit of a wedge between Alison and myself, especially once she had experienced the ignominy and pain of Andrew's adultery. She had never approved of Michael, even as Anna's husband. 'There's something essentially untrustworthy about him,' I remember her remarking to me very early on in their relationship. I hadn't dared tell her about the two of us for over a year after it had started, and when I did she went completely silent, her lips pursed. At last she said, 'I ought to call Anna right now. I ought to just pick up the phone and tell her that her best friend's screwing her husband, and she should get shot of them both.'

I'd half willed her to do it, though I knew Anna would be furious and hate me. But I also knew that no matter what he had done she would not let Michael go that easily; and that he would never leave her, not for me. Partly, it was her money, but it went deeper than that in a way I did not want to examine too closely.

In the end Alison had told me exactly what she thought of me. Then left a long pause, adding, 'If you ever screw Andrew I'll kill you.' She managed to keep a straight face for all of thirty seconds. But I knew she kind of meant it.

We'd done our very best to patch up our friendship since then; but the spectre of infidelity was always there with us. I was deeply touched that Alison had turned to me in the depths of her misery. So, as a poor form of repayment, I rolled out all the funny stories

I could muster: how on an early date Michael had taken me to a smart Chinese restaurant; how I'd been desperate to make a good impression, yet while eating my noodle soup had inhaled so hard that a strand had whipped across my chin, leaving a red weal which promptly blistered in a highly unattractive fashion; how we'd made love in a bluebell wood and he'd run a naked half-mile trying to get rid of an earwig that had crawled into his hair. How Anna had one day turned up at my flat and Michael had spent four hours freezing his nuts off in the garden shed.

I got quite carried away with this heady rehearsal of what had been for a lot of the time an anxious, emotionally unprofitable experience. It was a relief to talk about it at all, let alone make it into an entertainment for someone. I began digging out ever more excruciating anecdotes, often at my own expense, and soon Alison was giggling.

At last, I found myself staring down at the surface of the table, at the gouges and stains that marked its antique surface. At the beginning of its existence it would have been a smooth sheet of pine, honey-coloured, clean and wholesome; but even then it would have had its natural knots and whorls. None of us were perfect; and life made us infinitely less so. Tears of self-pity pricked my eyes.

'Ah, well,' she said softly, seeing that I had come to a halt. 'He always was a shit.'

At least we agreed on that. I told her about the break-up dinner. 'He gave me a book as a farewell gift. Let me show you.' I dug in my handbag and brought out *The Needle-Woman's Glorie*.

'Good grief,' she said after a while, turning it over in her hands. 'I'm pretty sure this was one of the batch Andrew unearthed from the attic a couple of weeks ago and sent up to Michael to sell for us. In fact, I'm sure of it, because it was one of a pair, and that struck me as odd. How weird that you've ended up with it.'

This statement hit me like a rabbit-punch. So, he hadn't even *bought* the book for me; and, in addition, by giving it to me, he had cheated Andrew and Alison out of whatever money they could have sold it for. I felt terrible. 'Oh. God. Perhaps you should have it back.' I paused. 'Or I could give you something for it?'

'Don't be an idiot. It's yours. Anyway, look, it's been defaced: he probably wouldn't have been able to sell it in this condition anyway.' She peered at Catherine's tiny pencilled handwriting, then she sucked in her breath. 'Hang on,' she said, 'did you do this?'

'No!' I was shocked that she would think I would deface such a lovely, ancient thing.

'It's just . . . well, your writing is so similar.'

I frowned. 'Is it?'

'Apart from the funny *s* and curlicues, yes. It's not a typical secretary hand: it's more cursive, freer of form. See, here, how the *g* loops up, just like yours? And she – I take it she was a "she" – dots her *i*'s a little way to the right, just like you do.' She held the book up to the window, screwing up her eyes. 'And, see here – this italic *a* – no one else I know forms their *a*'s like that.'

I write my *a*'s the way they are printed in books, rather than making the usual *o* with a tail. My frown grew deeper.

'That's really odd. It's never struck me at all. Even so, I'm not sure you're right.'

Alison pushed her chair away from the table with a screech of wood on wood and walked off into the dining room. When she came back, she carried a notebook and a pencil. With a knife from the kitchen block, she sharpened the lead to a needle-point.

'There you go,' she said, sliding notebook and pencil across the table to me. 'Go on: write something, write it as small as it is in the book.'

'Write what?'

'Whatever you like – no, hold on.' She opened the book some-where in the middle, turned the page sideways and scrutinized it closely. 'Write this: "An old Ægyptian woman came to the scullery door today", and that's "Ægyptian" with an "Æ" ligature –'

'A what?'

Alison rolled her eyes. Despite her wild times at university she had come away with a good degree and had always regarded me, affectionately, as a bit of an intellectual dullard. 'AE run together, you dope. "An old Ægyptian woman came to the scullery door today. She came on . . ." I can't read the next bit.'

I took the book from her. 'I think it's "a mule".' I passed it back.

'"... and was arrayed most strangely with bells and scarfs, her face and hands almost black" – that's "black" with an *e* on the end.'

I duly wrote it all down. I had to admit that when we held my version close to Catherine's, the two were more similar than I had expected. But I still said stubbornly, 'Mine has more of a slant, and the verticals are longer.'

'You've just taken up more space than she has; she had to squeeze it in wherever she could. Mind you, it's surprising that she was able to write at all – she's not an aristo or anything, is she?'

I shook my head. 'No, but I think her mother must have been educated, and it sounds from what she says at the start as if her mistress might have taken a bit of a shine to her and encouraged her.' I paused, staring at what I'd written. 'Egypt's a very long way from Cornwall,' I said dubiously. 'Are you sure that's what it says?'

'It's the old word for "gypsy" – they thought they came from Egypt. Some of them probably did.' She paused. 'Did you say Cornwall?'

I had forgotten to explain that small detail. 'Um, yes. She's called Catherine Anne Tregenna – Cat, for her initials – and she worked at a manor house in the seventeenth century, somewhere around here, in fact. Ken – something.'

'Kenegie?'

I looked at her in surprise. 'That's the name, yes. Why, do you know it?'

Alison's eyes were wide. 'It's the name of the Elizabethan manor house – we're within its old boundaries. In fact, we had a load of old rubbish from the manor house stuffed in our attic. Good heavens, that book must have been here for the best part of four hundred years: she probably lived right on this estate!'

The back of my neck prickled. 'Is the manor house still here?'

Alison hesitated. 'It's probably not what you expect.'

I looked at her, waiting.

'It's ... well, the Elizabethan house is still there, though it's been renovated to within an inch of its life. They're turning it into executive apartments.' She snorted. 'As if there were a load of aspiring executives converging on Penzance. And the rest of it is a sort of holiday village now.'

'A what?' I was horrified.

She spread her hands. 'You can't blame people: Cornwall's the poorest county in England. All that's left down here is tourism and fishing, and precious little fishing, given all the EU restrictions and the foreign factory ships. People have to make their money in any way they can.'

'I suppose so.' The picture she painted was rather different to the one I had been cherishing.

'We could walk down there later, you could see it.'

'Mmmm,' I said non-committally. Shards of mundanity were beginning to puncture the illusion I had been happily constructing. Cat's neat, secretive little jottings had been my escape from the unpleasant realities of the world. Poking around the place she had lived in meant sharing her with Alison, and I realized I didn't want to share Cat with anyone.

'What was her name again?' she muttered, flicking to the title page. Her eyes lit up. 'Catherine Anne Tregenna. You know, I think there are Tregennas somewhere in our family. In fact I'm sure there are. Or Tregunna. Or was it Tregenza? There's a greengrocer in Penzance called Tregenza's; then there's Tregenna Castle at St Ives. I wonder if we're all related? I've got the family bible somewhere . . .' Her face fell.

'What is it?'

'It's in the attic,' she said flatly.

'Oh.' I didn't feel like volunteering for that task.

'I have to go up there again sometime, I suppose . . .' She left the sentence hanging, as if I was meant to finish it in some way.

I said nothing, but I felt her eyes on me like a weight.

'I'll go,' I said heavily at last. 'If you can tell me where to look.'

She stood on the landing at the bottom of the stairs while I went up, her hands clutching the newel post like claws.

The attic space was as bright and fresh as the rest of the house, but a lot more untidy. A huge Velux window set into the hidden roof slope to the north of the house let in a wash of daylight for which I was profoundly grateful. Along one end ran Andrew's desk, piled high with papers. The computer sat there blank-screened and resentful. No one had switched it on in the best part of a fortnight. The suicide note, Alison said, had been propped up against the monitor. In the centre of the room ran a huge wooden beam. A length of rope remained attached to it, its end severed as if by a sharp knife – by the police, I imagined, since Alison had not been able to bring herself to touch the body. I tried not to look at it, but my eyes kept straying back. It was bright blue, of some man-made fibre – nylon or polypropylene – and looked rough to the touch, hard to make a good knot with. I wondered where Andrew had learned what knots to tie, whether his fingers had fumbled as he pulled it tight. I imagined how its coarse texture would cut into the delicate skin of the neck, and had to push the thought away.

'Can you see the boxes?' Alison called up, sounding falsely cheerful. 'They should be beside the big wooden plan chest.'

That at least was hard to miss: an old architect's plan chest dominated one end of the room beneath the gable, three cardboard boxes in a jumbled tower beside it. The top one was thick with dust; they obviously hadn't been opened in a while.

I hoisted the top box down and opened it. Andrew's face stared out at me, florid and grinning, and his presence suddenly filled the room. I dropped the box, and photos spilled over my feet. Alison and Andrew, Andrew and Alison – the AA, or 'fourth rescue service', as friends had jokingly termed them – a hundred, two hundred images of them taken together and singly: in groups at weddings, on boats, on holiday, in overalls working on the house. Twenty years of bright Fujicolor history packed into a dusty old box.

'Sorry!' I called down. 'Dropped something.'

I scooped the photos up and crammed them back into the box, averting my eyes from these images of another, better world. The second box contained old notebooks, diaries, a faded visitors' book, but nothing that looked like a family bible. That left the last box. I wrestled it open. Under a bundle of yellowing newspaper lay a huge, musty-smelling object. I levered it out. Its leather cover felt damp to the touch, and it smelled of mildew, though the box and attic space seemed dry and weatherproof, as if it brought its own climate with it.

'I've got it!' I called down. As I hefted it, something shifted from inside its back cover and several pages of foxed, brown-edged paper dislodged themselves. For a moment I thought the whole thing was disintegrating; then I realized they were loose. Old letters, at a glance. I shuffled them carefully back inside the cover and took a last look around the attic space where Andrew Hoskin had taken his life. Despite the bright light streaming in through the window, the room seemed oppressive, as if not only the beams and joists and tiles of the roof were bearing down on me, but also the sky, the stars and the heavens beyond. Suddenly I felt a wash of utmost despair. I was a tiny, worthless speck of life in a huge universe. What did I think I was I doing here? I was wasting my time, wasting my life. There was nothing for me here; indeed, possibly nothing for me anywhere. I had no job, no family, no man, no children, no prospects; and certainly wouldn't find them in Cornwall. Moreover, I was a woman, and faithless. The thought came to me, clear as a clarion call, that I should leave at once, just *go away.*

Clutching the bible, I fled down the stairs, already calculating the length of time it would take me to pack, call a taxi and make my way to Penzance Station.

'What on earth's the matter?' Alison's eyes were blue-rimmed and hollow. She looked like a stranger, an intruder in the house. All I wanted to do was to barge past her and get out.

I put a hand out as if to push her away. 'I –' And then the feeling passed. I blinked.

She took the bible away from me: I probably looked too unsteady on my feet to be carrying it. 'Let's go downstairs,' she said firmly, tucking the huge volume under her arm. She put her other arm around me. 'You look in need of a cup of strong tea.'

And, just like that, she had switched from being the victim to the carer, and I was the one in need of looking after. Perhaps, I reflected as I followed her down to the kitchen, that was exactly what she needed, this reversal in our roles.

There were no Tregennas listed at the front of the family bible. Lots of Pengellys and Martins, Johns and Bolithos; some Lanyons and Stephens and even a Rodda, a name I recognized from the tub of clotted cream Alison had in the fridge; but not a single Tregenna. I didn't know whether to be disappointed or relieved.

9

Catherine

July 1625

An old Ægyptian woman came to the scullery door today. She came on a mule & was arrayed most strangely with bells & scarfs, her face & hands almost blacke . . .

When the knocking came at the scullery door, Catherine was in the kitchen taking down a list of provender dictated by Lady Harris. The air was thick with the fragrant aroma of furmity, which Kate Rowse, the cook, had been boiling up all morning. The smell alone made Cat's stomach rumble: Kate had added spices, butter and rum to the wheat porridge, and she wasn't sure she could wait as long as the noon meal.

'Go see who's there, Catherine,' Margaret Harris said, without moving an inch from the larder. She turned back to the cook. 'Quite how we've managed to run through so much flour in a month I cannot imagine.' Lady Harris, like her husband, ran a tight ship.

Visitors to Kenegie were not infrequent, and came for all manner of reasons: beggars to request alms, though they were not encouraged, for the Master donated generously to the parish and preferred to see the parson attend to the matter of charity; gamesmen offering a fine hare or a brace of pigeons; Market-Jew fishermen with their wares strapped in a withy basket on their backs seeking a groat for a mackerel, a penny for a pollock or thruppence for one of the great eels that lurked beneath the offshore reefs.

Outside the scullery, tying the halter of a bone-thin mule to one of the ornamental bay trees, was what appeared to be an old woman: but, if so, she was like no other old woman Cat had ever encountered. This bizarre little person wore a brightly coloured headscarf tied at the nape of her neck, vast hoops of gold in her ears, a bodice of patchworked fabrics and a voluminous pair of breeches caught close at the ankle by silk scarves and ropes of tinkling silver bells. But it was not even the impropriety of the breeches that gave Cat such cause for amazement; it was the colour of her skin, which was a most remarkable brown, as dark as a conker. A couple of years back some vagrants claiming to be Ægyptians had turned up in Penzance with a travelling show; but they had blacked their skin with a liquor of oak galls – as had become evident when the Constable had consigned them to the stocks and upturned the water butt over them. Two days later they'd been lashed out of town, never to be seen again, which Cat had thought was a great shame; true gypsies or no, they would have provided some exotic entertainment, a glimpse of another, more glamorous world.

She opened the door a crack. 'What do you want here?' she whispered. 'You'd best be off quietly, for the folk here don't look well upon your kind.'

The crone regarded her with an eye as bright as a blackbird's. 'A girl with her head afire and goodness in her heart: now there be a fine sign for a murky sabbado.'

Cat stared at her. 'Whatever are you talking about?'

The gypsy leaned against the door frame and peered into the scullery. 'Yon settle looks fair for resting a bundle of old bones that have been jounced since dawn's light.'

'I really can't let you in,' Cat said nervously. 'Much as I'd like to – I'd get into trouble. There's a bench in the garden, though; you could sit on that and I could perhaps bring you something to drink before you go on your way.'

The old woman continued to gaze at her, unblinking. 'There be trouble coming your way whether or no you let me in.'

Cat took a step backwards. 'What sort of trouble?'

'I'll take some repast for that, my maid,' the Ægyptian said, sniffing the air like a little pug dog and setting her foot over the threshold.

'Ah, no, you'd best come with me,' Cat said quickly, before the situation got out of hand. She slipped out of the scullery door, leaving it on the latch, and drew the woman away across the garden, out of sight of the kitchen windows. The crone sat down on a bench beneath the apple tree and eased her feet out of her long leather shoes with a great sigh. 'Treacherous as the serpent in Eden,' she complained, glaring at them and rubbing her bunions with a great claw of a hand. 'I paid good silver for them at Exeter; by Plymouth I was in agonies.' She paused, then straightened up. 'I'll be needing new shoes in Penzance, I think.'

When Cat said nothing to this, the old woman rolled her eyes. 'Be a good maid and give me a bit of silver, and I'll tell your fortune.'

Cat caught her breath. 'Are you a moon-woman? One as reads the path of life in a girl's hand?'

'The spirits have bestowed that gift upon me,' the old woman said modestly. 'Though it tends to work the better for the touch of silver.'

'I have no silver; but I could get you something to eat, if you're hungry. There's some bread fresh baked.'

The old woman snorted. 'Can't wear loaves on my poor ruined old feet, can I?' she demanded.

Cat desperately wanted her fortune told. But she had given her last coin to her mother the day before and would not be paid till the coming Monday.

'The bread is good,' she urged. 'And there's furmity in the pot.'

At the mention of the furmity the crone sat up straighter. She gave Cat a wide, lop-sided grin which showed off her strange collection of teeth. 'Ah, furmity: now that's worth a fortune to me. But, mind, if you want good spirits to guide your future, maidie, best make sure there's plenty of good spirits in it, eh?'

Cat ran back to the scullery, wondering how on earth she was going to make away with a bowl of furmity without being seen.

'Who was it?' Margaret Harris called sharply as Cat entered the kitchen.

'A poor, hungry old woman,' Cat said, not meeting her eye.

'Another of them vagabonds, looking to steal our victuals no doubt!' Cook clucked.

Cat drew herself up. 'She's a poor old crone, bent almost double and riding the world's thinnest mule. I sat her down in the shade of the orchard.'

Margaret Harris strode over to the window and stared out at the unfortunate beast. 'Lord save us, the wretched thing's eating my lavender! Kate, go at once to the yard and tell young Will to take it away and give it some barley.' She turned back to Cat. 'You can take the old woman one of yesterday's loaves and draw her up some water from the well. Beggars can't be choosers.'

Cat reached for one of the flagons, but Lady Harris caught her hand. 'Do have a thought, child: these wandering people carry all sorts of diseases with them from the cities. We want no pox or pestilence here. Surely she must have her own drinking vessel?'

Then, as if her maid might already be infected by her contact with the vagabond creature, Lady Harris left the kitchen at speed.

Cat caught up one of the twelve new round loaves which stood cooling on the rack where Cook and Nell had placed them earlier. Then, recklessly, she took down an old pewter bowl and dipped it swiftly into the bubbling furmity pot. The crock of rum was on the floor; hefting it, Cat poured a good dash into the bowl, and over her shoes into the bargain.

'God's teeth!' Now she would have to wash them at the well or go round all day stinking of liquor, which certainly wouldn't enhance her already tarnished reputation. Clutching bread and bowl to her bosom, she ran back to the orchard.

The gypsy's fingers fixed on the furmity bowl like a falcon on a mouse. For a second the two women stood there, connected only by the pewter dish, and Cat felt a strange low thrumming in her bones. Then the Ægyptian broke the connection sharply. Holding the bowl close, she scooped the porridge into her mouth, barely drawing breath as she wolfed it all down.

'Not enough rum,' she pronounced at last, wiping her mouth and handing the empty bowl back to Cat. The loaf she stowed away in some great hidden pocket of her pantaloons.

Cat pursed her mouth. She had expected if not gratitude, then at least some acknowledgement of her trouble. She stuck her hand out, palm up, hoping that at least the spirits would be more gentle towards her, but the crone pushed her hand away. Cat had the sudden, distinct impression that she did not want to touch her. 'You said you'd read my hand!' she said sharply. ''Twas for that I brought the furmity and the bread and risked the wrath of my mistress.'

''Tis not the wrath of thy mistress thou needs fear, maidie,' the crone returned. She winked, horribly. 'I'll cast the stones for thee, but do not blame me if thee like not what thee hears.' And so saying she delved into the other capacious pocket of her breeches and drew out a little leather pouch that jinked as she moved it. 'Touch the stones, maidie, and think of the things that most trouble thee,' she instructed, and Cat did as she was bid, thinking of Rob and her fear of captivity, of the altar cloth and her dreams of escape. They felt cold and smooth, like pebbles from a stream, except for a roughness on one side.

'You must draw four stones, one at a time, and put them down there, on the ground.'

Cat's fingers caressed the stones, as if to pacify them, to soothe their predictions. Then she selected one and put it down. On the upmost surface three scratched lines had been inscribed into it like a crooked letter *c*. 'That's for thy past,' the crone said. She peered at the stone like a thrush regarding a worm. 'Now there's a mystery,' she said cryptically. 'A wild mix of blood you have there, my lover; and blood will out. Take another.'

Cat frowned. Her second stone bore a pattern like two broken links in a chain.

''Tis a time of change, but the results of this change will depend on your perseverance.'

Cat's jaw firmed. If perseverance was what it would take to get her out of here, perseverance she would have. But if they were going to marry her to Robert by the end of the summer, then perseverance would hardly serve. 'For how long must I persevere?' she burst out. 'I fear there are some things that may not be endured or turned back, whatever I do.'

The old woman clacked her teeth. 'Patience, birdie. Take a third.'

She watched as Cat put it down next to the other two. A stone bearing a zigzag line. 'Ah, the lightning bolt.' She made a face. 'The casting down of vanity and the wrath of God.'

Cat frowned. Now the Ægyptian was sounding like Nell Chigwine. 'Are you quite sure? Is there no other reading of the sign?'

'Don't question the stones, maidie. Unless you want worse.'

'I don't think I believe your stones!'

'I'll stop, then, and be on my way.'

Cat sighed. 'No, please don't. I'll hear the rest, if it please you.' She took a fourth stone quickly out of the bag and put it down. The symbol on it was shaped like a roughly hewn *r*, but all in angles.

The gypsy burst out laughing. 'There it is, there it is!' she crowed. 'I knowed it, I did. Ah, but the spirits speak loud to Old Maggi atimes. There she is, as bold as day: *raido*, the journey. Ye'll be going a long way, birdie, a very long way from here, and at the end of your journey will be a union between Earth and Heaven, all your dreams come true.'

Cat regarded her suspiciously. The promise of a long journey was exactly what she most wished for: all the way to London, with any luck. But the talk of a union between Heaven and Earth taxed her, for might that not mean that the journey was one's path through life, culminating in death and the ascension of the soul? Which was all very well, but surely was applicable to each and every one of God's children. She suspected the old woman kept a store of such charlatanry for her customers, hoping they would go away content with such generalities.

'Catherine Anne Tregenna, whatever do you think you are doing out here, consorting with such a creature!' Margaret Harris came storming down the path towards them.

Cat's face flamed. The pewter bowl lay in clear view, and the Mistress was sure to recognize it as one of her own.

'And you!' The Mistress of Kenegie's fury was now directed towards the old gypsy woman. 'Take your devilry away from here directly or it'll be the worse for you. Invoking the spirits will see you burned as a witch. You are lucky that I am a Christian woman and do not hold with the loosing of a soul by such violent means –

but if I find you on my land again beguiling any of my retainers, you may be sure that the Constable will drive you into the sea off the Gurnard's Head, and you'll meet a number of your own kind among the bones down there. Now take your mangy animal and away with you: and don't you stop in Penzance or I shall know of it!'

She grabbed Cat by the arm, then recoiled. 'By the Lord's wounds, Catherine, you stink of liquor! You add another malfeasance to your tally, my girl. Why a good man like Robert Bolitho should ever wish to take such a one to wife, I cannot imagine. You had best mend your ways, or he'll look elsewhere and you'll find yourself a spinster, or worse.'

The old crone scrabbled up her stones and stowed them away. Then she straightened up and looked Lady Harris full square in the face.

'Great sorrow will fall on this place; and nothing I can say or do can stay it. Thy life be long, Lady of the Mount.' She turned away. 'But thy husband will be in his grave ere long,' she uttered hoarsely. To Cat she hissed, 'Thee, birdie, need not fear marriage.'

Cat stared at her. 'Why ever not?'

'Because as Catherine thee'll never be wed in this world,' the Ægyptian said, and limped painfully away.

That night, in the confines of her narrow cot, Cat pondered the old woman's words. She had been thinking about the gypsy's pronouncements all day; they had woven a complete cat's cradle of a tangle in her head. Sometimes she thought she had pulled a thread away from the muddle and that it shone bright and clear in her hands: that she need not fear marriage, for she would not be wed. But then that thought was spoiled by the realization that if she were never to marry, then that was a fearsome thought indeed. To be consigned to work all her days away at the whim of whatever household she fetched up in, to depend on the charity of others: was that not even worse than marrying Robert, who, while dull and not the least bit rich, was at least a decent, hard-working man who would keep her in whatever comfort he could afford? Then she thought about the great sorrow the Ægyptian had spoken of.

Was the pestilence coming again to this corner of Cornwall? It had already carried off her father, a tough and sturdy man; if it could bring him low, it could sweep all in its path. Or would war explode suddenly on their peaceful shores, as it had at the end of the last century? The gypsy had told her, though, that perseverance would save her, so surely neither war nor plague was destined to take her life. And what of the long journey she had been promised, which would finish by uniting Heaven and Earth? That was in the end the question that vexed her most.

Perhaps she would be taking the road to London after all, to live in a great house and move in high society, and who knew then what her future might be? Even though the memory of Sir John Killigrew pawing her made her hot with shame and disgust, it proved that great men found her pretty enough to kiss; and maybe the Ægyptian was plain wrong when she said Cat would never marry. After all, she had said that 'as Catherine' she would never wed 'in this world': perhaps another world awaited her in another place. If the Countess of Salisbury took her away from here, to be her private embroiderer and maid, perhaps that fine lady would have a pet name for her.

This thought carried her to the matter of the altar cloth, for surely such a great project was all about perseverance? Fired by conviction, she drew her design out from beneath the bed, unrolling it with care.

The Tree of Knowledge stretched before her in the candlelight, stylized and elegant. Birds sang in its branches, flowers of all types bloomed in a blaze of glory, small creatures played at its foot. On either side of its trunk the man and woman leaned, their bellies pressed modestly against the wood, Eve's hand fixed around the fruit that promised knowledge and damnation.

Cat gazed long and hard on her design, and the more she looked upon it, the more she became convinced it contained the key to the conundrum. She traced its graceful contours, running her fingers over the rough linen as if it might somehow speak.

'A long journey,' she whispered to herself. 'A union between Earth and Heaven.'

And suddenly the cat's cradle was unravelled and there the answer lay: the Wood of Life, with its roots buried deep in the Earth and its branches reaching up to Heaven, reuniting the worlds of the sacred and profane in a single elegant symbol. For Cat, that was enough. She had her sign; her destiny was clear.

Tomorrow, after church, she would devote her free afternoon to working on the altar frontal that would save her, would carry her on a long journey and provide her with a fine new life, away from Rob, away from Kenegie, away from Cornwall, as she had always dreamed it would.

IO

I was in the garden with Alison a few days later when my mobile phone rang. We'd just come back from the solicitor's office in Truro where they were handling the probate of Andrew's will. There had been an accident on the A30, causing a huge tailback of traffic, parking in Truro had been difficult, the clerk had lost a crucial form which required Alison's signature, and we were both tired and a little fraught. Relaxing in the canvas chairs with a new piece of embroidery – a simple scarf with peacock feathers worked into the corners in a combination of satin stitch and chain – with the larks singing high overhead, and a glass of chilled Chenin Blanc, was proving wonderfully recuperative. So when the harsh polyphonic noise of the ringtone sounded, it was a most unwelcome intrusion. How unwelcome I was not to guess.

'Hello?'

Stupidly, I had not checked the screen before answering. Michael's voice caught me unpleasantly by surprise.

'Ah, you're still alive, then?' He sounded faintly disappointed. 'I left you several messages, but you never replied,' he accused.

I said nothing.

'Where are you?' he pressed.

'I'm down in Cornwall with my cousin Alison, though it's none of your business where the hell I am.'

There was a pause, an intake of breath at the other end of the line. He wasn't used to hearing me feisty and self-sufficient, let alone downright rude. Then he laughed. It was, I thought, a rather nervous-sounding laugh. 'How amazing. So am I. In Cornwall, that is.'

Alison reached across the table and took my mobile from me.

'Hello, Michael. Yes, that's right, she's here with me. Trevarth Farm, just above Gulval, in the hills north of Penzance.' She listened for a moment, then nodded. 'If you've got the Landranger map, it's clearly marked. Just ask anyone you see on the road if you can't find it; or call Julia for more instructions once you're closer. We'll expect you in forty minutes. There's a crab salad for tea; I hope you're not allergic to shellfish.' She pressed the red button, closing the connection, and handed the mobile back to me.

I stared at her. 'What on earth did you do that for?'

'You two need to make a civilized end to your affair, for Anna's sake. Shake hands and start behaving normally towards one another. After all, you can't avoid each other for ever, and you might as well do it while I'm here as referee.'

'That's easy for you to say, but I'm not ready to see him again. I'm going to have a shower,' I said stiffly, pushing myself out of the chair.

'Put on your red dress!' she called to me as I went in. 'It makes you look really pretty.'

When I came back down again forty minutes later, clean and tidy from my shower, my hair bound back, my make-up refreshed and the red dress on simply because it was the only thing that didn't require either washing or ironing, I found that Michael had some-how already arrived. He was sitting with his back to me in an old deck-chair, knocking back a glass of wine and chuckling at some-thing Alison had just said, looking annoyingly at home.

'Where's your car?' I demanded crossly. 'I didn't see it in the drive.'

He swivelled at my voice. 'It's lovely to see you too,' he returned, struggling to rise from the deck-chair. I prayed for a painful tangle of collapsed wood and limbs, but Michael managed to disengage himself without serious mishap, looking typically elegant in a cream linen shirt and a pair of stone-coloured chinos. His eyes swept over me, taking in the contours of the red dress appreciatively. 'I took a taxi; it seemed the most sensible option to let a local do the legwork. He knew where it was at once.'

I was damned if I was to be so easily charmed; or chastely kissed. I stood there with my hands on my hips feeling suddenly furious at the effect he still had on me. 'What are you doing here? In Cornwall, I mean.'

He turned back to Alison, grimacing. 'I see what you mean.'

I drew up a chair a little way from the table and sat down, glaring.

'I, ah, had a little business down here. Some property of Anna's she wants to sell. She sends her love, by the way.'

The mention of her name made me go cold. Anna had links with Cornwall? Goose bumps stood out on my arm as if a sudden breeze had caught me. I gave him the sort of flat-lidded look I imagine cats give those they most despise. 'Oh, I see. Freeing up a bit of capital for a second honeymoon, are you?' I said acidly, and he had the grace to look away. 'Where is it, then, this "property"?'

'Mousehole village, a cottage that's all, but derelict. Anna's had a tenant in it for ages, and he's just passed on. It came to her on her twenty-first birthday, but this was the first she told me of it; she's a secretive little thing sometimes.'

'So where are you staying?' Alison asked.

'I'm booked into a little hotel there. Bit pricey, but I guess I can't begrudge my fellow Corns an honest dollar. Or even a dishonest one.'

I stared out across the garden to the valley and the sea beyond. Through the bright lattice of trees I could just make out the tower of a church above the seafront at Penzance and a little stretch of the glittering bay beyond. Mousehole lay a few miles away, past the headland which marked the westerly extent of Mount's Bay. I recalled from Cat's little book that it was where a fishing skiff called the *Constance* had been found washed up, all its crew missing and a 'Turkish blade' stuck in her planking.

'I'd love to see it,' Alison said. 'The cottage. Some of these quaint old places have so much character, especially when they've been left to rot for a while. I could give you some advice on how to do it up, get a good price for it.'

I glared at her, willing her to stop. It was just the sort of project

Alison needed to distract her from the misery of Andrew's death; but selfishly all I could think was that every bit of profit made out of the cottage was a contribution towards Michael's new life with Anna. If I thought about them at all (and I had tried very hard not to) I wished them poor and discontented, not rich and happy.

But Michael was animation personified. He leaned across the table and patted her arm, giving her the smile that lit up his face, the one I thought he reserved for me. 'Great. Come down tomorrow – I can't say I'm looking to do much with the place, just get it into shape and put it on the market as fast as we can, but I'd love to know what you think. As Julia can tell you, I've not much gift in the matter of interior design – my Soho flat's been cheerfully rotting about my ears for years, but I don't think you'd find it very quaint!'

At this point, I could stand it no longer. Pushing my chair back so violently that its feet scraped the granite with an unforgiving screech, I headed for the shelter of the house, feeling two pairs of eyes drilling into my back as I retreated.

I fled upstairs and flung myself face down on the bed, all my emotional elastic snapped and flabby. Tears that I had been holding back for ten days spilled out in a torrential flood. I made so much noise, I didn't hear the footsteps on the stairs or the opening of the door; so when the mattress gave suddenly as someone sat down, I sprang up with my heart hammering.

Michael sat there, looking at once appalled and shamefaced. He pulled a large and crumpled handkerchief out of a pocket and wiped my face with it, smearing unglamorous strings of snot across my cheek. Furiously, I pushed his hand away and ran into the en suite, shutting the door behind me. There, I splashed my face with water and stared at myself in the mirror. Daylight is a teller of harsh truths: I never understand why people design their houses to let more of it in. Unless you have the tight, gleaming skin of a fit twenty-year-old, daylight will cheerfully illumine every wrinkle and blemish, every sag and bit of dullness, leaving you feeling like an age-old, careworn hag, even after you've exfoliated every atom of dead skin away, moisturized with cream that costs more per ounce than pure frankincense, and applied with care and expertise the world's most expensive make-up. I had done all these things less than an hour ago; now I looked like a hurricane victim.

Viciously, I rubbed my face clean with a flannel and, without the slightest enhancement or disguising mask, went out to face the lover who had rejected me. Let him see the effect he has had, I thought; let him see the damage done.

But when I came out, I found him with his back to me, hunched over. He looked upset; I knew the contours of his body so well, I could tell even from this view that he was agitated.

'Why did you come here?' I said quietly, and was glad that my voice did not tremble.

He started guiltily, got up and turned to face me. In his hands he held my book, his parting gift to me.

I strode across the room and took it from him, cradling it against my chest protectively.

'Alison's been telling me about the book,' he said, sitting back down with what seemed a feigned nonchalance. 'It sounds fascinating.'

'It is,' I said, hugging it closer.

'I'd love to have a proper look at it.' He held his hand out, and for a moment some traitorous instinct in me believed he was reaching for me.

'I'm sure you would.'

'Julia, don't be angry with me.'

'I think I have every right to be angry with you, don't you?'

'I never meant to hurt you, truly I didn't.'

'Then what are you doing here, rubbing my nose in it – all that stuff about bloody Anna's bloody cottage? How can you imagine it's OK for you to just turn up out of the blue like this? I came three hundred miles to get away from you and now here you are, in my face, reading the bloody book you gave me as a goodbye-and-get-stuffed present!'

By now I was yelling at him, all reserve gone. He went pale; he had never coped with extremes of emotion well.

'Calm down. Please. I wanted to know you were all right, so I phoned your mobile a couple of days ago, and Alison answered it. She said she was worried about you, so I volunteered to come down and sort out the cottage for Anna so that I could see you.'

I glared at him, thinking. Alison and I had gone swimming at the lido a couple of days ago, a lovely old Art Deco affair down on the seafront where you could paddle endlessly around an enormous seawater-filled space, gazing at the cerulean sky and St Mary's Church and pretend you were on the Riviera. I remembered seeing Alison on the phone at one point as I lazily breaststroked my way around the deep end, but I hadn't realized it had been my phone.

'Very gracious of you, I'm sure.'

'Not really.' He shrugged. 'Truth is, for . . . er . . . various reasons we're going to need some extra cash.'

I had to suppress the small, mean smile that rose up inside me. Not such a bed of roses after all. Well, that was some consolation.

'In fact, it's a funny thing, but the book' – he gestured towards it – 'came from a house clearance down here. It must have been down here in Cornwall ever since when was it, 1634?'

'1625.' He obviously didn't know I knew it had come from the very house we were sitting in. I could have let it go, but somehow I didn't want to. 'Alison said she and Andrew sent it up to you along with a load of other old books. To sell for them.'

He reddened. 'Ah. Well, I thought you'd appreciate it, it being an embroidery book and all. Kept it for you for a while, actually, then forgot all about it until . . . well, you know. So, really, I gave it to you in error: in all honesty, you ought to let me have it back again when you've finished it, so I can sell it for Alison. Funerals cost a bit nowadays, and I gather Andrew was rather on his uppers.'

What a snake he was. As soon as he got his hands on it I knew he'd sell it, all right, but I bet the full price fetched would never make it into Alison's pocket. 'When I've finished reading it, then, perhaps,' I lied, and watched his face soften with relief.

'Come here, old thing,' he said at last, holding his arms wide.

Like a mindless automaton I found myself walking towards him, and then my head was resting on his shoulder, and I could smell the ironed-linen smell of his shirt and a trace of his usual cologne, heated by his body, beneath. He cupped my head against him, and I felt the beat of his pulse quicken. The book dug uncomfortably into my breast as he held me closer, and, suddenly aware of my weak stupidity, I pulled away, cheeks flaming.

'Go away,' I said. 'Don't do this.'

He rubbed his face and I remembered how many times I had lain propped up on my elbows over him easing away the tension lines on his forehead with the pads of my fingers.

'It's not so easy to forget you, Julia, whatever you may think; it's not been easy for me these past weeks.'

'Good. Now go away.'

That night, I stayed in my room and immersed myself in Catherine's book. Midnight passed, the moon rose, and the stars wheeled, but I did not see them. When the owl hooted in the woods at two in the morning, I was still reading, because the notes in the margin had suddenly revealed themselves to be not just a needlewoman's daily journal but a devastating historical puzzle.

II

Catherine

Sunday, 24th July

I wryte this I noe not where, in darknesse & feare for my life, nay, my very sowle. It ys five daies since they came uppon us, five daies & nights of horror. I have seene sights no woman shuld witnesse, borne indignitie & terrors no Christian shuld be subjected to, & where it all will end, if not in agonie & deth, I can not conceive. All around ys misery & paine, stink & creweltie. May bee we are all ready dead & have passed on to purgatorie. But surely even Hell can not bee worse than this awefull fate that has overtaken us? May the Lord have mercy on me & on my fellows & save us from our inhumayne lot, but I feare He has turned His face from us & heares not oure cryes ...

'Cat . . . Catherine!'

She turned quickly, to find her cousin Robert standing in the hallway, wearing his Sunday best and a hangdog expression. His blue eyes were beseeching. For the past two weeks, since the Master had spelled out her destiny, Catherine had barely spoken a word to him.

'What do you want?'

'I've come to take you down to the town. Matty said the two of you were going to the chapel in Penzance to hear the new preacher, so I thought I might come with you. Besides, there's a sea-fret hanging over the bay – I thought you'd not want to get wet –'

Cat's chin came up sharply. 'We can walk, thank you, it's only two mile or so.' She glanced down regretfully at her best stockings, the ones with the clocking at the ankles. She had embroidered them herself, and they were very fine: the thought of them getting wet or, worse, muddy, was infuriating. But she would not go with Rob if she could help it.

At that moment Matty appeared. When she saw Robert Bolitho, her face broke into a huge and happy smile. 'I saw the trap outside; are you come with us down to the town, Rob? It's fair mizzly out: you can't even see the Mount through it and I warn't looking forward to the walk, though Nell and William have already set out, I see.'

Cat sighed; there was no avoiding it now. 'Nell Chigwine's going to the chapel of Our Lady? Why isn't she going down to Gulval as usual with the rest of the household? It was the one reason I could fathom out that might make joining Mother and Uncle Ned today a little more bearable, that at least I wouldn't have to endure Nell watching me during the sermon, waiting for the preacher to make a reference to Eve's sin so that she can smirk at me.'

Matty grinned. 'It'll be a change, Cat; 'sides, if I have to sit through another of Mr Veale's long sermons I'll likely drop off. I din't get a wink last night with them gulls squawking their heads off on the roof right over me. The Reverend says God created all creatures with a purpose and a plan, but I can't see what seagulls are good for at all. I rubbed my knuckles raw yesterday cleaning their mess off the courtyard, bleddy things.'

Cat leaned in towards her and said softly, 'It's said they cry with the voices of the dead who've not yet passed over.'

Matty recoiled. 'But they're right over my head!' she wailed. 'I hear them walking around!' Her eyes filled with tears.

Rob shot Cat a furious look, then he put an arm around the distraught housemaid. 'Let's get you in the trap, Matty. When we get back I'll see what I can do about clearing their nests off the roof above your room, shall I?'

Matty gazed up at him adoringly. 'You're a good man, Robert Bolitho. Cat don't know how lucky she is.'

The mist was still thick as they trotted out of the drive on to the road that wound steeply down towards the sea. It swathed the countryside, trapping the heat of the land so that the air was muggy and hard to breathe. Sea-frets like this were not a rare phenomenon during a Cornish summer and would most likely burn off when the sun rose higher, but to Catherine the enclosing mist made the ride down to Penzance claustrophobic. She felt the hedges pressing in on her, the seedheads of the docks showing the rust-red of old blood, the towering foxglove stalks now bereft of all flowers, as if they had been stripped by some malign hand. She stole a glance at Rob, at his broad, blunt profile and the unruly strands of straw-yellow hair escaping from his hat. Could she bear to wake to see that face on the pillow beside her day after day, year after year, with the cows lowing in the byre behind her cottage wall and the gulls screaming on the roof overhead, and these same small horizons framing her world? Something inside her contracted. Until the Master had forced the betrothal upon her, she had regarded her cousin fondly; now she could hardly bear to sit beside him in a carriage and have people look upon them as a couple. The gypsy's words of hope had been proved false: in a month she and Rob would be man and wife, for the banns were posted and several yards of Spanish brocade had been bought by Lady Harris from the best draper in town (who just happened to be Cat's uncle, Edward Coode, so no doubt a fine deal had been struck), as bright as the sea that the mist veiled this day. She had not had the heart to make a start on it. To sew your own wedding dress when every time you looked at the fabric made you wish it were your shroud was not likely to imbue your gown with all the luck you would need to carry you through married life. Worst of all, her one possible avenue of escape – in the shape of the Countess of Salisbury's visit to her mistress – had been closed down. She had been embroidering the altar cloth for the past two weeks; then last Thursday a courier had brought the letter from Lady Cecil explaining that she would be spending the summer at Framlingham and that she hoped now to travel with her husband when he came to inspect the Mount in the autumn to assess the case for new armaments. That night, Cat had folded the altar cloth away beneath the bed. She had not touched it since.

As the trap drew along the seafront road, she gazed across the cloud-filled bay. St Michael's Mount made its presence felt only as a vague, massy shadow. The tide was in, but nothing stirred on the sea; the boats were moored up for the day of rest, and even the seabirds had tucked their heads under their wings. Cat played with a loose thread on her sleeve. Normally she would have addressed the repair with alacrity, darning in the escaped thread with stitches so neat and fine none but she would have noticed the mend, but, truth be told, she found she had neither the energy nor the will to begin the task. With her fate laid out straight before her and no apparent chance of escape, she felt as shadowy and indistinct as the castle on the isle: an empty, lifeless thing trapped in a restless sea.

The road ran around the harbour, along the quay, past the warehouses and the fish sheds and St Anthony's Well, and then rose steeply up Quay Street to the chapel of Our Lady on the headland. They passed a stream of worshippers toiling up the hill, all no doubt eager to hear the new preacher speak. He was a Puritan come all the way from Liskeard, Cat had heard, which had made her heart sink further: her uncle was a recent convert and as head of the family was determined that they should all follow his example. Many of those who made their way to the chapel wore simple garb; and not all of them, Cat suspected, because they were poor folk. Indeed, she recognized fat old Alderman Polglaze and his equally large wife, Elizabeth, huffing and puffing along all in plain black relieved only by white lace collars and cuffs. The irony was, she thought, that some decades back they'd have looked just like the Spanish Catholics they so despised, give or take a ruff or two. They passed the Constable, Jim Carew, and old Thomas Ellys and his wife, Alice, the boatbuilder Andrew Pengelly and his son Ephraim, Thomas Samuels and his sister Anne, the Hoskens family from Market-Jew and old Henry Johns, who had the big house up near Lescudjack. It looked as if the preacher would have a very fair turnout. Then someone called out to them, and Cat turned to see Jack Kellynch grinning like a shark on the other side of the street.

'Hoy there in the coach! You look like a gentleman born, Rob Bolitho, trotting by with your soon-to-be lady wife at your side; but, oh, poor Matty all alone in the back!' And with that, he ran across the road, caught hold of the side of the trap with both hands, swung himself up over the wheel and vaulted into the back seat alongside the blushing housemaid.

Cat turned to regard him solemnly, though inwardly she seethed at his description. 'I'm surprised to see you on your way to Preacher Truran, Mister Kellynch. I'd have thought, with your upbringing and sinning ways, the confession box would be more to your taste than listening to some old tub-thumper.'

Jack laughed. 'Don't you let my old man hear you talk like that or he'll put you over his knee and beat some godfearing ways into you, *Mistress* Catherine. Even my ma can't talk him out of his passion for the minister. Ah, look, there they are now: wave to them, Matty, like a real queen!'

Near the top of Quay Street came Isacke Kellynch, followed by his little dark wife, Maria, their second son, Jordie, and daughter, Henrietta, whom everyone called Chicken. Matty, red as a beetroot now, raised a feeble hand. For a moment Isacke Kellynch stared at the passing carriage, then his bright blue eyes bulged. 'Get down out of that fancy wagon,' he bellowed at his son, 'and use your two legs as the good God gave you.' But Jack just threw back his head and laughed.

At the top of the hill Robert drew the horses to a halt, got down and handed Cat out of the trap. He waited, holding her elbow, until Jack and Matty had passed into the crowd. Cat pulled her arm away crossly. 'Now Matty has gone in without me and everyone will tease her about Jack, and you know she is sweet on him, and he's just dallying with her, it means nothing to him and she'll get her heart broken,' she said, all in a rush.

Rob gave her a queer look. 'You don't know much about Jack Kellynch, do you?'

'I know that he's a brigand and a buccaneer, a rare nighthawk with a girl in every port.' And far too flash and handsome for a turnip like Matty, she thought, but did not say.

'You're wrong,' Rob said, shaking his head. 'You're always so obdurate in your opinions, Catherine, that sometimes you can't see what's right before your eyes.'

'If it's not bad enough that I've come to hear the boring old preacher sermonize, now I have to listen to you too!'

'If you don't want me here, then I will go. But Jack will make Matty his wife before the year is out: mark my words.' He dug in his pocket and brought out a little package wrapped tightly in a piece of blue silk. 'Here: I want you to have this. You can open it later, in the presence of your family; or privately if you prefer.'

Her fingers closed on it. Inside the silk the hidden object was small and dense and hard. 'What is it?'

'A token of our betrothal. It was my mother's,' he said shortly. 'She would have liked you, even though you do not care for me one whit.' His jaw was set; it had cost him dear to say what he knew to be the truth, but if Sunday was not the day for speaking what was in his heart, then he knew not when else he might do so. They were so rarely alone, especially now that she avoided his company.

Cat stared at him in dismay. 'It is not you, Robert; not alone. It is here – Kenegie, Cornwall, this life. It is not what I planned for myself. Not what I dreamed of.' Her fingertips investigated further, discovering that the heart of the object was absent. A ring. A betrothal ring. She pressed the little parcel back into his hand. 'Do not give it to me now, Robert. Wait for a better time, when there are not harsh words between us.'

He looked at her so piercingly that she felt sure he could see right into the core of her. At last he nodded. After a pause which indicated a hard internal wrangle, he said, 'Perhaps I can find work elsewhere in the world. I would not have you give up your dreams, Catherine.'

And then he turned and walked away, leaving her breathless and confused.

'Catherine!'

She turned to find her uncle bearing down upon her. Edward Coode was a tall man, as bald as a snake, and with about as much warmth. Beside him, his wife, Mary, was the picture of florid health, her vast bosom barely confined by the boning of her corset. Their two small sons ran along the churchyard wall, hitting one another with sticks, until old Annie Badcock the witch turned her evil eye upon them and they went to hide their faces in their mother's skirts.

'You will sit in our family pew with us today, Catherine,' her uncle said severely, thus putting paid to her hopes of sitting with Matty at the back of the church, where she could write her notes in privacy and avoid the gaze of Nell Chigwine. She carried her book, writing stick and a little knife for sharpening its lead in the little bag she wore at her waist. Her journal entries had become too personal to allow for others to happen on them, and, even though she knew neither Polly nor Nell could read, she suspected that if either found the book they would render it up to Lady Harris – the one out of well-meaning intent, thinking it misplaced, the other out of sheer spite. The idea of their mistress, or anyone else for that matter, perusing her words made her stomach lurch in horror.

'Good day, daughter.'

Jane Tregenna had not succumbed to her Puritan brother's plain ways. She wore a deep blue robe with silver inlay in its bodice and at the wrists, and a collar of fine lace.

'For goodness' sake take off that dreadful coif!' And before Cat could unstring the cap, her mother had yanked it from her head. 'Your hair is your crowning glory; do not hide it away. And, oh, that threadbare old gown!' she declared, under the disapproving eye of her brother. She tucked her arm through Cat's and marched her towards the church. 'I am not entirely happy about this matter with Master Bolitho, Catherine; but Ned has overruled me. Lady Harris assures me Robert will have a good living at Kenegie and succeed Parsons as the steward, which is not a bad position, I suppose.' She sucked her teeth, so that all the little lines of discontent around her thin lips deepened to crevasses. 'But I have to confess myself a little disappointed; I had thought you might catch one of the Harris boys.'

'You make them sound like fish, Mother, there for the taking.'

'They say a cunning fisherman can land a whale, if he's so minded.'

'Well, even if I were so minded, Margaret Harris is not. She watches me like a hawk and keeps her lads well away from me, all the time throwing Rob in my path. But what's done is done; this is not a subject I much wish to discuss.'

Her mother pursed her lips. 'I'm sure your uncle will have more to say at dinner. He is most delighted that you are to be settled.'

At that moment the sun struck through the mist and the spire of the chapel gleamed in golden light.

'God is smiling on us.'

This was intoned by a tall, weathered-looking man with an eagle's beak of a nose, a bald pate and a froth of white beard, who now continued: 'From Heaven the Lord looks down on the Earth and all the nations shall revere His name, and all the kings of Earth His glory.'

He turned his fierce gaze upon the crowd, one by one; and one by one they scuttled inside. At last his glance came to rest on Annie Badcock, standing on the other side of the churchyard wall. A curious expression played across a face as wrinkled as a withered apple, an expression made grotesque by the old woman's mis-matched eyes: the blind one stared right back at him, but the sighted one looked out over the misty bay.

'Won't you come in, goodwife, and offer your heart to the Lord?'

Old Annie Badcock raised up her face and grinned her gummy grin, the one that gave small children nightmares. 'Nay, bless thee, Preacher. I've never been nobody's wife; nor good neither! I'll stay out here like the old sinner I am and save my own soul.'

'None but the Lord can save thy soul, old woman.'

'Be that as it may, I'm off to my cot, Walter Truran.' And then she swivelled her good eye in Cat's direction. 'If thee has the sense the good God gave thee, ye'll get back in the carriage with thy young man and lay down in his arms. Mark what I say: ye'll regret it if ye don't.'

Some of the listeners laughed at Cat's discomfiture, but her uncle was furious. 'Get away with you, you foul beldame, and stop talking such blather. Shoo! Shoo, now!'

For a moment the old woman held Cat's eye, then she threw her shawl up over her head and was gone.

Jane Tregenna clicked her tongue. 'It really is time Penzance had a madhouse like Bodmin wherein we can sweep up all such leavings.'

'That's not very Christian of you, Mother,' Cat said crossly. What could the old besom mean? Did she know Rob; indeed, had he put her up to it? With these thoughts in her head, she followed her uncle into the chapel of Our Lady and took her seat on the outside of the family pew.

'I will show you the eight particular properties of a man without Christ!' the preacher roared suddenly, and a hush fell throughout the congregation.

This was what they had come to witness, this was what they wanted: a proper bible-thumper, all hellfire and damnation.

'First, every man without Jesus Christ is a base man. Though you are born of the blood of nobles, and though you are of the offspring of princes, yet if you have not the royal blood of Jesus Christ running in your veins, you are a base man.'

And he transfixed them all with his bright blue eyes.

'Second, a man without Christ is a bond man. This it says in John 8:36: if the Son shall make you free, then are you free indeed, for if you do not have an interest in Christ to free you from the slavery of sin and Satan, you are slaves: slaves to sin, to the Devil and to the law!'

A woman in the middle row began to rock and moan, a raw, ragged sound that went on and on. It was Nell Chigwine. Cat sighed. The Reverend Veale never subjected his congregation to such fierce words; he adjured them to treat one another with Christian charity and took them gently through the parables and the psalms. She wished she was sitting with the Kenegie household in her usual place in Gulval Church, where she could peruse her little book . . .

The preacher's balled fist hammered on the pulpit and Cat came to herself with a start.

'Fifth, he is a deformed man. A man without Christ is like a body full of sores and blotches. He is like a dark house without light and a body without a head, and such a man must be a deformed man.'

The preacher's voice lowered, and he gazed out at them sorrowfully, as if they were all already lost to hope. 'Sixth, he is a most disconsolate man. Without an interest in Christ, all your comforts are but crosses, and all your mercies are but miseries.

'Seventh, he is a dead man! Take away Christ from a man and you take away his life, and take away life from a man and he is a dead lump of flesh!'

The echo of his words rang around the rafters, and one of the small children in the front row burst into noisy tears and had to be shushed by its mother. Into the small pause caused by this disturbance came a roar and a crash. The heavy wooden door at the back of the chapel rebounded off the stone wall.

Preacher Truran glared at the latecomer. His chest swelled as if he was about to deliver a bellow of outrage at such rudeness. Then his eyes bulged in disbelief and his jaw dropped.

One by one, the congregation turned to see who had reduced their fire and brimstone preacher to such unlikely silence. Cat craned her neck, and at that moment a gang of men burst into the church, howling like banshees. They wore long, dark robes, their heads were shaved, and they brandished curved, wicked-looking swords. Swords just like the one she had glimpsed on the table in Kenegie's parlour; like the one discovered in the wood of the abandoned fishing boat *Constance*. Their skin was as dark as the gypsy woman's, the whites of their eyes brilliant by contrast. A dozen ran down the nave, crying, '*Allah akbar!*'

Pirates, thought Cat, barely able to breathe. Her heart hammered against her breastbone like a trapped bird's. Turkish pirates.

Alderman Polglaze lurched to his feet. 'Who are you?' he demanded of the first man down the aisle. The man laughed, showing an array of white teeth; with his greying beard and his long face, he looked like a wolf. The Alderman was used to being listened to and obeyed. He was also rather short-sighted. 'How dare you interrupt our worship? If you want alms, you must wait outside until the service is over. Get out of here at once!' He put out a hand as if to draw a meeting to order. The raider felled him with a casually brutal blow. A woman screamed. Mistress Polglaze was on her knees at her husband's side, shielding him from the scything sword that would surely follow. But the raider merely reversed his blade and struck her with the hilt so that she collapsed on top of the Alderman. They lay there in a vast mound of fabric and flesh, unmoving. Their children began to scream, setting off all the other children around them. In the front row a toddler wailed hysterically, its face purpling.

One of the raiders flourished his blade in front of it, lips drawn back from his teeth like a snarling dog. '*Skaut!*' The child's noise subsided abruptly to a terrified snuffle.

More men were arriving all the time, shouting in a strange, guttural language, brandishing swords. Jim Carew, the Constable, feeling some doomed sense of duty, caught hold of a raider's arm and tried to pry his weapon away from him. The man drew a curved dagger from the belt at his side and buried it in Carew's neck. Blood spouted in a graceful arc, covering all those within a four-foot radius.

As if they had been in doubt as to the nature of the intrusion until the moment death's shadow fell over Constable Carew, there was pandemonium as the congregation panicked. 'Lord save us!' 'Save our souls!'

At the back of the church, Jack Kellynch vaulted over the pew, dragging Matty with him, and headed for the vestry door, only to be cut off by a knot of robed men. 'Get back, infidel dog!' one of them grunted. Jack stopped, looking from one to another as if reckoning the odds, but Matty hauled on his arm. 'No, Jack,' she urged. 'Do what he says.' When it looked as if Jack would keep coming, the first raider said something unintelligible to his fellows, then pushed Jack roughly away with a kick to the midriff so that he cannoned backwards into Matty, who in turn took down three people behind her.

Ever more pirates were pouring through the door – twenty, forty, fifty – until it was impossible to count them. Suddenly the little church was crammed with din and the heat of bodies. Fear was tangible in the thick air. Into the midst of the chaos came a tall figure, who pushed through the knot of men at the door and made his way down the nave, kicking out his dark-blue robe with every stride, and the pirates fell back and made way for him. His skin was the colour of polished walnut, and a length of burgundy cotton had been wound around his head, the fabric falling in folds to his shoulders. He wore a silver belt and heavy silver bracelets on his dark forearms, and his scimitar was richly damascened. The man looked about him, taking in the bodies on the floor, the wailing children, the terrified women, the white-faced men. With his long straight nose and his keen black eyes he looked like a bird of prey: capable, controlled and ruthless, Cat thought, and felt a chill run through her. Her instincts were soon borne out, for the turbaned raider shouted something in his language to the pirates, and they ran to obey him, fanning out to ring the congregation. He, meanwhile, came to a halt in front of Preacher Truran. They stood eye to eye, and then the pirate laughed and in a fluid dancer's movement leaped behind the minister, who suddenly found the damascened blade at his throat.

'Keep your seats and still your tongues or I kill your imam!' he cried in heavily accented English.

A terrified hush fell and everyone sat down, immediately subdued like children caught at play by a fearsome tutor. The pirate chief looked them over with no small satisfaction.

'You come with us,' he enunciated clearly. 'There will be no resistance, no fight. You come with us to our ships, and we not hurt you. You try to run or fight, we kill you. You understand? Is very simple.'

Someone started to pray, very fast, very quietly, 'From lightning and tempest, from plague, pestilence and famine, from battle and murder, and from sudden death, good Lord, deliver us.'

'Save us, Lord save us.'

'Oh God, oh God, oh God.'

'Jesus, save us.'

'Is good that you pray to God,' the pirate chief said consideringly. 'For the soul is fragile thing and must be reinforced by prayer. But no more of this man Jesus Christ, for he is mere prophet, flesh and blood like you and me, and no use in saving souls. Now on your feet and make no struggle. Come now, quiet and good.'

One of the pirates picked up Alderman Polglaze as if he were no more than a sack of turnips and slung him over his shoulder. Another urged a groggy Mistress Polglaze to her feet and pushed her ahead of him up the aisle.

No one struggled; no one dared. Out into bright sunlight and the deserted streets of Penzance they stumbled, to be met by a clear view of three ships moored in the bay: a fine caravel, its furled sails brilliant against a turquoise sea, and two smaller, lighter-built vessels with strange, triangular sails. Cat blinked and stared: details leaped out at her, perverse and super-real: a seagull sideslipping through the blue sky overhead, as if the world went on as usual; Nan Tippet's heeled red slippers clacking on the cobbles like a donkey's hooves; Henrietta Kellynch sucking her thumb and gazing at the pirate, who pushed her brother Jordie along at swordpoint as if they were part of some elaborate charade, as if the 'obbyoss might at any moment break out of a side street with a pipe band and a colourful crowd of mummers dancing behind it and everyone would laugh. A tortoiseshell cat on the wall of the quay, which watched them incuriously and continued to wash its face with its paw, its eyes pale gold and inimical. Old Thom Ellys rubbing his mouth with a ringed hand over and over, his wife hanging on his arm asking what was happening, dear, where are they taking us, where are we going?

Where indeed? Cat wondered. Someone pushed her hard in the back, and when she turned it was to find one of the foreign brigands glaring at her and saying something in his harsh, unintelligible tongue. She shook her head, flustered, and he pushed her again and laughed at her incomprehension, showing a wide black gap in his mouth where several teeth were missing. Somehow this was more terrifying than all the rest.

Approaching the quay now and having espied the ships, Mayor Maddern suddenly addressed himself to the leader of the pirate band. 'I have money, good sir. Look, I have five angels here, and half a dozen crowns, all fine gold!' He drew a pouch from his belt and rattled it. 'Take the money and let us go.'

Someone whistled. It was a lot of money to be carrying. Someone else muttered about embezzling county funds, while behind him another called, 'Is that for all of us, John Maddern; or is it just for you and your fat wife?'

The Mayor reddened – from shame or fury – and flung himself around to confront the caller. The pirate chief barked out a laugh. He snatched the pouch from Mayor Maddern's hand and upended it into his palm. Then he turned to his men and said something loud and fast, and they all started to laugh uproariously.

The turbaned pirate swept the Mayor a mock-bow. 'Thank you for your contribution, fat man: I take as first instalment.'

'First instalment?'

'Of your redemption, of course.'

'Redemption?'

The raider grinned. 'There are birds at the Sultan's palace who have just such trick. I am told they are intelligent, but I think they repeat only sound without comprehending sense.' He paused to enjoy the Mayor's evident discomposure, then continued smoothly, 'The redemption of your person: your ransom. For your wife' – he considered the large woman grasping her husband's arm, her eyes as round as saucers – 'she seems a well-built woman, which many men like. She should fetch good price. I suggest maybe four hundred pounds for pair of you.'

Curiously, it seemed it was the sum that outraged Maddern rather than the concept of ransom. 'Four hundred pounds?' He could not help himself. 'You must be mad. That's a fortune!'

'Less first payment of' – the pirate scanned the coins in his hand, calculating – 'two pounds and sixteen shillings. That will be three hundred and ninety-seven pounds and four shillings in the money of your country. Though I am happy to take Spanish reals and doubloons too.' He paused cruelly. 'Start thinking who pay and how, or you soon find the fat of your flesh wasting away on a galley slave's bench!'

Mistress Maddern began to sob; and it looked as if her husband might do the same.

They were at the water's edge now and still no one had appeared. If they had seen the raiders, they had shuttered up their windows and sat quiet as mice within, hardly daring to breathe. Or perhaps they were at prayer in the chapel of Raphael, or at All Saints' at Market-Jew, oblivious to the disaster that was being played out so close at hand. They would be singing the closing psalm at Gulval now, Cat thought, Sir Arthur and his family, Rob and the rest of the household, unaware that in the bay below them lay three pirate vessels at anchor which had stolen into the haven of their wide harbour under the cover of a sea-fret and now waited to make off with sixty of their countryfolk.

Down at the harbour wall a host of small boats bobbed cheerfully up and down on the quiet sea, blue-painted wooden skiffs that looked little different to those used by the local fishermen; and now the raiders moved among the crowd, with harsh voices dividing them into bands which each boat might bear away to the distant ships. Maybe it was now that the grim reality of the situation struck home – the idea of this being their last touch of Cornish soil – and suddenly there was a great hubbub, and Jack Kellynch and a couple of the lads were swinging away with their fists. One of the pirates cartwheeled into the harbour with a splash, his curved sword arcing through the air with the light breaking off it so bright it hurt the eyes to watch it fall. The raiders laid about them mercilessly, and this small insurrection was soon and savagely settled, leaving Thom Samuels lying groaning on the ground, his blood running crimson between the cobbles, the fingers of his severed right hand slowly unfolding from the fist he had made like a flower unfurling in the sun.

In no time they were in the skiffs and away, too cowed by this sudden burst of violence to offer any further resistance.

Cat allowed herself to be bundled aboard a little boat like the piece of rude merchandise she had now become. She crouched in the bow, crushed up against two crying women whose names she did not know. None of her family were in the same boat, and she found she could not bring herself to look at the two men who rowed them away from the quay. Instead she stared out past them to the place she had so long and so fervently prayed to leave. She had never seen Penzance from the sea before; had never once set foot in a boat, for all that she was Cornish born and surrounded by this gleaming, sleek ocean. It moved under the little boat like a live thing, disorienting her further. She shielded her eyes from the sun and gazed and gazed at the receding shore. Surely someone would come? Someone must at least see the great ships and wonder what they were doing here. They would have passed right by St Michael's Mount, right past its battery and its guards, and no one had so much as raised an alarum. Of course, they had slipped by in the fog; but now the ships lay in full daylight, bold and massive and arrogant, pennants flying, men on their decks. Were the garrison also at prayer, or were they more likely sleeping off a heavy headful of ale with the Governor away for the week's end? If its lookouts and gunners were senseless and snoring, it mattered little how many guns Sir Arthur petitioned from the Crown, Cat thought, remembering that day barely a month ago when Cornwall's great men had gathered at Kenegie.

Then the shadow of the tallest ship fell cold across her, and when she looked up it was to see two great flags flying high from its masts. The first was a graceful pennant bearing three crescent moons. The second was a huge dark-green banner on which an arm wielded one of the long curved swords, and beside it a skull resting on a pair of crossed bones grinned down at her.

12

In less than an hour they had been loaded up and stowed in the hold. Their hands were manacled in cold iron, and they were then locked, in groups of eight, to a succession of long bars running across the width of the hold. There was barely room to sit, let alone to lie, and it stank to highest heaven.

The congregation of St Mary's Chapel of Penzance were not the first captives to be taken by the pirate gang, for another fifty or more poor souls watched them herded in to share their already foul conditions: men whose eyes glowed fever-bright in the gloom, whose faces were gaunt and sunken. They watched in silence as the newcomers were shoved into their places and locked down, as blows and imprecations rained down, for they had long since learned it was wiser not to aggravate their captors.

Once the doors to the hold banged shut above them and darkness descended, the questions started.

'Which vessel have they taken you from?' This in a thick accent not that of Penwith. 'Must a been a big one, with all these women and children.'

'Vessel? Nay, it was no vessel we was taken from. 'Twas ashore in Penzance,' supplied a man's voice: Cat thought it might be Jack Kellynch.

'Ashore?'

'Aye, they stormed the church and took us while we were at prayer.'

There was much shock at this. 'I never heard of such a thing. Never in my life.'

'It was an easy mark on a Sunday morning.'

The ship's timbers groaned as the vessel got under way, and by the pitch and roll of it they could tell they were away into the sea. Then some began to weep, the shock of their situation being made worse by the realization that many others shared their fate – strong, able-bodied men from far and wide in the West Country, who had been able to do nothing to escape their captors – and that no one had attempted rescue.

Some time later a number of their captors entered the hold. For the most part, they were small, wiry men with gleaming black eyes and heads shaved to leave only black top-knots. They spoke quickly to each other in the harsh, noisy language of their country. They wore their robes tucked up at the back between their legs and fastened at the front through their belts, and they picked their way as fastidiously as cats through the filth, distributing pans of water, dry rusks of dark bread and a handful each of small black fruits among the prisoners. No one said anything to them; they took the food and water, and waited till the men had gone again.

'Eat and drink everything they give you,' came a voice. 'Or you'll not last the voyage.'

Cat sipped at the water. It was brackish and had a strange, acidic taste.

'Dip your bread or you'll break your teeth,' another man called into the gloom. 'Don't mind the taste: 'tis only vinegar, or so they tell us.'

Next she put one of the small dark fruits into her mouth, and almost spat it out again at once, it being both bitter and salty and with a hard stone at its centre. She had never tasted anything so horrible in her life. 'Here,' she said to the woman next to her. 'Take mine. I don't want them.' She watched as the woman bit into the black fruit and chewed and chewed, the expression on her face never appearing to change. 'I've had worse,' she said. 'Saltfish and soused herring; rotten cheese and seal-flipper. Whatever these little things are, they ain't so bad. If thee don't eat, birdie, thee'll waste away, and thee're only a tiny thing as 'tis.'

'Who are these monsters and what will they do with us?' a woman cried out plaintively. With a shock, Cat realized it was her mother and turned to stare into the darkness, but it was hard to see anyone's features in the gloom. She sounded unhurt, which was some small comfort.

A man laughed. 'Pirates out of Sallee; and they're taking us to the Devil.'

At this there was a commotion. Then, 'Where is Sallee?' cried several voices at once.

'Dick'll tell thee: he's been there afore. The man's a regular Jonah on the ship to Tarshish, he is: he has no luck. Tell 'em thy tale, Dick Elwith.'

In the aft of the hold a man coughed. A deep voice rumbled out into the darkness. 'When I were a child my father told me that they that go down to the sea in ships shall see the Lord's wonders; and so I purposed as soon as I was a man that I would give myself as a sailor on a London merchant vessel. And so I did; but my true motive was for material gain, and maybe that is why the Lord has cursed me, for I was driven by more than curiosity into the Lord's creation and the wish to acknowledge His works and cry Him praise. I thought to amend my lot in life, and to rise by enterprise; but that was not to be my destiny.

'It was 1618 I was first taken. Our ship was making her course for the Madeiras, laden with salt and beef, but in the early morning, about a hundred leagues off the Rock of Lisbon, we saw a sail to windward of us, who gave us chase. We made what sail we could from him but to no avail, for he gained upon us little by little no matter what course we took, or how hard we put her to it. At last, at the rising of the moon, he came close enough to hail us and inquired whence came our vessel. We answered "London"; and when we asked the same of him, he answered "from Sallee" and laughed, and then we realized he was a Turkish pirate vessel and fired off a broadside upon him, but he sheered off. We tried sailing in all ways but found we could not wrong him, no matter what we did. He kept astern of us all day and all night, and in the morning put out Turkish colours, so we answered with English, and, having no more powder in our store, were forced to surrender, whereupon he grappled us close and set a hundred men upon our decks, who fell to cutting away the rigging till our ship was disabled and we were obliged to yield. They took us all off and scuttled our brave vessel and took us to Sallee, a Moorish port of northern Africa –'

'Africa?' a woman wailed. ''Tis a continent of savages half a world away! Oh, shall I ever see my home again?'

Many others now cried out their anguish at hearing this dire news. Cat sat dumbstruck, her mind a wilderness.

'Let the man speak: for clearly he has survived his experiences, even if he has had the misfortune to be taken by the same colour of pirate a second time.' Cat was sure this was the voice of the preacher, Walter Truran, for its resonance filled the wooden bowels of the boat, just as it had filled the wooden frame of the church; and she was soon to be proven right as he continued: 'The Lord does not willingly afflict nor grieve His children, but we provoke Him to take His rod into His hand and lay it smartly upon our backs because that folly which is bound up in our hearts will not otherwise be lashed out of us. Thus He taught Judah, by the captivity of Babylon, to prize the freedom of Canaan.'

'Amen!' cried a man, and 'Amen' other voices averred.

'I haven't earned His rod!' someone else complained. 'I do not deserve to be taken by heathens –'

'Shut up the lot of ye canting souls: speak on, Dick Elwith, and tell us what fate awaits us in this Moorish place.'

'We were all taken into the marketplace there and stripped for all to see, and I had some knowledge of the sea and ships and thus was I sold to the master of a raiding vessel, and because I would not turn Turk they put me to an oar. Three year I rowed, chained like a beast. I prayed to die, but the Lord had other plans for me. One day we were caught by a Dutchman, possessed of twenty guns and a determined skipper, and with his brave men he over-hauled the pirate vessel, taking it back as a prize to his homeland, and from there I made my way home – no richer but much wiser, and I swore never to put to sea again.'

'What went wrong that thee find thyself in the same predicament once more?'

Dick Elwith gave a great sigh. 'Me. I was what went wrong. Greed got the better of me, so it did. Having no money and no prospects on land is a hard thing, and, wishing for a wife I could tup without putting a bag over her head, I decided to make enough that I could take my pick, so I took service once more on a ship that sailed only in home waters, and foolishly thought myself safe. We ran passage between Plymouth and France, but never further afield than that, and thought ourselves safe enough. We were in the British Sea two weeks back when three ships were sighted flying Dutch colours, and we thought little of it, for their merchantmen are often seen in our waters and no trouble comes of it. So we let them get a lot closer than we should; but before too long we saw the true stamp of their faces, and I cried to the captain, Mister Goodridge – who sits here now beside me – make sail and flee, for I know the type of men who sail this ship, and they are no Dutchmen, but corsairs out of Sallee, and they mean to take us as slaves! And Mister Goodridge exclaimed in some horror and ordered us to luff up with all our sail, but to no purpose, for before we could make port we were overtaken. And as soon as they had taken us aboard they ran up their own colours, three crescent moons on a green ground and the pavilion of Sallee, which shows a scimitar raised in anger above a skull and crossed bones.'

Cat closed her eyes, remembering the effect that the sight of those sigils had had upon her.

Another voice, presumably that of the unlucky said Captain Goodridge, now intervened. ''Twas the Devil's own work, such trickery. How were we to know they were Turks?'

'It would have done thee no good had thee known and made sharp speed away, for these Sallee Rovers are swift and ruthless sailors and they never give up the ghost.'

After this, the stories came thick and fast. In that hold was a collection of prisoners from a dozen vessels, with a dozen tongues between them. There were Spaniards, and Flemish-speakers, and Devon men; two Irishmen and a whaling man from Newfoundland who had returned to see his family at Hartland. Fishing boats had been taken as well as merchantmen; but the raid on Penzance had been the first time the pirates had taken captives from a town, and the only time women and children had been captured.

'I'm sorry for the stink and the filth,' one man said solemnly. 'They treat us as they would a herd of pigs, for we eat and we shit and we sleep where we sit.'

Several women cried out in horror at this, but Dick Elwith rumbled a laugh. 'Nay, not pigs, man, for the Turk cannot stomach a pig and will have nothing to do with them, neither to rear nor to eat. We'd be better off as swine, for then they would have left us be.'

'"The swine, though he divide the hoof and be cloven-footed, yet he cheweth not the cud; he is unclean to you,"' quoted the preacher. 'Leviticus, Chapter 11. If you wish yourself a lower beast, man, you shame the Lord's creation and damn your very soul.'

The ship lurched and heeled over to starboard, and there was a great groan from the sailors, who recognized the new rhythm and pitch of the ocean. 'We'll be in the sea lanes now, heading south, and they'll not stop now till they hit land,' one said lugubriously. 'All the way to Morocco.'

'How long will that take?' someone asked.

'A month, with fair winds and good weather.'

'And if there's a storm?'

Dick Elwith laughed, but it was a sound with no mirth in it. 'If the ship founders, we drown.' And he shook his chains as if to illustrate his point; at which there was much lamentation.

Preacher Truran called for quiet. 'Stay thy fears: do not let our captors know they have cowed our spirits. Our strength lies in the Lord, and He will comfort us and protect us from the devils who have taken us. Harken to the words of the psalm and gird up your courage!

'Hear the right, O Lord, attend unto my cry, give ear unto my prayer, that goeth not out of feigned lips. Let my sentence come forth from Thy presence; let Thine eyes behold the things that are equal. Thou has proved mine heart; Thou has visited me in the night; Thou has tried me, and shalt find nothing; I am purposed that my mouth shall not transgress. Concerning the works of men, by the word of Thy lips I have kept me from the paths of the destroyer –'

A hoarse laugh rudely punctuated here, but the preacher merely raised his voice and kept on.

'Hold up my goings in Thy paths, that my footsteps slip not. I have called upon Thee, for Thou wilt hear me, O God: incline thine ear unto me, and hear my speech. Show Thy marvellous loving kindness, O Thou that savest by Thy right hand them which put their trust in Thee from those that rise up against them –'

The second interruption was less easy to ignore. Light and noise broke abruptly into the hold as the door was opened from above, and four men bearing lanterns and swords descended into the gloom, yelling in their dreadful, guttural speech and lashing out at random with great knouts of knotted rope. The first of them reached Walter Truran.

'Shut noise, infidel dog!' he cried in a rough approximation of English, and whipped the tarred rope viciously across the preacher's face.

Undeterred, the preacher squared his shoulders and roared on. 'Keep me as the apple of Thy eye, hide me under the shadow of Thy wings! From the wicked that oppress me, from my deadly enemies, who compass me about –'

Now there was a shining blade pressed against his throat. The preacher swallowed and at last subsided into silence.

One of the other pirates brought out a key and unlocked the bar to which the Reverend Truran was shackled. He slid the bar free and gestured for the four men who had been attached to it to get up, while the next pirate unlocked the bar to which Cat and three other women were shackled. 'On your feet! Up, now, get up!'

They did so unsteadily, for the ship was rolling, and in the semi-darkness it was hard to get one's balance. One of the women – Cat had seen her in the market of a Tuesday but did not know her name – clutched at her sleeve, nearly pulling it off, and, as she staggered to regain her footing, Cat felt the sole of her shoe sink into something soft and slimy. A foul smell permeated the already foul air. All she could think, inconsequently, stupidly, was that her best stockings would be ruined, and her bewildered thoughts were still running in this foolish direction when she emerged at last upon the deck, whereupon a great blast of sharp salt air served to clear her head admirably.

In the waist of the ship, the pirate chief sat on a carved wooden chair with his feet up on an ornamented box. On his left a man in a white robe and turban sat crosslegged with a board of smooth, pale wood in his lap and a writing implement in one hand. On the pirate chief's other side a bulbous glass jar stood on the ground, half full of some clear liquid. The container tapered to a graceful point and was decorated at base and lid with perforated silver cuffs. A long tube, with purple silk and tassels wound around it, snaked up from the halfway point of this remarkable container, terminating in an ornate silver beak that he held to his lips. As the captives were whipped into view, the corsair took a long draw on the beak, making the liquid in the glass stir and bubble. Closing his eyes, he inhaled blissfully, then exhaled a great fragrant cloud. Truly, Cat thought, seeing him wreathed about by curls of smoke, he is the very Devil, with his fierce profile and his strange, dark skin, sitting there on his chair as if upon the throne of Hell in triumph over us poor sinners.

He waved his hand at the pirates who had freed them from the hold, and they came forward, driving their captives before them. One of them prodded Cat painfully in the back, but when she turned to complain at such unmannerly treatment, she saw he was a man with blue eyes, carrot-coloured hair and a skin darkened only by a vast multiplication of freckles, utterly unlike the outlandish-looking foreigners who made up the rest of the crew. Seeing her surprise, this man grinned at her and dropped a slow, insulting wink. 'Not expectin' an Englishman among this possel, eh, my bird?'

Cat's jaw dropped. 'And not only an Englishman but a West Country man, from your accent,' she said, horrified. 'For the love of God, can you not speak for us and save us from these savages?'

The other laughed and spat. 'I have no more love of your God than our fine *raïs* there: I turned Mahometan two year back. Gone is my birth name of Will Martin, and now they call me Ashab Ibrahim – Ginger Abraham – which suits me a darn sight better. In Plymouth I were a poor and despised man, a turner of staves and apprentice cooper, till I was pressed into what's left of His Majesty's navy, may God rot their souls; then along came my saviours and sank our fine ship, took me and my fellows captive. So I turned renegado and went to sea with these fine picaroons. Now I have a house in Sallee, two wives priddier than all the women of Devonport put together and more gold than I could have made in three lifetimes. *Allah akbar.* God is great! And do you know how I came by such a fortune?'

She shook her head, though she already suspected the answer.

He leaned in closer, conspiratorial. 'For each slave we take and sell, I shall have a hundredth share for my part in the capture. If we get all of 'ee to Sallee alive and kickin' and in good enough fettle for the market, I'll make a proper packet, and that's for sure!' He winked again, lewdly. 'Mebbe I'll buy 'ee myself, me 'andsome: I bet that priddy hair could keep a man warm a'nights!'

Cat stared at him, aghast. If even Christian men had turned against their fellows in such a cruel fashion, there was surely no justice in the world.

'Ibrahim?' It was the seated man who had spoken.

Will of Plymouth, now known as Ashab Ibrahim, snapped to attention. 'Yes, Al-Andalusi?'

'Silence! Only I speak now.'

The renegade hung his head.

'You there, man in black robe.' Al-Andalusi indicated the preacher with the beak of the strange device from which he had been smoking. 'What your name?'

Walter Truran threw back his shoulders and looked the pirate chief in the eye. 'My name I shall keep between me and my God.'

The raïs sighed. 'How we ask family for ransom if you not give me your name?'

The preacher looked even more outraged. 'Ransom? Sir, my soul is my own; I shall not have my family blackmailed into buying it back from whatever godforsaken corner of the world you are taking us to!'

'Sir – raïs – my name is John Polglaze, and I am Alderman of the town of Penzance. Return me and my wife now to the bosom of our family, and I promise you will be handsomely rewarded.'

Al-Andalusi said, 'Write it down, Amin. All information useful,' and turned his attention to the Alderman. 'You not poor man, I can see by your girth. Empty your pockets and show me your hands.'

John Polglaze frowned at him, not understanding the request.

'Ibrahim!'

The renegade caught hold of Polglaze and rummaged expertly through his clothing, coming away with a handful of coin and a pair of handsome rings. Then he took the Alderman's arm and turned the hand palm up for his captain's inspection. The raïs grunted. 'So white and soft, you no good in galleys or working in field, you last a week, no more! So how much they pay me for you?'

Alderman Polglaze looked flummoxed. 'I . . . I . . . ah . . . I don't know, sir . . . er, raïs.'

'Four hundred pounds?'

The Alderman went white. 'Impossible! Never.'

Al-Andalusi waved a hand. 'Say four hundred pounds, Amin. One hundred fifty for John Poll Glez, and two hundred fifty for his wife. Is she comely? What her name?'

'Elizabeth, sir, but –'

'Ah, like old Queen, excellent. She good friend to Morocco, bring us much trade, timber with which to build ships, many guns, enemy of bastard Spanish. Amin write down two hundred twenty English pounds for wife Elizabeth Poll Glez: her name earn discount. Three hundred seventy pounds for pair.' This he repeated in his own language for the benefit of his scribe, then waved Polglaze away. 'Next.'

The next man was a fisherman in his thirties, spare and short in stature, his face almost as brown as the pirate's, except where crow's-feet had left white streaks around the eyes, but his muscles were like whipcord. His pockets contained no more than a ragged kerchief, two groats and a pocket knife, which the raïs weighed in his hand, then tossed back to Ibrahim.

'Henry Symons of Newlyn. My family are poor: thee'll get no money for me from them.'

The raïs laughed. 'Can you row?'

Symons looked puzzled. 'Aye, of course, and sail.'

The pirate said something in his own language, and the clerk wrote it down, smiling.

The next man was older, and his seafaring days were long spent. Cat recognized him as old Thomas Ellys. Arthritis had swollen his joints and age bent his back. His silver thruppenny bit was still in his pocket, ready for the collection, along with a yellowed bone comb. The raïs inspected his hand, which was callused and rough, confirming that he was a worker, and no rich man's father. He turned to the clerk, and they debated for a few moments; then the pirate called for one of his men, made a curt gesture and indicated the old fisherman. Without a word, the crewman jostled Thomas Ellys away to the ship's side and without ceremony upended him over the gunwale. There was a pause, a splash, and then silence.

'You barbarian!' the preacher started. He stared out at the rolling, empty sea. They were already far from land; even a young, fit man had no chance of gaining the shore from here. 'May the Lord Jesus Christ have mercy on his soul.'

The raïs shrugged. 'We short on provisions: cannot waste on useless old man who no one ransom and who fetch nothing in auction. If your Jesus care for his soul, he will arrange miracle.' He held the preacher's furious regard coolly. 'It was Romans first called my people *barbari*, "the uncultured"; but they ignorant and so are those who use same word after them. My people call ourselves the Imazighen, "the free men": we are Berber and proud. At home in mountains I speak language of my own people, with business partners in the kasbah I converse in Spanish, with fellow corsairs I speak Arabic and the lingua franca of ports. I speak also some English and a little Dutch. I have read every page of the Qur'an and from curiosity some of your bible. In my collection of books I have copies of Ibn Battuta's *Travels*, poetry of Mawlana Rumi, Ibn Khaldun's *Mukaddimah* and Al-Hassan ibn Mohammed al-Wazzani's *Cosmographia Dell'Africa*; I have read them all. Now, tell me who the barbarian?'

'To steal innocent human beings – women and children – from their homes and sell them into slavery is the act of a barbarian.'

'Then all great nations of world also barbarians – Spanish and French, Portuguese, Sicilians and Venetians. I manned an oar for year on Sicilian galley, have many scars on my back. English also: your great heroes Drake and Hawkins also barbarians. And they far worse than the corsairs of Slâ, which ignorant call Sallee, for they took captives solely for personal profit and treated their cargoes with contempt.'

'And you do not?'

'I am *al-ghuzat*, warrior of Prophet. My men and I carry *jihad* – holy war – into seas and on to shores of our enemies, take captive many infidel for sale in our markets. Money we raise from such trade is invested in welfare of our people and glory of God. Is pleasing to Most High that riches of infidels be returned to Allah.'

'Then not only are you a barbarian but also a heretic!' The preacher's eyes were flashing now. His beard flapped in the wind. He looked, Cat thought, like one of the Old Testament prophets, like Moses calling down the ice-storm upon Egypt.

Al-Andalusi leaped to his feet, knocking the pipe over so that smoke and water poured across the deck. 'You not use that word to me! The Spanish called my father heretic. Inquisition broke his bones on their vile rack, but they never broke his spirit.' He turned and shouted at three of his sailors, who ran to do his bidding. In no time they had returned. One carried a stave of iron with a flattened end; the other two a small brazier. The latter was set down on the deck beside the raïs, and the first man at once set the end of the stave to the coals in the brazier and held it there till it glowed red, then white. Walter Truran watched it with something approaching fascination, unable to take his eyes from it. Then he started to pray.

Al-Andalusi shouted an order, and the men tore the boots from the preacher's feet.

'You have such faith in your crucified prophet, now you for ever honoured by bearing his mark.'

And with that, he gestured to the men, one of whom held the preacher down while the other applied the iron to the man's white and wrinkled soles. Cat closed her eyes; but she could not erase from her senses the sound of the brand as it burned through the skin and sizzled in blood, nor the stink of burned meat which rose into the air.

While the preacher lay moaning on the deck, Ashab Ibrahim rifled his pockets, coming away with an ivory-handled fruit knife, a handful of small coins and a little leather-bound psalter. This last the raïs flicked through with some curiosity, then tossed back to the preacher. 'If you not give me your name, you go down on manifest as the Imam.'

'Give me no heathen title! My name is Walter Truran, and you can write beside it "Man of God". But I warn you now, there is no one from whom you can extort a ransom.'

The raïs shrugged. 'You have strong spirit and strong back. Perhaps galleys take you. Or perhaps Sultan Moulay Zidane will be amused by your rantings. Your feet will not be bound until all have seen what happen to those who think to defy me. From today know whenever you set foot on ground you tread on symbol of your bastard religion; and that is how it should be.'

Now Cat was brought before the captain of the pirate ship. So frightened was she by the Reverend Truran's ordeal that she could hardly bear to look upon his tormentor. She kept her eyes on her feet and prayed silently that he would pass her quickly by. Even the mire, discomfort and darkness of the hold was preferable to this. Her knees shook uncontrollably.

'What your name?'

'Catherine,' she started. Her voice was the squeak of a mouse. Drawing a breath, she tried again. 'Catherine Anne Tregenna.'

'You wear green dress, Cat'rin Anne Tregenna. Why?'

This was such an unexpected remark that her head shot up, and she found herself looking the raïs in the eye. His gaze burned into her. 'I . . . ah . . . it is an old dress, sir.'

'Green is colour of Prophet. Only his descendants may wear it. Are you descended from the Prophet?'

Horrified, Catherine shook her head, her tongue stuck fast to the roof of her mouth.

'Take off! Is insult to Prophet to wear his colour unless entitled.'

Cat's eyes widened. 'I . . . can't . . . it laces up the back . . .'

Al-Andalusi leaned forward. 'A woman cannot dress herself must be dressed by a slave. Are you rich woman, Cat'rin Anne Tregenna?'

What was the right answer? Cat searched for inspiration. She reasoned it were best to suggest that keeping her whole and fit for ransom would be worth while; she did not want to be thrown overboard, branded like the preacher or, worse, passed as a worthless bawd to the bestial crew for their pleasure. She squared her shoulders. 'I am Catherine Tregenna of Kenegie Manor, and I am not without means.'

The raïs translated this for the scribe, who wrote quickly on his block. 'Turn around,' he told her then, taking an ornamented curved dagger from his belt.

Fearing the worst, Catherine did as she was told, and waited for the cold blade at her throat. Instead, there was a shearing sound and an ease of pressure, and suddenly the green dress lay around her ankles, leaving her shivering in her cotton shift. Instinctively, she crossed her arms over her chest, feeling the eyes of the crew crawling over her pale white skin like the unclean touch of insects.

Al-Andalusi bent and shook out the fabric. From it fell the little pouch, which at once he snatched up. 'What this? Is bible or prayers to your god?' He brandished her little book.

All at once, she felt a powerful sense of ownership. No one must touch her book; her most secret thoughts lay within. Without thinking, she reached out and took hold of it. For a moment, their eyes locked; then the pirate released his grip on the soft calfskin cover. 'It is a book on embroidery,' Cat said in a low voice. 'See, here –' She opened it on a page she had not yet written on, showing a spray of stylized flowers which might be reproduced on a cuff or a pair of stockings. 'It contains patterns to copy. Like this.' Daring now, she raised her petticoat an inch or two to show him the fine clocking at her ankles.

He tilted his head to examine it. 'And you have done this work yourself?'

'Yes.'

The raïs said something to the scribe, who added something to the list he made. Then he tossed the little pouch back to Cat. 'Women of Sultan's court pay much for work like this. Perhaps you teach them new patterns.' His eyes narrowed. 'And perhaps Sultan Moulay Zidane pay me well for such addition to his harem, particularly with such white skin and hair colour of sunset. We set price of eight hundred pounds for such rare prize.'

Eight hundred pounds! It was a huge sum. Cat clutched the pouch to her chest with her heart hammering. Foolish, foolish wench, her head scolded her. Thinking you could outwit a man like that. Now he has set such a price on your head that no one can ever afford to redeem you, and you will end your days in some foreign land, pining away for the sound of an English voice or the touch of Cornish rain, for Rob and kindness and all the ordinary things of the world which you have spurned, and all for vanity. One of the pirate crew threw a thick woollen robe over her head and led her back down to the hold; she stumbled before him as if in a dream, one from which she might never be able to awake.

13

Those who have also been taken captive call the pyrats who have taken us the Sallee Rovers & say they come from Moroco on the Barbarie Coast in Afrik, but when the old Ægyptian told my fortune & said I would voyage a very long way & that at the end of my journey I would find a union between Earth & Heaven, I had not thoghte of anny thing so terrible as this. How I wish I had not prayed for such a destiny. If God sees me He ys surely smylyng now at my vanitee . . .

It had been hard to sleep after reading these last entries in Catherine's little book. I had just about got my head around her descriptions of daily life at Kenegie and the petty frustrations and jealousies of living in a small, closed community. I had taken the more unfamiliar words and spellings in my stride, skipping those that continued to evade me; but now she had completely thrown me. I had been enjoying her acid comments about her co-workers, her fierce anguish at being forced to marry her cousin, who struck me as a decent-enough man; I had even been rather looking forward to discovering something of what a seventeenth-century wedding entailed: the domestic details, the dress, the meal arrangements and of course Cat's reaction to becoming a married woman. I found myself charmed by this long-dead girl, felt caught up in her distant life, her hopes and fears. I wished too to know more about the altar cloth she had started, whether the Countess of Salisbury ever reappeared. I wanted to hear that that fine lady and Cat's mistress had been suitably astonished by the ambition of her vision and by her skill in executing her grand design when she finally presented them with her Tree of Knowledge. I had – I should admit now – rather hoped to track down this magnificent artefact and make it the subject of a distinguished magazine article, suitably illustrated and as elegantly written as I could manage. I had even – God help me – entertained the idea of asking Anna for a few useful contacts in placing such a piece.

The brief and bloody encounter with the raiders had astonished me. I had lived in Cornwall for my first eighteen years, and no one in all that time had so much as mentioned the words 'Barbary' and 'pirate' in the same breath. I did not know what to think: did all the history of the region I had ever been taught rest on a false foundation; or was Cat a fantasist, earthing out her anxiety and boredom by means of some wild fiction? If it were the former, then I had to find out whatever I could on the subject. I decided that after accompanying Alison and Michael to view the cottage at Mousehole, I would make my excuses and visit Penzance Library to trawl the internet and the local history shelves for whatever I could find about Cornwall in the mid 1620s.

A little voice nagged at the back of my mind: how likely was it that, snatched by slave traders, Catherine could have taken and kept her embroidery book and her writing implement with her and managed to continue her journal in the desperate conditions of such a ship's hold? And, if she had managed such a feat, then how had the little book ever made it back to this country and, more specifically, to Alison's house, so close to where Cat had been taken from in the first place? But if Cat *had* been driven by her own difficulties to take shelter in fantasy, the story she had created would surely make her England's first writer of prose fiction, predating Daniel Defoe by almost a century. Either possibility rendered the book a valuable object; and, as such, made me even more determined to keep it away from Michael.

We parked on the outskirts of the village and walked down its winding main road, exclaiming in delight as we rounded the corner and emerged suddenly into a wide, sunlit harbour.

'How extraordinary!' Michael's eyes shone as he took in the array of small, brightly coloured craft bobbing within the protective arms of the quay, the tumble of cottages lining the steep hillsides around the cove.

If you removed the cars and the yachts, the streetlamps and the tourists, it was a scene that had changed very little in a couple of hundred years, I thought wistfully. There were not many places left in the world like this, and most of those had lost a lot of their soul, but Mousehole retained something of the rare conviviality of a village in which a local community lived out their lives and watched the tourists come and go like the tides. Outside the grocer's a blackboard had been attached to the railings overlooking the harbour; on it someone had chalked in large unsteady letters, 'Happy birthday, Alan, 73 today!' A group of elderly women who evidently shared the same hairdresser – one who had perfected a single style of grey-helmet perm – was gathered at the bus stop, gossiping cheerfully. As we passed, I heard one of them say, '. . . and he got up and went off down to the boat, never even noticed she were dead' – which for some reason merely made her listeners chuckle, as if it was the sort of oversight men here made all the time.

'It's up here,' Michael announced after consulting a hand-drawn map. Even from where I stood, I could tell it was Anna who had made it. Anna was just the right person to draw maps: neat, precise, painstakingly accurate. If she'd been charting oceans at the time of Magellan, there would have been no fanciful monsters curling up out of the deeps, no 'heere be dragons', no siren mermaids or other unnecessary curlicues, but merely the legend 'open water'. It was probably this very lack of imagination that had enabled Michael to continue his illicit liaison with me all this time.

The street he led us up was too narrow for traffic. Instead, people had filled it with effusive containers of flowers and bizarre prehistoric-looking plants like giant, fleshy black rosettes; outside one particularly eccentric dwelling was half of an old rowing boat with terracotta pots of geraniums ranged along its thwarts. Anna's cottage was limewashed and had shutters of a pretty faded blue. Seagull droppings mired the windows and chickweed grew on the roof, but even so it was exquisite.

Inside, however, the chocolate-box illusion was dispelled. Dark, dingy and filthy, the cottage exhaled a great gassy breath of mildew and damp as soon as Michael opened the door. The low ceilings were yellowed, not just with age but with nicotine; the old man who'd rented must have been a pipe-smoker. The armchairs were stained and threadbare along the arms, and the back of one had been ripped down to the stuffing where a cat had used it for sharpening its claws.

'Poor thing,' said Alison. 'It is in need of some care and attention, isn't it?' For a moment I thought she'd spied the resident pet, gone feral since its owner's demise; then I realized she meant the house.

Michael smiled wryly. 'That's what the estate agent said, but all I thought she meant was that it could do with a lick of paint and some new carpets.'

'Ah, estate agents,' Alison said. 'What do they know?'

Boxes had been stacked against one wall marked 'Books' and 'Crockery'. Michael made immediately for the first of these piles, took down the top box and started emptying it on to the floor, eyeing the contents avidly. Did he suspect there were more antiquities like *The Needle-Woman's Glorie* hidden away down here? I crouched beside him to examine what he had brought out of the box. The top layer consisted of paperbacks gone brown with age, the sort of fiction that had long since passed out of fashion – Second World War novels and luridly packaged American detective stories. Nothing of interest there.

'How long has this place been in Anna's family?' I asked idly.

Michael frowned. He picked up a plain-jacketed, ex-library hardback, flicked to the title page, scanned it, shook the book in case something had been hidden inside it and then discarded it with the rest. 'Oh, ages. I don't know.'

'It seems to have been stuck in a time-warp,' I persisted. 'Hasn't Anna ever been here?'

He looked up at me unhappily. 'Not as far as I know. Why would she?'

'Well, I'd want to have a peep at my inheritance. Seems a bit cavalier to take the weekly rent and just let it fall into rack and ruin. I feel quite sorry for the poor old man who lived here.'

'Look, it's nothing to do with me. I just came down to go through the stuff that's left, make sure the clearance people didn't miss anything important.'

'Like the book you gave me?'

Catherine's little book was in my shoulder bag. I felt it there, emanating such strong signals I was almost surprised Michael couldn't sense its presence.

'Stop sniping, both of you,' Alison snapped. 'Come on, Julia, let's have a poke around.' She took me by the arm and fairly wrestled me out of the living room. We ducked our heads under the lintel and found ourselves in a small dark kitchen.

'Can't you try to be civilized with one another?'

I made a face. I was wishing I hadn't come. It was easier to nurse my righteous hurt away from Michael. Besides, Cat's story was haunting me: I had a sudden powerful urge to run outside into the sunlight, away into the open with her little book.

'I think I'll go for a walk,' I told Alison. 'I've got a bit of a headache.'

She looked surprised. 'Oh, OK. Do you mind if I stay for a while?'

'Do what you want.' It was rude, but I didn't feel much like making the effort. I was still angry at her for encouraging Michael to come down here.

By the time I got back to the living room, Michael was on his third box.

'Anything interesting?'

He shook his head, looking grim. 'A load of old rubbish.'

'All you deserve,' I said under my breath and marched out of the door.

I wandered off to find myself a suitably quiet and sunny spot in which to sit and read, but I had not gone more than a few yards before a tiny old woman beckoned to me. As I got closer, I realized that she was suffering from some kind of strabismus, which had caused her left eye to be directed in a different direction to her right one. Feeling embarrassed, as if I had mistakenly reacted to her call when she was in fact hailing someone else, I turned, but there was no one else on the street. 'Hello,' I said cautiously.

She came down the hill towards me. 'You're searching for something, my dear.'

'No – just wandering around, taking in the sights.'

Her smiling face was as softly wrinkled as the leather of an old Chesterfield sofa, one eye looking over my shoulder, the other unnervingly focused on my chin. I had no idea which one to respond to. She leaned in closer. 'I can tell you are searching,' she insisted. She patted my hand. 'It will be all right, you'll see.'

She was obviously a bit mad. I smiled. 'Thank you, that's nice to know. You live in a lovely village, and I'm going to have a jolly good look around it now.' I stepped away, but her grip tightened.

'What you are searching for you will have to travel to discover,' she urged me. 'And what you find will not be the thing you thought you went to find. It will be' – and here she beamed at me as if bestowing the blessing of all the angels – 'far more wonderful than anything you have imagined, it will remake your life. But if you stay here fate will catch up with you. Annie Badcock never lies.' A cloud drifted over the sun, and she broke the connection between us suddenly. 'They were here.' She winked at me. 'They came across the ocean and took them away. People have forgotten; they have forgotten all the important things. But the past is stronger than they know. It is a great black tide which will sweep us all under in the end.'

And with that she was off, limping away down the hill without a goodbye or even a backwards glance. I stood there, staring after her, nonplussed. Had she read my mind or was she just crazy? But perhaps, that irritating little voice at the back of my mind prompted, perhaps she really knows something. *Annie Badcock*. The name was vaguely familiar, but I couldn't remember where I'd come across it.

★

'If you took down the internal wall between the old scullery and the breakfast room, you could open up the kitchen and make it a lot brighter.'

There was light in Alison's eye. She looked as if she might burst into hysterical laughter or tears at any moment. Perhaps poking around the old cottage had reminded her too much of renovating the farmhouse with Andrew. But there was a determined thrust to her jaw: she needed a project, for the money as much as for the distraction. We were sitting out on the terrace at the Old Coastguard Hotel, finishing a bottle of rosé after eating local fish and Cornish cheeses, and as soon as the waiter had cleared our plates away, Alison had covered the table with sketches and notes.

Michael was in her thrall, nodding and asking questions. 'And you think all this could be done for how much?'

'Sixteen, seventeen thousand. I know some good local crafts-men, and you could use me as project manager. I'd be happy to oversee it.'

'I'll talk to Anna, see what she thinks. It makes sense, though, I can see that. No one's going to buy the cottage in the state it's in at the moment.'

'Not full of old rubbish,' I added helpfully.

He pursed his mouth, which made him look prissy and mean; I could see the old man he could soon become if he allowed the negative side of his personality to hold sway. When he turned back to Alison again it was with his left shoulder held higher, as if to block me out of the conversation. Pain lanced through me, but I said as blithely as I could manage: 'I'm going to take the bus into Penzance. I'll see you later, Alison. I'll get a taxi or something.'

'Oh, OK.' She frowned, as if expecting an explanation.

'Some things I need to buy,' I said, not wanting her to see that I was feeling territorial and upset. I got up and slung my bag over my shoulder.

'Aren't you going to say goodbye to me?' Michael said, looking put out.

'I was under the impression we'd said goodbye some time ago,' I said coolly. I felt his eyes on me as I walked away.

Half an hour later I was tucked away on the first floor of the local library with an ancient PC and a dodgy internet connection. I Googled 'barbary pirates cornwall' and waited. Seconds after I clicked 'search' I was offered the choice of over twelve thousand entries containing this unlikely combination of words. I picked a few at random and in a very short space of time had begun to feel as if I were inhabiting a sort of alternative universe in which an entire buried history existed under the surface of the world I knew.

According to various sources – academics, amateur historians, official state papers, the occasional survivor's account – over a million Europeans had been abducted and enslaved by North African pirates between the early sixteenth and late eighteenth centuries. A fraction of the estimated twelve million Africans taken and sold in slavery in the Americas, but still a hugely significant number. Between the 1610s and the 1630s Cornwall and Devon lost a fifth of their shipping to corsairs, and in 1625 over a thousand sailors and fishermen from Plymouth and the Cornish and Devon coasts were taken and sold into slavery. The Mayor of Bristol reported that a Barbary fleet had captured Lundy Island and there raised the standard of Islam, and that this little island in the Bristol Channel then became a fortified base from which they launched raids on the unprotected villages of north Cornwall and Devon. The raiders came to be known as the Sallee Rovers, since they operated out of the Muslim stronghold of Salé, just across the river from Rabat in Morocco, and included a ragtag collection of disaffected privateers from various seafaring European nations who had ensconced themselves there alongside the remarkably mixed population of the area, which already contained native Berbers, Arabs, Jews and 'Moriscos' – Muslims expelled from Catholic Spain, where many of their families had lived for generations. In the Barbary states these Europeans found men eager for revenge on the Christian world which had persecuted them, men with the resources, the wit and the will to carry a seaborne war to the very shores of the enemy; a war, moreover, sanctioned and blessed by the ruling powers and driven not only by the greed for wealth but also by the fervour of religion.

One of the most effective raiders had apparently been an Englishman by the name of John Ward, who had turned renegade shortly after King James I signed a peace treaty with Spain, thus cutting off Ward's legal opportunities to attack the Spanish treasure fleet. He made for North Africa, converted to Islam, taking the name of Yussuf Raïs, and started training up the locals in the knowledge of navigation and in the use of sailing swift vessels. He became the admiral of the Salé fleet, vowing to 'become a foe to all Christians, bee a persecutor to their trafficke, & an impoverisher of their wealth'. One particularly intrepid corsair chief, Jan Jansz – a Dutchman going by the adopted Muslim name of Murad Raïs – apparently sailed all the way to Iceland from Salé and stole four hundred captives out of the harbour-city of Reykjavik to sell at a premium, with their milk-pale skin and white-blond hair, in the Barbary slave markets.

I found mention of a letter from the Mayor of Plymouth in April of 1625, warning the Privy Council that he had spoken with an eyewitness to a fleet of ships ('thirtie saile') about to set out from Salé in Morocco bound for our shores bent on the capture of slaves; clearly, the authorities of the time had not acted on the information.

It was the final entry I followed up that sent shivers running down my spine. Quoting the state papers of the time, a Lebanese expert on the period described how in the summer of 1625 Salé corsairs took out of a church in Mount's Bay 'about 60 men, women and children, and carried them away captives'. For several moments I sat there, trembling. I read and reread the entry to make sure I had not misunderstood it. Then I took out the little book Michael had given me, laid it on the table and stared at it, feeling the synchronicities wreathing around me like ghostly threads. Here I sat in a library in Penzance, Mount's Bay, with my left hand on the soft calfskin cover of an extraordinary seventeenth-century memoir and with my right on the hard, smooth plastic of a computer mouse, old technology and new connected by a human bridge spanning four centuries of history. And now my head knew what my heart had already accepted: that Catherine Anne Tregenna had indeed been snatched from Sunday service by ruthless pirates, to be sold in white-slave markets two thousand miles and two continents away.

Just at that moment, as if the electricity of that connection had somehow arced across another emotional gulf, my mobile phone rang. It was Michael.

I should have switched it off and let him stew; but the disapproving faces around me panicked me, and I ran outside to take the call.

'Hello?'

'Why did you run off like that? And what about that parting shot – "I thought we'd said goodbye some time ago"? That was hurtful.'

I almost laughed. 'You're hurt? What about me? It was you who ditched me, not the other way round. You've no right to feel hurt.'

'I know, I know; and I was wrong. I should never have done it.'

'Never have done what?'

'I should never have walked away from you. I can't do this, Julia. I can't not have you in my life. I miss you.'

Every dumped woman dreams of having a man say such a thing to her. Every dumped woman practises a number of killer lines with which to squash the insect that crawls back thus. Unfortunately I couldn't think of any of them. Instead, what came out was 'Do you?' in a horrible, yearning whine.

'Meet me tonight. Come and have dinner with me at the hotel. You could stay, if you wanted to.' And then he made a sexual suggestion that sent a shock of electricity through my entire body.

'I really don't think that's a very good idea . . .' I said.

'It may not be a good idea, but it's an idea that always works for us. Come on, you know you want to. And afterwards you can read me to sleep with embroidery hints from your little book.'

It was like having a bucket of cold water upended over me. 'I can't,' I said firmly. 'It's too soon, you hurt me too much. I need to think about what I want, what's good for me. And I don't think spending the night with you tonight is good for me at all. Go take a long walk and a cold shower. I'll see you tomorrow.'

Shaking, I rang off, then switched off the phone for good measure. When I got back to my seat in the library, I found that the internet connection had crashed.

14

Catherine

1625

Wee have beene at sea now for the best parte of two weekes, but yf wee reach Sallee alive it will surely bee a miracle, caughte as wee are between wyld seas, starvation, disease & the violent conduct of oure captors. All ready wee have lost some of oure original number, viz. three children & two of the men taken captive before us, who bore woundes from their capture off Plymouthe. This verie mornyng old Mrs Ellys expired at last from weaknesse & shock of losyng her poore husbande, but no one has taken her bodie, she lyes in the ordure & addes to the stink. My mother ailes, & there is no thyng I can do for her. We have no comforte of light or clene aire & are plagued by flyes & maggots & I have heard the scuttle of rattes along the timbers of the shippe. It ys as well they do not feede us moore, or the mire & vermine would bee worse. No one seeyng us now would ever knoe that wee are not all of the same estate for wee appeare all as poor wanderyng ragged beggars herded together like in a pygges stye . . .

There were days when Cat simply wanted to lay her head down against her companion and die, days when she could no longer bear the stench and the captivity, the pangs of her gut or the terrible, suffocating miasma of hopelessness that had stolen over the whole miserable human cargo. At the beginning, outraged by their treatment, there had been talk of insurrection, of overcoming those who came to feed them – holding them down and drowning them in the shit and piss that made a second sea within the ship, of stealing the keys to their shackles, arming themselves with whatever they could find and storming the ship. They embellished the fantasy of this revolt with loving detail: how they would take the raïs and put out his eyes with the same brand that had burned the preacher's feet; how they would strip him bare and throw him overboard for the sharks and laugh as he was ripped limb from limb; how they would hang the renegade Englishman now known as Ashab Ibrahim from the yardarm, but not before removing the male appendage he must have submitted to heathen circumcision when he first turned Turk; how they would take captive the remaining crew and confine them in this very stinking pit of a hold, then sail for a home port and hand them over to the authorities as hostages against those unfortunate Englishmen still held in the port of Sallee.

Captain Goodridge told how he had heard of a successful insurrection by captives aboard an Algerian vessel. The prisoners had managed by some means or another to bribe one of the Europeans in the crew to release them and furnish them with weapons, and they had killed the captain of the slavers and run the ship back to Plymouth with all speed and honour – whereupon they had roasted a pig on the quayside and paraded it in front of the Mahometan picaroons, threatening to force them to eat it till they wept in abhorrence.

Privately, Cat thought the captain had most likely confected it himself to raise their spirits and his own. In the end, it had not worked. At the very mention of pork, many of the captives had groaned and salivated, reminded afresh of their hunger, while others had retched and added to the noisome liquids that swilled around their feet.

It had not taken long for such rebellious talk to evaporate: a few more days of discomfort, some foul weather which left them bruised and shaken, and the sudden death of the first of the children, a little boy, who had been overcome by fever and flux, and their spirits, such as they were, were broken. The boy's mother wailed over the tiny body until the raiders came down and took it away. Then she shrieked hysterically that they would eat it, and none could comfort her or assure her they would do nothing of the sort: for no one was entirely sure that such was not the case. The sound of her howling haunted their hours, waking and asleep.

After that, one by one, they fell ill. Two more children succumbed to the fever: a girl of three and a boy of eight. Cat had known the little boy – he came to the manor with his mother on feast days, and she had played Club Kayles with him in the garden. He suffered for several days, but by the time he died Cat found she could neither cry nor pray. She wondered if the first inability was because there was some lack of feeling within her; or whether it was simply that she could produce no more tears for a want of water. As to the second: she knew that her faith had failed her. It was hard to believe that a god who cared sufficiently for his flock could allow children to die in such a terrible manner.

Within a week, nineteen had been taken by the flux or other ailments: strong men, young men, sturdy women, lively children. Thom Samuels, whose wound suppurated until his arm went black; Captain Goodridge, whose ship had been taken in the British Channel; Nell's husband, William Chigwine; and little Jordie Kellynch, who had been coughing for days before being taken from the church; Annie Hoskens of Market-Jew and old Henry Johns of Lescudjack. Her own youngest nephew, little Jack Coode.

Walter Truran healed with remarkable speed, despite the conditions. There were those who believed the symbol of the brand itself protected him; others whispered of a miracle. But the women who had lost children shot him sidelong looks which clearly showed their inner feelings: they wished God had spared their own at the preacher's expense.

At last, with the spectre of losing the entire precious cargo before him, the ship's chirurgeon made an appearance, rather against his will. A tall thin man with a long grey beard and hooded eyes barely illuminated by the lantern he carried, he was accompanied by two of the raiders, one of them Ashab Ibrahim, a cloth clamped to his nose and mouth with one hand. The other hand firmly propelled the doctor into the hold.

'Who here is sick?' Ibrahim called.

His question was met by a great wave of noise, and the chirurgeon looked aghast. He said something in rapid Arabic to the renegade, who shook his head. 'Well, do what you can, then.'

The chirurgeon made his way gingerly between the benches, examining a tongue here, the white of an eye there. Some he shied away from touching: they were obviously beyond saving. When he came to a woman two rows in front of Cat, he recoiled. The woman turned her head, moaning, and with a shock Cat recognized her as Nell Chigwine. Thin strings of vomit fell from her lolling chin to her filthy dress; sweat beaded her forehead, and her breathing was shallow. The doctor shook his head and backed swiftly away, gesticulating. He stood in front of the renegade and talked with such vehemence it seemed he was in a fury. He pointed at the sick woman, then indicated the filth on the floor. He waved his arms, shouting. At last, Ibrahim shrugged and bent to unlock the bar which held the shackles in place.

'Get up!' Ibrahim said, and kicked at the man on the end of the row when he did not respond. 'Stand up!'

The man lumbered to his feet, his face a mask of agony as unused muscles protested, and stood there swaying with the rocking of the ship. A fisherman, then, Cat thought, watching as he moved automatically with the motion of the vessel. Nell staggered and collapsed. 'Get up!' the fisherman hissed. 'Your life depends on it.' He caught her under the arms and hauled, and she clutched at him. It looked as if she would fall again, but some inner force of will exerted itself, and she drew herself upright, looking more corpse than breathing woman.

The renegade chivvied the first group of captives into line, then turned back to address the hold at large. 'We're takin' you up on deck one group at a time for some air on the chirurgeon's instructions. Anyone who can't make it up the stairs on their own two feet will be thrown over the side. One person from each row will clean up your shit before going on deck. Then you will return with a bucket of seawater and sluice your area.' He took a metal pail from the second crewman and threw it to a woman in the first group on their feet. Cat averted her eyes as the woman scooped the filth into the pail and selfishly prayed that this awful task would not fall to her.

She watched three ragged coffles of prisoners following these instructions, leaving and after a while returning, cleaning their area, taking their stations once more. Her feet itched to move; she could almost taste the briny air that awaited her. At last, after what seemed an interminable amount of time, Ashab Ibrahim came to her row and unlocked the bar. 'Up, all of you.'

They lurched upright and stood there uncertainly, trying to balance. To her horror Cat found that after two weeks cramped into a crouch her legs did not want to support even her reduced weight, and she fell across the man in the row in front of her, who swore in protest.

The renegade caught her by the arm and dragged her to her feet. 'Can't afford to lose 'ee overboard, my bird: precious cargo, you are.' He leered.

Affronted, Cat forced her muscles to obey, shuffling along in the heavy woollen robe they had given her, her chains clanking painfully against her ankles. Someone else had landed the task of cleaning the row.

At the top of the steps, the fresh air hit her like a fist. For a moment she felt dizzy, disorientated. She had to close her eyes against the sudden light and hold tightly to the sides. Someone pushed her in the back. 'Move on, can't you?'

Up on deck she stared at the swathes of blue that assaulted her vision: a great vivid sky, streaked with high clouds like mares' tails; an endless ocean beneath frothing with white caps. The shimmer of the sun on the sea and the whiteness of the belling sails hurt her eyes so that she had to look down at the solid darkness of the wood beneath her feet. Two weeks, she thought (they had all been counting, judging the passage of time by the changing quality of darkness in the hold); two weeks without sight of the world or fresh air to breathe. She had never realized how lucky she was simply to exist at Kenegie; to wish for more than simple pleasures had been a raw vanity.

They stumbled across the deck, impeded by their chains, threw the filth overboard (out of the wind, if you please, as the renegade laughingly instructed them), drew up bucket after bucket of seawater and scrubbed their filthy skin and clothes. Salt stung their sores; strong men cried out in pain.

The crew watched them, their black eyes as inimical and assessing as those of the Kenegie farm cats. While they joked with one another, Cat wondered what they were thinking: were they mocking their captives, commenting on the weakness of these poor pale creatures? Were they totting up their likely prize money, the prices they would fetch at auction; or were their thoughts running along darker lines? She huddled under the robe, using it as both washcloth and towel. How they must despise us, she thought, filthy as animals, crawling with lice, feeble and diseased. They have reduced us to this state so that we are less than human, and that is how they now see us: cargo which must be kept alive to earn any sort of price, as nondescript as sheep. And she kept on scrubbing as if the dirt would never come off.

She was still in this almost trance-like state when she was surprised by a cry, and a man on the foredeck started to chant in a strange singsong voice:

'Allah akbar. Allah akbar. Achehadou ana illah illallah. Achehadou ana mohammed rasoul allah. Achehadou ana mohammed rasoul allah. Haya rala salah. Haya rala salah. Haya rala falah. Haya rala falah. Qad qamatissaa. Qad qamatissaa. Allah akbar. Allah akbar. Laillah illallah . . .'

The entire crew stopped whatever they were doing and walked quickly to the buckets of sand set at intervals about the ship. Each man dipped his hands in the bucket and rubbed the sand between his palms like soap. Then they ran their hands over their faces, three times, as if washing. They took another handful of sand, then 'washed' their right hands, then their left, to the elbow, again three times. Cat stopped her own washing and watched, fascinated. She looked around and found that the other captives were doing the same thing. It was like a Mystery Play, she thought suddenly, remembering when as a child her father had taken her to see the mummers when they visited Truro – something you didn't quite understand but could not take your eyes from. The mummers had frightened her with their strange costumes and their chanting voices: the Devil with his skin rubbed black with ashes, his wild red hair and the sheep's horns stuck on his head; the angels in white sheets swaying and pacing, back and forth, back and forth, mesmeric but unsettling. But at least the mummers had been at a safe distance, and she had known she was going home afterwards.

Now the crewmen turned to the left-hand side of the ship and stood facing an older man in a white robe with the hood up over his head. They waited, silent for a few moments as if deep in thought, even the most savage-looking of them; then they went to their knees and stayed like that without a word for a minute or more. Finally they prostrated themselves, touching their foreheads to the deck: once, twice. Cat realized, with a sudden shock, that they were praying, and that their captain was among them, no distinction made between him and the men of his crew.

They rose, and followed the same ritual again, and the prisoners shuffled uncomfortably. No one knew what to do; there was no hiding place on the ship, nowhere to escape to, except the great wide, empty sea. One by one, they tore their gaze from the praying men, and that was when John Symons saw the ship.

'Ship!' he whispered hoarsely and pointed.

Cat and the others turned, shading their eyes against the glare. There it was on the northern horizon aft of them, a big square-rigger, but still too far away for the colour of the pennants streaming from its topmast to be discerned.

'Spanish,' declared a man who had been on the merchant vessel taken by the pirates in the Channel.

'Caravel ain't no indication,' grunted Dick Elwith. 'These Sallee Rovers've got ships of all sorts – pinks, xebecs, brigantines, cogs and caravels. Origin ain't the thing, it's who sails in her that counts. And there's no point straining your eyes for the colours, as I knows to my misfortune, for they'll fly any nation's flag for convenience before changing it for their own damned sigil.' But, even so, he screwed up his eyes and scrutinized the approaching vessel with all his might.

What difference did it make if it were a Spanish vessel? Cat remembered the stories of how the Spanish had fired the houses of Mousehole, Newlyn and Penzance, and the church at Paul. They did not inspire her with much confidence of better treatment at the old enemy's hands than from those of their captors. And if they attacked the pirate vessel, what then? She could see the gun ports on the bigger ship now: if it turned those guns upon them, what chance did they stand? Was it better to be blown to pieces or sold as a slave? She abruptly felt so sick that she had to stagger to the gunwale and vomit over the side.

Maybe it was her sudden movement that caught the raïs's eye, for at that moment he looked away from his prayers. His eyes widened, and then he was on his feet and running, shouting instructions. There was an immediate frenzy of activity as the crew leaped up from their prayers and took up their designated stations at sail or gun. Two men fled up the rigging on the main mast for a better sight of the other ship; from the deck, someone drew down the corsair flags.

The prisoners stood like trees in the eye of a storm, still among the chaos. The raïs pointed at them. 'Get them below!' he shouted to Ashab Ibrahim and his subordinate.

Dick Elwith darted a look at the approaching renegade, then at the ship, as if calculating something. Cat saw him give a little, inturned smile, then he winked at her. 'Can't go through it all again,' he said softly. 'I'd rather take my chances with the Spanish or go down in Davy Jones's locker than be whipped bloody working a galley's oar.' And with that he levered himself up on to the gunwale and dropped like a stone over the side of the ship.

Ibrahim ran to the gunwale, but there was nothing he could do. 'Bleddy idiot,' he stormed, watching the sea foam subside where Elwith had plunged in. 'He coulda made a fine corsair if he hadn'ta been so stiff-necked. All you gotta do to turn Turk is say a few words and lose a little bit of useless skin. 'Ten't a lot to give up for a life a darn sight better than 'e 'ad before. Now all 'e'll see for 'is trouble is to feed a few fishes.'

'He's going to swim for that ship,' Cat said furiously.

''E en't swimming anywhere with them shackles on 'im.' And he grabbed her by the arm. 'Down below with 'ee, while we take care of business.'

★

Back down in the hold they huddled in their rows, waiting and listening, but it was only when the first of the guns roared that they realized the two ships had engaged. The woman on the left of Cat – who up till now had said barely a word to her, locked in her own private misery – gripped her arm suddenly.

'My name is Harriet Shorte,' she said. 'If I die and you live through this, I want you to let my husband know what happened to me. Nicholas Shorte is my husband's name, everyone calls him Little Nick. We have a cot in Market Street, Penzance, they all know us there. We argued on the Saturday night before I was taken – he said he en't no Puritan, and he don't want his sons brought up Puritan, and so he took the children to St Raphael and St Gabriel's instead.' There was a boom, and the ship shuddered from stem to stern, as if God had struck it with his fist. Tears began to run down her face; Cat saw the gleam of them even in the dark. 'I wish I'd listened to him. If I hadn't been so cross-grained I wun't be here now. I shoulda been with them, I should never have gone off alone in high dudgeon.' She swallowed. 'I told him . . . I told him . . . to go to the Devil, and then I stormed off. This is God's punishment to me, I know it, I know it . . .' And she broke down sobbing.

Cat placed her hand over the other woman's. 'I promise if anything happens to you, I'll let him know. But it won't, you know: you'll be fine,' she lied. If their ship was struck again, if a cannonball blew apart the hold, how would any of them survive when the ocean rushed in through the hole? Chained to the iron bars as they were, they would drown, each and every one.

There came a terrible grinding sound all down the right of the ship, followed by the report of muskets and muffled cries a long way off. For some while there was a storm of sound, like thunder, overhead; then the ship gave a great lurch and the water in the bilges sloshed and they were moving again, at some speed, it seemed.

More muffled booms, at a greater distance, and the ship rocked as its own guns recoiled from firing on the other vessel. At last there was quiet, just the creaking of the timbers and the low rumble of the sea.

'They're trying to outrun her,' said a gruff voice. 'They're out-gunned, and they've got to run.'

'What does that mean for us?' cried Jane Tregenna. 'If they catch us, will they sink us?'

'More like they'll try to take her. She's an old ship but still serviceable, a decent prize for any captain. And there will be a price on the heads of these pirates; they'll be rewarded for the captives they take, and they can use the bastards to trade against their own. From what these other lads have said there must be a fair few Spanish souls mouldering away in Barbary dungeons, or striped by a galley master's whip.'

'The Spanish have no love for the English,' rumbled Walter Truran.

'They'll have no love of thee, that's for sure,' laughed another man bitterly. He had an Irish accent. 'But I'll not tell them ye're no Catholic if ye don't.'

On they sailed and night fell, and no one came down to bring them sustenance at the usual hour.

'Something's up,' Isacke Kellynch opined sagely.

But, even as he said this, the hatch opened and Ashab Ibrahim appeared with two of his fellows, one of whom wore a bloodstained turban, the other a bandage about his arm. The captives looked to one another and said nothing: where was their food?

'Do you not have even a little fresh water for us?' Jane Tregenna asked querulously.

'We en't here for your convenience,' Ibrahim said. 'I have the raïs's orders to carry out.'

At this there was great commotion and many among the prisoners began to shout and curse.

'Shut yer holes or I'll stop 'em for ye!' Ibrahim roared. He stamped down through the hold until he reached Cat's row, where-upon he took a great iron key from the chain about his waist and unlocked the bar that held them. The man on the end started to rise, but the renegade shoved him roughly back down with a boot. 'Not you, cur! I want the girl.'

Cat's fingers tightened instinctively on the bar. She feared the worst, and he saw it in her face and laughed. 'Stupid chit, it's not what you think. The raïs wants you.'

Somehow, that was worse. 'But why?' she asked in a small voice. The raïs frightened her, and not just for his casual violence against the preacher: there was something fearsome in his demeanour, in his very eye. The renegade switched at her knuckles with the knout of his rope.

'Leave go and do as you're told,' he growled. 'He don't confide his desires to me, the Djinn.'

'Djinn?'

'That's what some of us call him. A djinn is made by God from subtle fire: fire that doesn't give away its presence by the sign of smoke. Ah, it's a good name for him, for they are angry spirits, the djinn, powerful and malevolent. But don't ever call him that to his face, for he won't thank 'ee for it.'

Cat got to her feet unsteadily, as if she were about to go to the very Devil.

Out on deck, the moon cast its sombre light upon the ship, illuminating pale, splintered wood on the starboard gunwale, a fallen mast, its rigging all in a tangle, patches of charred wood where fires had broken out. A team of men was engaged in freeing the sail from the fallen mast, cutting it away, while trying to salvage as much good rope as they could.

They passed through the waist of the ship and climbed the stairs to the aft castle, and wherever they passed dark eyes followed them.

On the tall upper deck Cat scanned the ocean, but found no sign of the Spanish ship. It seemed they had outrun it after all, which was surely a victory of sorts for the pirates, yet they seemed silent and subdued. A number of them bore visible wounds, while a few lay groaning against the sides. Others hunched over strings of beads, muttering quietly as if in prayer.

Down an elaborately carved companionway they went. Lanterns burned here, casting blooms of golden light on to the panelled walls and illuminating leaves and acorns etched into the wood, as if in commemoration of the great oaks which had given up their timber to the construction of the ship. Despite her circumstances, Cat admired the delicacy of the designs. They reminded her of tapestries she had seen in the great hall at the Mount, tapestries of Flemish origin: it was puzzling to see the same motifs on a heathen pirate vessel.

At the end of the companionway Ibrahim stopped at a low door and knocked. A moment later it opened, and he exchanged a few words of Arabic with the man on the other side. The door opened wider, and Ashab Ibrahim pushed Cat into the chamber beyond and shut the door behind her.

It was like walking into another world, a world out of a dream. Everywhere she looked there was something extraordinary. Brass lanterns hung from the ceiling, their perforations sprinkling out dancing patterns of candlelight which played across carpets of scarlet, blue and gold wool, intricately carved little round tables with tooled gold tops, a tall silver flagon, a collection of ornate glasses, ivory boxes, silver incense burners, silk hangings, the great, decorated water pipe she had seen up on deck. A little cage of what must be songbirds hung swaying from a hook, though they were not singing now.

'Come here,' commanded a voice from the shadows, and Cat's heart lurched.

She stumbled and pitched face forward into the dark. She cried aloud and flung out her arms, expecting to hit wood, but her fall was broken by a mound of cushions of bright wools and silks. Even so, the breath went out of her. Carefully, she levered herself upright.

'Is good that you prostrate yourself to me,' said the voice. 'For I am the master of this ship, and therefore the master of you.'

Someone caught her under the arms and hauled her to her feet.

'Bring light,' the raïs demanded. 'So that she can see what she must do.'

Cat struggled now, for it was horribly clear what was expected of her: the raïs, Al-Andalusi, lay half naked on his bed, draped only in a sheet. 'No!' she cried. 'No! Leave me be! It is dishonourable of you to treat a poor maid so, to force her against her will!'

There was a pause, then a short laugh that turned into a pained cough. 'Ah, you think I intend to violate you.' The raïs shifted slowly so that the light fell across his face. She saw that he wore no turban and that his shaved head bore an ugly stubble. It made him look smaller and more vulnerable, a vulnerability that was further emphasized by an unhealthy pallor and the sweat that beaded his brow. 'Alas,' said Al-Andalusi, with a small, courteous gesture of the hand. 'I wish I could fulfil such fantasy, but *maa elassaf*, sadly I am not. Also, you stink like goat, which not very arousing even if I feel ardent. Which I hope I shall again soon, *inch'allah*. No, you here because I wounded and chirurgeon dead.'

Cat stopped stone-still. 'I don't understand,' she said at last. 'I am not a chirurgeon.'

The raïs closed his eyes. 'I know that. You have other . . . skills.' He said something rapidly to the man who held her, and he took Cat by the arm, more carefully now, and led her to another part of the cabin separated from the bedchamber by a beaded curtain and pushed her gently through the gap between the hangings. Inside this enclosure she found water heating in a metal bowl over a brazier, and a pile of linen beside it.

'You wash,' the raïs told her from his bed. 'You wash good and change robe. I not in habit of putting myself into hands of infidel, but Allah wills it, for he has taken Ibn Hassan from me, and I have no choice. Now give Abdullah your clothes.'

Gingerly, she removed the soiled garment and passed it through the curtains, where it was taken from her grasp, leaving her standing in her shift and stained stockings.

It was as if Al-Andalusi heard her hesitation. 'Take rest off and give to Abdullah. He will wash and give you later. There are clean clothes for after you wash. Please be . . . what is word? Exact.'

'Thorough,' she corrected, without a thought. Her hands flew to her mouth. What was she thinking, correcting this barbaric chieftain so?

There was a pause on the other side of the curtain. Then, 'Tho . . . ruh,' he repeated slowly, as if storing the word away for future use. 'Thorough, yes.'

Cat did as she was told, and suddenly her shift and stockings were gone, leaving her clutching the precious little bag containing *The Needle-Woman's Glorie* and her plumbago stick: her last connection to another life. Putting it carefully aside, she sorted through the pile of linen and found a pair of wide cotton breeches, a sleeveless tunic and, underneath these, an over-robe of white wool so soft and finely woven that she could not refrain from running her hand over it as if over one of Lady Harris's house cats. Then she took up the washcloth folded beside the bowl, dipped it into the hot water and started to scrub herself clean. This was so much better than the cold seawater of the previous day, which had left salt scurf on her skin, that she luxuriated in the sensation of it, almost forgetting that barely six feet away, on the other side of a flimsy curtain, was a naked man; a man moreover who was both a pirate and a heathen, and therefore a monster. At last, washed and clean for the first time in a fortnight and more, and dressed in wonderful comfort, and her wet hair wrapped in a piece of cotton, she emerged.

The raïs regarded her curiously. 'Much better, Cat'rin Anne. Now you look like a Berber.'

'Catherine,' she said.

He waved his hand. 'Too complicated. Be content with Cat'rin. You here because of skill with needle.'

Cat stared at him. 'You've brought me here to embroider something?'

'Embroider?'

Cat indicated one of the tapestried cushions. 'Embroidery.'

Wordlessly, he twitched the sheet aside.

The flesh of his flank was split a hand's span from breast to waist. The wound gaped wide, offering the obscene sight of muscle and a skim of yellow fat. Blood oozed darkly with the slightest movement.

'That not all. Move sheet away from leg.'

Cat knelt to do as she was told. Beneath a thick bandage a ragged hole had been bored through his thigh.

'Musket wound. Other sword. Both Spanish.' And he spat. 'Doctor killed, and none of crew can use needle. You sew wounds.'

145

'I . . . I can't.'

'You will.' His voice was hard. 'If you do not, your mother die.'

'My mother?'

'Jane Tregenna, no? You not alike, but she said she your mother. She go over side if you do not.' He left a few seconds for this to sink in. 'And if I die, they put you both in sea.'

They brought her a sailmaker's needle, thick and cumbersome, and thread for the same task. She made them sharpen the needle on a whetstone and, while they did it, unravelled some lengths of silk from one of the hangings and boiled them in the water over the brazier.

'Bring pot,' the raïs told her, indicating a squat glass container topped by a heavy stopper. 'And open it.'

She took it from one of the small tables, opened it and frowned. 'Honey?'

He nodded. 'Put into wound.'

Despite herself, Cat grinned. 'My grandmother used to do that when we hurt ourselves as children. She said it would stop corruption of the flesh.'

He raised an eyebrow. 'She did? My *jeddah* taught me this. My *jaddhi*, grandfather, he kept – how you say . . . zzzzz?' His hand traced the movement of an insect.

'Bees. My grandfather still does.' A wave of nostalgia overcame her at the thought of the cottage at Veryan, tiny and snug, where her grandfather kept a log fire burning and her grandmother smoked hams and bottled fruits for the winter. She had not seen them since her father died, for her mother wanted nothing further to do with her husband's family, considering them of low estate and referring to them unkindly as 'peasants'. For the first time Cat realized that in this, as in so much, her mother was wrong-headed.

The honey was a thick, deep brown, more solid than liquid, not at all like the pale golden nectar with which she had first written her name, drizzling it from the honey-spoon on to a slice of her grandmother's freshly baked bread. She sniffed it and recoiled. It smelled extraordinarily strong, powerful and heady.

'The . . . bees that make it feed only on wild mountain plants,' the raïs said, watching her face. 'It is strong magic.'

'Magic?' Cat snorted, unable to help herself. 'There's no such thing.'

'You very sure of that.'

'I am.'

'And miracles, and fate?'

Cat's jaw set in a long, hard line. 'My mother always said that our fate is in our own hands, and we must make our way as best we can, for no one else will do it for us, and when I had my fortune told by an old Ægyptian woman, she said I would live to see Heaven and Earth reunited, and that my dreams would come true; but here I am, a prisoner on a pirate ship bound for some horrid place where I am likely only to find hardship and death. So, no, I don't believe in miracles or fate.'

'Only Allah holds the keys to our *kadar*. He know everything, he design everything. Our souls cannot decide where we are born or when we die: only Allah make such decisions. He has plan for all of us, and we must accept what he sends.'

Cat stared at him, spoon poised over the 'magic' honey. 'Then it does not matter whether I put this in your wound or not, nor if I sew the flesh with care: if you die, it is God's will, and so I do not understand why you went to such trouble to have me brought here, nor threatened me and my mother to make me do *your* will.'

Al-Andalusi shifted uncomfortably, his eyes closed against the pain. 'Is bad when women try to argue like men; and for infidel woman is worse, for you cannot comprehend will of God, is foolish to try. You make me impatient now: perhaps I put you over side now to save my head from noise of your tongue. Yet it seem Allah sent you to me, so he must have his reasons. Now put honey on wounds and sew them shut, and we see in time what his plan reveals for you, and for me.'

Cat pursed her lips, dug out a spoonful of the honey and pressed it into the wound on his leg. His muscle twitched as she pressed: she felt the hard flesh jump like an animal under her touch. She snatched a glance at him, but he was staring at the flame of the lantern overhead, his dark eyes inscrutable. She moved up to the wound on his flank. Here, the skin was lighter than that of his face and arms, and as smooth as any woman's; smoother, certainly, than Matty's. It felt like silk beneath her fingers, though the wound itself was horrible to look upon, and so horrible to touch that as the honey went in she had to look away before she retched.

'Now sew, with smallest stitches,' the raïs said hoarsely. 'This body God's body, and it must be fit to do his will.'

Cat threaded her needle with the boiled silk and, putting all other thoughts from her mind, applied herself to the loathsome task.

15

So nowe I lye here in the pyrat captaines cabin where I must stay to tend him, writyng this by the lyght of a candel-lantern, in far greater ease than my poore mother, aunte & uncle & others in the hold belowe. What must they thinke that I shuld bee here all these daies alone with the Turkiss raiz, even though he bee weeke unto deth & like to die? No goode thyng, I am sure. Many would saie I should not wayte for his wounde to carrye him off, but take my chaunce to kill hym now for the crewelties he has visited upon good Christian folk, but once the captaine ys gone we will bee at the mercie of men like Ashab Ibrahim which seemes to mee an even worse fate, so I wille do what I must to keepe him in lyfe & hope the Good Lord wille take pitie on us ...

Al-Andalusi was a strong man and had borne many wounds as a warrior and corsair, but the one that good Toledo steel had made in his flank looked sure to cut short his life, for the flesh swelled and festered, despite the thyme honey and the skilful way Cat had closed the skin.

For three days he resisted the fever that threatened him, sweating and shouting in his sleep and taking nothing but water with lemon juice squeezed into it. After this, the fever broke, and he was able to eat a thick gruel of chickpeas and garlic. They brought him hard bread dipped in olive oil every morning, but he passed half of it to Cat, and watched as she ate until not a crumb remained. 'I protect investment,' he told her when she protested. 'Sultan give me a fortune for such prize; and thin women he like not.'

The air of the cabin stank of his sweat, which the garlic made rank; then the wound began to putrefy, and that rendered the smell a thousand times worse. In his lucid moments he spoke to the men who visited him in rapid Arabic, issuing orders, asking for weather reports and the ship's position, his eyes unnaturally bright in his increasingly gaunt face. Catherine sat silently in the corner of the cabin as she had been told, and watched. Most of the men who came to the cabin ignored her; but some stared at her with undisguised hostility and touched amulets around their necks. Others still undressed her with their eyes, and she began to dread the inevitable day when the raïs lost his battle for life.

When Al-Andalusi finally lost consciousness and started to rave in his sleep, the second-in-command, a severe-looking bearded man by the name of Rachid, sent the renegade Englishman to sit guard over his captain.

'He don't trust 'ee, girlie,' Ibrahim leered at her. 'Thinks you're poisoning our raïs.'

Cat glared at him. 'And just how am I supposed to be doing that?'

'Merely with your infidel presence. Rachid considers it an affront to God that you be here.'

'Then send me back down to the hold with the rest of my people.'

The renegade laughed. 'Oh, I don't think the *khodja* meant only that as a vile Christian you are poisoning the air of our raïs's personal chamber – though you may be sure he does think that; no, our *khodja* thinks it an affront that Christians breathe the same air as the rest of us in the world. If he had his way your head would be on a pike adorning the harbour at Penzance, along with every other infidel he could execute.

'Besides, what sort of reception do you think you'll get from the poor starving bastards below when they see you looking so clean and plump, eh, my bird?' And when she opened her mouth to answer, he stopped it with his hand. 'I'll tell 'ee exactly what they'll think, my 'andsome: they'll think you're the Djinn's whore. They'll think he's been fucking you stupid all this time, and he's only sent you back down into that hell-hole because he's finally got tired of your little white arse.'

Tears pricked Cat's eyes, not merely at the probability of this unjust scenario, but at the stench of the man, who now pressed himself up against her. Beneath the obvious sweat and stale urine on him was a smell of smoke and of a pungent herb which made her head spin.

'When he's gone' – the renegade indicated the supine raïs with a tilt of his head – 'I'm going to take you for myself; and then I'm going to do to you all the worst things what them folk below imagine is already your lot. Except that when I'm tired of you, I won't send you back down to the hold. Oh, no. I'll pass 'ee on to provide a little comfort for the crew, eh?'

Cat's head came up fast and caught him hard under the chin, so hard that Ashab Ibrahim bit his tongue. Blood spurted; the renegade swore. He drew back his fist.

'You little bitch!'

Something spun through the air, an arc of silver, and Ashab Ibrahim pitched forward, howling. From his right shoulder blade a small, curved knife protruded, its ornamental red tassel swinging wildly.

'Show respect, you runagate! Faithless wretch, apostate son of sow, coward who chose Islam to save rotten skin! You treat no woman so, not on my ship, or any other of the Slâ fleet!' The raïs wheezed hoarsely, following this invective with more in his own tongue, and Ibrahim picked himself up in terror and fled the chamber, leaving an alarming trail of blood behind him.

Al-Andalusi collapsed on to the cushions, gasping. 'Cat'rin, go to door, call for Abdal-haqq. Go!'

Cat scrambled to her feet and did as she was bade. The companionway swallowed her words; she called the unfamiliar name again, louder, until the flames in the lantern-sconces shuddered and the sounds echoed out of the wood. At last, she heard the sound of voices and running feet. A third time she called for Abdal-haqq, and then she ran back inside the cabin.

But by the time she got there, the raïs was dead.

★

151

Some moments later the man called Abdal-haqq slipped through the door. He took in the scene with quick black eyes which belied his grey beard and age-worn face.

Kneeling by the pirate captain's unmoving body, blood seeping into the soft white wool of her robe from the wounds of the renegade, Cat looked as guilty as she felt. She sprang aside, but the man merely glanced at her and waved her away with a dismissive hand. He shook the raïs by the shoulder, touched his forehead, then his neck. Then he barked something at Cat.

'What? What? I don't understand.'

The bearded man muttered crossly; then he pulled himself upright, pushed past her and disappeared into the back of the cabin, stopping only when he reached the ornate cage in the shadows where the silent songbirds slept. He opened the cage door, reached in and took something out. 'Fire,' he said urgently. 'Where is?'

Amazed to find another pirate on this godforsaken ship who spoke English, Cat blinked. 'I'll get it,' she said, and did. She dragged the brazier out from the screened area and set it down in front of Abdal-haqq, and he blew upon it, making the coals glow cherry-red. Then he took up the tongs that lay across the brazier's bars, transferred the contents of his hands to them and thrust the tongs into the coals.

Cat cried out in horror. What she had thought was a songbird was another type of beast entirely, a sort of bizarre reptile, for its skin had tiny scales like those of a lizard or a snake, though it was like no lizard or snake she had ever seen. The creature coiled and writhed as it hit the embers, and from its strange beak of a mouth there spiralled a long purple tongue. Its extraordinary armoured eyes whirled; its scaled skin fizzed and burned. A moment later there was what seemed a small explosion in the brazier.

Abdal-haqq nodded, satisfied. '*Mezian, mezian.*' He picked up the beast by one tiny clawed foot, carried it to his captain's bedside and passed it two or three times under Al-Andalusi's nose. Cat understood this was some form of arcane magic. The smell of the burned creature – repulsively pungent – pervaded the cabin, making her eyes water. Quite what effect a burned lizard could have on the warring humours of a man, let alone a dead man, she could not imagine; but abruptly the raïs gave an almighty sneeze and sat bolt upright.

Cat felt her knees dissolve and abruptly found herself sitting on the floor. She had heard of corpses that made sudden involuntary movements, and even of some that spoke a last word – indeed, it was common knowledge that Mary of Scotland had moved her lips for a good quarter-hour following her beheading – but she had never heard of a corpse that sneezed.

'*Labas aalik?*'

The raïs subsided on to his cushions. He grasped the old man's hand with both his own. '*Labas, allhamdullah. Shokran, shokran, Abdal. Barrakallofik.*'

The two men conversed quietly. Then the old man turned to Cat. 'English renegade put evil eye on our raïs. The *al-boua*, the chameleon, help for now. But for that the infidel must die. *Then* the raïs get better.' He patted the curved dagger that hung from his silk bandolier. 'It will give me great pleasure.'

Cat watched him go, feeling more than ever that she was trapped in another world, one in which death visited swift as a hawk, in which the dead sat up and spoke, and in which the normal rules were refracted like light through water; a world in which magic was both tangible and more powerful than logic, custom or sanity.

And now Ashab Ibrahim, who had in another life been an ordinary seaman from the West Country, was to be executed. He had thought himself safe in this outlandish place because he had clothed himself in its garb, adopted a foreign name and religion; but since this had all been mere disguise rather than any honest transformation, it had not saved him. She felt no fellow feeling for the man who had once been called Will Martin, no genuine regret that he should be killed at the whim of the raïs; what preyed upon her terribly was the sense that it had been the renegade's threat to *her* that had earned the ire of the raïs. But, if that was the case, why had Al-Andalusi lied to the old man? To save her shame, out of some strange form of respect? But if Ibrahim *hadn't* cursed the raïs, then how was it that the magic of the burned lizard had revived him? It was all too baffling. Tears began to pour down her face.

'Why you weep?'

She turned, surprised to find the raïs watching her, and her thoughts felt naked to his gaze. She looked away, discomfited, wiping the tears away with the back of her hand.

'Do you weep for the renegade?'

Shocked, she stared at him. 'No, of course not.'

'Then why you weep?'

She shook her head, furious now. 'I don't know.'

'Because you thought me dead?' There was a wicked glint in his eye.

'No!'

'Many women would weep if I die.' He paused, watching her reaction. 'I have large family.'

'How many children do you have?'

His expression hardened and closed. 'I have no wife, no children. I have aunts and cousins and their children to provide for, in Slâ and in mountain villages, very many who depend on me, and I work hard for them. Every spring I sail with Slâ fleet, I raid, I take Nazarenes as prisoners, and if they resist, I kill them. In summer or autumn I go home with captives, sell them in souks, divide money among crew, backers, the *marabout*, my family, my community. Everyone profit a little, spiritually and financially, from holy work of the *ghuza* –' A violent bout of coughing silenced him.

Red-eyed, Cat regarded him. 'You're weak and should sleep.'

'I sleep when I dead, and I not dead yet, despite efforts of bastard Spaniards.' He spat copiously, then declared, 'Bring chicha.'

Cat looked towards the ornamental pipe. 'I don't think that's a very good idea.'

He snapped his fingers. 'Bring!'

His peremptory tone galled her. She leaped to her feet, grabbed up the pipe and shoved it at him. 'Oh, take the blasted thing and poison your wounds with its foul-smelling smoke! You are a monster and a zealot, and I would not care a damn if you were to die this very minute!'

154

The raïs's fingers closed around the stem of the pipe, but there was no strength in them. With a crash, the pipe hit the floor and shattered in a shower of glass and water and pungent herbs.

Al-Andalusi swore in his horrible language, a guttural explosion of sound; then he fell back against the cushions, sweating profusely. 'I think I keep you for my household; but I see now you are . . . *kambo* and stupid and would break everything I have of beauty and value.'

'Good, for I have no intention of being a slave in some heathen pigsty!'

His eyes narrowed. 'You insult me?'

Cat decided it might not be wise to explain the exact import of her words. Instead, she bent and began to clear up the broken glass, averting her eyes from his furious expression, but the raïs was not to be diverted.

'What this word you said? What this "sty"?'

His gaze bored into the top of her head. 'A pig-house,' she said, very low, regretting her temper now.

'So, you despise me, do you, little infidel? You think I am ignorant "heathen", man who live like unclean pig, in filth and dirt? Perhaps you think we all like that in my country, that we no better than animals?' He bit off each word so that it rang in her ears, sharp and cutting.

She swallowed. 'No.'

From above there came an agonized scream, a scream that hung on the air and then was cut abruptly short. Cat closed her eyes. So ended the life of Will Martin of Plymouth; and, if she was not very careful, that of Catherine of Kenegie would soon follow.

She was saved by the pirate's weakness, for soon after this he fell asleep, drowsing fitfully through the rest of the day and night. The next morning his fever had broken, and he came to without need of another burned chameleon, somewhat to Cat's relief. She took him the food that one of the crewmen had brought to the door at first light and watched as he picked at it. She had after long thought come to a kind of decision.

'Yesterday you asked me why I wept. I will tell you. I wept because I do not understand your ways. I do not understand why you had Ashab Ibrahim killed. I do not understand anything about this "evil eye" or how the burning of the lizard brought you back from the dead. I do not understand why you have stolen us away, and why you believe it is right to do so. I do not understand why you hate good Christian folk so. I understand none of it at all; and, most of all, I do not understand why you keep me here in your cabin. I wept because I am used to understanding the world I live in, and now I understand nothing at all.' All this came out in a rush.

The raïs closed his eyes as if pained. 'Women . . . Why they ask so much? We not here to understand world; we here to *be* in world and give thanks for it. And I have only just woken up.' He gave a deep and heartfelt sigh. 'I tell you why renegade dead: because he act as if my authority on this ship gone, as if I already dead. No one treats my captives ill without my order.'

Cat took this in silently. Then she said, 'Abdal-haqq said he had put the evil eye on you, and that was why he had to die.'

The raïs made a non-committal gesture with his piece of bread. 'Abdal-haqq very wise. When he tell the crew I say this why the renegade must die, they will not question my decision. They are . . . how you say? Afraid of curse and such like. They will put bag over his head and throw him in sea so he cannot turn evil eye on them too.'

'But what is the evil eye? How can an eye hurt anyone?'

'There is old Berber saying: "The evil eye can bring a man to his grave, and a camel to the cooking pot."'

'I don't know what a camel is.'

Al-Andalusi laughed. 'Are all your people so ignorant? I cannot explain camel to you: a camel is itself, and all men know its worth; but evil eye is like a light. You can see it, feel it or hurt others by using it. It can make harm or death, but you can never hold it in hands; all you can do is avert it, by luck and by will of Allah.'

'So which was the lizard: luck or the will of Allah?'

Al-Andalusi rolled his eyes. 'Disputing with women bad for health: already I feel my strength waning. Is clear to me now that stars in firmament must be female, and each month poor moon is worn down by their incessant tongues. The chameleon is strong magic, but if it works or not against evil eye is determined by Allah. More than that I cannot explain to infidel.'

'Why do you hate us so, and call us "infidels" and "Nazarenes"?'

'Do you know nothing of world? Christians have made war against my people for thousand years. They persecute us cruelly and use religion as excuse. My family is dead at hands of the Nazarenes, and I alone left to avenge them.'

'Oh.' In a small voice she asked, 'What happened?'

He looked away. 'Why you want to know?'

'To help me understand' – she made a helpless gesture with her hands – 'why you do this, why I am here . . .'

The raïs regarded her steadily. 'I do not have to justify my actions. Besides, is not story to tell a child, let alone Nazarene child.'

'I am *not* a child. I don't even know if I am what you call a "Nazarene".'

'You are Christian, no? Follower of prophet Jesus the Nazarene?'

Cat bit her lip. Nell and Mistress Harris were constantly chiding her for her lack of Christian values. She did not know what she believed, what she was any more. She had been baptized in Veryan's font and had prayed silent prayers to the baby Jesus, to the Son and the Father and the Holy Ghost in times of stress. But that was before the raid. Now she could not understand how a god who cared for his people could allow an entire congregation to be taken by heathen raiders while at prayer, then let them waste and die in such foul conditions – men, women and innocent children. It tested the faith of the strongest believer, and she had never been that. But she was no Mahometan, so what could she say? Eventually, she shrugged. 'I suppose so.'

'Then you my enemy, and I tell you why. My mother's grand-father's father came from Rabat in Morocco, but he leave because no work, so he join colony of Moors in Estremadura, in mountains of Spain; my mother's grandfather and father born there and then my mother too: four generations of her family – you understand? – they live there, they work, they make trade, make community prosperous. My father was trader, he travel all over Morocco, bring salt and gold and ivory from south-west, from Tafraout to north coast, and then to Spain; and take fine Spanish steel, swords and guns back. One visit, he stay my mother's family and meet her, ask for her as bride. Next trip they marry; then he take her home to Morocco, to mountains of Atlas, where I born. But she very sick for home in Spain, miss family much, spoke no Berber, no Arabic, only Spanish; so when I five, we move to Estremadura to be with her family. Then Spanish king Philip decide all Moors must leave Spain, no matter how long they live there or how Spanish they become. Some our family, they see signs of persecution early, and they leave – my uncle, some cousins – they take everything they can carry and go back to Morocco; but my father angry. He already moved all he had to be in Spain, his business is good there: why he should leave, just for being Muslim? He refuse to leave; they make him Catholic by force. It great shame for him; but my mother beg him support it. They stay longer, but all time it get worse, he treated like dog, disrespected, cheated in business; then finally Inquisition come. They take my father away in night; next morning my mother put me on mule and send me down mountain trail to be with cousin who leave for Morocco. All sisters cry because I leave. They all babies. "We join you there," my mother promise, but I knew I never see them again. I cry all the way down the mountain. It is last time I ever cry.'

Cat's eyes were round. 'And did you ever see them again?'

He swallowed. 'I not know my family's fate for a year. I went with cousin to Slâ and found two uncles and other cousins living there. I wait for my father and mother and sisters, but they not come. At last my uncle said one night, "Come with me. There is a man, Spanish prisoner." I went to kasbah in New Slâ where ship had come in with captives. This man, he blacksmith in Hornachos, but when Moors left he no work, he became soldier. He told me Inquisition racked my father to death. They drew his arms from his sockets, left him rot in prison cell.' He closed his eyes. A tiny muscle in his cheek twitched and jumped.

Looking down, Cat found her knuckles were white where she

had been gripping her skirts. She did not dare ask the question she wanted to for fear of what the answer might be.

'The soldiers came for rest of my family two days after taking my father. They rape my mother and kill my sisters. My mother die of shame and grief. I was ten years old. My sisters were two, four and seven. I should have stayed and defended them . . .

'The blacksmith, he saw. He said he tried to stop them, but I knew he lie. My uncle gave me knife to kill him. He was first Nazarene I kill; at age of eleven. Now I have lost count.

'I swore revenge so my cousins make me apprentice to a great corsair: Yussuf Raïs, once Englishman called John Ward. English treat him ill: call him hero when he take foreign prizes for Crown, and villain when he take them without letter of marque, so he renounce Christianity and come instead to Islam, make war on Nazarenes. He once said me, "If I meet my own father at sea I rob him, and sell him when I had done." He was good teacher. I sail with him five years. When he went to Tunis, he give me this ship. He die three years ago; I bless his name. Now I operate under *usanza del mare*, code of corsair: I bring much money, many captives, back to my people, kill many Spanish, many Nazarenes, *damara'hum Allah*, may God destroy them. Is both my revenge and holy work. I cannot bring down Inquisition or Spanish throne, but I can wage war against its religion and wreak what havoc I may.'

His eyes flashed, and with a shock Cat remembered the same expression on the face of her grandfather as he recounted tales of the Bloody Queen, half-sister of the great Elizabeth, who had burned three hundred Protestants at the stake and threatened to bring the Spanish Inquisition to English shores to turn the whole country Catholic. The Spanish were roundly hated in Cornwall; he had himself lost a leg in an action against a Spanish privateer. And she remembered how only two years ago, when King James had sent a delegation led by his favourite, George Villiers, the Duke of Buckingham, to attempt to win the Spanish Infanta as the Prince of Wales's bride, there had been much fury and riotous talk in Marazion; how Thom Samuels had spoken of taking up arms if

England were to have a Spanish queen, and Jack Kellynch had punched him, since his own mother was Spanish. It was rather extraordinary to find that her own people had anything in common with this violently zealous pirate. It was also extremely disconcerting to discover how moved she was by the story he had told: for a moment, at least, he seemed less a monster and more a man who had a reason to do the terrible things he did.

She found she had been staring at him; when he looked up suddenly and met her eyes, she found the intensity of his gaze uncomfortable and had to look away.

'But I still do not understand what you have against the English,' she said at last. 'Especially if you sailed with an Englishman and he gave you his ship. It wasn't the English who killed your family, it was the Spanish, and England is at war with Spain again, just as we were under the old Queen, so they're our enemies as much as yours.' She paused. 'And Cornwall's really a separate country all its own, not really part of England at all.'

Al-Andalusi gave a short laugh. 'I have raided the Spanish coast so hard there's no village we haven't struck. They well fortified now; too many guns. So I take Nazarenes where I find them. Your people not well prepared: no guns, no defences, very easy.' Seeing her face fall, he said more kindly, 'Here, Cat'rin – take bread and eat. If you tend me until I well you need be strong.' He handed her the remains of the small, hard loaf. 'Dip in oil to make soft or you break teeth. Broken teeth lose me money at market. And take some of these too, good for digestive organs.'

Heaped on a brightly coloured earthenware plate on the table beside him were a number of the salty black fruits she had so disliked and some round, squashed-looking objects that resembled nothing so much as miniature turds.

Cat wrinkled her nose. 'No, thank you.'

'Take,' the raïs told her. 'Is good.' He picked one up and held it out, and, when she hesitated, thrust it at her with greater insistence. 'With my people, hospitality important: to refuse is insult.'

She took a small bite. Sweetness flooded her mouth so that she gasped. It was not in the least what she had expected, for it tasted remarkably like the preserved medlars the cook bottled each autumn from Kenegie's orchard. 'Oh . . .' She took the rest whole, saliva breaking from the corner of her mouth.

Al-Andalusi looked on, eyebrow cocked sardonically. 'Is fig,' he said. 'In some traditions it was the fruit Eve gave to Adam from the Tree of Knowledge.'

'In the bible that was an apple!'

'In our tradition, according to Qur'an, it was apple also. And when Adam swallowed mouthful of fruit it stuck in throat and made lump all men have.'

'The Adam's apple!' Cat cried, astonished. 'We call it that as well.'

'We are, perhaps, not such strangers to one another as you think.'

16

The raiz saies that in two daies our shippe wille come in to Sallee Port in Moroco. After whych tyme I knowe not what wille become of mee. The raiz ys nowe on hys feet & I have seene lyttle of hym. I have not beene sent back down belowe but am kept here in the cabine. I was in hopes that hee would allow my mother to joyne mee heere, but he just turned from mee and I dare not aske agayne. I feare my future, for on account of my foolish lye hee stille thinkes wee are of a riche familly who wille paie a grate ransom for oure return. But hee also threttens mee with being solde to a sultan, who I beleeve ys lyk unto a kyng in ther countrie, for hee saies I wille fetch a goode price at Sallee's market wyth my redde haire & faire skyn. How I wishe I had took old Annie Badcock's advyse & gone home with Rob to Kenegy . . .

'Why did you shoot off like that, Julia? It looked really odd, you know.'

I regarded her steadily. 'I really can't bear to be around him.'

Alison made a sympathetic face. 'Sorry. I've just made it worse, haven't I? Look, if you'd rather I walked away from the renovation of the cottage, I will. It's only money.'

'Did Andrew leave a lot of debts?' I felt awkward asking. 'I could help you out, you know.'

She smiled, and her eyes filled up. 'It's probably not as bad as I think it is. I haven't dared look at the statements, haven't felt up to it. But I could do with a bit of work, if only to have something else to think about.'

'Of course you must take on the cottage, if you want to do it. Don't mind me.'

'It's just that . . .' She looked embarrassed. 'Well, I may have got a bit carried away with telling Michael what could be done with the cottage: he seemed quite fired up by it. In fact, he called Anna, and she's coming down tomorrow to discuss what we might do.'

'Is she?' I was horrified. Had Michael suggested Anna visit before or after he had called me? If before, he must have decided it would be his last chance to see me before she arrived. If after . . . I felt sick. Was it his way of punishing me for turning him down? I knew there was the purely practical matter of the cottage, but something told me there were other, darker reasons. 'Does Anna know I'm here with you?'

'Um, yes,' she said. 'Sorry. When Michael came off the phone he said she sent her regards and was looking forward to seeing you.'

Cold iron in the heart. 'I can't stay. Can't do it.'

Alison rubbed her forehead. 'God, what a mess. Isn't it better to get it out of the way? Try to get things back to normal?'

I shook my head. 'It's too soon. I just can't face her. Not feeling strong enough yet.' My mouth twisted suddenly; I thought I might cry.

Abruptly tears started to spill out of the corners of my eyes, and a moment later Alison welled up too. She hugged me. 'I'm so sorry. God, now we've both got the waterworks going.'

I gave her a wobbly smile and pulled myself together. 'Sorry, I'm being pathetic. It's only a stupid affair, one that should never have started. I brought this on myself, but you –'

She waved her hands at me. 'Don't.' She gulped. 'Look, don't you think it might give you closure, put a proper end to it?'

'No, I'm just not ready.'

'To be honest, I don't think Michael is either. He talks about you a lot when you're not there.'

My traitor heart leaped up.

'Oh, and he asked about the little needlework book too, whether you'd finished it yet. He seems to think it might be valuable.'

'If it is, Al, you should have it back.'

She shook her head. 'He gave it to you: it's yours, Julia, honestly. And don't you give it to him without getting a receipt, OK?'

I grinned. 'Because we all know what an honest man Michael is, eh? You know, Al, I really should get back to London for a bit, just to make sure the shop's OK, try to get myself straight.'

Alison shrugged. 'You do what you have to do.' She put her hand on my arm. 'It's been great having you here, you know, Julia: I've really appreciated it.'

'I was glad to be able to do it,' I said, and meant it.

'It'll all work out for the best in the end. I mean, there has to be a reason for it all, doesn't there? There are days when I think there really is some huge great tapestry of a plan out there, and we're all woven into it – this fabulous complex pattern of life and death, full of recurring motifs and waves of colour, and we're each one tiny thread in the weave. And then there are the days when I know that we're on our own, and it's all a horrible mess and our own fault.' She sighed. 'But there are some amazing coincidences going on. I mean, how weird is it that Andrew should have sent those books up to Michael, and one be about embroidery, just your thing, and contain the journal, and that Michael should spot it and think of you? Let alone that Catherine should come not just from Cornwall, but right here at Kenegie? There was a load of old Kenegie stuff in the attic, you know, odds and ends, books and broken furniture. Probably been dumped there when they were renovating the manor, been mouldering away for centuries.'

'Mmmm,' I said, feeling uncomfortable. 'Synchronicity, I guess.'

'Have you read any more of it? Is she still working on the Countess of Salisbury's altar cloth? Do you think she ever finished it?'

'We'll probably never know.'

'Well, why don't we walk down to the manor house and have a look at where she lived? Before you go back up to London.'

Reluctantly, I agreed.

By the end of the afternoon I very much wished I hadn't. Visiting Kenegie Manor had been a grim experience. Alison had told me that it had been developed into a holiday complex, but I hadn't really thought about what that might entail, so the sight of dozens of ugly little bungalows and chalets jammed together in what must have been Lady Harris's prized orchard and gardens was dispiriting. This was compounded by the harsh primary colours of the children's playground, the acre of car park, the modern annexe housing the swimming pool and racks of tourist-information leaflets inviting them to a host of lurid artificial attractions – stately homes with tropical butterfly collections and teddy bear exhibitions, petting zoos and miniature railways. It seemed the whole of Cornwall's heritage was being prostituted in much the same tawdry way. Adjoining the annexe was the manor house itself. Tall Tudor chimneys were about the only feature that spoke honestly of its origins. The granite stonework had been refaced and repointed, the windows and doors had been replaced, and where the knot garden and herbs had once grown there was now a paved concrete courtyard. A large estate agent's board on the way in had boasted that the Grade II listed manor house was being redeveloped into stunning modern apartments. It gave a number to call for viewings.

'We could call the number and pretend to be prospective buyers,' Alison suggested.

I shook my head wearily. 'No, thanks.' I was already feeling glum enough. Who could do this to such an historic old house? How could English Heritage allow such a commercial insult to one of the county's treasures? I said as much to Alison.

'It's probably been messed around with so much down the centuries that there wasn't anything original left to preserve,' she said, shrugging. She stuck her head in through the open front door. Distant sounds of hammering wafted through the corridors. Then there came the sound of booted feet on bare boards, and a man in a yellow hard-hat and overalls appeared, a claw hammer in his hand.

'Hello,' he said. 'Have you come for a viewing?' He peered over our shoulders. 'Is the agent with you?'

'We've got an appointment for later,' Alison lied cheerfully, 'but we thought we'd get here early and have a bit of a nose around. You know what agents are like, always hurrying you past the things they don't want you to ask awkward questions about.'

They both laughed, complicit.

'Well, you might as well come in, then,' the builder said. 'Have a poke around. It's not like there's anything to nick. Not unless you're partial to cordless drills!' And with a hearty chuckle he waved us through and tromped off to destroy some other part of the house.

If I had been feeling downcast before, now I was properly disillusioned. What trace of Cat and her seventeenth-century life could survive amid all this new plasterboard and wiring, the litres of brilliant white emulsion and multiple phone lines? There was no trace of any of the previous inhabitants. Even my overactive imagination couldn't picture the shades of Sir Arthur and Lady Harris among the seagrass matting and the double-glazing; or of Robert Bolitho and Jack Kellynch amid the sterile concrete pathways; or Matty and Nell Chigwine among the soulless melamine and stainless steel of the fifteen identical new kitchens. I bet no old gypsy women came to the scullery door now, seeking a groat and a mug of furmity, or whatever the modern equivalent might be.

As I followed Alison miserably from room to room, it became ever clearer that wherever the soul of Catherine Anne Tregenna rested, it was not here.

That night I dreamed. It was inevitable after the turmoil of my day. None of the images that stayed with me in the grey light of dawn illumined the problems I faced, but rather seemed to emphasize them. Anna in a hooded cloak, in her hand a great curving knife, dripping blood. People shouting at me in a language I did not understand. The smell of burning. Michael pleading with me for his life. I dozed, I re-entered dream situations, I surfaced; went under again and finally came back to full consciousness feeling a weight of dread pressing in on me.

Alison knocked on the door. 'Are you OK? It's late: gone ten.'

'Damn!'

I had meant to take the first train home out of Penzance, but in the end we didn't make it to the station until lunchtime. As we stood on the platform, watching the passengers from the just-arrived London train disembark and make their way through the throng of friends and relatives waiting to meet them, Alison said suddenly, 'Isn't that Anna?'

My heart fell like a stone into the pit of my stomach. Out of the first-class carriage stepped a dark-haired woman in an expensively tailored jacket and straight-legged jeans which slid seamlessly into a pair of glossy, high-heeled brown boots. Despite the looming horror of the social situation about to explode around me, I found myself admiring her effortless style.

I turned to run, but Alison caught my arm. 'Look, you're just going to have to brazen it out. What's worse, saying hello for five minutes on a station platform with your escape ready to chug off into the distance, or dodging around for the rest of your life trying to avoid her?'

She had a point, though I couldn't see why we couldn't just nip into the station café and hide while she walked past, and said so. Alison pulled a face. 'Don't be stupid: she's bound to spot you, and then it'd be obvious you were trying to avoid her. Besides, if she thinks I'm playing the same game, she's hardly going to trust me to do up her cottage, is she?'

So there I was, waiting like a sacrificial lamb, knowing that my execution came ever closer, watching my ex-lover's wife tow her dinky little silver suitcase down the platform towards us, her perfectly made-up face showing no sign of having registered our presence.

I had seen Anna only intermittently in the last seven years; enough to witness her changing fortunes and style, and in some way to envy them. But, as she approached, her eyes fixed on the tarmac in case it was booby-trapped, I realized with a shock that she had aged. Dye and clever cosmetics can hide a lot, but what they cannot hide are the erosions caused by catastrophic life experience. Lines were deeply incised on either side of her beautifully painted but downturned mouth. She walked right past us and out into the sunlight without seeing us at all; and it struck me that I was watching the passage of a deeply unhappy woman.

I pondered that for some time on my return journey. I knew in my gut that the depth of grief I had seen etched into her face was that of a woman who has known for a very long time that her husband is unfaithful to her, a woman who has borne his infidelity silently and let the mask slip only in private, or in an unguarded moment such as the one I had just witnessed. I sat for three hours – through Exeter, through Taunton, as the train crossed the ancient landscapes of the Salisbury Plain – remembering my times with Michael. I revisited his body, every inch of it, clothed and naked, in repose and aroused. I cried, very quietly, with my face pressed against the window so that no one could see. The train rushed through Hungerford; by the time we stopped at Reading, I had put Michael away from me, shut all my memories up in a box and stowed it away in a dark attic corner of my mind.

It was with some relief that I closed my own front door behind me after the weeks in someone else's house, and felt its familiar shades and contours enfold me.

I dumped my suitcase in the bedroom and went to make myself a mug of tea. Then I wandered from room to room, reacquainting myself with my home. Perhaps I was tired and fraught, or perhaps my mind was playing tricks with me, but little details of the flat kept catching my eye. Had I really left the Sunday papers so untidy under the desk? Had the books on the shelves to either side of the fireplace always been so higgledy-piggledy? I didn't remember leaving the cardboard box full of files out where it was now, nor the bureau lid open. I frowned.

In the bedroom I found that the drawer of my bedside table had not been properly shut, the faulty catch not engaged. There was a knack to it, and only I had it. Someone had been here. Someone had broken into my flat.

In sudden panic I raced back into the front room, but the entertainment centre appeared untouched, all its little silver hi-tech boxes still wired in place. My paintings still hung on the walls, my old laptop still sat on the desk, and no one had bothered to steal the few pieces of jewellery my mother had left me.

I frowned. Not a very successful burglary, all in all.

When I finally realized what must have happened, my knees gave way and I suddenly found myself sitting firmly on my Afghan rug.

Michael had been here. He had let himself in using the key I had given him six years ago. He had made this unforgivable invasion, failed to find what he was looking for, and then had the gall to follow me to Cornwall. The complete and utter bastard.

I felt sick. Was Catherine's book really that valuable? If it was, why had he given it to me in the first place? And what would he do next once he found that I had returned to London? Was I in danger? Would he hurt me to get hold of it? In that moment, I realized I didn't really know the man I had been sleeping with for seven years at all.

I called Alison.

'Don't worry,' she said. 'I'll keep them down here. They're planning to stay for a couple of weeks, anyway: it'll give you some breathing space. If Michael leaves, I'll call you.'

For the next fortnight I devoted myself to cleaning my flat thoroughly, for the first time since I had bought it. I threw out fifteen black sacks of rubbish and felt oddly cleansed myself: catharized. And after I had done that, I put it on the market and handed the key to the agent. I didn't want to live there any more.

I moved into a rented flat in Chiswick, sold the lease on the shop to a girl who'd just graduated from St Martin's and wanted somewhere from which to sell a line of gorgeously silly clothes, and my stock (what little there was of it) to a woman I'd met at a craft fair the previous year.

Then, feeling absurdly rootless and light-headed, I took myself to Stanfords on Long Acre and bought all the guidebooks they had for Morocco.

★

The night before I flew, I had misgivings. I called Alison.

'Look, I'm going to Morocco tomorrow. I thought someone ought to know, just in case anything happens to me.'

There was a shocked silence at the other end of the phone. 'You're going *alone?*' she said at last, disbelieving.

'Um, yes. But I'll be staying at a lovely place, a *riad* – an old merchant's house in the capital, Rabat.' I gave her the address and contact details. I had had a long conversation with the woman who ran it, who spoke beautiful fluent French, which stretched my stuttering schoolgirl French to the limits and beyond. But Madame Rachidi had been reassuring and helpful. There was a guide who would walk with me around the city, she said, a cousin called Idriss who was well educated and knowledgeable about the history of the area and who spoke excellent English. This would mean I'd be safely chaperoned from any 'unwanted attention', as she put it. I didn't really know what she meant.

'But Julia, it's a Muslim country. You can't go alone.'

'Why ever not?'

'It's dangerous. The men over there, well, if they see a Western woman on her own, they'll think she's fair game, that she's asking for it. It's a very sexually repressed culture, with the women all covered up and sex before marriage illegal – Western women must seem like prostitutes to them, flaunting everything they've got. And you're blonde –'

'Oh, come off it!' I snapped. 'You're sounding like the *Daily Mail*. It says in the guidebooks that you just have to cover up a bit more than usual and be sensible. Madame Rachidi says I'll be fine.'

'Well, she would, wouldn't she? She wants your lovely English money.'

'Anyway I'll have her cousin Idriss with me.'

'Julia, you've got to be joking. You don't even know him – he might be the problem personified!'

'Look, I only called to let you know,' I said crossly. 'And to give you my new mobile number. I'll call you when I get to the riad, OK?'

I heard her sigh. 'Well, if I can't deter you.'

'I fly tomorrow at ten, I should get there mid afternoon.'

'*Inch'allah.*'

'Oh, very funny.'

17
Catherine
August 1625

The days were long and empty once Al-Andalusi was sufficiently recovered to resume his duties as captain. Each morning the raïs would rise at dawn with the first call of the prayer leader, wash himself with ritual care using the cold water in the bowl behind the traceried mahogany screen and, taking up a stick his men had fashioned for him, limp down the companionway and up on to the deck. Cat would not see him again until sundown.

At first she found it hard to fill her hours. She would lie in the semi-dark, waiting for the knock at the door which signalled the arrival of the food with which she every morning broke her fast – a little hard bread, some oil, honey rather less dark and pungent than that with which she had cleansed the raïs's wounds, and from time to time a strange hot drink flavoured with some herb and a great deal of sugar, which she would drink down greedily. The call to prayer came again at mid morning and once more as the sun climbed high, and still he would not return. After a few days she realized that she missed his company, and that gave her concern. Surely she should hate her captor and wish death upon him? She thought about her family and compatriots in the stinking hold below, how astonished they would be to see her living in such luxury, and felt more guilty than ever. A few days before she had plucked up enough courage to ask the raïs to allow her mother to join her in the cabin, but he had turned his hawk's face away from her without saying a word, and she was not sure he had even understood her request. Something hung in the air between them, awkward and unspoken, some tension she could put no name to. At times she thought it was because she had seen him at his weakest and most unguarded, and he was ashamed; at others he seemed obscurely angry with her and would sit moodily, staring into a candle flame, or reading a small leatherbound book, his lips moving silently, as if she did not exist.

She would wander about the cabin, intrigued by the exotic objects he had collected there – running her hands over the intricately carved little tables with patterns of brass and mother-of-pearl and ivory inset into their polished tops, the lanterns with their star designs punched out of the metal, the gorgeously coloured fabrics of the wall hangings. There was a pair of sturdy silver bracelets, set with studs and stones, their surfaces etched with swirling lines, which opened on a hinge and closed with a long pin on a chain. They were so large she could slip them on without moving the pin; they settled comfortably over her bicep, though the raïs wore them at his wrist. She examined the odd crystalline substance in a little brass dish set over coals which he often heated after his evening prayer; its powerful scent still perfumed the cabin the next morning. It infused her clothes, and she could smell it in her hair even after she had washed it, which she did occasionally merely to pass the long and solitary hours. She wrote in her little book, taking the opportunity to fill the tiniest spaces with writing even she could barely read; she lay among the cushions and wondered at the strangeness of people who would sew pearls and gems into an object created for comfort; she picked at the smoked meat and dried fruits left for her midday repasts; she even managed to develop a taste for olives.

Today, when the knock came at the door, she opened it to find not only food for her lunch but also some squares of fresh white linen lying on the ground outside. Placed carefully upon them were a spool of fine black wool and a ship's needle.

Astonished, she gazed up the companionway, but whoever had brought these treasures had departed post-haste, barefoot and silent. She gathered them up, took them in and spent the afternoon amusing herself with some blackwork designs of her own making: a decorative cross-stitched band of zigzags and circles. Then, with the plumbago stick, she sketched twining leaf motifs, to which she added two birds. She was still stitching the last of these when the raïs returned to his cabin, but she was so absorbed in her task that she did not hear him arrive. She looked up to find him framed in the doorway, the candlelight throwing his features into relief, exaggerating his high cheekbones and full lips. His expression was unreadable, his eyes in shadow, the whites visible as a thin line beneath the iris. How long he had been there, standing with his hands pressed against the jamb, watching her, she did not know. Flustered, she put the sampler aside, covering *The Needle-Woman's Glorie*.

'May I see?'

'It isn't finished.'

He held out his hand. Reluctantly, she passed it to him, watched as he examined it, turned the fabric over, handed it back. 'We believe it is wrong to show realistic representations of living things.'

He watched as her face fell and went on more kindly, 'There is story, a hadith. According to Ayesha, who was Prophet's favourite wife, Mohammed came home one day from expedition and found in one corner of room a hanging she had ornamented with embroidered human figures. At once he pull it down, saying: "On Day of Resurrection worst punishment shall be reserved for those who seek to imitate beings created by God." And so chastened, Ayesha took down hangings and cut them apart, avoiding human figures, to make pair of cushions.'

Cat felt quite sorry for Ayesha: her husband sounded a fearsomely pious man. She frowned. 'But I'm not really seeking to re-create these things, just to show a simple version of them, interpreted in my own way.'

'Is that which is presumptuous.'

She thought for a moment. 'But isn't it just another way to appreciate God's works? To think about them for yourself?'

The raïs closed his eyes, considering. After a while he said slowly, 'In the south of my country, in the mountains where my father's tribe comes from, the women weave images of camels and sheep into their carpets; but they are peasant women: they know no better.'

Cat flushed. 'I'm no ignorant peasant! Where I come from it is considered a great gift to be able to represent the beautiful things of our world.'

Al-Andalusi regarded her solemnly. 'God is beauty and he loves beauty. Camels are things of great beauty, it is true. And so is woman in a fury. I am not sure which I like better.' And then he smiled and held her regard, until she looked away, uncomfortable.

Her hands were shaking; she did not know why. Gathering up the linen, the skein of wool and her little book, and hugging them to her, she said, 'When will we arrive in Slâ?' She had learned to pronounce the Barbary port after his own fashion, though it was ugly to her ears.

'We cleared the Cabo de São Vicente yesterday; if the wind is good to us we arrive later tonight.'

That was sooner than she had expected; much sooner. Cat could hear the blood beating in her ears. 'And what will happen to me then?' she asked.

Silence stretched out between them like a wire. What did she want him to say? That he would keep her to be ransomed to her family back home? But with her mother and uncle on the same vessel, she did not even know to whom she might write, let alone how such a letter might make its way back to Cornwall – which now seemed another world, in another time. There was her cousin Rob, and Rob alone, who might care enough to work for her release; but could he prevail upon the goodwill of Lady Harris to speak to her husband on Cat's behalf? Somehow, she could not imagine that, even if he did so, Lady Harris would care much for the welfare of one she regarded as at best a servant, and at worst a wanton coquette. Neither could she conceive of Sir Arthur giving such a huge sum of money into the hands of foreign corsairs for an uncertain return, for why would he bolster the fortunes of the very enemies it was his duty to defend the coast against? The other possibilities – that the raïs would give her into the hands of the man he named the Sultan, or sell her to the highest bidder at the slave markets Dick Elwith had spoken of – were too terrifying to contemplate further. The final scenario – that he would keep her for his own household, as he had once intimated, before declaring her too clumsy – gnawed at her. She knew she shouldn't hope for such an outcome, that to enter the domicile of a barbarian pirate whose sole aim in life was to murder and steal from her own people was to be regarded by civilized folk as a grim fate; but if her duties included such simple tasks as teaching his womenfolk her needlework skills, then surely to be a servant even in this foreign land was preferable to being sold to a stranger who might use her for who knew what dire purpose? Now she was shaking, courage failing.

'I do not know,' he said. 'I have not yet decide.'

She looked up, startled. He was staring at her, dark and intense.

'Come with me, Cat'rin,' he said suddenly, holding out his hand. 'You shall see stars shine down on Africa and moon rise over city that is my home.'

He wound a length of cotton about her head and face, leaving only her eyes naked to the sight of his crew, and she wondered at his reason, for he had never covered her before. But this time as she passed, instead of staring at her with curiosity or hostility, the crewmen bowed their heads, and none bothered her. They went down the companionway into the waist and walked the length of the ship. Above them, the sails cracked – great squares of white on the main masts, and elegant triangular sheets on the mizzen – and in the black sky above a heavy yellow moon hung, tinged with red as if with blood. A hunter's moon, they'd call it back home, Cat thought, and wondered what it presaged for her future. Stars were scattered across the firmament, thousands of them, and so bright, particularly one. She found her eyes drawn to it, for it blazed like a silver beacon overhead.

'Shining One,' Al-Andalusi said softly. 'Al-Shi-ra. Egyptians named it Star of Nile and predicted rising of floodwaters by its appearance; Romans called it Dog Star. In old religions, it guard way into Heaven – do you see great bridge of stars that lie beneath?' And when she looked, she could see a glowing swathe of milky white, a bridge between Earth and Heaven. 'And there' – he turned her about and pointed – 'to north shines Al-Qibla. From its position we can determine direction of Mecca, sacred city of Prophet.'

'But that's the Pole Star!' Cat cried, astonished. Rob had shown it to her so many times that now she could find it for herself. 'I know that one. We call it the Fisherman's Star: they use it for navigation.'

He smiled. 'Sailors use it thus, also. I have sail to many places in world using that star as guide. To Valetta and Sardinia, Constantinople, Cabo de Verde, even as far as Newfoundland.'

To Cat, these were merely names; but they sounded exotic and far-flung. And she, who had never travelled further than the Bartholomew Fair at Truro and had wished so hard for wider horizons, was now looking at the savage land of Africa.

With the Pole Star at their backs, the wind drove them on towards a line of indistinct dark shadow rising from the foam-flecked sea. They stood there in silence, watching the land come closer.

'That is Morocco, Jezirat al-Maghrib – island where sun sets; my home.' There was something in the vibrant tone of his voice that made her turn to look into his face. His eyes shone, reflecting the moon; but they blazed from within as well, making him almost demonic in his fervour. She shivered, and looked away.

Gradually the indistinct revealed itself, moment by moment, rendering up the outline of cliffs, a breakwater washed by surf, a slender tower whose tiled roof glinted silver-green in the moonlight, a wide-mouthed river flanked on either side by massive fortifications. Whatever it was that Cat had been expecting of her first sight of the dark continent, it was not such evidence of a powerful martial culture, or anything so shockingly contrasting as the ethereal tower.

'Slâ el-Bali – Salé the Old' – the raïs indicated the settlement on the left bank – 'and Slâ el-Djedid – New Salé on other side. I have family in both cities – among the Hornacheros of New Salé and followers of the Sidi al-Ayyachi in old city, which give me rare perspective, unusual advantage in my dealings. They will all be glad to see what I have brought them!' He called something to his crew, and a man unshuttered a lantern once, twice, three times. Answering lights flashed from the top of the fortress, and he laughed. 'They already know it is one of their own: they well remember this pretty ship, and no other would dare to enter river by night. It is treacherous even in the brightest sunlight, for all it bears the tranquil name of Bou Regreg.' In his tongue the word sounded as harsh as the call of a crow – *bu-rak-rak*.

'What does it mean?' she asked, eyeing with dread the looming fortress, the myriad robed figures moving around its battlements and gun emplacements.

He thought for a moment, his brow furrowed. 'Yussuf Raïs told me it was in your language "Father of Reflection", for on calm day when river lies as still as a sheet of tin you can see all of Heaven reflected in it; but a man must reflect carefully when he steers his ship in its waters, for beneath gleaming skin lies hidden sandbar that has broken backs of a thousand ships; and a thousand more have foundered in its winding channels.' He paused, then smiled. 'Is good to come home, triumphant and with great success.' He closed his eyes, ran his hands down his face, kissed the right palm and touched it to his heart. '*Shokran lilah.*'

Triumphant. Successful. Bringing a shipload of Christian slaves, most of whom were bound, if the stories below deck were true, for the galleys and the slave markets, for ill use and beatings, for torture and enforced apostasy, and ultimately death in a strange land. Something hardened in her heart against the confusing feelings he stirred in her. Words welled up and spewed out before she could stop them.

'You tell me about the terrible things the Spanish did to your family and say that you carry holy war to the Christians as just revenge and on behalf of the Mahometan people. But if your religion says it is right to treat anyone the way you have treated the innocent men, women and children in the hold of this ship, who lie in filth and die of disease and ill treatment, then I say it is a wicked, cruel religion and that your god is not my god!'

She saw the fury in his eyes; she saw his hand make a fist which trembled with the effort it took him not to strike her. Time seemed to stand still. She stared at him till she thought her knees would fail her, not knowing whether she had said a stupid thing that she would have a short lifetime to regret, or whether she had touched home a point that might give him pause. But, just as she thought the latter might prevail, he shouted, and seconds later she found herself seized by two crewmen who came running at his summons.

'I have not time to dispute with you. I have the Bou Regreg to navigate and ship to dock. Is not my habit to argue with women. You will be taken back to your people: your fate shall be their fate. No one question my religion or my god. No one insult memory of my family. I thought you worth more, and not just money. But you same as rest, ignorant and faithless. You could have lived like queen in most beautiful house in kasbah; now you take your place on blocks with rest.' And he waved the men away and turned his back on her.

18

Casablanca Airport was bewildering. Seas of people engulfed me as soon as I stepped into the main concourse: travellers in expensive European designer clothes, men in sharply cut suits and sunglasses, others in flowing djellabas, West African women in bright prints and fabulously wound turbans, extended families herding children and trolleys buckling under the strain of overstuffed bin-bags, saran-wrapped suitcases and cardboard boxes. I passed a roomful of men kneeling on prayer mats, a football team in matching shell-suits, innumerable security staff in military uniforms and out-sized sidearms. All around me swirled a Babel of languages. My schoolgirl French was not up to interpreting the muffled announce-ments over the tannoy or the confusing signage; by the time I had queued for an hour at the correct security point, haltingly answered the immigration officer's questions ('*Vous voyagez seule, sans votre mari?*' 'No, no husband . . .' His eyes bored into me), located the baggage-reclaim hall and retrieved my bags, and at last stumbled out into the oven-hot air of the exterior, there was only one vehicle left in the taxi lane. It was a Mercedes, and not just any Mercedes, but an ancient stretch limo. I stared at it in disbelief. Must be waiting for a local celebrity, I thought, but as soon as I laid eyes upon it the driver fairly flew out of the door and seized my bags. I held on, equally determined. '*Combien à la gare de Casa Port?*'

'For you, three hundred dirham, madame,' he answered me in perfect English.

'I'll give you two hundred.'

'Two hundred and fifty.'

'Two hundred.'

He looked pained. I thought he was about to lecture me on

starving his children, but he merely gestured at the Merc. 'Such beautiful car, how I can maintain on such little fare?'

There was no answer to that, so I just shrugged and smiled.

He sighed. 'Such beautiful eyes; for your eyes I take you for two hundred.'

'My train for Rabat leaves at five: will we make it?'

'*Inch'allah*. Is in the hands of God.'

Feeling distinctly nervous now, I watched my cases being swallowed by the boot, then took a seat in the back. When a second and third man appeared at his call, I dug out my mobile phone and got ready to call Madame Rachidi at the riad, hoping that she would have some useful advice for me, or at least alert the local police on my behalf. The driver took his place behind the wheel and his friends disappeared from sight around the back. I whipped my head around, paranoid – only to find them bump-starting the car. At the third attempt, it roared to life.

Great, I thought. I am alone in a foreign – a really foreign – country, with a man who's already complimented my eyes, and now has two mates sitting up front with him, heading for a city I've never yet visited, in a car that may break down at any minute. Perhaps Alison had been right.

My qualms were on the way to full-blown panic by the time we approached the outskirts of the city, and the driver swerved wildly across three lanes of traffic to take an abrupt detour into the suburbs. The typically bland motorway down which we sped at alarming speed into the city had offered no clue to the flavour of the country in which I had arrived; but suddenly we were in the *bidonvilles*.

The driver must have seen my expression in his rear-view mirror, because he turned around, one hand still casually draped over the steering wheel at what felt like sixty-odd miles an hour, and told me cheerfully, 'There is camera and police. Always they stop me, is very expensive!'

I tried not to imagine all the worst things that could happen to a woman on her own in the slums of Casablanca and applied myself to taking in the unfamiliar new environment that fled past the windows of the slewing car. Crumbling adobe houses and tin shacks between which ran alleys of beaten red earth frequented by a Third-World mélange of little black goats, skinny chickens, bone-thin cats and ragged children; cars rotting away under the blazing sun, weeds pushing up through the rusting carcasses of broken bicycles; lines of washing flapping in the dusty breeze; bright carpets hung over terrace walls; roofs of corrugated iron sprouting a forest of satellite dishes. Two men squatted beside an electricity pole playing a draughts-like game with coloured bottle tops and stones; others sat on doorsteps, smoking and staring into empty air. A woman robed from head to toe in white cotton washed unfeasibly large garments in a small tin bath; she raised her head to watch our passage incuriously, then returned without any trace of reaction to her task: the stretch Merc was clearly a frequent visitor through this insalubrious quarter.

Then, just as abruptly, we were back on the main road again, and the slums had vanished in a cloud of dust. Moments later we were speeding through a thoroughly modern city – creamy-white low-rise apartment blocks, shop windows, billboards and traffic lights, not that anyone seemed to take any notice of them. The blare of car horns was deafening: it seemed that every jam, every hold-up, every awkward manoeuvre was someone else's fault. Ten lanes of traffic converged in a lethal-looking knot at every major junction. If their horns weren't working – or even if they were – motorists stuck their heads out of the window and helpfully offered to others gems of basic driving advice. Three-wheeled bicycles to whose front ends were appended unwieldy cartloads – of fish, of vegetables, of scrap metal – wove a dangerously unstable path between the cars and buses. Sometimes suicidal pedestrians wandered into this appalling mêlée, but we passed too quickly for me to see whether they survived. We drove past glittering hotels, chic boutiques, showrooms displaying top-of-the-range cars, designer kitchens, flat-screen televisions. The three men in the front of the Mercedes joined in the general rush-hour conversation, shouting oaths, shaking fists and wagging fingers, and the charms and amulets hanging from the rear-view mirror pirouetted wildly.

The will of Allah was that I should arrive at Casa Port Station in one piece, and just in time to catch my train to Rabat. My driver, Hassan, shoved his way to the head of the queue to buy my *billet simple*, persuading the guard to allow him through the barrier, carrying my bags right on to the train for me, finding my designated seat and stowing my luggage safely above my head. He shook my hand vigorously. '*Bes'salama. Allah ihf'dek. Dieu vous protège.* God go with you.'

He absolutely refused to take a tip, leaving me staring after him open-mouthed with amazement and gratitude.

My carriage was largely comprised of business people, judging by the number of briefcases and laptops on display, and a surprising percentage of these were women, some dressed entirely in Western clothing, others in full-length pastel robes complete with hijab, while others went bareheaded. Each one wore a quite extraordinary amount of make-up: full-cover foundation, powder, lipstick and pencil, blusher, thick black eyeliner, eye-shadow, highlighter, eye-brow pencil, all very expertly applied – and exquisite, high-heeled shoes. Kohled eyes watched me covertly – *poor woman, travelling on her own; no children, no sign of a wedding ring, and so inelegantly dressed too – has she no pride in herself to be wearing such old jeans and ugly trainers, and not a trace of cosmetics?* No matter how swiftly they looked away, I could read their thoughts in an instant. The men smiled at me kindly: perhaps in their eyes too I was worthy of pity. One young man, keen to show off his English, asked me if I was visiting his country for the first time, and what did I think of it, and did I need somewhere to stay in Rabat, because his family would happily take me into their home. I told him it was my first visit, that what little I had seen of Morocco so far seemed fascinating and I was looking forward to discovering much more; and that yes, thank you, I had arranged my accommodation in Rabat. I watched his face fall.

'If you need a guide –'

'That too is arranged.'

He fixed me with an earnest look. 'You must be very careful about guides here in Morocco, sometimes they are not what they seem, I mean they are not to be trusted and may tell you many lies. It can be dangerous for a lady who travel on her own.'

The woman opposite me caught my eye and held my gaze for several heartbeats, then looked away.

'Thank you for your kind advice,' I said, smiling. To signal that our conversation was at an end, I dug out my *Rough Guide* and applied myself to it, nerves jumping. I felt his regard on me like a physical touch, and my skin began to crawl. He's only being friendly, I told myself fiercely, he's concerned for your welfare.

I went out into the corridor and phoned Alison.

'Hi. I'm here.'

'Where's "here"?'

'On the train to Rabat. It gets in in about twenty minutes.'

'You OK?'

It was reassuring to hear her voice. I thought about her question for a split second, felt foolish at my paranoia, smiled. 'Yes, fine, actually. People are really pleasant and helpful. How are you?'

'Great. I was going to phone you later. Something amazing's happened. We've found something – you'll never believe it, it ties up with Catherine's book.'

I waited, pins and needles tingling at the base of my skull. Alison said something inaudible. 'What? Say that again?'

'Sorry, it's just that Michael's here. I'm going to hand you over.'

A pause.

'Julia?' Michael's voice, a continent away.

I closed my eyes, remembering the last time we had spoken. 'Go away,' I said softly.

'What? Julia, I can't hear you. Look, you've got to come back – get a flight tomorrow, Anna and I will pay for it – we really need the book, you won't believe what we've found –'

'Go away,' I said, and turned the phone off, my heart hammering.

A portly middle-aged man in a tunic and wide trousers waited for me in the concourse of Rabat's main railway station holding a handwritten cardboard sign bearing the legend MME LOVEIT. I walked right past him before it clicked. A fit of the giggles threatened to consume me. Mastering it, I retraced my steps. 'Hello. I'm Julia Lovat.'

His face broke into a huge, gap-toothed grin. '*Enchanté, madame. Bienvenue*, welcome, welcome in Maroc.' He waddled up and pumped my hand effusively, and at once relieved me of my suitcases.

'Are you Idriss el-Kharkouri?' I asked. He was not at all what I had been expecting: somehow, from the refined tones of Madame Rachidi, I had pictured an elegant cousin with a scholarly air and the ability to march me around the city at speed, filling my head with arcane knowledge. It did not look as if Idriss was in the habit of walking anywhere at all; nor did his lazy smile intimate the razor-sharp intellect of an expert guide. But I knew nothing of what might lie behind the façades of this culture: perhaps I should not leap so swiftly to judgement.

He looked puzzled, so I repeated my question, adding: '*Idriss, le cousin de Madame Rachidi, mon guide?*'

Now he shook his head vigorously. '*Ah, non, non, non, désolé, madame: Idriss ne pouvait pas m'accompagner. Il est occupé ce soir. Moi, je suis Saïd el-Omari, aussi cousin de Madame Rachidi.*'

Another of Madame Rachidi's cousins, I slowly translated for myself, following in his wake as he staggered along with my cases, not realizing, or perhaps disdaining, the efficacy of the handle and wheels. Popping open the boot of a small rusting blue Peugeot bearing an official taxi sign, he stowed my luggage, helped me into the back, performed an illegal U-turn and headed at speed down the main road of a city that looked as blandly European as the centre of Casablanca. Monumental government buildings, a vast post office, rows of modern shops, municipal gardens lush with colour, office blocks, car parks. As the nondescript trappings of a modern city sped past me, I allowed my mind to hover for a moment – like an insect over a Venus flytrap – over my brief conversation with Alison and Michael.

Whatever could they have found that was so important it would prompt Michael to offer to pay my fare back? And what, my guts clenched, had he said to Anna about it all? Before I had left London, aware of the many perils that can befall a traveller, I had taken the book to a copy shop in Putney and carefully photocopied every page, laying the book as flat as I could without damaging the spine, and using the most complicated graphics settings the machine offered to capture as best I could the soft pencil script. It had taken me several false starts, a great deal of finicky care, well over an hour and cost the best part of ten pounds, but it was worth both cost and effort for some peace of mind. A more prudent person would probably have left the original at home and taken the copy with them, but I could not bear to be parted from the object itself, so I had lodged the copy with my solicitor.

My hand strayed to the bag on my knee. Delving inside, I caressed the cover of *The Needle-Woman's Glorie*. I have often wondered whether pet owners stroke their animals for their own or the pet's benefit; now, the feeling of the soft calfskin under my fingers calmed me, reassuringly solid and present, and I suspected it might be for the former reason. I held Catherine's book pressed to my chest as we passed from the modern city through an archway into the crumbling terracotta pisé walls of the old *medina*.

Immediately I was craning my neck, all thoughts of England forgotten. This was truly foreign territory. People thronged the streets – old men in hooded robes, veiled women, teenaged boys in a mixture of garbs from the downright medieval to the saggy jeans and bling of classic hip-hop culture. Music pervaded the air: percussive and insistent, traditional North African voices mingling with the occasional throb of drum and bass. The taxi dodged at a snail's pace through the flow of people on bicycles, mopeds and donkey carts, giving me a privileged view of market stalls overflowing with produce, narrow alleys bordered by tall, windowless houses with ornate doors of aged iron-bound wood, elegant towers topped by shining green tiles, wrought-iron gateways offering a tantalizing glimpse of hidden courtyards verdant with orange trees and bougainvillea. We turned a corner and a great wailing voice shivered on the twilight air: the muezzin, the call to prayer. I closed my eyes, listening – '*Allah akbar. Allah akbar. Achehadou ana illah illallah. Achehadou ana mohammed rasoul allah. Achehadou ana mohammed rasoul allah. Haya rala salah. Haya rala salah . . .*' – and suddenly felt myself inside the heart of Western Islam.

Some minutes later the spell was broken as Saïd hurled the taxi up on to a broken sidewalk, and the engine shuddered to a halt. I looked around. By now it was full dark, and here particularly so, the only brightness visible being the blue-white fizzing light of a man arc-welding his car across the road, an activity which threw off alarming shadows that leaped and danced like dervishes. Something moved fleet and close to the ground in my peripheral vision. I whipped around, and it froze in mid-pace: a black cat, thin as a stick. Its eyes flared at me as the welder's light reflected in them, then it flicked its tail and vanished into the night.

'*Allez, madame*, with me. Dar el-Beldi this way, *par ici*.'

I followed him down an alleyway so narrow I could touch it on both sides without stretching out my hands. The houses had walls of rough adobe and were incised with grand doorways. In one of these an old woman sat crouched on a doorstep. As we approached, she smiled up at Saïd, and her eyes were all white with cataracts, shining up at me like those of the cat. She stretched out a dry, brown bird's claw of a hand. '*Sadaka all-allah.*'

Despite being laden with my bags, Saïd stopped, dug in a little pocket set aslant in his tunic, withdrew two coins and pressed them into her palm.

'*Shokran, shokran, sidi. Barrakallofik.*'

He was already past her, stepping into the shadows opposite and knocking on a vast iron-studded door. A small door within the door swung inwards, and golden light flooded out on to the alley. There was a loud staccato burst of Arabic between Saïd and the person on the other side; then he waved me forward. I skirted the old beggarwoman with a nervous smile and fled into the welcoming light of the riad.

19

To Sir Arthur Harrys
Master of St Michael's Mount
Kenegy Manor House, Gulval Hills, Cornwall

24th daie of August, anno 1625
Sallee, in Barbarye

My duty be remembered to you, & may your health in the Lord be goode.
Pray, from the goodnesse of your hearte pay the person who brings you
this post from us poor captives in Sallee, where wee lye in the handes of
crewel tyrants, at whose behest I wryte this letter, in feare of my lyf.
Myselfe, & those I liste belowe represent all those who were taken
from the attack on Pen Sants and survive to this daie, that ys alle who
have not perished of the voyage or of other paines & endurances, or
beene taken away I knowe not where. Sir, I must beg your supportation,
for there ys no one else wee maie turne to for our deliverance, & I knowe
you to bee a goode Christian man who would not willingly see your
countryfolk left unredeemed & forced into apostasy. Every daie they
offer us threats & blandishments for turning Turke and becomyng
Mahometan, & I feare some maie bee perswaded rather than face the
galleys or the bastinadoe. I liste heere those peple whose fate I knowe,
but there were taken many more, & I knowe not what has become of
them, or what wille become of us in the long weekes it maie take for this
post to reach you.
Viz. of youre owne householde:

Catherine Anne Tregenna, ladys maide – £800

Eleanor Chigwine, house keeper (your servant William Chigwine perished on the voyage) – £120

Matilda Pengellye, house maide – £250

Others taken from the church in Pen Sants:

Jane Tregenna, my mother, widow – £156

Edward Coode, Esq., draper – £100 and wyf Mary (my uncle & aunt) – £140. I feare both my nephews are lost

John Kellynch, fisherman of Market-Jew – £96, sister Henrietta – £125 & mother Maria Kellynch – £140

Walter Truran, preacher – £96

Jack Fellowes, farmhand of Alverton – £96, wyf Ann – £180 & children Peter & Mary, twelve & eight – £280 the paire

Alys Johns – £250 & her child James, five – £104

Ephraim Pengellye, fisherman of Pen Sants – £96

Anne Samules, spinster of Pen Sants – £80

Nan Tippet, widow of Pen Sants – £85

I knowe not why the price they have putte on mee ys so hie. I knowe that I am not worthie of such costlie sum, sir.

Of Mayor & Ann Maddern, & Alderman Polglaze & Elizabeth hys wyf, I knowe not how they fayre, but I am towlde they are to be ransomed separately.

There are also wyth us others taken from various divers places, marriners from shippes & ports around the West Country, but they have made their own testimonies, so I wille not trouble you wyth such heere.

May it please you Sir Arthur the Mahometan corsaires who holde us claim a ransome of some three thousand four hundred and ninety-five pounds (or seven thousand Spanish doubloons) for the return of all those of whom I wryte. It is a fearfull summe of money & I knowe not whence it maie bee raised, but I do pray you that some meanes bee found to redeem us from our miserable fate, & that our sighs will come to your eares & move you to pitee & compassion. Deny us not in your prayers if you can do nothyng else, & please remember mee kindly to Lady Harrys, who has my gratitude every daie for her goodnesse in teaching me my letters, & pray also pass my greetings to my cozen Robert. As Preacher Truran saies, we did never so well understand the meaning of that psalm penned by those poore Jewes held in Babylonish captivity till nowe: 'By the waters of Babylon we sat down & wept when we remembered thee, O! Sion.' O! Cornwall, how we do miss your greene hills & vales, the clene aire & the free & ordered lives we once enjoied, now that wee are confined in darknesse & filth in feare for oure lyfs & limbs.

I am towlde in London there maie bee merchant shippes who stille have trading contacts in this region. If you have an opportunity thus to do, I pray you maie sende worde within a month or six weekes, or for sure wee shall perish in this terrible place.

Thus ceasing to trouble you, I rest
Your most dutiful & obedient servant
Catherine Anne Tregenna

20

Catherine

August 1625

Cat laid aside the pen and sighed. In truth, she had no hopes that her former master would even receive the letter she had just drafted, let alone be minded to act on her entreaties. Three thousand, four hundred and ninety-five pounds, of which she knew a full eight hundred to be her own redemption price. It was a fortune: at Kenegie she had been paid just eight pounds a year, from which was deducted her bed and board; Matty earned barely four. Cornwall was a poor county: there was never enough money to go around. Taxes and tithes had to be scraped together; doctors' fees were a luxury – many a child had sickened and died because its parents could not find a shilling for the chirurgeon. The cost of a decent burial forced many families to cast themselves on the mercy of the parish for the price of the simplest service. Cat had witnessed the use of sackcloth as a winding sheet; even once a body blessed by a mendicant priest for a bowl of gruel and taken by night by one of the local fishermen to be consigned to Davy Jones's locker.

'Done?' The large, rough-faced, rough-handed woman into whose care Cat had been thrust now stood before her, hands on ample hips, waiting impatiently.

Cat nodded reluctantly. 'It's finished.'

'Give.'

She handed over the sheet of paper and the woman took it and stared at it suspiciously, turning it around and around in her callused fingers. Cat could tell that the woman could not read a word of what she had written, but she made a satisfied noise and rolled the paper into a scroll.

'I take to the Djinn.'

Cat frowned. 'Al-Andalusi?'

In response, the woman hissed at her and bustled off into the shadows. Cat sank back into the cushions and tilted her face up to the sunlight, which streamed down through the twining jasmine, releasing its confectionery scent into the still air. She was sitting at a table set within a recess to one side of a tiled courtyard. Overhead, in the vines that climbed the intricate trellis to the balcony that ran around the whole inside square of an elegant two-storeyed house, tiny reddish-brown birds sang. An orange tree spread its limbs across one corner of the courtyard; in the opposite corner a small patterned rug had been set, its once-bright colours faded by the sun, and in the centre of it all a fountain splashed into a raised marble bowl scattered with pale-pink rose petals. The light and scent and exquisite artistry of this tranquil place were so far removed from the vile *mazmorra*, the pitch-dark and stinking of shit and piss holding-pen in which she and the rest of the captives had been thrown, that all she wished for now was to be allowed to remain here, even if it meant writing the wretched letter a thousand times over.

She had spent only three days in the mazmorra (reckoned by the cries of the muezzin, for no sunlight penetrated their cell), but already it had replaced every other image for Hell that her mind had ever conjured. They had all been confined together – men, women and children – in such filthy conditions that it was clear their captors cared little whether they lived or died. Early this morning two men had come for her, calling her name in an accent so heavy that it had taken several moments of confusion before anyone realized it was Cat who was being summoned. They had bundled her up in a black robe and veil, tied her hands and dragged her, stumbling and blinking, through the narrow streets to this house. She had been pushed into a cool, dark room, the door thudding closed behind her. The contrast between the blinding sunlight of the streets and the dimness of the interior had been disorientating, so that when the familiar voice had broken the silence, she had fair leaped out of her skin.

'So, Cat'rin Anne Treg-enna. How you like your new quarters?' And he had laughed, a cruel sound which brought stinging tears to her eyes. He snapped his fingers, and a black-skinned boy, who had been squatting silent in the shadows, sprang to open a shutter. Sunlight flooded the chamber, gilding the walls and pouring in an amber wash over the handsome furnishings and the man who reclined on the cushioned divan.

Al-Andalusi was garbed in a robe of cerulean-blue embellished with swirls of golden embroidery, his head swathed in a white turban. He looked like the embodiment of gracious summer, and in contrast Cat felt more than ever the lice-ridden, filthy savage she had in such a short time become.

'You will write the letter of ransom on behalf your fellow townsfolk,' he had told her. He outlined the form the letter should take, the money that should be demanded, ignoring her gasp of horror. 'You will tell them how terrible are the conditions in which you live; also that we beat you mercilessly and threaten you daily to convert to our faith –'

Cat stared at him. 'No one has been beaten since we left your ship,' she said boldly. 'And no one has made any attempt to force us to your religion.'

Al-Andalusi's eyes glittered. 'B-a-s-t-i-n-a-d-o-e,' he spelled out and made her repeat back to him. 'Do you know what it means?'

Cat shook her head.

'One is laid upon the ground and the feet are drawn skyward, then the soles are beaten till they are black. I am told is excruciating. No one withstand such pain long: they soon scream away their faith in the false Son and embrace true belief in Allah. You will include it in your letter.'

'I cannot understand why you should wish me to say such things.'

The raïs laughed. 'Why your people should pay if your life and soul not in mortal danger?'

'They won't pay.' Cat's chin came up. She felt furious – at the deceit, the cruelty, his deliberate enjoyment of her situation.

He impassively watched her colour rising. At last he shrugged. 'Then you will live and die in Morocco.'

*

194

The letter had, unfortunately, met his requirements. The two men who had brought her from the mazmorra returned; she went with them, unresisting. Something had gone out of Catherine Anne Tregenna on that day. A glimpse of paradise had been afforded her, then whisked away, like a conjuring trick, leaving her soul in a darker state than it had been in before. At the door they took the black robes from her, though they fit her mood, and pushed her back into Hell.

'Had enough of you already, has he?' shouted one man. She could not see his face in the darkness.

'He has his choice of whores, no doubt, the Turk.'

'Cat is no whore, Jack Fellowes: may you burn for your words!'

For a moment Cat thought it was her mother who had defended her name, but her mother would never have used the short form of her name: it was another who had spoken. The indignation in the voice tore something in Cat's heart. Matty: dear, faithful, silly Matty, still defiantly alive and hale enough to care what was said about her friend.

Cat started to weep, for the first time since they had been taken, and now the voices came thick and fast, some trying to soothe and calm, others jeering and coarse. She sat crouched with her knees to her chest and her hands over her ears, rocking back and forth, trying to shut out the noise. Using every fibre of her will, she recalled the details of the fragrant courtyard and the cool quiet of the house. The rose petals on the water, the mosaic tiles in radiating patterns of blue and white and gold, the fruit glowing in the orange tree, the fretted trellis-work supporting the tumble of sweet-smelling flowers and the little hopping birds; the carved cedarwood ceiling in the raïs's chamber, the thick woven carpets and sculpted wooden furniture; the elaborate costume of the little black boy and the tight crimp of his hair; the rich fabric of the raïs's robe, and the gleam of his eyes in the gloom . . . For a moment, a small voice in her head questioned her: why do you not seek to recall the details of your life in Cornwall to comfort you? She answered it silently that she could no longer remember that life in sufficient detail for it to serve her purpose; but, even as she thought it, she knew that to be a lie.

The next day two guards came with the *patroona* to the prison. For the first time the captives were sorted into male and female, the children standing with their mothers or nearest relative. They took the women and children first. Out they stumbled into the street, their eyes squinting in the merciless sunlight. The guards chained them expertly into a coffle, taking care not to touch their infidel skin except with the cold iron of the leg-rings, displaying as little reaction to the state of their piteous charges as they might to a herd of hobbled goats being taken to market.

Cat stood in line behind little Nan Tippet. The widow was at the best of times a short woman, and now her head was bowed, leaving Cat's view of the city known as Old Salé unimpeded. It was hard to believe she had been out in these streets the day before, for she recognized nothing of her surroundings, but in truth she had been bewildered and hampered by the unaccustomed veil; in a dismal daze, she had taken nothing in. Now, though, it was as if the town demanded her attention, as if it shook its foreignness at her like a gypsy's tambourine. The streets through which they passed were alive with people – men hauling bony donkeys whose backs were bowed beneath their burdens, ragged children who ran behind, hitting the beasts with sticks and shouting raucously, gaudy-hatted water-sellers with animal skins about their shoulders, men with long beards and prying eyes, blind beggars, cripples lurching along on uneven limbs, women robed from head to foot, balancing enormous baskets on their heads or backs, staring curiously through the eye slits in their veils at these fair-haired, pale-skinned savages in their outlandish rags and tatters.

'*Imshi!* Move!'

One of the guards poked Cat with his stick. She had herself stopped to stare. On the corner of the street, a man played a flute to a swaying serpent in a pot; his partner held another snake in his hands, demonstrating to a small crowd of onlookers that it would not bite them, but no one took the writhing creature from him.

The air was filled with heat and flies and noise and dust and spices. Cries and music, the braying of an ass, the squawk of chickens, the smell of dung. She glimpsed goats skittering away down an alley between tall, windowless houses, pursued by a band of brown-skinned children. Cat stumbled on, her senses assaulted with every step.

At last they turned into one of the narrow side streets, and the patroona led them to an enormous, brass-studded door, which was opened by a slender woman wrapped in a robe of midnight-blue, the selvedges of which were embroidered with a series of bright geometric patterns. Cat fixed on the one thing in this alien world she could comprehend. Such a simple design – a child of seven could embroider it. Given such fine fabric and a choice of silks, she could make such a robe exquisite, for all its voluminous asexuality.

The patroona embraced the other woman and kissed her four times on the cheek, and they chattered companionably. The prisoners had been marched at speed by their guards, hit with sticks if they hesitated or stopped, and now it was as if there was no hurry in the world. The greetings finally over, they were ushered into a tall-ceilinged room, at one end of which sat a cowled woman at a desk with an inkwell before her and a quill in her hand. She tapped this impatiently up and down, and beneath the desk her scarlet-shod foot tapped away at the same tempo.

Released from their leg-irons, they approached the desk one by one and via the patroona gave their names, ages and marital status, which the clerk took down in her own approximation of the strange foreign sounds. Shortly, they found themselves in two groups. On one side of the room Jane Tregenna stood with her sister-in-law Mary Coode, Maria Kellynch, Ann Fellowes, Alice Johns, Nell Chigwine and Nan Tippet. On the other side, Cat, Matty, Anne Samuels and the two children, James Johns, aged five, and little Henrietta Kellynch – known as Chicken – who, detached from her mother, clung to Matty as if she would never let go.

The patroona and the slender woman walked among them; then the latter tapped Alice Johns with her stick. 'The *amina* says "Take off robe!"' the patroona barked at her. She plucked at Alice Johns's filthy dress and gestured wildly.

Alice gawped. 'Off! Take off!' The patroona took hold of the skirt and began to haul it off her. Alice clutched the dress to her and began to shriek. The slender woman hit her smartly across the back with a long, supple switch, making her shriek even louder. The switch was raised high and came down again with a thwack.

The captives exchanged horrified glances. 'Off!' Under the barrage of blows and cries, Alice capitulated, standing as unresisting as a punished toddler as the dress was dragged over her head, leaving her standing in her stained cotton shift. At twenty-five and with only the one child to her name, Alice Johns was a handsome young woman, despite the ordure and grime that adhered to her skin. The patroona and the amina poked and prodded at her, chattering in their strange tongue, feeling the muscles in her arms, examining her hands, her feet, her teeth. From time to time the clerk would consult a large manual on the desk and call out a question, which the patroona would roughly translate. When Alice failed to understand the patroona's heavy accent and odd phrasing, she was hit again, this time across the hamstrings.

Now they were pulling at her shift. Alice began to weep. 'No,' she pleaded. 'No, no!' But there was no resisting them. Off came the shift, leaving Alice pale and naked to their eyes. Desperately, she covered herself with her hands, drawing herself inwards as if she would disappear. The captives stared at the floor, feeling Alice's shame as keenly as if it were their own, knowing their own time for this ritual humiliation would soon come. Cat felt the little bag in which she kept her book and pencil pressing against her skin beneath the robe she wore. If they were to strip her, she would surely lose it.

'*Murtafa-at*,' declared the slender woman, slapping Alice's hands away from her breasts, and the patroona nodded vigorously. At the desk, the clerk scribbled away.

Alice was at last dismissed. Now the patroona took hold of Maria Kellynch. Seeing her mother move forwards, Chicken detached herself from Matty, dashed across the distance between them and fastened herself to Maria's leg like a limpet. 'Let go!' the patroona shouted and tried to pry Chicken loose, but all the little girl would do was wail and grip tighter. At last the amina stepped between them. With surprising gentleness for someone who had but lately been lashing people with a switch, she ran a hand over the little girl's hair and spoke soothingly into her ear. So amazed was Henrietta by this that she stopped crying at once and gazed up at the Moroccan woman with huge eyes. '*Eh-daa, a bentti. Shhh.*' The veil fell away from the amina's face, and Cat saw with surprise that she was strikingly lovely, with great dark eyes and arching brows, a long, straight nose and skin of a luminous olive hue. Then, with a practised flick, the veil was at once back in place, as if she felt the weight of the other's regard.

Now Maria was subjected to the same scrutiny as poor Alice Johns, the patroona and the slender woman poking at a fold of loose skin at her belly, the slight sag of her breasts. The patroona shook her head and called a word to the clerk, who added it to a column on the other side of the page.

Next came Nell Chigwine. Head high, she stared the patroona in the eye. 'I shall disrobe without being ashamed of the body the good Lord gave me. I shall take off my garments and place them under my feet and tread on them, as Jesus did, and then shall you see a good Christian who is not afraid of your heathen bullying.' She hauled off her ruined dress, shift and drawers, flung them down on the ground and stood there before them all, an awkward arrangement of angles and bones and tufts of pale hair.

Someone tittered. The patroona exploded into a whirlwind of sound, shrieking and battering at Nell with her hands. At last in a fury she bent, grabbed up the clothing and threw it at her. 'I not tell you disrobe!' she barked. 'You no *murtafa-at,* no use, thin stick woman!'

Ann Fellowes, Nan Tippet and Cat's aunt, Mary Coode, were variously examined and at last Cat was called forward. The woman in midnight-blue regarded the djellaba she wore with interest, plucking at the sleeve and running the fabric between her fingers. Then the amina turned to the older woman and jabbered animatedly. The patroona made an assessing face, then nodded and responded at length. Cat's heart began to pound. *The book*, she thought, *they must not take my book*. This suddenly became vitally important, as if within its calfskin cover resided what little was left of her identity.

'Off!' The patroona glared at Cat. 'Take off!'

How to hide her book from their prying eyes? Cat stared at them, trying to win precious time in which to think. Then she shrugged the robe off carefully, so that the bag came into her hand, and, as she stepped out of the folds of fabric, she dropped the bag softly behind her.

The slender woman pounced on the robe and shook it in front of the patroona as if making a point.

'Where you get djellaba?' the patroona demanded of Cat on behalf of the other woman.

'I was given it,' Cat said, covering herself as best she could with her hands and her long red hair. She felt like Eve, in the Garden, for the first time in shame of her body. 'By the raïs, Al-Andalusi.' She watched the two women exchange outraged glances, then the slender one dropped the robe and flew at Cat, raining blows down upon her. Fire burned her skin as the flexible switch found its mark. The other women looked on open-mouthed, but no one dared come to her aid. Weakened by her confinement, Cat was slow to react; even so, she was taller and more sinewy than the Moroccan, and fuelled by anger. Launching herself at her assailant, she managed to haul the woman's veil from her and tangle hand and weapon in the fabric, but moments later the patroona and clerk had her pinioned on the floor, adding bruises to the red weals on her pale, pale skin.

The midnight-robed woman adjusted her clothing, then spat accurately upon Cat's exposed back, and to this insult added a barrage of invective.

What happened next would remain with Cat to her last day as a moment of supreme humiliation, for now the women forced her legs apart and minutely examined her private parts. Then they had what seemed a heated argument, the patroona turning Cat over on her back. 'You virgin or no?' she demanded.

Eyes huge, Cat nodded, which started another storm of discussion. In the midst of this she pushed herself gingerly to her feet. There was the little pouch, lying on the stone floor. Some of the other women were staring at it as if expecting something monstrous to spring from it. Cat wished they wouldn't: it was only a matter of time before they drew the amina's attention. With a clever hand, she swept it up and turned to join her compatriots.

For a moment she thought she had got away with her deception; but the amina had sharp eyes. Cat heard the switch whistling through the air before the blow landed. Had she not turned, it would have fallen less harmfully on the back of her head, but as it was she caught the full force of the blow in the face, and in the shock of pain dropped the bag. In an instant, the amina had grabbed it up. She flourished the book at Cat. 'What is?'

Tears were streaming down Cat's face now, generated by a potent mixture of pain and rage and shame. She shook her head, unable to speak. The amina opened the covers and gazed inside. The patroona and the clerk joined her scrutiny. Together they puzzled over the strange diagrams, the pencil markings.

'It's my prayer-book,' Cat said at last, inspired.

The patroona frowned. 'Prayer?'

Cat put the palms of her hands together. 'Prayer.'

The three women conferred. 'For your religion?' the patroona asked.

Cat nodded. Nell Chigwine made a choking sound, as if swallowing outraged denial. The amina flicked through the pages, stabbed her finger at one of the designs and spoke urgently to the clerk, who nodded.

'Khadija say this blasphemy,' the patroona pronounced. 'She not care it your religion, for your religion blasphemy too. The robe you stole and the book will go to fire, as will your soul.'

After that, proceedings passed in a blur. What seemed an age later, after poor Matty Pengelly (but curiously not the aged spinster Anne Samuels) had also been subjected to the shameful inspection, they were all marched out of the room and herded by the patroona through a maze of cool, dark passages, until they reached a door from which billowed forth great clouds of vapour.

Here, Jane Tregenna came to a halt. 'Do they mean now to boil us alive?' she asked.

'*Imshi* – move, get in!' In comparison to the older woman, the patroona was enormous. She was struck all at once by the gauntness of Cat's mother's face. She had till now tried hard not to look beyond that point, but a single glance was all that was needed to take in the knife-edge collarbones, ribby chest, sunken belly and fragile limbs. Her mother had always cut a fine figure, with her sweeping farthingales and neat curves shaped by her tightly laced corsets; but now she looked old and defeated, a woman with one foot hovering over her own grave. Of them all, Cat suspected herself to be the only one not broken by the cruel voyage, for she had eaten while they had starved, had slept in linen while they wallowed in their own filth; and the flesh was still on her, hale and full. No wonder they had all – both her own women and the Moroccan – thought she was the pirate chief's whore.

There was no resisting the patroona: there was no point, and nowhere else to go. They trooped into the steamy gloom, whereupon they were set upon by a quartet of young girls wearing tightly wrapped white robes and caps, who scrubbed them till their skins were raw. Had she been able to, Cat would have scrubbed hers harder still, till the blood came; and even then it would not be enough.

'I will never wear your vile Turkish garb!' Nell Chigwine, her greying hair in rat's tails and her white skin blotched with unsightly red, folded her arms and glared defiantly at the patroona. 'Bring me decent Christian clothing, or nothing at all!'

The others stared at her, some with reluctant admiration, some in fear, as if she might bring down punishment upon them all.

The patroona had heard it all before, in a dozen different languages. Captives had passed through her hands from Spain, from the Canaries, from Malta and France and Portugal. She had dealt with them all, just as she had those unfortunates traded in tribal disputes and local wars – the captured Berbers of the bled and the mountains, the black-skinned women brought by camel-train from the hot lands to the south. Her community depended on the money raised by the auction of these prisoners: it financed not only the holy war carried on by the corsairs like her master – whom some called the Djinn and others the man of Andalusia – but also the rebuilding of the kasbah, their houses and souks, the schooling of their children in the fine *madrasas* and the maintenance of their shrines. It paid alms to the poor, the widowed and the crippled. It kept them all alive in the hand of Allah. It was sacred work, and she did it with a vengeance.

All this was clear in her tone, if not her words, as she railed at Nell Chigwine; but Nell also had righteous anger coursing through her tough old bones, and she pushed the patroona against the door jamb. The patroona had eaten well – not just today, when she had broken her fast with fresh bread and Meknès honey, with eggs and tomatoes and onion with cumin, but for all of her life. She had eaten well, and she had washed linen and hoisted baskets and pots and children till her forearms were as muscled as any man's. When she pushed Nell Chigwine back, the older woman's feet went from under her instantly on the wet tiles, so that she fell catastrophically, arms flailing for balance. She came down with a crash, her head striking the delicate zellije tiling on the wall to add a fifth colour to the starry mosaic, an unwonted scarlet amid the white and blues, and she lay there as still as stone.

Up on the auction platform that afternoon, Cat stared out at the throng who had gathered in the Souk el-Ghezel. The market square was packed with would-be buyers, and with those curious to see the new slaves the Djinn had brought back from his latest foray into enemy territory. The majority were in long robes, many of them bearded and turbaned, but through the crowd there strode others who reminded her of the Plymouth-born renegade who had turned Turk to become Ashab Ibrahim – lighter-skinned men in European dress who swaggered like lords at a feast, pushing their way to the front as if it were their due. Traitors, she thought bitterly. Men who had turned coat against their own, and all for money. Anger bubbled up inside her. How dared they come to mock and gloat over decent Christians treated so; or, worse, come to purchase a woman they would never have won honestly in their own country?

The women of Penzance were not the only chattels to be auctioned in the slave market this day. Strings of coffled male captives were being led around the other side of the square, paraded as proudly as stud horses at the spring fair. They wore nothing but a winding of white cotton about their loins, and their prices had been written in charcoal on their chests. None of them were captives from the hold of their ship; evidently, other corsair vessels had returned from the oceans and shores of Christendom with their own cargoes of snatched slaves.

As they went, the *dilaheen* cried out the qualities of their charges, encouraging the gathered buyers to outbid one another for those best for the galleys, for private armies or for hard labour in the fields. Some were proclaimed as shipbuilders, as sailmakers and gunners; these would fetch the highest prices. Most were fishermen, hardy men with weather-beaten faces and sinewy arms. Bidders felt the muscles of the slaves, prodded their chests and bellies, examined their teeth to be sure that the ages the auctioneers claimed for them were accurate. Now came more women, their skins almost as dark as the flimsy robes they wore, and on their backs numbers had been chalked in white. Cat watched in horrified fascination as a man pulled the robe away from one woman and began to feel the fatness of her arms and legs. She had never seen skin with such an ebony sheen, but the would-be buyer seemed inured to such exoticism, and kept prodding merely to ensure the woman was fit and healthy. Was she pregnant? He touched her belly, and would have explored further had not the dilaheen pushed him away, not angrily but with a jest.

'We are no more than animals to them,' Jane Tregenna remarked in disgust. 'They will select us for breeding or work us to death.'

'Perhaps the letter Cat had to write will save us and Sir Arthur will send the money to redeem us,' Matty started, but the older woman rounded on her.

'You have not the brains of a country mouse, Mathilda Pengelly! Do you really think the Master of Kenegie has money to spare for such as we? Or that if he did manage to raise such a sum, that these savages would not take it and keep us and laugh at him? Or that once we are sold into diverse places, they would concern themselves with finding us and returning us to our homes? And that's if the letter even reaches him, which I severely doubt.'

No one said anything to this, for there was nothing to say. Already shocked by the death of Nell Chigwine, the women felt a deeper gloom descend upon them, and they faced a new uncertain future, one in which they might be sold to any man who bid for them for whatever purpose pleased him, or sold on to another in who knew which godforsaken part of this strange world, where they might live apart from their fellows among heathens who spoke no word of English and had no care for them save that they justify their cost.

Now came their turn to be paraded for sale. As they shuffled down from the dais, the auctioneer in charge of them checked them off against the list the amina's clerk had made that morning, then began to call out his high-pitched cry in his barbaric tongue. Maria Kellynch and Chicken were sold first as a single lot, quickly followed by Ann Fellowes and her little girl Mary. There were no takers for Anne Samuels or Nan Tippet. Matty, Alice Johns and her son James were bought by the same bidder – a formidable-looking man in rich robes, his long black beard oiled into ringlets, with gold adorning his ears and forearms. He carried an ornate staff and was attended by two boys in livery, just like footmen from a wealthy European house.

When he came to Cat, the dilaheen paused. Then he raised up his voice to an even higher pitch and pulled back her veil so that her fiery hair was exposed to the view of the crowd. At once, the throng surged and people began to shout and wave bids in the air. Cat firmed her jaw, though her knees had begun to knock. Now that it came to the moment of her sale, she found that she was terrified. Even the squalor of the mazmorra was preferable to standing on the edge of this abyss. Who would buy her? The fat merchant with the avid, greasy face? The thin, cruel-looking man with the hooked nose and austere robes of unadorned white who made no sound, but moved a hand discreetly as the bidding spiralled? The two young men at the front of the crowd who devoured her with their sly black eyes? The coarse-faced renegade swaying from the effects of alcohol, leaning on his equally inebriated friend? She had thought him an Englishman; but when he shouted out it was in a language she did not recognize, and any hope she might have had that she could persuade her buyer to keep her safe until her ransom arrived, or on the pretext of such happening, disappeared. She looked from one to the other, nausea rising in her gullet. Then one of the young men darted forward and something flashed in his hand.

Suddenly, a small, curved dagger was coming at her. Cat wailed and tried to run; but her leg-irons hindered her, and she stumbled and sprawled full length on the ground, taking Nan Tippet and Matty down with her. After that it was chaos: people yelling and shoving, a woman screaming on and on. Cat pushed herself to her knees just in time to see the dilaheen lash out at the young man who had attacked her. The dagger spun away, flashing in the sun, and by the time Cat had got to her feet the young man and his friend were gone.

Then, as if nothing out of the ordinary had occurred, the auction-eer called for the resumption of bids. The crowd pressed forward again, and he pointed his stick at one after another, noting their offers. A lull followed, during which it seemed she had been sold; then a tall figure in a dark-blue turban at the back of the crowd raised his hand. He made a complicated gesture with his fingers, and the dilaheen dipped his head as if in some form of assent. There was a collective gasp, and the crowd turned to see who it was who had closed the deal, but the tall figure was already moving away again. They muttered and fell back, grumbling and disappointed, for the most part uninterested by the remaining lots.

'He tried to kill you,' Matty whispered urgently, as they were ushered away while the monies and promissory notes were paid over. 'Why did he do that?'

Cat had no idea. How could she?

'They hate us,' Jane Tregenna said, white-faced. 'They hate us and would see us all dead.' She touched a hand to her daughter's face, a tender gesture such as Cat could never recall receiving from this woman in all her life. 'We may never see each other again after this day, Catherine. Remember that you are well born: your blood is better than you know. Be proud and uphold your honour before God in this heathen land.'

21

'You must be Madame Lovat, yes?' The speaker was a tiny woman in an elegant dark robe and a pale silk hijab.

'Julia, yes. Are you Madame Rachidi?'

'Do call me Naima. Let me show you to your room: leave your bags here, Aziz will bring them. Was your journey good, comfortable?'

I followed her through long, softly lit corridors out into an open courtyard. Wrought-iron tables and chairs had been set around a central fountain, to whose square splash-pool someone had added handfuls of fragrant rose petals. Ornamental lanterns scattered skeins of patterned light at each corner of the courtyard; a pillared arcade ran around the sides, and above stretched a gallery of cedarwood overgrown by a froth of jasmine and bougainvillea. As if to add the final perfect touch, a crescent moon hung in the empty black space overhead. I sighed. 'This is so beautiful, Naima.'

'*Barrakallofik*, Madame Lovat.' She looked away with a private smile then, walked to one side of the courtyard, unlatched a pair of double doors and pushed them open. Inside lay a chamber out of the *Arabian Nights*. A huge canopied bed spread with snowy covers and tumbles of silk cushions, lush carpets upon a polished stone floor, brass-topped tables bearing a tray of coloured glasses and a carafe of water, lanterns, candles, two low carved chairs. An upholstered banquette ran along one wall beneath a shuttered window which gave out on to the courtyard. The perfume of roses and incense floated through its curlicued grille. Beyond an archway on the far side lay an exquisite bathroom with shiny-plastered walls, intricate mosaic tiling, two basins of beaten gold, a deep bath of what looked like softly streaked marble and a separate shower cubicle – all lit by flickering candlelight. Now I was speechless. I imagined owning a bathroom like this: if I did I'd live in it. My skin would be permanently wrinkled and prune-like.

'Milouda has prepared a tajine, in case you are tired and prefer to eat here tonight,' Naima Rachidi said from the doorway.

I whirled around, caught in my reverie. 'That's very thoughtful of you.'

'I'll set a table in the courtyard for you. It'll be ready in half an hour, if that would suit you? Then you have time to unpack and bathe before eating.'

'Thank you so much.'

'*Tanmirt*.' She inclined her head. '*Marhaban*. You are most welcome.'

I smiled at her. 'Your English is wonderful. I'm afraid my Arabic is non-existent.'

She made a face. 'My English I learned at college here; but my family is Berber: we prefer to speak our own language. I'm sure Idriss will teach you a few words, if you would like.'

Idriss. I'd almost forgotten him. Would he fit in with the romantic idyll his cousin had created here? It seemed a tall order. I ate the tajine at one of the tables in the courtyard, wondering over its complex spices and unfamiliar ingredients. The lamb melted on my tongue, and when I swallowed it left little fireworks in its wake, a burst of citrus and chilli and garlic and what seemed a dozen more subtle tastes as well. When Milouda – a bustling older woman in white leggings, headscarf and a billowing knee-length tunic – came to clear my greedily cleaned dishes, I asked her what was in it. She told me what I already knew, then tapped the side of her nose in that universal gesture of complicit secrecy.

'*C'est magie*,' she said, and refused to elaborate further.

I slept well that night but was visited by strange dreams, which the gilded notes of the dawn muezzin wrapped around like a golden cord. I lay there, half asleep and half awake, shivering with the thrill of being alone on this alien continent; yet I felt safe and cared for, and when I went back to sleep it was for another four hours of dreamless rest. I awoke at last to the sound of the little birds in the courtyard and the gentle fall of the fountain's waters.

I had finished my breakfast and had settled back with a strong coffee and my guidebook, listening to the chatter of two French tourists at the adjoining table, when a shadow fell across me.

'Good morning.' English spoken with a faint accent I could not place, but which might have been American. I looked up. The sun was behind him so that I could not see his face; when he moved, the light struck me full force and I had to look aside.

'What are you reading?'

I spread the guidebook flat on the table. ' "The exodus to Africa of the Moors exiled from Spain continued steadily throughout the sixteenth century up to the end of 1609, when Philip III decided to expel all the Moors definitively from Spanish soil. His final edict, in January 1610, was both general and imperative and demanded that all Muslims, whether they had at any time or for any period converted to Catholicism or not, leave the country at once. It was a decision which was to have dire consequences. The first expulsions in the previous century had already caused a vigorous development of piracy in the Mediterranean; this radical new measure would greatly increase the insecurity of the seas, giving direct rise to resettlement of Salé by those Moors who for almost two hundred years were to become the most active of the Barbary pirates." '

He took the empty chair beside me as I was quoting this passage, crossing one long linen-clad leg over the other. I could feel him listening intently, and when I came to a halt and looked up again, he nodded. 'A reasonable summary, if a little thin on detail, and not entirely accurate.' He had a grim face, all sharp angles and fierce lines. He could have been anywhere between thirty and fifty, for his head was close-shaven and his regard was knowing. His long, straight nose and high cheekbones of burnished copper gave the impression of a feral hunter, smaller than a lion, more dangerous than a wolf; but then he smiled, and the original impression was immediately replaced by less perturbingly predatory similes.

'Are you staying here?' I asked.

'You could say that. I visit so often that it has almost become my second home.'

'You sound as if you're quite an expert on Morocco.'

He inclined his head. 'You could say that also.'

His sharp black eyes were laughing at me. With sudden force I realized why. 'Oh, God, I'm sorry. You must be Idriss. I thought you were a . . . a visitor occupying one of the other rooms, you know, appearing so casually like this at the breakfast table and sitting down, speaking such good English . . .' Colouring now, I could feel the blush rising in my neck, always the worst sort. I had taken him for a tourist because he spoke decent English and therefore couldn't possibly be Moroccan; and I had blasphemed, in front of a Muslim.

He bowed. 'It is I who should apologize, interrupting your *petit déjeuner* so rudely and without introducing myself. Allow me,' and he offered his hand across the table. When I took hold of it, he shook it gently. '*La bes*. I am Idriss el-Kharkouri. *Marhaban.*' And he spread his fingers across his heart. 'Welcome to Morocco.'

We made a little more small-talk, then he went away across the courtyard and returned bearing a fresh pot of coffee and an ashtray. 'Do you mind? A filthy habit, but one many Moroccans share. We should all be dying from lung cancer; but it is usually diabetes that carries us off first.'

'Go ahead.' I declined the cigarette he offered me. 'Why diabetes?'

'Have you tried our whisky?'

'I thought Islam forbids alcohol,' I said naively.

He grinned. 'We like to call mint tea "Moroccan whisky". It makes us feel the deprivation less sharply.'

'Milouda made me some tea last night. It was . . .' I thought back. 'Rather sweet.'

He laughed aloud. 'Just wait until you see how much sugar goes into a pot. You'll never drink it again. French women have a fit of the vapours when they realize what they've cheerfully been sipping at all holiday long. But for us, sugar is more than just a sweetener: it's a symbol, of hospitality, of good luck and happiness. A married couple will be given a sugar cone as part of their bridal gift: it's traditional. Our economy was founded on sugar and salt – sugar brought out of the south, salt from Taghaza in the Sahara, on the main caravan route between Timbuktu and Morocco. It was all shipped out of the ports on the north coast – Essaouira, Safi and Anfa, as well as here at Rabat-Salé – to every country in Europe; your English queen Elizabeth who defeated the Spanish did a good deal of trade with Morocco. But that was not just for the sugar, but for saltpetre to be used in gunpowder, for ivory, silver, gold and amber, Meknès honey and beeswax too. And, in exchange, they brought us guns to use against the Spanish.'

I was going to enjoy being guided around the city by Idriss, I decided; for all the grimness of his aspect, he was a veritable mine of information. 'So what went wrong? Why did the pirates start preying on the English coasts if we shared an enemy in Spain?'

'My enemy's enemy is my friend, you mean?'

I nodded.

'An ancient Arab saying . . .' He paused. 'You're interested in the corsairs of Salé – might I ask why? Even in our country, it is not a subject much spoken of.'

'A family legend,' I said evasively. 'An ancestor was stolen by Barbary pirates to be sold into the slave trade, or so I'm told.'

'They were corsairs,' he corrected me, 'not pirates.'

'What's the difference?'

'Pirates are freebooters, operating only for their own gain. The corsairs brought their spoils home and divided the money they fetched among the crews, the ship owners and the community. It was a very well-regulated trade, you see. The corsairs of Salé hunted with the mandate of the state, and were called the *al-ghuzat*, a title once used for the soldiers who fought alongside the Prophet Mohammed. They were hailed as religious warriors carrying a holy war into the seas against the infidel.'

I frowned. 'But they still traded with us "infidels"? That seems just a touch hypocritical!'

He shrugged. 'Look around you, read between the lines in your newspapers, on your television – is it really so different today? For decades, Europe and America have been selling arms, both officially and on the black market, to the very people you now label "terrorists". War and business, always they go hand in hand – it's realpolitik. Nothing ever really changes, human nature is what it is.'

'And so history goes on repeating itself, over and over in some dreary loop of greed and corruption and compromised ideals?'

'Come,' he said, getting to his feet. 'Let me show you what you came here to see, and we'll leave the politics behind, to discuss over dinner.'

Dinner? That seemed rather presumptuous. I shot him a look, but he was already clearing away the coffee things with a practised ease that suggested years of helping with domestic chores. Yet he didn't wear a wedding ring: perhaps such was not the custom among Muslim men, though surely he must be married and have a brood of children. Indeed, perhaps he had more than one wife? Wasn't polygamy still legal in this culture? I realized how very little I knew about Muslim men.

Outside, the sun was a hammer on my head: I hid at once beneath a wide-brimmed straw hat and sunglasses.

'We are in the old medina here,' Idriss informed me as we walked up the alleyway outside the riad, 'the ancient part of the city. There's been a settlement here since the Carthaginians and Romans. Nothing much has changed for hundreds of years; we are a conservative people, we like to maintain our traditions.'

Women wearing full-length robes and headscarves and carrying baskets of market goods were gossiping, slapping hands and laughing loudly at the end of the street. Their glances flicked over me as Idriss and I passed, but the rhythm of the gossip didn't miss a beat. We turned a corner, followed another of the labyrinthine alleys and emerged suddenly into a wide-open space through which six lanes of traffic roared and honked. On the other side of the city-circular rose tall, crenellated red stone walls, pitted with the erosion of ages and arrow slits, and punctuated at intervals by arched gateways.

'Wow. That looks as if it's seen some action.'

'That's the Kasbah des Oudaias – begun by the Almohad Sultan

Abd el-Moumen in the twelfth century to defend the area against attack from the sea. His son, Yacoub el-Mansour, continued the work, creating these great ramparts around an existing convent – hence the city's name of Rabat, which means "fortified monastery". It was from here the soldier-monks set out for holy war in Spain in the Middle Ages; and later, in the seventeenth century, it became the base for the corsair republic's holy war against Christendom.'

'You're beginning to sound like my history teacher at school. We spent all our lessons taking down lists of dates, and none of us learned a thing.'

'I'll do my best to spice it up for you.' He sounded both disdainful and hurt at the same time.

I didn't know what to say, so I let him take my elbow and ferry me across the lethal road into the shadow of the great walls.

As we entered the arched gate, a young man dived out at me. *'Vous voulez un guide, madame? Moins cher –'*

Idriss barked a barrage of words at him, and the young man fled.

'I'm sure he didn't mean any harm,' I said, taken aback by his ferocity.

'Unofficial guides give Morocco a bad name. They pester tourists, and some of them prey on unattended women. It's not to be encouraged.'

'All I wished for was a guide, not a guard dog,' I said, smiling.

He looked at me coldly. 'Dogs are dirty animals not sanctioned by the Qur'an. I'd appreciate it if you didn't call me that.'

I opened my mouth to explain that I had meant no insult, realized I was only likely to dig the cultural hole deeper, and shut it again. After that we walked in silence for a time, until we turned a corner between tall, rough stone walls and came out into a central garden of exquisite design. A criss-cross of tessellated pathways partitioned areas designated for herbs and oleanders, flowers and banana palms, all growing in perfect order. Wooden lattices spanned a number of the squares and supported the climbing plants whose close-knit leaves gave some respite from the boiling sun. Oranges glowed in the trees and arcades ran along the edges, offering shady

214

niches where people sat and read or contemplated their serene surroundings.

'Beautiful,' I breathed. 'Just like a miniature Alhambra.'

'It's called the Andalusian Garden, but actually it was laid out by the French in the colonial period, with the Alhambra in mind.'

'Ah.'

'But the palace behind it, which is now the museum, was built in the seventeenth century by the Sultan Moulay Ismail: perhaps your ancestor would have seen it: the Sultan had many European slaves. When was he taken?'

'It was a she. And according to the . . . the family story, it was in the summer of 1625.' Instinct warned me not to mention the needlework book.

'That's earlier than I would have thought. The corsair republic wasn't founded until 1626, and the raids were at their height later in the century.'

'Oh.' I was suddenly once more full of doubts. 'Maybe the legend is just that; or they got the dates wrong.'

'I have a friend at the university we can ask, if you're serious about this.'

I laughed nervously. 'It's just curiosity, really.'

He gave me a hard look. 'You've come a long way, alone, out of mere curiosity.'

We took a narrow alleyway off the main thoroughfare, which wound its way steeply between tall houses with walled gardens, turned a sharp corner and came upon a group of children gathered around something glowing like gold in the sunlight. I bent to see what had them so entranced, and the children made way for me with huge grins. In the centre of the circle were eight day-old chicks, scrabbling around like popcorn in a pan as they pecked up the grain the children had scattered on the cobbles.

Idriss hunkered down beside me. He said something to one of the boys, who dissolved into laughter, open-mouthed and gap-toothed, and gabbled back at him. Then the child – quite without formality – caught my hand, turned it over and dropped one of the chicks into my palm. It stood there uncertainly, its tiny legs shifting minutely for balance, weighing almost nothing, its pale down flaring in the sun just like a dandelion clock. I could feel the beat of its heart pulsing fast in counterpoint to my own. Then Idriss put his hand on my forearm, and it was as if someone had touched a live wire to my skin.

'Abdel here says you can keep it.' His solemn gaze held mine.

My jaw dropped. Such generosity from a child – but how could I respond? Idriss smiled at my discomposure. Then he shooed the chick off my hand and back on to the cobbles among its fellows, dug in his pocket, took out a couple of coins and gave them to the boy, cupping a hand over his close-cropped head. '*Tanmirt*, Abdellatif. *Bes salama.*'

This little incident transformed the rest of the morning, as if events took their cue from its lightness and magic. I stopped worrying about the book, about its authenticity, about Michael, and gave myself up to Morocco: to its warmth and generosity, its exoticism and its crumbling, pungent, ever-present history.

It would, in any case, be hard not to enjoy the day, for the kasbah offered up marvel after marvel: mazes of little winding streets lined with rough-plastered houses painted in blue and white, their windows adorned by intricate wrought-iron grilles, their doors of weather-silvered wood studded with heavy nails. Vivid cascades of bougainvillea and jasmine, glorious tumbles of climbing roses.

At last we came upon a lovely mosque with a tall minaret, and here Idriss stopped. 'This is the Jamaa el-Atiq, built in the twelfth century by the Sultan Abd el-Moumen. I don't mean to bore you with dates and dry facts, but it is worth mentioning that this is the oldest mosque in Rabat.' He gazed upwards, the lines of his face softened by the sunlight, which turned his black eyes a lustrous chestnut-brown.

'Can we go in?' Given the elegance of the outside, I was curious to see the interior.

Idriss stared down at me. 'Of course not.'

'Why not?' I bridled. 'Because I'm a woman?'

'Because you're not a Muslim.'

'Oh.' I laughed, without humour. 'An infidel.'

'Indeed.'

'Charming.'

'Come, let me show you where my ancestors brought your infidel ancestor.'

'Actually,' I said, following him up through the maze of streets, 'I think you'll find that the Christians called the Muslims infidels too.'

He had the grace to smile.

Up on top of the kasbah was the semaphore platform, a huge gun emplacement offering astonishing views over the ocean and across to a gleaming white town on the other side of the wide stretch of water.

'Our river is called the Bou Regreg – the "Father of Reflection",' Idriss said, sitting on the wall. 'It is a beautiful name, no? I do not know who called it that, but there have been people here since the earliest times. Three separate city-states developed. Out there, across the river, was Slâ el-Bali – Old Salé, the port that served the opulent kingdom of Fez. In the seventeenth century it became the hub of the region's slave trade, and the heart of radical Islam. Across the water' – he pointed behind us – 'lay Rabat, where the rich Jewish and Moorish merchants eventually settled. We are standing in what was Slâ el-Djedid – New Salé. When Philip of Spain expelled the Moors from Andalusia in the early part of the seventeenth century, many returned and set about reconstructing here the city that had been abandoned. They were welcomed with open arms: they brought considerable wealth with them – wealth and an indelible hatred of the Christians who had persecuted them. The ruler of this area, Sultan Moulay Zidane, gave them money to raise the ramparts and a garrison to guard the fortress, which became known as the Kasbah Andalus.

'To begin with they repaid him by paying over a tithe from the cargoes they took, but it wasn't long before they stopped paying taxes to the Sultan altogether. They didn't need his aid, or his protection. Salé is strategically placed: the Strait of Gibraltar is very close. They funnelled all the mercantile shipping as if through the neck of a bottle: all the corsairs had to do was to pounce as ships emerged; then, being faster and knowing the coast better than any pursuers, they sailed back into their home port with great speed. Do you see the disturbance in the water there?'

I followed his pointed finger and saw where a line of surf ran across the river's mouth, and nodded. 'Yes.'

'There's a sandbar hidden beneath the surface. Only a small shallow-keeled ship could pass over it. And if that didn't stop them, the narrow channels would. You'd need an expert to navigate a passage through them. The wreckage of a lot of foreign ships litters the sea bed there.'

'So why did they start stealing people?'

'Because they soon realized they could make a lot more by taking the crews and selling them at the slave auction. Besides, if you were running galleys into the Mediterranean, you needed crews of oarsmen to pursue the rich prizes.'

'But why the women?'

'Why do you think? For the purpose for which men have always stolen women.'

I flushed. Poor Catherine.

'I'm hungry,' I said suddenly to change the subject and got up off the wall. 'What can we eat?'

He thought for a moment, a deep vertical line appearing between his eyebrows. 'Do you like fish?'

'Sure.'

'Then I have an idea.'

We walked down the right bank to the river's edge, where a number of high-bowed, bright-blue wooden boats were pulled up on the shore. On a little makeshift jetty people were queuing to get into one of these clinker-built boats. Idriss gave the ferryman two coins, handed me in over the gunwale, then joined me. The ferryman – a dark-skinned, emphatically bearded man who eyed me with barely disguised hostility – poled us into the river's channel and across to Old Salé, and I walked into another world.

Men in djellabas, their faces shadowed by their hoods; women veiled in the full Muslim niqab, covering everything but their eyes;

not a European to be seen. Self-conscious within moments of stepping on to this left bank, I wound my hair up into a knot and stuffed it under my hat. We walked past stall after stall selling the day's catch. Men sat on stools beside the stalls, gutting and filleting, bombarded by a blizzard of screaming seagulls, their tunics smeared with blood and scales. I stepped carefully between stinking pools of fish detritus, rather dreading my lunch; but Idriss guided me by the elbow to an open-sided café on the shore, and there we dined like sea kings on the freshest fish I had ever tasted, accompanied by great slices of lemon, new-baked bread, butter and oil. At the end, licking my greasy fingers, I counted the backbones mounded on the paper in front of me. Fifteen. I stared at them in disbelief. I had eaten fifteen fish, and not all of them small. Idriss, however, had a significantly larger pile than I, and was still eating with deep concentration, applying himself to the task with intense care so as to waste nothing. He ate like a man possessed, like a man who didn't know where his next meal was coming from.

'So,' I said as casually as I could manage, 'tell me about your family.'

'What do you wish to know?'

'Do you have brothers, sisters, parents . . . in-laws?'

'In-laws?'

So much for subtlety. 'Are you married?'

Idriss shook his head. 'No.'

'Never?'

'Never.'

He was not exactly being forthcoming. 'Why not?' I pressed.

He put down his fish. 'It has just . . . never happened.' There was a pause as I wondered what to say next, then he said into the silence, 'And you?'

'Ah, no. Same reason.' I could feel my lips pressing together as if to keep the unsavoury truth imprisoned safely behind the bars of my teeth.

'That surprises me.' His dark eyes scrutinized me with the same ruthless attention he had applied to flensing his fish. 'Here we say, "A woman without a husband is like a bird without a nest."'

At that instant the waitress passed: I signalled her urgently, but it was to Idriss she spoke. He began to dig in his pocket, but I pushed two hundred dirhams across the table. 'On me, please.'

I could feel the waitress's keen gaze flickering between us and could imagine exactly what she was thinking, but at that moment all I wanted was to be out in the air, refocusing our conversation back on to the safely dead and buried.

The medieval squalor of the river bank gave way to a sudden burst of modern development, wide streets lined with French colonial villas, and after that the ochre walls of the old city reared up.

We passed into the medina by the Bab Bou I Iaja, and from there into a wide square containing lovely gardens. Idriss led me through these and out the other side into a street where the houses almost touched one another across the narrow span. Little shops were set into niches, selling ironware, shoes, jewellery, groceries, mobile phones, computer parts – it was bizarre to see evidence of the modern world in this medieval setting. Scents began to fill the air – fish, which seemed ubiquitous in this part of the city, spices, frying food and other less identifiable smells. We turned down an alley, and there was shade: looking up, I saw that the alley was covered by a rough thatch of reeds. Around another corner and we were in the heart of the souk, the traditional market. It was like an anthill: a heaving mass of humanity, noise, music, shouting, laughing, sizzling oil, all confined within this labyrinth of tunnelled passages. I didn't know what to look at first: the sensory overload was total. Things loomed out at me as we wove our way through the jostling shoppers: exquisitely worked leather goods, shoes and slippers the colour of jewels, clothing, brassware, piles of bright fruit, olives and candles, garlands of dried figs and apricots. Spices had been ranged in perfectly formed pyramids, their colours vivid, their scents pungent, persuasive – the reds of powdered chilli and paprika, rich browns of cinnamon and nutmeg, paler cumin and ginger, the yellow ochre of turmeric, stars of aniseed, spikes of clove. The smells became rank, and then we were surrounded by stalls of meat selling objects I could hardly believe I was seeing –

cows' feet, ears, noses; sheep's heads, goats' heads, veiny white testicles, piles of tripe.

'Ugh.' I held my nose.

Idriss laughed at me. 'I forgot your delicate Western sensibility. Come, we'll go this way.'

We passed more odd sights – a woman surrounded by geese, ducks and rabbits, with people gathered around her to choose their dinner for the night. Bundles of dried snakeskins hanging from the rafters. A cage of monkeys, and one of some strange-looking reptiles with swivelling eye-sockets and little hand-like claws. We passed them at a clip and were some way further on before I realized what they were.

'Weren't those chameleons in those cages back on the corner there?'

'I should imagine so. Some people use them against the evil eye.'

'What do you mean "use them"?'

'If you have a specific trouble, you can throw a chameleon on the fire: if it explodes, then your trouble will disappear with it. But if it just melts down,' he said, shrugging, 'then your trouble is here to stay.'

'You are joking.'

'We are a very superstitious people, we Moroccans.'

'So are the English, but I don't think we'd ever throw a living creature on a fire merely out of superstition.'

'No? What about all the witches you burned? I believe your Queen Elizabeth even burned cats at her coronation.'

'She did not!' The idea of our sensible, stolid old Queen doing anything so barbaric made me laugh out loud.

'The first Queen Elizabeth – she burned them to prove that witchcraft had been purged from her kingdom.'

'You are a fund of arcane knowledge.'

We turned another corner and emerged into a market square. In the middle of it, an old man was weighing fleeces into a huge pair of brass scales. 'This is the wool market,' Idriss said. 'The Souk el-Ghezel. In the seventeenth century it was one of the places where Christian slaves were auctioned.'

I stood there looking at the old man and the brass balance. With his flowing white beard and his long cream djellaba, the wool-seller looked as if he might very well have stepped out of the same crowd that witnessed the corsairs' prisoners being auctioned at the slave blocks.

What would those untravelled, sequestered people of Cornwall's Penwith peninsula, most of whom had never crossed the River Fal, let alone the River Tamar, have made of this supremely alien place? It continued to shock and amaze me at every turn, yet I had travelled to a dozen countries in the world, and been exposed by television to images of hundreds more. Already traumatized by their abduction and the horrors of their voyage, they must have moved through these foreign streets as if in a drugged-out, psyche-delic dream.

Idriss's touch on my arm brought me back to myself. 'Let me show you something else. I think you will like it.'

He led me around the city walls until we reached a monumental gateway, towering twenty feet and more above us. Despite its enormous size and the massive nature of the stonework, it possessed astonishing beauty, for the arch seemed poised overhead as if held by some invisible inner tension between the two towers on either side and by the delicate traceried net of its mystical, interweaving patterns and scripts.

'This is the Bab Mrisa,' Idriss told me as we both gazed up at it. '"The Little Harbour". In the seventeenth century, before the river silted up and changed its course, the corsairs sailed their ships right into the fortified heart of the city through this gate. It was through the Bab Mrisa that your Robinson Crusoe was brought. "Our ship making her course between the Canary Islands and the African shore, was surprised in the grey of the morning by a Turkish rover of Sallee,"' he quoted suddenly.

I stared at him.

'I majored in English for two years. One of the visiting tutors was a Defoe enthusiast – I read them all – *Journal of the Plague Year*, *Moll Flanders*, *Roxana*.'

What on earth would a man from a Muslim culture make of a

rumbustiously bawdy romp like *Moll Flanders*? I couldn't imagine. 'You're better read than me,' I said laughingly, but also rather uncomfortably, for I began to suspect that it might be true. 'But tell me: why do you have a touch of an American accent?'

His hand went to his mouth. 'Really?' He thought about it a beat too long. 'My tutor was American, I guess that's why.'

'He seems to have made quite an impression.'

'She.' He turned away and started to walk so fast up the thorough-fare into the city that I had to run to catch up.

'So, Idriss, what do you do – what's your job, when you're not shepherding tourists around the sights? Are you teaching at the university yourself now?'

'I drive a taxi.'

'Oh.' I didn't know how to react to this. His cousin's house was opulent, and he was clearly well educated. So, although I was sure that driving a taxi was a perfectly good and respectable occupation, it wasn't what I had expected.

'And you?'

I laughed. 'Good question. At the moment I don't do anything at all.'

'You aren't married, you aren't employed, you have no children, no?'

'No, no children.'

'So, Julia Lovat, if you were to disappear somewhere in the backstreets of an obscure Moroccan town, would nobody miss you?' He turned to scrutinize me, and with the sun behind him I could see only the glint of his eyes.

He had struck a painful chord: who, indeed, would miss me? A few friends, eventually. Michael, but only because he wanted the book. Alison, certainly . . .

I stared at him, suddenly terrified. 'I want to go back now. I'm very tired.'

He looked puzzled. 'Of course,' he said.

It was late afternoon by the time we made it back to the riad, and I was indeed exhausted. My feet ached, my back ached, and my head was stuffed with images and information. All the way from Old Salé to Rabat's medina, I kept myself going with the promise of a long, fragrant soak in the beautiful bath that awaited me in my room.

But, as we stepped across the threshold, Naima Rachidi intercepted us. She said something very fast in their shared language to her cousin, who looked visibly shaken; then she turned to me.

'Your husband was here looking for you.'

'My . . . husband?'

'Yes. I told him you were taking a guided tour of the city and wouldn't be back till this evening, so he said he would go for a walk and come back later.'

I could feel my eyes growing huge and round. 'Ah . . . thank you. How . . . how was he looking?'

She frowned. 'How? Tired, a bit annoyed, though he was very polite.'

'I mean, are you sure he was my . . . husband? Could you describe him? Perhaps it's a mistake.'

'About fifty, middle aged. Taller than you, not as tall as Idriss, dark hair – how you say – bald, here.' She touched her temples. 'Dark eyes, not big built, a bit of fat here –' She indicated her belly.

Naima Rachidi was a very observant woman, though I wasn't sure Michael would have approved of her description, particularly her significant overestimation of his age or her hawk-eyed pin-pointing of the beginnings of a spare tyre. The light-headed feeling was returning, along with a horrible nausea. I took a deep breath. 'Did he say when he'd be back?' I could feel Idriss's glower as a tension in the air behind me.

Naima shook her head. 'No, but he said that he had left you a note in your room.'

'In my –!'

'I'm sorry, should I not have let him in?'

'No, no, it's fine.' I ran a hand over my face. 'Thank you.' I turned, dreading Idriss's reaction, but my guide's dark face was inscrutable. I managed to blurt out: 'And thank you, Idriss. I very much enjoyed the day.' And then I ran away.

My room looked as if a bomb had hit it. Michael had tried so carefully to cover his tracks at the London flat, but he'd made no effort to hide his search here. The bedclothes lay in a rumpled heap on the floor, my suitcase had been upended in the middle of the room, the wardrobe doors flung open, my clothes thrown everywhere. Even the bathroom toiletries lay scattered and the towels left piled up on the edge of the bath.

I clutched my bag to me. I had meant to leave *The Needle-Woman's Glorie* safe in the riad when I went out that morning, but somehow couldn't bear to be parted from it: perhaps some sixth sense at work; perhaps Catherine herself had been prompting my actions.

An envelope had been left on top of the disaster that was the bed. Very symbolic, I thought, my heart thumping.

My name was scratched on it in Michael's terrible scrawl, so there could be no mistake. He had followed me all the way to Morocco, had tracked me to this very room. Shaking, I opened the envelope. There were some sheets of paper inside, one folded around the rest. The top one read:

I must talk to you (see enclosed).
I'll be back at 6.
M

The next sheet was a photocopy of an old-looking letter. I scanned the beginning and made out:

To Sir Arthur Harrys from hys servante Robert Bolitho, this 15th daie of October 1625.

Sir, I wryte this in the offices of Messrs Hardwicke & Buckle, shippers of the Turkey Company, Cheapside, London . . .

Suddenly the room was stifling. Heart beating a sharp tattoo, I refolded the papers and tucked them into the back of Catherine's book, which in turn I stowed deep inside my handbag. Then, in a flurry of panic, I stuffed my belongings into my suitcase and canvas bag, and hauled both out into the courtyard. For all my tiredness, for all the riad's comfort and beauty and elegance, I could stay here no longer.

'Running away?' Idriss sat at a table, cigarette in hand, a curl of smoke spiralling up into the roses above him. His long dark eyes regarded me curiously. 'I thought you might want help.'

'What sort of help?'

'Well, you said you'd never married . . . and now a "husband" turns up, and you look as pale as the moon. I thought I could offer my services.' He eyed my bags. 'Even if it's just as a porter.'

'I need somewhere to go, just for the night,' I said in a rush, but even as I said it I knew that was exactly what I did need: somewhere to stay, somewhere to hide from Michael. 'Can you recommend a decent hotel? I hate to let Naima down, and of course I'll pay her what I owe her, but I can't stay here.'

Idriss stubbed out his half-smoked cigarette. 'Here, let me take your bags. I will talk to Naima, don't worry about that.'

A few minutes later I found myself sitting in the back of a small blue Peugeot with a taxi sign on top of it. Amulets and sigils hung from the rear-view mirror, twirling wildly as the elderly suspension groaned under the weight of my luggage.

'Where are we going?' I was alone in Africa. Now that I had left the riad no one knew where I was; no one would miss me if I disappeared. Could I trust Idriss? I remembered how nervous he had made me that afternoon and felt doubt gnawing at my stomach, as insistent as a plague-rat.

'I am taking you to my home,' he said without turning.

Which didn't make me feel any easier.

22

Robert

To Sir Arthur Harrys from hys servante Robert Bolitho, this 15th daie of October 1625.

Sir, I wryte this in the offices of Messrs Hardwicke & Buckle, shippers of the Turkey Company, Cheapside, London, to keepe you abrest of my travails. I have taken upon myselfe a large decision, one that ys onlikely to meete with your approval or blessing . . .

Rumours as to the fate of those who had disappeared that cruel July morning from the church in Penzance had flown around West Cornwall like bats chased out of a belltower. Some had blamed the Devil, others the hand of the Lord after the rantings of mad Annie Badcock; but Andrew Thomas shamefacedly admitted to seeing the marauders putting in to Penzance Harbour when he should have been at church, having stayed away with a pounding ale-head after too late a night at the Dolphin. At the time, he'd thought the drink had tainted his senses; but when the hue and cry was raised he realized that his vision of a band of dark-skinned, turbaned, scimitar-wielding raiders arriving and then shortly departing with a large number of his fellow townsfolk in captivity, including the Mayor and the Alderman, had been no alcohol-induced haze but the very truth. Three ships, he had reported to the town council, weeping and shaking and wringing his hands. One fine caravel and two foreign-looking vessels carrying lateen sails and open decks. He knew them as xebecs, though it was a long time since he had traded in Mediterranean waters, where last he had seen such things. It was this detail, and his description of the vessels' crew, which suggested the identity of the raiders: pirates of Barbary, famed for their boldness and the violence they used towards their captives, who were most likely bound for Argier or Tunis, maybe even thence to the court of the Grand Seigneur, the Great Turk, in Constantinople.

When word of Cat's letter reached Rob, he had been standing in the farmyard at Kenegie, staring at a piece of harness that he held in his hands without the slightest idea of why he had taken it from the barn or what purpose he had meant to put it to. George Parsons had come upon him in this unusual state (for Robert Bolitho was known as a practical man who applied himself with thorough attention to his work and was ever quick and alert). He had to repeat his name three times before Rob replied. Ever since the raid Rob had found himself thus distracted: all he could think of was Cat and whether she was still alive. He existed in a sort of limbo, living from day to day, waiting to discover where she might have been taken, waiting for the time when he might decide on a course of action. Rob was not a man much given to introspection, so the effect that Cat's theft had upon him was a shock in itself. He found himself dithering over the most ordinary and automatic task, his mind wandering in the middle of a sentence; he woke at odd times in the night, not knowing who he was, or where, or why. He was beset by nightmares, for a time even thinking himself haunted by some angry spirit, before he realized it was his own guilt which plagued him. His thoughts swung wildly: the raiders should have taken him, not Cat. He should have stayed with her at the chapel to defend her from the barbarians, instead of riding away to Gulval because of a sharp word or two. Had he so little determination? He had not even managed to persuade her to take his ring, which he now regretted with real force, as if somehow it might protect her, mark her as his own, even magically bring her back to him.

'Rob, Rob! Robert Bolitho – the Master's calling for you. In the parlour, now.'

His head had come up slowly, as if he rose through the deep waters of a dream. 'Beg pardon, George, what did you say?'

'There's a letter come from Catherine.'

A letter? How could that be? Letters were civilized communications undertaken by educated folk and men of business, not from the squalor of a foreign pirate vessel sailing in who knew which godforsaken waters.

Even so, he found his feet making his decision for him.

Arthur Harris had been sitting at the parlour table, a ragged sheet of paper in his hands. It was the quality of the missive which struck Rob at once, for it looked at once well travelled and authentic, and the paper on which it was written was thicker and more yellow than the paper they used at Kenegie.

'This has arrived by various convoluted means from Catherine, or so it seems. Is this her hand?'

He flourished the letter at Rob, who stared at it as if it might contain the very secret of the universe, which in that moment, for him, it did. He blinked, then nodded. 'It is, sir.' His knees began to wobble; he leaned forward to let the table take his weight.

'Sit down, Robert. A messenger brought it this morning from Southampton.'

Rob's heart had at that moment leaped up. 'She's in Southampton?'

The Master of the Mount held up a hand. 'No, no, Robert, let me finish. He brought it from the offices of a shipping company there. The captain of the *Merry Maid* delivering his cargo to his masters in that harbour told how he was intercepted by a merchant-man sailing under the protection of the Porte, who had it from a Turkish trader out of Barbary.'

'Barbary?' echoed Rob, his heart sinking as rapidly as it had risen. It seemed his worst fears had been realized, and his face must have betrayed his horror, for Sir Arthur nodded grimly.

'And not merely Barbary but the town of Sallee, which is, I have heard, a veritable nest of sea-devils, home to the most fanatical of pirates and scavengers. There have been some hundreds of fishermen and merchantmen taken from our seas to the Barbary shores, but they say no Christian ever comes back alive from Sallee. Many of them are tortured into apostasy and succumb to Islam out of fear for their flesh, if not their souls.'

Rob had closed his eyes. It was not only the fate of Cat's soul he feared; the thought of her tortured and ill used made him groan aloud. The content of the letter had not reassured him. Eight hundred pounds? Where could he ever raise such a sum? Already, he was calculating wildly: advances on his wages, the sale of his few worldly goods, a loan here or there, some charity. He might raise, what? Fifty pounds with great good fortune. Some part of him knew he should care for the fate of the other captives so cruelly taken – for Cat's mother and uncle and aunt, for the death of the little nephews, for Matty and Jack and Chicken and the others – but all this was just a distraction from the one thing that really mattered: that Cat was alive, at the time of writing, at least. If he could sell his soul to redeem her, he would.

That day he completed his chores in record time and with massively increased efficiency. He then begged audience of Lady Harris, whose heart, he thought, might prove softer than her husband's, and felt sudden wild optimism when she immediately waved him into her sitting room. Unfortunately, he found Sir Arthur had already talked with his wife, and when he raised the subject she pursed her lips.

'I am sorry, Rob. I know you were set on making her your wife. But such an immense sum! Were she the worthiest young woman in Penwith, I'd still have the same answer for you. Eight hundred pounds is the ransom of a queen, not a little jade like Catherine Tregenna. Better you settle your heart elsewhere and find yourself an honest wife from an honest family. Besides, there is not only Catherine to consider, but our fellow townspeople: we cannot be seen to favour one above another.'

Colouring furiously, he had pressed her again until at last she said wearily, 'If you are so determined to save the girl, you had best seek out her father.'

Rob's brow wrinkled in consternation. 'Madam, he is dead these past many seasons.'

'Would that were true. Poor John Tregenna: a stolid man and not greatly to Jane's taste; but he did not deserve to give his best years to raising a whelp that was not his own only to die early of the plague. If you would ransom Catherine, you had best visit Sir John Killigrew at Arwenack.'

A hard knot formed in his throat, and he could not speak. An hallucinatory image of the two flame-haired figures standing too close in the courtyard earlier that summer came to him suddenly, and he knew at once that Lady Harris spoke the truth. But how could John Killigrew not take one look at the girl who carried his blood and not know her for his own?

'Here.'

He looked up. Margaret Harris was holding something out to him. His fingers closed around it before he realized that it was a pouch of coins.

'Don't tell anyone I have given you this. For all her faults, Catherine is still dear to me, and if there is any chance of saving her and Matty, I hope that you will do your best to redeem them. You are a resourceful young man: maybe you will be able to find a way of using this small token on their behalf. The thought of two young girls in the hands of such wicked heathens is too much for me to bear.'

She turned away; but Rob had seen the glitter of her eyes.

The meeting of the town council, chaired by Sir Arthur in the absence of Mayor John Maddern, came to no useful conclusions. There was much recrimination. Why had the lookouts not seen the ships sail in? Why had the guns of the Mount not defended the town? Why had the Vice-Admiral of Cornwall not foreseen the danger if there had, as had been reported, been a dozen and more attacks up and down the coastal waters before the attack on the church? Why were there rumours that the Lord High Admiral, the Duke of Buckingham, was sending English warships to assist Cardinal Richelieu of France against the Huguenots, rather than policing the West Country seas? And what was the point of all this talk of war with Spain if there was already a war on their doorstep, a war against terror from the sea? Did the new King not care about his own citizens? More than one voice declared grimly that Cornwall was too far from the heart of things for anyone to care overmuch about their fate.

Two hours were wasted thus before anyone got to the nub of the matter: whether there was any way to raise the demanded three thousand, four hundred and ninety-five pounds, and, if there was, whether they could obtain any assurance that the captives were still alive and would be returned. Town funds were negligible; and that was before the next letters arrived from Salé demanding ransoms for Mayor Maddern, Alderman Polglaze and their wives.

Petitions were circulated and collections raised. Penzance and Market-Jew, and the outlying communities of Sancreed and Madron, Newlyn and Paul, contributed what they could, right down to Widow Hocking with a single penny, and blind old Simon Penrose with two groats. Even after seven hundred and eighty people had made their contribution, the total raised was little more than forty-six pounds, and that included five pounds from Sir Arthur and ten from the Godolphins.

'We must petition the sovereign,' Sir Arthur sighed. 'Though I foresee no success in doing so. Parliament has been dissolved, and I do not know when they will sit again, so mistrustful of them is King Charles. The only man he trusts is Buckingham, and I have no way to Buckingham. All we can do is to make public the plight of our captives and hope that some pressure can be brought to bear. But whether any funds will be forthcoming seems unlikely: the treasury is tight-fisted, and war against Spain will cost heavily. I have been begging the Crown's aid in rearming our defences these past years with little joy. Perhaps our patron the Earl of Salisbury may be of some aid, though he has not the air of a serious man, for all his heritage and education. Henry Marten might know of a way to the King: he is considered the most influential of our local men.'

'And Sir John Killigrew?'

'Why ever should Killigrew concern himself with this affair? Penzance means nothing to him. You may try him of course, but I have never heard that man risk effort or money on behalf of any but himself.'

'I will ride over to Arwenack this evening.'

His master snorted. 'The Master of Pendennis is not at home. He's investigating some new business venture up in London with the Turkey Company or suchlike. When I saw him last week he tried to persuade me to put in with him – as if I had spare capital to burn in one of his wild schemes!'

It was found that even though Parliament was not convened, Sir Henry Marten was in London, where plague had that summer struck hard, taking with it several of his wife's relatives and leaving their estates in some state of confusion. It was decided that Rob should make the trip to London without delay, bearing letters of recommendation and petitions signed by the relatives, neighbours and friends of the captives. He set off an hour later with a string of three horses, and had ridden one lame even before he reached Gunnislake.

London was a noxious place. Rob had thought Bodmin on market day bad enough, with its roaring mongers, rattling carts and cacophony of creatures both four- and two-legged, but London was unimaginably worse. He was so unprepared for its immensity, its sights and its fumes that had he not been compelled by his mission, he would have turned and run the three hundred and more miles back to Cornwall on his own two feet without a backward look. The owner of the first inn he stopped at took one look at him and turned him away: he'd been sleeping in barns and under hedges all the way from Cornwall to save every penny of the money Sir Arthur had given him for his expenses; and the horses were in no better fettle. Fear of plague was still rife, and strangers were not welcome. The next inn was so raucous and stank so badly that he took no more than one step over the threshold before turning and fleeing. At his third stop, the innkeeper recognized his accent as 'that of an honest man' and let him kip down in the stables for the night, and one of the maids took pity on him, for the sake of his big blue eyes, as she told him till he blushed, and took away his shirt and breeches for washing. When she slipped beneath his blanket as he slept, he awoke with a start, shouting, and she put her hand over his mouth. 'We ain't got no cat,' she said perplexed. 'Now shut your noise and buss me.'

He left before dawn, at speed and still dressing, feeling dirtier than ever, for all that his clothes were fresh.

When he asked for directions to the address of the residence he sought, most people laughed heartily. 'Someone's having you on, lad,' one man said. 'Such folk never open their doors to a tyke like thee.' But when Rob showed him the letter he carried, he became more respectful and at last indicated the road he should take. 'Best visit a barber before thee goes a-calling on a lord,' the man's wife advised.

Rob felt his chin. In his rush he had brought no shaving gear with him, and he could feel how the hair had sprouted haphazardly in a week on the road, over his lip, down his jaws: he would have mutton chops in no time. The thought repulsed him. He remembered how Cat had poked fun at George Parsons, at the way his facial hair grew out in bright ginger bushes despite the thinning grey above, and resolved to put himself in the hands of a barber forthwith.

Two hours later, his face scraped raw from the intimate attentions of a not-very-sharp razor, he finally found himself in the Strand, a place of great resort lined with grand stone mansions and arcaded walkways filled with elegant shops. The house Rob sought was the grandest of all – more of a palace than a house, keeping the world at bay behind ornamental gardens in which labourers toiled and swept. One of these waved Rob and his animals angrily away as he made to pass inside the gate. 'You can't come in here, the Master sees no beggars.'

Rob showed him the letter from Sir Arthur, and the man squinted at it myopically. 'Don't mean nothin' to me,' he said suspiciously. He called to a boy wielding a rake. 'Go fetch Master Burton and be quick about it.'

Rob waited, shifting from foot to foot with impatience. After what seemed an age, a white-haired man in a rich blue tunic and velvet breeches came walking gingerly down the path towards him, his cane ringing on the stones. 'Who are you and what's your business at Salisbury House?'

Rob handed him the letter. The man broke the seal without ceremony and scanned its contents. When he looked up again, his expression was quite different. He handed the letter back to Rob. 'Follow me,' he said briskly, and returned up the path at twice the pace, his stick rattling out a smart tattoo to the clack of his heeled shoes.

Rob was led into the house through a door of magnificent proportions and left in an antechamber that was larger than the whole of Kenegie Hall. Its panelled walls were lined with portraits of grim-looking men who glowered down at him unforgivingly. If he had been on any other than pressing business, he would have felt so deterred by their unblinking black eyes and forbidding visages that he would have made his excuses and departed; but that was, he considered, probably why people were left here to await their appointments: so that the proud heritage of this powerful family could impress upon them the insignificance of their own humble origins. All around him, some of the greatest men of the kingdom – Burghleys and Howards – gazed down imperiously, uninterested in the painter who had captured their image or in those who would later view them. He stood beneath a huge portrait of the current earl's late father, a man dressed plainly in Puritan attire despite his title of Lord High Chancellor, and studied the lines of that cold, aloof face with its fox-red beard and tired regard. For all his wealth and power, Rob thought, he did not appear a man who had been much contented with his lot in life. The portraitist had opted to hide from view the reputed hunched back; he had, however, captured a strained look in those crafty eyes, the eyes of a spymaster, a man who had seen too much, including the fate that awaited him just a few years later, that swift and shocking fall from grace, from power, from wealth and eventually from life itself. Rob squared his shoulders as he heard footsteps tapping down the hall outside and turned to meet the present incumbent of the title: the second Earl of Salisbury, William Cecil.

But it was a woman who stood framed by the oak doorway: a beautiful, fragile creature with a pale face made paler still by a judicious use of expensive cosmetics, and huge dark eyes framed by tumbles of ringlets. She wore a gown of voluminous rose-pink silk, cut square and low enough across the breast to reveal a silky white cleavage nestling in froths of exquisite Flemish lace, which Rob tried hard not to stare at. Instead, he applied his gaze to the great diamond that hung around her neck on a choker of black satin, and the ornate bone fan which she held in her right hand. It was impossible to guess her age.

After pausing to make her entrance, and to observe her effect on the visitor, she walked towards him, extending a long-fingered white hand encrusted with rings. 'I am the Countess of Salisbury: and who might you be, pretty young man?'

Rob, remembering his manners, bowed so hastily and low that a particularly huge ruby almost took his eye out. 'Robert Bolitho, my lady, of Kenegie Manor in Cornwall. I bring a letter from my master, Sir Arthur Harris, for the Earl's attention.'

Lady Cecil smiled sweetly. 'My husband is otherwise engaged. Perhaps you might let me see the letter? Andrew said it mentioned something about Barbary pirates – so fascinating, so romantic!'

'It is not a very romantic story, madam, nor one likely to entertain a lady like yourself,' Rob said, smiling back. It was unfortunate that the Earl was not available, but to see his wife was the greatest good fortune for his own private quest. 'But I would indeed crave your indulgence if you would hear the tale, for it concerns someone of your acquaintance, at least,' he said, then amended hastily, 'You have acquaintance of her work, I believe.'

The Countess tilted her head towards him like a sparrow. 'Really? Well, then, we shall take a bowl of coffee in my chambers, and you shall tell me all.'

'Sixty people, in a single raid?' Lady Cecil blinked and blinked. 'How very audacious of them.' She leaned forward. 'And tell me, did you catch a glimpse of these bold pirates, were they very cruel of visage and Turkish in their dress? I imagine them all glittering eyes and jutting beards, like Saladin, flourishing their shining scimitars and calling on the name of their god.'

'I did not see them, my lady. I was at Gulval Church with the Harris family.'

Her face fell. 'Oh, *quel dommage*. And what will they do with their captives? Will they go for slaves to the Great Turk, do you think? I hear he is a monster who has a harem of ten thousand women, and that his palace is paved with gold. Ah, Constantinople, I would so love to visit Constantinople, to see its domes and minarets, to walk inside the Sancta Sophia and breathe the ancient air of Byzantium – though I believe it is forbidden for a woman to enter there, or indeed a Christian. I should have to disguise myself as a Mahometan pilgrim!' She clasped her hands. 'I would stain my skin with walnut dye, fashion myself a beard and wrap myself up in robes with a dagger at my waist and coloured leather slippers, just like the chiausch who was here this spring to visit the King as an envoy of their sultan!' She clapped her hands together at this delightful image. 'He brought lions and tigers, you know, for the Royal Menagerie. Such a pretty gesture, I thought. But *he* didn't look much like a pirate: in fact, he was a little fat –'

'Lady Cecil, I beg pardon for interrupting . . .'

The Countess was not used to such plain speaking: she gaped, then started to fan herself agitatedly.

Rob dug inside his jacket and drew out a paper-wrapped packet which he unfolded with immense care. 'I wanted you to see something.'

'Great heaven!' The Countess smoothed her hands over the thing Rob had spread out. 'This is remarkable work.'

It had been a last-minute flash of inspiration which had prompted Rob to run up to Cat's room before leaving Kenegie. On the threshold he had paused, as if a fraction of her might linger there out of time and he might surprise some ghostly apparition before it had time to vanish again. As he entered, he felt profoundly he was intruding into a space that was still full of her being: he could almost smell her in the air, a faint aroma of musk and roses. The half-finished altar cloth had been easy to find underneath the bed, the first place he had looked. He had stowed it inside his shirt and ridden away with it next to his skin until he realized he would likely stain it with his sweat. It was a sacred object in essence and in association: he did not wish to mar it.

Now he gazed upon the work Cat had undertaken in secret, by candlelight, in the privacy of her attic room and remembered their visit to Castle an Dinas earlier that summer, how she had voiced her desire to join the Broderers' Guild, how he had tried to dissuade her from over-ambition.

'The design is exquisite, visionary.' Lady Cecil traced the path of the serpent twining about the trunk of the tree, touched a finger to the gold of Eve's hair, the blush of the apple.

'The design is Catherine's own.'

The Countess looked up, startled. 'Her own? I thought Margaret and I had agreed I would send my own man down to pounce out the design for the young lady to stitch. I must admit I was tardy in arranging it, so much to do with the children, the management of the house . . .' Her voice tailed off as she was caught up in the details of the embroidery again. 'But Christopher would never have dreamed of anything as *alive* as this. It's quite wonderful.' She paused. 'Why have you brought it to me incomplete?'

Rob swallowed. 'Catherine was taken by the raiders. She was made to write the ransom note, from Sallee in Barbary. They have demanded eight hundred pounds for her return.'

The Countess's laugh rang out. 'Eight hundred pounds? For a serving girl? Even for a girl who can sew like this, that's an extraordinary sum. Did you know you can purchase a baronetcy for a mere thousand?'

He hung his head. 'I have vowed to redeem her.'

The Countess smiled indulgently. 'Sweet boy. How much have you raised so far?'

'Next to nothing, though I would pledge myself to work for nothing for as long as it would take to pay the debt. Cornwall is a poor county, and Cat's close family were taken with her by the raiders.'

She sighed. 'Such a true heart is worth a fortune. Would that I had one at my disposal. But all this' – she indicated the rich apartment, her dress and jewels – 'well, my dear, it's all show. We don't own the palace, it belongs to the Bishop of Durham; we have just this wing. My husband would kill me for saying so, but our debts are really quite immense. William's father died owing more than thirty thousand pounds, and as for my own family . . .' She spread her hands. 'It really would be very lovely to have you come and work for us here in some capacity to earn your Catherine's redemption fee, but you see how it is.'

Rob saw how it was, with a sinking heart.

'Do leave the altar frontal with me,' she cooed. 'I shall commission someone to complete it for our church at Framlingham.'

'I cannot do that,' Rob said softly. 'It is all I have of her.'

The Countess pursed her lips. 'Wait here.' She clicked out of the room and returned a few minutes later bearing a leather pouch. 'Here,' she said, placing it in his hand. 'It will not redeem your Catherine, but it may go some way towards helping, and it seems a fair price for the work she has thus far done. My husband is likely too drunk to miss it: if he does I will remind him that he lost the sum at cards last night.'

The pouch contained the best part of fifty pounds in gold sovereigns and angels. Beneath a chestnut tree just beginning to lose its leaves, Rob counted it out with a hammering heart. He was sad to lose contact with Cat's embroidery, but the touch of her hand would be more welcome by far than the touch of something that hand had worked, however fine. He stowed the gold carefully away with a prayer of thanks to the mysterious workings of the Lord, and set off on his next errand: to find Sir Henry Marten and deliver his second letter and the petition of the people of Penzance. 'Go to his townhouse in Westminster,' Sir Arthur had told him, writing down the address. 'He has an abrupt manner and does not suffer fools lightly, so keep your wits sharp and your tongue civil. He can be somewhat trying, but we need his help.'

After the splendours of Salisbury House, Rob was unprepared for the squalor surrounding the seat of the country's power. The streets of Westminster were filthy and stank of swamp gases, piss and ordure. Flemish merchants cried their wares in heavy accents, drunks stood propped against walls bearing mugs of pepper-spiced ale or vomited into sewers already overrun with waste, cooks' stalls sold meat pies, pigs' trotters, porpoise tongues and fried cows' ears. Rob was glad he had stuck to plain fare: a small loaf of fresh-baked bread and a lump of salty yellow cheese eaten as he walked through Long Acre.

He passed the huge structures of St Stephen's, where the Parliament sat when in session, and the royal Palace of Westminster, wherein lay also the Law Courts, and found himself experiencing a kind of ecstatic terror at their vast, dark masses, akin to the time he and Jack Kellynch had taken a skiff beneath the forbidding green-stone cliffs of the Gurnard's Head, and he had imagined being shipwrecked on the foam-battered rocks below. These towering buildings were inimical: their scale too grand, too imposing, to encompass him within their context. Passing out of their shadow, he stood in awe for a time beneath the north façade of the great Abbey, marvelling over its arching buttresses and Gothic pinnacles, its jewel-like glass windows and intricate carvings. Ambushed by its magnificence, he felt something spring suddenly wide in his head, like a flower opening beneath unexpected sunlight. For a moment he thought he might summon the courage to go in, but at the last he did not dare. Its beauty was too much for a simple man to bear. Besides, he had already been followed by a man with a pocked face and shifty eyes, who'd asked him if he wished to go with him to his house, and he became aware of how much of a country yokel he must look, with his mouth hanging open and his eyes wet with amazement: a pathetically easy mark for even the most amateur footpad or sneak-thief. Indeed, the narrow lanes around the Abbey were frequented by many shady types, who assessed him as he passed but seemed to decide he had nothing on his person likely to warrant the effort of robbing him, an irony which would have made him smile, were he not so nervous of their attention. He was glad that he had left the horses at a livery stable in Seven Dials; but the pouch of gold weighed heavily against his flank, and he blessed his sense in wrapping it well enough to prevent the coins chinking as he walked.

Sir Henry Marten's house was just off Broad Sanctuary, and with great good luck he was at home, though not in the best of tempers.

'And what does he expect me to do about it?' he roared, having scanned Sir Arthur's letter.

Rob, who had not been asked to sit down, clenched his knuckles. 'I believe, sir, that he would have you raise the issue with other eminent men with Cornwall's best interests at heart with a view to putting the petition before the Privy Council so that we may plead for monies from them to ransom our captives back.'

'Ransom? From whom?'

'From the raiders, sir, the men of Sallee who stole them.'

'The Sallee Rovers are a company of pirates, and with pirates there is no treating or confederacy! They are traders only in terror, in blood and fanaticism, and His Majesty's government must never sully itself by so much as considering their crazed demands.'

'My betrothed, Catherine Tregenna, was taken,' Rob said low, the cords on his neck beginning to stand out with the strain of not taking the man by the throat. 'And I am resolved to save her. I have already collected over fifty pounds for her ransom fee alone.'

Sir Henry Marten stared at him. 'That is a remarkable achievement, young man, but you might as well spend it on sack and piss it down a drain. Giving these scum money will do nought but encourage them in their trade. It merely serves to validate their wicked practices. Besides, they'll not be parted from your Catherine if she's pretty: women fetch high prices in their markets. They'll take your money and send you to the galleys, and no one will be any the wiser.'

'I understand what you are saying, sir, but, with respect, I am determined on my course.'

The Cornish MP sighed. 'I do not blame you for wishing to save your young lady from the filthy hands of such heathens, but I can assure you there is never any good to be had out of trading with infidels, let alone those who believe themselves carrying out some bizarre holy war against Christendom – they have no honour, they believe in nothing, and there is no reasoning with them. If we must parley with such heathens, then at least it should be with someone who has proper authority – their sultan or suchlike.'

'Could you place a motion to do that, sir? The Countess of Salisbury mentioned an envoy from the Barbary States who has met with the King. Perhaps he might be prevailed upon –'

Henry Marten snorted. 'All that impostor did was to drain the resources of the merchant company who defrayed his expenses and depart with a shipful of "gifts". Lad, there are over two thousand captives held in filthy conditions across the Barbary States – in Algiers and Tunis as well as Sallee –'

'Two thousand?' Rob was aghast. 'If there are so many of our folk rotting in slavery, why has nothing been done? Our coasts are unprotected. I know our people are poor and held to be of little account in great places like London, but this is scandalous.'

'Do you think we've not tried to find some way of saving them? Armed expeditions have spectacularly failed; so, against all sense, we are trying diplomacy. We've established a consulate in Algiers, but so far all we've managed through strenuous effort is the release of forty poor souls, more dead than alive. And Sallee is quite independent of the rest of Barbary; 'tis a nest of vipers, and even seasoned expeditioners have had no luck. Give me your petition: I will add it to the rest. Go home and tell Arthur it is a fool's mission to try to bring these people back. He would do better to devote his energies to pressing again for more guns for the Mount – that way he can prevent others being taken.'

Rob squared his jaw. 'Thank you for your time, sir. You might remember when you return to the bosom of your family that the stolen captives include eighteen women and twelve children among their number, two babes in arms and three elderly widows. According to Catherine's letter, at least two of those children perished on the voyage. How many more will die in slavery while we sit back and refuse to make contact with their captors? I trust you will do what you can on behalf of our people.'

He crossed to the door, then turned back. Sir Henry was looking somewhat purple in the face.

'I wonder, sir, if you might know where I might find the Turkey Company? I seek Sir John Killigrew, for I would speak with him.'

Marten's face became purpler still. He fixed the lad with a grim look. 'If you have any sense at all, you'll go straight back to Cornwall. London is no place for a decent young man, and the Turkey Company are completely unscrupulous.'

Rob made no move to leave, and at last Sir Henry sighed. 'Very well, then. I know not where the Turkey Company operate, even if they have such things as offices, but you might make inquiry at one of the goldsmith's on Cheapside, for they all seem involved in some tricksy scheme or another. But have a care, Robert Bolitho, for Killigrew's a worse brigand than any of your Barbary pirates.'

An hour later Rob found himself wandering in Cheapside, a spacious high street teeming with life and lined by houses which had been extended upwards by three, four or even five storeys, so tall and unstable-looking to Rob's untutored eye that he was afraid to walk beneath their eaves for fear they would at any moment collapse upon him. Crowds thronged the area, and the noise was abominable. As soon as he was able, Rob took himself off the main thoroughfare and into the labyrinth of streets which surrounded it, where there were to be found the headquarters of every craft guild in the city – the ironmongers and carpenters, mercers and saddlers, haberdashers, drapers, cooks and coopers and cordwainers. The bakers were situated on Bread Street, the dairymen on Milk Street and the fishmongers on Friday Street. He found the goldsmiths at work between Bread Street and Friday Street on, unsurprisingly, Goldsmith's Row.

He went from workshop to workshop, but none there knew the name of John Killigrew. He was thinking about giving up his fruitless search and was bemusedly staring up at the sign for the Company of Merchant Tailors – which showed on one side of its arms a Turk riding a bizarre-looking animal like an enormous cow with a grotesquely long neck, and on the other a black man astride a great lion – when he was accosted by a pimply young apprentice, who followed him to the end of the street and tugged on his sleeve.

'The man you seek is with some merchants of our acquaintance.' The lad stood there expectantly while Rob glowered at him.

'Where would I find these merchants?' he demanded.

The boy held out his hand, the fingers burned and pitted from the motes of molten metal that were a daily hazard of his trade. Sighing, Rob dug in his pocket and brought out a groat, but the apprentice snorted derisively and would not be satisfied until the Cornishman picked out two whole pennies. He gave the lad one, whipping the second out of his reach. 'Take me there and you can have the other.'

The apprentice paled: an achievement, given the pastiness of his face. 'My skin is worth more than two pennies.'

'I doubt it,' Rob told him. 'But I'll not tell him how I came by knowledge of his whereabouts.'

Greed warred with fear, and triumphed.

By the time they arrived in an anonymous backstreet, Rob was completely disorientated; but one glimpse of a head of red hair through a grimy window immediately eradicated any such mundane concerns. He tossed the boy his penny and knocked on the door. A suspicious silence fell within, then, after someone peered out of the window, the door opened, a hand shot out and Rob was dragged inside.

'What the – I know you!' Killigrew frowned, searching his memory.

Rob was hard to miss, with his immense height and corn-yellow hair; he did not look much like a city man. 'Robert Bolitho. I work at Kenegie for Sir Arthur, who said you would be in London.'

John Killigrew grimaced. 'God damn the man, is he spying on me? My business is my own and as honest as any.'

'I come of my own will on a personal matter. I would talk with you alone, sir, of Catherine Tregenna and her mother, Jane. Jane Coode, as was.'

The man's expression changed. He looked around at the two other men in the room, whose demeanour had become attentive, avid. 'Come with me.'

Killigrew pushed Rob before him into a dusty, sparsely furnished back room, shut the door and turned to confront him. 'The woman is nothing to do with me now: it was a long time ago that she worked at Arwenack.'

'The best part of twenty years, which is, interestingly, her daughter Catherine's age.'

'And what has that to do with me?' Killigrew blustered.

'Sir, I have it from an impeccable source that she is your daughter. There is no point in denying it: she has inherited the same fox-red hue of your hair. You might recall your . . . encounter with her, in the courtyard at Kenegie some weeks back.'

A flicker of reaction showed in the pale eyes. 'I have bastards strewn the length and breadth of the county: it is hardly shocking news to any who have acquaintance of me. And nothing happened between me and the girl: if she says it did, she is lying to cover up an indiscretion of her own.'

'Both mother and daughter at this moment lie in fear for their lives in some filthy slave prison in the Barbary States.'

'The Penzance raid by the Sallee Rovers?'

That was indeed the name that had been given the bold raiders. Rob nodded. 'A ransom note arrived last week. They want . . . a very great sum of money to redeem the captives.'

Now Killigrew laughed. 'And you have come to me in search of this "great sum"? You have hit upon the wrong man altogether if it is charity you seek, for I have none, as you must surely know from my reputation, which I have fostered long and hard. Or did you think in some way to blackmail me? There is no profit to you in that, I can assure you: I care not one whit what anyone thinks of me. Moreover, I care not at all what happens to Jane Coode or the whelp, though I have to admit she has turned into a comely wench. What do you say to that?' He thrust his face belligerently at Rob.

Rob bit his lip. None of his meetings today had taken the course he had hoped or expected. 'I beg your pardon, sir, for taking up your time. There is evidently nothing more to be said on the subject, and I must seek another avenue to save Catherine.' He turned on his heel as if to leave, but Killigrew called him back.

'Wait! Tell me, what would you do to save her?'

Rob stared at him. 'Anything. I would do anything in the world if I could bring her safely home.'

'Are you not in Arthur Harris's employ?'

'I am.'

'But you might consider other offers?'

'It would depend entirely on what was entailed, and the likely outcome. Is it legal?'

Killigrew paused. 'Would that make a difference?'

Rob swallowed. He had been brought up to fear God, to love his country and to abide by the law; but neither his country nor the law seemed able to offer him the means to save Cat; and perhaps God's way did not always follow the straightest and most obvious path through the darkness. 'No, sir, it would not.'

'Then it seems, Robert Bolitho, that you may save me a long, uncomfortable and probably dangerous voyage.'

'A voyage?'

'There are great fortunes to be made in Barbary. We have something the Moors want badly – and they have much that we wish to have in return. Morocco is a country rich in resources: it seems foolish that we cannot trade openly with their . . . merchants. Now it seems we might add one other small item into the balance – but I warn you, this is not a charity mission but a business venture. If you undertake this voyage, it will be on my terms. A ship sails for North Africa tomorrow before the winter seas close in; and, if you satisfy me that I may trust you, you may take my place on it. If you help my proxy to strike the deal I seek to make, then you may add your Catherine into the bargain, but no other, do you hear me?'

'There is her mother, and her friend, Matty . . .' Rob began, already feeling the guilt gnawing at his vitals. 'And many other poor souls we might help. And I cannot simply disappear without letting the Harris family know where I am: they have been good to me; they would worry were I not to return, and Sir Arthur would likely come looking for me –'

'Stop! We will walk to Hardwicke & Buckle, who are outfitting the expedition, and I will explain your part in this venture to you.

You may write to your employer from there to give your notice, but you will tell no one of my involvement in your decision or discuss the nature of the trade: is that agreed?' He held out a hand; and Rob took it, his heart pounding. As they shook to seal the deal he felt that he was shaking the hand of the Devil himself and about to risk not only his life but his very soul.

23

The house to which Idriss brought me was on a narrow street on the southern edge of the medina. Children watched curiously as we passed, Idriss carrying my bags. One small girl, her dark eyes lit by the orange sodium lamps, tugged on my sleeve. '*Baksheesh, madame.* Please, *danke schön.*'

Idriss said something in rapid Berber, and the children ran away, shrieking and laughing.

'Not the first time they've seen a tourist, then,' I said wryly.

'Little monkeys, they know they should not beg, I have told them often enough.'

'You know them?'

'They are my nieces and nephew, the children of my brother Rachid and his wife, Aïcha.' He stopped at a wooden door whose blue paint was barely a memory, inserted a key and led me inside. This house was a far cry from the splendid grace of the Dar el-Beldi: bare lightbulbs harshly lit a narrow hallway lined to half height with brightly coloured, mass-produced tiles of geometric design. I could hear foreign voices emanating from the rooms off the hall and a television blaring out. Idriss called something over the hubbub, and two women appeared suddenly at a doorway and began to chatter loudly. They came flying out and engulfed me in a cloud of perfume and spice, warm flesh and billowing fabric. I was kissed many times on both cheeks; my hands were wrung. '*Marhaban, marhaban,*' the older of the two said over and over. *Welcome.*

At last they stepped back. 'My mother, Malika,' Idriss said, indicating the elder of the two, a lady of indeterminate age, her face criss-crossed by lines like a contour map of a life filled with emotional incident. 'And my *belle-sœur*, Aïcha, who is married to Rachid.'

The second woman grinned at me. She was young – maybe still in her twenties – and wore a tunic, denim jeans and a bright silk scarf which she now drew up over her dark hair. 'Good day,' she said. 'Idriss say you English. I speak English a little. Come, come with me. I show you room.' And she took me by the hand and drew me after her up three flights of tiled stairs to a room on the top floor. 'This Idriss room,' she informed me cheerfully. 'You sleep here.'

'And where will Idriss sleep?' I asked nervously.

'In salon. Is no problem. I bring you clean things.' She bustled about the room, whisking off the blanket and bedlinen with a practised flourish, and was gone in an instant, leaving me alone to inspect my new quarters. One bed (single), one bedside table, a lamp, a chair, a wardrobe, a bookcase, an old-fashioned candlestick, the candle half burned down. On the back of the door hung a robe of ankle-length dark-blue wool with a pointed hood, like a Sylvestrine habit, reinforcing the impression that I had somehow stumbled into a monastic cell.

Aïcha returned with her arms full of linen. As we made up the bed, I asked, 'Do you live here too?'

'Of course. Is family home. Is me and husband Rachid, our children Mohammed, Jamilla and Latifa; Idriss, his mother Malika, his brother Hassan and Lalla Mariam, when she not in the mountains.' She ticked them off on her fingers one by one. 'When other family visit Rabat they stay with us too. While you stay, you are one of our family.'

'Thank you, it's very good of you.'

She pressed the flat of her hand to her heart. '*Barrakallofik.* Is our honour.' As we spread the striped blanket over the bed, she added, 'There is bathroom next door so you can wash before eating. Come down when you ready.'

If I had thought Idriss's bedroom spartan, the bathroom was positively rustic. A narrow cubicle next door was tiled from floor to ceiling. A tap protruded from low down on the left side; high above was a plastic showerhead. A water bucket, wooden stool, soap, shampoo, a mug containing three razors, a broken mirror on the back of the door, a small white towel and an ominous-looking hole in the floor completed the scene. I found myself remembering wistfully the luxurious bathroom suite I had left behind at the Dar el-Beldi and had to push the image fiercely away. Damn Michael.

In the kitchen I found Idriss rubbing aromatic oil through a mound of steaming couscous, surrounded by a cloud of vapour like a genie emerging from his magic bottle. Behind him, his mother ladled a savoury-smelling scarlet liquid into a huge earthenware bowl. They were laughing and talking loudly in Berber, and at one point she held out her hands palm up and Idriss slapped them with his own so that grains of couscous jumped in the air like specks of molten gold, and then they were shrieking with laughter and chattering again like school friends rather than mother and son. Feeling as if I were intruding, I turned away.

'No, no, come in.' Idriss's long almond eyes were shining: he looked a different man to the taciturn, grim-faced guide who had shepherded me around Salé that afternoon. 'Here, taste this – is it too spicy for you?' He held out a spoonful of the scarlet liquid. 'Europeans don't always like much chilli.'

I tasted it. Flavours seethed along my tongue, fiery and delicious. 'No, that's wonderful. Really. What's the Berber word for "delicious"?'

'*Imim*,' he told me.

I touched his mother's arm. '*Imim*,' I said, pointing at the sauce. '*Imim, shokran*.'

Her face creased into a thousand wrinkles of pride as she gabbled away at Idriss, flashing her kohled eyes at me, then back at him. Idriss shook his head then rapped her knuckles with the spoon and the volume of their discussion rose by another decibel. At last, she shooed him out of the kitchen, and he took me with him into a small sitting room lined with banquettes encircling a low, round table.

'What was she saying?'

He looked embarrassed. 'No matter how I try to explain, she seems to think you are my girlfriend.'

Now I was embarrassed. 'I didn't think people had "girlfriends" here.'

He looked at me curiously. 'What do you mean?'

I spread my hands. 'Forgive me, I don't really know anything about your culture. The guidebook said something about sex before marriage being illegal in Morocco. Especially between Moroccans and foreigners.'

His face went very still. 'Many things that are illegal still happen,' he said stiffly. 'But there is a social code here, and people try to respect it. That is perhaps the difference between my culture and yours.' He paused, as if assessing the effect of this strike, then added, 'My mother also said you are very beautiful.'

I felt myself colouring furiously. 'I don't think anyone's ever said *that* about me before.' It was meant as a light-hearted remark to fend off such an unexpected statement, but as I said it I realized it was true. Not even Michael had said that of me in all of the time we were together: especially not Michael, as tight with his compliments as he was with his emotions, and his money.

'Well, then, you have surrounded yourself with people who do not value the truth, or maybe do not wish to see it.' And before I could say anything to this, he disappeared again.

When he returned it was with a huge platter of couscous – a mountain of yellow grains studded with slices of courgette and carrot, squash, green beans and fennel, and gilded with the glistening spicy sauce. He was soon followed, like the Pied Piper of Hamelin, by a crowd of people, everyone talking at once: his mother, Aïcha, three children (including the little girl who had accosted me outside), a tall, grave young man in a suit, introduced as Aïcha's husband, Rachid, another who looked like a younger version of Idriss ('my brother Hassan, means "handsome" in Arabic: it suits him, no?') who was all smiles and charm, with a pair of sunglasses balanced on top of his head, and an older couple ('my uncle and aunt') – a man in a well-worn robe and a dumpy woman with iron-grey hair who nodded solemnly at me, then winked.

Everyone took their places around the table, on the low sofas or on leather pouffes dragged in from other rooms, and at once began to eat fast and neat with the fingers of their right hands, rolling the couscous and vegetables expertly into little balls. The older man made a large pellet of the mixture and flipped it nonchalantly into his mouth from an arm's length away, much to the delight of the children, who made as if they would try to emulate him until Aïcha chided them. '*Mange, mange,*' Idriss's mother exhorted me, proud of her French.

I smiled weakly and caught Idriss's eye. He was watching me expectantly, as if waiting to see how I would handle this tricky situation. I set my jaw. I would not, I decided, be such a feeble European as to ask for a plate and fork. I plunged my fingers into the grain mountain and almost yelped, for it was extraordinarily hot. Then I hit on the idea of using a piece of carrot like a spoon and managed to get a large mouthful down me without scattering it all over the table.

The tajine at the Dar el-Beldi the previous night had been toothsome, but this was yet another venture into the world of spices. More subtle than Thai seasoning, more complex than Indian food, more demanding than Chinese, it was a rich and powerful experience.

'Here.' The young man who looked like Idriss pushed a piece of soft orange pumpkin towards me. 'Is best: we call it Berber cheese.'

'*Shokran.*'

They all nodded in approval at my mastery of the language, and soon everyone was picking the choicest morsels out of the mountain and pressing them upon me until I could eat no more.

Later, much later, as it seemed – after I had fended off questions about my life, my family, my friends, my marital status, life in London, why I was in Morocco, how I knew Idriss, and why I was staying with them – I found myself up on the roof terrace, smoking the first cigarette I had touched in twenty years. It tasted horrible, but I persisted with it anyway. My nerves had been rattled so many times today that I felt I needed to do something to break the pattern.

Idriss leaned against the wall, the smoke from his cigarette curling up into tranquil night air. 'So tell me, Julia, why it is you hide from this man who calls himself your husband?'

I sighed and took a final drag on the cigarette to delay the need to respond. I had been waiting for this question ever since we had left the Dar el-Beldi and I still didn't know how I was going to reply, whether I would trust this stranger with the truth or whether I would offer a strategic lie. Down below us lay the remains of a little market: striped tarpaulins jerry-rigged over scaffolding posts, drifts of rubbish, strewn vegetables. A thin cat sat in the middle of this, having taken back its territory for the night, grooming an outstretched leg. At last I said, 'I have something he wants, something valuable.'

In the darkness it was hard to tell whether the gleam in his eyes was one of mere curiosity or of avidity. 'He must want this thing very much, to have crossed continents to find it.' He dropped the end of his cigarette and ground it underfoot until its glow was extinguished. 'Or perhaps it is you he wants.'

'I don't think so!'

'You say that very definitely and, if I may say so, with some bitterness.'

I stared at him, then looked away.

'Is he your husband? Or perhaps he was once your husband?'

'No. Not now, not ever. Why are you so interested, anyway? You've only just met me.'

'Julia: I never saw a woman look as terrified as you did this evening at the riad. Something about this man has frightened you, and I do not like to see that. But I promise you, here you are safe: my house is your house and while you are here you are a member of my family. On my honour: no one can threaten you here.'

Tears pricked my eyes. I leaned my forehead against the balustrade, and it was cool and rough against the flush of my skin. 'You said earlier you know someone at the university who's an expert on the corsairs?'

He nodded. 'A friend, yes, Khaled. He is a historian, he lectures there.'

'Have you known him a long time? Is he trustworthy?'

'He is a good man, a friend of my father since their childhood together in the mountains. He is like an uncle to me. If you ask me if he is worthy of trust, then yes, most certainly, yes.'

'Could we go to see him tomorrow, do you think?'

'He will be teaching in the morning, and after that he will visit the mosque, but maybe he can see us in the afternoon. If you like I will call him.'

'Thank you.' I glanced up, feeling some relief.

But he was not looking at me. Instead, his eyes were fixed on the night sky behind me. 'Look!'

His hands were warm on my shoulders as he spun me around just in time for me to see a star tumble through the black air. 'Oh!' In the north-west sector of the sky, right over the distant sea, another fell, then another. 'Shooting stars . . .' I had not seen such a thing since I was a child of seven, sitting on the little pebble beach near our home with my father, when the future held unimaginable promises and everything was full of newness and magic.

'Beautiful, no? My *jeddah*, my grandmother, used to tell us they were the Devil's fireworks. But those are not stars that are falling but a meteor shower – the Perseids, at this time of year. It is great good fortune to see them.'

'Perhaps I won't need to burn any chameleons for a while.'

I felt his laughter as a vibration which trembled through his hands and into my bones. His breath was warm on the back of my neck; for a terrible moment I thought I was going to turn and kiss him. Tremors of intent ran through me. In a split second I had imagined the contours of that strong, dark face between my hands, the sensation of his lips upon me, his lean hands roaming beneath my shirt. Sexual tension grasped us; then I stepped quickly aside and broke free of it.

'Come with me,' I said, a decision made. 'I want to show you something.'

'This is the thing that Michael wants so much that he followed me to Morocco to get it.'

I took *The Needle-Woman's Glorie* from my bag and handed it to Idriss. Then I sat down on the bed as he moved the chair closer to the candle and bent his head over the book, touching its calfskin cover reverently, opening it as carefully as if its pages were the petals of a fragile and long-dead pressed flower. He scanned it silently, then he read out loud, haltingly and with many self-corrections: '*I feare my future, for on account of my foolish lye hee stille thinkes wee are of a riche familly who wille paie a grate ransom for oure return. But hee also threttens mee with being solde to a sultan, who I beleeve ys lyk unto a kyng in ther countrie, for hee saies I wille fetch a goode price at Sallee's market wyth my redde haire & faire skyn. How I wishe I had took old Annie Badcock's advyse & gone home with Rob to Kenegy . . .*

'I'm sorry, my English is not really up to this task: it is difficult for me to read. But, if I understand it at all, it seems to be the account of a female captive taken by the corsairs, written by her own hand?'

I nodded.

'Is it real?'

'It depends what you mean by real. I believe it's authentic, but I need an expert opinion.'

His eyes were shining. 'But this is extraordinary. If it is real you have here a piece of the true history of Morocco in your hands, Julia Lovat. It's a miracle, a magical window into the past. *L'histoire perdue.* I never heard of such a thing, not so early as 1625, and certainly not by a woman. *C'est absolument incroyable!*'

He kissed the book; then, as if by oversight, he crossed the room and kissed me, four times, on both cheeks. I could still feel the impressions of his fingers on my upper arms when he sprang away again.

'I am sorry, forgive me, please.'

I forced a laugh. 'There is really nothing to forgive. It really is an amazing thing, isn't it?'

'Truly. But one thing I do not understand – what are these pictures?' He indicated one of the embroidery patterns, a pair of pretty birds with their necks twined about one another, enclosed by a bower of leaves and roses.

'They're slips, embroidery slips,' I explained, taking the book back from him. 'Simple patterns for girls to follow in their needlework.' I mimed the act. 'To decorate their dresses, or things for the home – bed hangings, tablecloths, that sort of thing. Englishwomen spent a lot of time on this art through the ages. Some of us still do.' I retrieved my bag from the floor, placed Catherine's book inside and then drew out the piece of embroidery I was currently working on: the scarf with peacock's feathers flaring in gorgeous emeralds and aquamarines at three of its four corners. I thought I might change the motif for the last corner, but inspiration had not yet struck me.

'You did this?'

'You needn't sound so surprised.'

He smiled. 'It's just . . . well, I thought women like you were too busy, too modern, to spend time on such things. It's the sort of thing my grandmother might embroider. You must show her when she comes back from her visit. She loves the feathers of this bird, the *paon*; she has some in a vase in her room.'

'The peacock?'

'Peacock, yes. Jeddah will be here tomorrow evening, or maybe the next day: Rachid is driving to fetch her.'

I frowned. 'I'm not sure I'll still be here then. If we can see your expert tomorrow and get his view on the book so that I know what I'm dealing with, I'll probably take the train back to Casablanca immediately after and fly home the next day.'

An unreadable expression crossed his face. Then he said, 'Wait here.'

He returned a short time later with something draped over his arm.

'I thought tomorrow you might like to wear this, in case we pass your . . . Michael? in the street.'

It was a djellaba of midnight-blue, very plain, but of good-quality cotton, though the embroidered cuffs and hems were machine-stitched and unremarkable in style. With it came a length of white cotton to use as a hijab.

I laughed. 'I'll look like a nun if I wear that.'

He frowned. 'A nun?'

'Like a monk, a *frère* but a woman . . . a *sœur*?'

Now it was Idriss's turn to laugh. 'I do not think you could look like a *sœur* if you tried. Not with eyes like yours.'

I didn't know what to say to this, so I said nothing. Seeing that he had embarrassed me, Idriss bowed his head. 'I must go now and see my brother before he retires: there is something I would like my grandmother to bring with her from the mountains. I wish you good night, Julia. *Timinciwin. Ollah.*' He covered his face with his hands, kissed the palms, then drew them down to his heart. 'Sleep well.' And he was gone.

I opened the shutters and sat on the little prayer mat to watch the moon sail over the rooftops of the medina. How long I sat there I do not know. The muezzin rang out, and the stars wheeled, and I thought about Michael and how life had brought us to such a strange pass that he should have pursued me across continents to take back the gift that symbolized the end of our liaison. After a time it occurred to me that I could not picture him any more. I could imagine his eyes, his mouth, the shape of his skull, but I couldn't imagine them all together, couldn't see his whole face, or a single expression. Just who was it I had been having a relationship with all this time? The harder I tried to think of Michael, the more he eluded me; and after a while I began to believe that this in itself was significant, that I had spent the last seven years living inside my own fantasies, acting out a role with a man who came and went only when it suited him.

With all this playing through my head, I went to bed. It felt odd to be lying in a single bed for the first time since I was a teenager, odd but somehow comforting to be so constrained. Even so, I tossed and turned, my sleep interrupted by fragments of imagery from a day spent walking around Rabat and Salé, filled with veiled and hooded figures who chased me through narrow streets where I became lost in a maze of alleyways, or trapped in dead ends past doors that wouldn't open.

In the middle of the night I suddenly became convinced that

someone had followed me all the way to Idriss's home, that they had come into the house and entered the very bedroom in which I slept. I sat up, sweat running between my breasts and my pulse racing. There was no one there. Of course there wasn't. I lay back down with my heart hammering and willed myself to relax, but, try as I might, sleep would not come.

At last I swung my legs out of bed, padded across the room and lit the candle. The sky showing through the slats of the shutter was a deep, rich black: dawn was still a long way off. I decided that I would read some more of Catherine's journal, and perhaps that would help me sleep again. I positioned the candle on the bedside table so that it would provide a pool of light in which I might hold the book, then pulled my bag towards me and reached inside. My fingers felt blindly around among the contents: wallet, passport, mobile phone, hairbrush, make-up bag, tissues, chewing gum. In the second compartment I found only my embroidery, a notebook and pen.

But of *The Needle-Woman's Glorie* there was no trace.

I went cold all over. My immediate thought was that my dream had been no dream. But that was surely crazy. I got out, smoothing the blanket in case I had suffered a failure of memory and left it on the bed before falling asleep. Of course, it wasn't there. Neither was it on the floor, the chair or the bookcase. Given the sparsity of the room, there really was nowhere else to look, and I was left with no explanation other than that someone – Michael? – had indeed come into this room and stolen it while I slept.

I threw the djellaba over the T-shirt and knickers in which I had slept and made my way downstairs through the still, dark house. Anger carried me down two flights of stairs; but by the time I reached the third it was giving way to uncertainty. As I reached the ground floor, something made my heart skip a beat. Flickering light danced across the tiled corridor and threw sinister shadows against the wall, making me think, unwillingly, of the tales of the djinn I had come upon in the *Arabian Nights*, spirits formed of subtle fire, bent on torment and destruction, or leading astray the unwary and the foolish. I took a deep breath, pushed down my superstitious fears and approached the source of the light.

It came from the open door of the salon, wherein a single candle burned, casting a golden circle over the head of a figure hunched over a book. My book: Catherine's book.

As preternaturally aware as a drowsing cat, Idriss turned just as I stepped over the threshold. We both spoke at once.

'What are you –'

'I am sorry –'

We stopped and gazed at one another, each mirroring the other's dismay. Idriss beckoned me in. 'Come, sit with me, and listen to this.' And he showed me the page he read from.

They putte mee on the blocke & parted my robe to shew my red haire & white skin. They mayde much of my blew eyes & towlde how I was virgine & pure & many men made bidde for mee just lyke I was a prize yew untill I was sowlde & taken aside. That was the last tyme I saw my mother or my aunte which was a crewel partyng, but the worst separation was from my goode Matty & wee both wept sorely as they tooke me away . . .

24

Catherine

They covered her in a dark robe from head to foot and took her by mule from the marketplace through the streets of Old Salé. With only her eyes exposed, none could look upon her; she moved through the crowds, an anonymous woman on a starved mule led by a silent man. The silent man had a hard, fierce face and a bald head which gleamed with sweat in the sullen afternoon light. His hands were burned almost black by the sun, and he wore a dirty white robe tucked up between his legs and looped over his belt. When she asked him who had bought her and where they were going, he did not so much as turn his head. Had it not been for the chafing of the mule's sharp bones against her own, she would have felt as insubstantial as a ghost.

She looked to left and right, but what was the sense in seeking an escape? There was nowhere to run to, no one to help her. The thought of being sold into the hands of some stranger was terrible to her, but what was the alternative? To run through a strange city, only to be captured by a vengeful mob whose language she could neither speak nor understand? Or to throw herself off the city walls into the sea? She shivered. She had no wish to die yet.

They left the medina and came at last to the wide river's bank, where a boat waited, the oarsman leaning on his pole, silhouetted against the sombre waters of the Father of Reflection. As Cat stepped into the boat, she thought of the tales Lady Harris had told her of Charon, who ferried the souls of the ancient dead across the black river into Hades, a passage marking the relinquishing of their old life and the beginning of a new, grim existence. All she lacked was the coin in her mouth, Cat thought; that, and the loss of her memories. As the ferryman poled the boat away from the bank of Slâ el-Bali, Cat gazed into the water that spooled away behind them and thought of her old life at Kenegie, with its easy duties among people whom she might not always have liked but largely understood. She thought of the easy green and gold landscape of Cornwall, the grass and trees and gorse, the soft rain and hazy sunshine. She thought about her lost family: her dead father, her dead nephews, her mother stripped grey and naked. Turning her thoughts sharply from that painful image, she thought instead of her cousin Robert Bolitho, whose heart she had spurned, and wondered if she could ever have reconciled herself to the little life he had promised her. It was, she thought bitterly, a question she need never ask herself now, for that was her old life, and ahead lay another, which was the way of things. Better be like the dead and accept one's crossing over and not torture oneself with a future that could never be. Cat set her jaw and turned to watch the walls of Slâ el-Djedid looming before her.

On the water's edge waited another man holding the reins of another beast; but these two were quite different from the pair she had left on the river bank of Old Salé. This man was tall and garbed in a long red robe trimmed with gold; a scarlet turban covered his head and most of his face. From a gilded bandolier across his body hung a jewelled dagger, and silver bracelets clattered on his wrist as he raised his hand to greet the ferryman. Beside him stood a tall horse, its head small-boned, its legs long and delicate: a pure-bred horse that would show a clean pair of hooves to the hunters in Kenegie's stable. Its crimson saddle cloth was worked with gold, as were the bright tassels of its harness. If this man and horse belonged to her buyer, Cat reflected, he must be a man of great wealth, and one who wished that others knew it.

As the ferryman drew the boat up on to the shore, the horse stamped and tossed its head, but the turbaned man laid a hand on its muzzle, and it quieted. He stepped forward and pressed a coin into the boatman's waiting hand.

Ah, thought Cat humourlessly; *there it is: the payment for my soul.*

Then the man turned to her, picked her up as if she were no heavier than a child and set her on the horse's back. As wordless as his counterpart on the other side of the river, he led her through the streets of New Salé, beneath a great arched gate and into the Kasbah Andalus.

They made their way through a maze of narrow streets which wound up a steep hill, and the sound of the horse's hooves rang on the stone and echoed off the walls on either side until it sounded as if a small army were ascending. At last they arrived at a long blank wall broken only by a tall wooden door. Here the man came to a halt and, without knocking or otherwise announcing his presence, pushed open the door and led the horse inside. The dry and dusty outside suddenly gave way to verdant life: palm trees, fruit trees, earthenware pots overflowing with bright flowers. A boy as black as ink came running over, bowed to the man in scarlet and held the horse's reins as he helped Cat down. Two women emerged from a side door of a tall house and they too bowed to the man. Words passed among the three, guttural and harsh to Cat's ears, and then the women took hold of Cat, not unkindly, bearing her away with them into the cool shade.

The next few hours passed as in a dream. She was bathed in a room thick with steam and rinsed in another chamber lined with cold white tile, where she was rubbed with perfumed ointments; her hair was washed, and a sweet-smelling oil was applied to it by careful hands. Someone brought her a silk shift, which felt so cool and smooth against her skin that she almost wept. Over this, they placed an embroidered robe. Her wet hair was wrapped in a headscarf, and they gave her a pair of soft, red-leather babouches for her feet. Then she was taken to a tall-ceilinged room with a canopied bed. Here, spreading their hands as if to say 'this is for you', they left her, closing the door quietly behind them.

What now, Cat wondered. She had been so cleansed and seasoned with perfume that she felt like meat that had been prepared for a rich man's table. Was that what she was to become now, a rich man's plaything, a creature of the bedchamber? She shuddered, and waited.

No one came. After a time she got up and opened the tall carved armoire against the left wall and found therein neatly folded cotton shifts, head cloths, three more robes in rich fabrics and another pair of leather shoes. She closed it again, frowning. Was she in some other woman's room? She wandered to the window. Through the curlicues of its wrought-iron grille she could look down into a courtyard bright with marble and trees. Its geometrical design was soothing to the mind: a fountain in the centre sat within an eight-pointed reservoir from which four channels carried water to the corners and around the edges of the courtyard. Pots extravagant with blue and white flowers sat at counterpoint to the fountain, and at the outer corners, in raised square beds, stood four orange trees, their fruits glowing among the gleaming dark foliage. Its design reminded her of the courtyard at the house across the river where she had been taken to write the ransom demand, but this house was larger and finer by far.

Her mind again returned to the question of what manner of man had bought her. That he was wealthy seemed evident; but she knew the sort of enterprise that made men rich here, and probably the world over; being rich was clearly not commensurate with goodness or decency. But the house spoke of moderation and taste, of style and elegance. Everywhere she gazed there was evidence of the work of master craftsmen. Every possible surface and substance was decorated: the carved plasterwork which marked the transition between the gleaming walls and the high, coffered cedarwood ceiling; the walls were tiled to half-height with stylized starbursts, a motif which was echoed in the carving of the door, the tiles on the floor, the brass top of the table and the decorated glasses set upon it. It was, she had to admit, a pretty prison. But surely a prison all the same.

At last, exhausted, she lay down and slept. When she woke again, the sun was low in the sky, and she was very hungry. She went to the window. Three women, including the two who had bathed her, were at work down in the courtyard. One swept the paving, another watered the pots of flowers, while the third scooped rose petals out of the fountain. When they saw her looking out, one of the women beckoned her down. Cat went to the door, turned the great iron ring set therein and found to her surprise that it opened.

She made her way down a winding staircase and through the narrow corridor, following the light until she emerged in the courtyard. The women paused, then all of them started to talk at once – none, unfortunately, in a language she could understand. At last they seemed to realize this. One touched her bunched fingers to her mouth and mimed chewing. Cat nodded. Yes, she was hungry.

They brought her fresh-baked bread and honey, a bowl of sticky dates and nut-studded cakes, a silver pot of sweet green tea. She ate and drank it all, and the women exclaimed and brought more until she protested and waved her hands. They sat with her and shared out the second pot into tiny delicate glasses. The tallest of the three was called Yasmina, the youngest Habiba and the plump one Hasna, they told her. They had difficulty pronouncing her own name, so she settled for Cat.

'Where is the man who owns this house?' she asked. She drew an invisible turban around her head, got up and mimed a man's walk across the courtyard, until the women cried out with laughter. All she understood of their response was that he was away some-where – one mimed a horse, or it might have been a boat; they would never make mummers, Cat thought. But he was a rich man, a merchant and a soldier, she ascertained at long last from their acted bargaining and swordplay; handsome too, according to Hasna, who blushed, though the others waved their hands in denial. Too solemn, Yasmina mimed, making her face grim and angry; too old, Habiba suggested, and too sad, pulling her mouth down in the universal expression of sorrow.

'When will he come back?'

No one knew.

'What am I to do here?'

They didn't know that either. But the next day she opened her door and found outside a reed basket containing a roll of white linen, a dozen skeins of coloured silks and several fine needles of Spanish steel stuck through a book of red felt. So the raïs must have advertised her skills as an embroiderer, and her buyer had decided to test her ability. Perhaps her new master did not want her as a mere concubine after all.

Downstairs, she found Hasna and another woman waiting in the courtyard. Cat nodded to them.

'Good day,' said the other woman, bobbing her head.

Cat stared at her. 'You're English.'

'Dutch, in actual fact, but I speak your language well enow that your master pay me to translate with you.'

Cat noticed now that she spoke with an odd lilt and clipped the words in an unfamiliar way. She held out her hand. 'My name is Catherine Anne Tregenna. I was brought here as a captive from English shores.'

The other grinned, showing three gold teeth among the rest. 'Oh, yes, that I know. I am called Leila Brink, brought here by my pig of a husband, God rest his soul.'

'Oh, I'm sorry –'

'No need for sorry: none miss him, least of all I.' Her eyes were merry enough amid the black kohl she had applied in the local style. 'So, Catherine, what do you think of our city?'

'I don't know. I don't understand your ways here. It is all too strange to take in. A . . . a man tried to kill me, on the slave blocks,' Cat said. 'He cast a dagger at me.'

Leila sighed. 'Another attack. There are many fundamentalists here, to whom the presence of a living Christian is an eternal insult. Please do not judge us all by such mad creatures.'

That was a small relief at least. Then, 'Can you tell me the name and nature of the man who has bought me?' she asked. 'I have not yet had the pleasure of meeting him.'

Leila gave her an odd look. 'His name is Sidi Qasem bin Hamed bin Moussa Dib, a great benefactor and well-respected man, if somewhat grim of demeanour.'

'They tell me he is a merchant and a soldier.'

'That is right enow. He is a man with a good nose for a bargain and an eye to the main chance. He is also great patron of arts and such, not having wife and children to spend his fortune on.

He will be a good master to you if you do what he wishes of you.'

'Which is what?'

'He says you are a master embroiderer.'

Cat coloured. 'It was my aim in England to be such, but I never had the chance to train formally.'

'I have some knowledge of the craft. My father was a guild master in Amsterdam; some of the finest work in Europe passed through his hands.'

Cat bit her lip. 'What does he expect of me?'

'Come, you will see.'

Cat hoisted her basket and followed the Dutchwoman and Hasna through dark corridors and up a set of stairs which wound around and about, until they emerged into a cool, bright workroom in which a dozen or more women and girls were gathered. A number of low wooden frames had been set at intervals throughout the room, and women sat at them cross-legged, fitting them with lengths of linen cloth. On a wide circular table had been arranged a bale of thick white linen, more coloured silks, a pair of shears, several rolls of paper and some thin sticks of charcoal. Everything was very ordered, and as quiet as a schoolroom.

She smiled at the women uncertainly and sat down by one of the unoccupied frames, shuffling to sit comfortably in this unaccustomed position. The frame before her was not much like the little round withy-wood frame she was used to at Kenegie, with its spring mechanism and small surface. This was larger and more primitive, but, as she bent her head to fit a length of linen to it, she saw that it was more than serviceable, even though sitting cross-legged at it felt strange. When she looked up again some moments later, it was to find the gaze of all the women upon her, assessing, expectant.

She looked to Leila, confused. 'Are we waiting for the teacher to arrive?'

'There is no teacher here but you,' the Dutchwoman explained slowly. 'These women know only to work the simplest of peasant designs. Sidi Qasem is determined that you shall widen their repertoire. You shall be a sort of *ma'allema*, a teacher – but only of

266

embroidery. A true *ma'allema* would undertake some of their moral education too, though of course he would not expect that of you. He has other ambitions.'

'Ambitions?' Cat echoed, feeling all those dark, foreign eyes upon her.

'The royal city of Fez makes a great fortune each year from the fine embroidery it exports to the world. There are three thousand houses of *tiraz*, official factories of embroidery, operating there. Very fine work, traditional – very beautiful. But every *tiraz* make same thing, over and over; is boring and loses novelty. He wants New Salé to show Old Fez that it can do better, combining European techniques with Moroccan craft. You will facilitate this new industry for us. These women are just a beginning: you will teach them, and they will become *ma'allema* too and pass what they have learned to others. If you succeed, you will be like guild master. Sidi Qasem will be rich, and so will you.'

Cat felt faint. In Cornwall she had railed against the limits set around her, like a great unscalable wall. With her work on the altar frontal she had felt as if she had climbed three or four rungs of a giant ladder that might eventually enable her to peer over that wall. Here, at a single bound, she found herself astride the summit, but instead of a golden vista below there loomed a great, yawning void.

'What if I fail?' she asked, and her mouth was dry.

Leila shrugged. 'Is best not to fail.'

Cat touched her throat, where it felt as if her heart was trapped. What choice did she have? She must seize her fate and force down her fear. Perhaps she could achieve something extraordinary. Perhaps she could find the life she had always sought, even if it was on another continent, among strangers. She squared her shoulders. 'We had better start with the fundamentals. If these ladies can show me the sort of stitches they use, we can begin with that. Then tomorrow each can bring an example of the work she has already done, or something she has in the family, so I may have a better idea of the styles of embroidery made here. But I also need to see the sort of thing that is made in . . . what was the name of the city, Fez?'

'I am sure all that can be arranged. But a *ma'allema* does not sit on the floor among her students.' Leila held out a hand and helped Cat to her feet. 'You sit here.' She indicated a carved chair set before the largest frame of all. 'If you tell me what you need them to do, I will translate.'

Cat sat in the chair, which was low but wide, as if made for a much larger woman. Then she held up a hand. 'My name is Catherine, I come from England, and I will be your teacher in embroidery. You will each tell me your name, and then we will start with some simple stitches.'

And so began her first lesson.

On that first day she took them through some of the more basic stitches and was relieved to find that not all were unknown to them, although they called them by different names. Damask stitch, flat stitch and a type of darning stitch they were familiar with. She showed them, in addition, cross stitch, chain stitch and a simple herringbone, which made them laugh: to them it looked more like a stalk of wheat than like a fish. They showed her, in turn, Fez stitch, a sort of reversible backstitch producing work that looked the same on both sides of the fabric. She shook her head. 'It's very fine, but for most purposes it is wasteful: it uses a lot more thread. I think if you use a flat stitch instead, you will find you can achieve a similar effect on the only side of the fabric which is seen; and it is quicker too.' She demonstrated, but they pulled faces. Old habits die hard.

The next day each woman brought a piece of work from home. One brought a tunic decorated at neck, cuff and hem with a simple stylized design. It was neatly done, if unambitious. 'Very nice,' Cat said approvingly. 'Will you ask her what the pattern is?'

When Leila translated this, the woman – nut-brown and lacking a number of teeth – laughed and clacked her tongue, and Cat suspected she had demonstrated her foreign ignorance by asking the question.

'It is the tree-and-stork design,' the Dutchwoman explained.

'They have used it here for centuries. The stork is *baraka*, a good omen.'

Which was all very well, but what was a stork? Cat had no idea. Leila shrieked with laughter. 'Later I show you – there is a nest on the minaret.'

So it was a bird, then. Cheeks flaming, Cat looked back at the design. A bird with a long beak, she surmised, but was not much consoled by this.

Another woman had brought some long embroidered bands of a dense, complex design, with tarnished silver thread running through it. 'This is not local,' the translator said. 'It is very old and was a part of her great-grandmother's trousseau, and the old woman came originally from Turkey, she says. But this other piece' – she held up a simpler, monochrome band – 'is a ceremonial one for a man and comes from the Rif.'

'I like this very much,' Cat said. 'Much nicer than the Turkey piece.' The design was bold and emblematic, strong and confident in execution, and clearly made by someone with long experience of working in these materials and with these motifs. She picked up the other again and examined the workmanship. The silver had not been stitched through the fabric, but lay across the surface, held in place at tiny intervals by a sturdy neutral thread. 'Ah, this is couched – it saves the thread and makes sure the piece will not be stiff or buckled.' She smiled. 'Though I have never worked in silver, nor in gold either!'

'You will,' Leila promised. 'Sidi Qasem has many plans and a great deal of money.'

There were the braids and trimmings known as *mjadli*, wall hangings, or *hyati* – and a *sau*, a pretty decorated bath veil used to tie up the hair when attending the hammam. All these were homely, attractive objects worked in single colours with rudimentary skill. Then Habiba shyly drew out of her burlap bag a length of dark velvet that was so at odds with everything else they had seen that the women as one gave a gasp of delight.

'This is my *izar*,' she said. 'Or rather one of them. One half of a bridal curtain. For when I'm married.' And she blushed while the women drew it reverently out of its folds and caressed the soft velvet, one even touching it to her cheek. They had to climb, three together, giggling and staggering, on to one of the divans in order to give it its full height, and now it was Cat's turn to gasp.

The scope of the design was larger by far than any of the other examples the women had brought with them: someone had had remarkable ambitions. From a series of dense friezes alternating geometric patterns with stylized trees and plants there rose a recognizable minaret, which reached from the foot of the curtain full five feet to its apex, all the way down the right-hand side of the velvet.

'This is truly remarkable,' said Cat admiringly.

Habiba explained through the Dutchwoman that her mother and grandmother had made it together and that it was one of a pair. She had had to sneak this one out of the house, for the curtains were the most costly things the family owned, and her mother would have been angry that she should show it off so, and to strangers too; but you could tell by the way her eyes shone, Cat thought, how proud she was of it. The piece was having its effect on the other women too, for they exclaimed over it covetously, and Cat felt a sudden swelling of ambition inside her own breast. She could perform work like this – finer even, given the chance. She thought longingly of the altar frontal left behind under her bed at Kenegie, no doubt gathering cobwebs and mouse droppings, and for a moment she felt very sad that no one would see or praise her finest design. *I will outdo it*, she promised herself. *I will make something finer still, in this new world.*

Leila and Hasna had managed to gather a number of items made in Fez and other regions. Mostly, these were exquisitely worked pieces in dense monochrome: a scarf in red, a mattress cover in blue, and a pretty bed hanging in violet and mauve, touched with details of gold. The embroidery on these pieces was professional in comparison to that of the more rudimentary examples, the stitches finer and more regular, the patterns more exactly replicated, and the work reversible too, which showed considerable skill.

She had somehow expected to be daunted by the Fez work,

thought it might be beyond her capability, and that of the women who were to be her students. But, with a good eye, a careful design and strict training, a child could work these pieces. What they lacked was fluidity and individuality, she thought privately, remembering her Tree of Knowledge. Even the slips and patterns in *The Needle-Woman's Glorie* would show them a thing or two. How she wished she still had her little book. Never mind, she told herself fiercely. That belonged to my old life; this is now. I still have my two hands and my imagination, and that is what counts.

'Leila,' she said, and there was new purpose in her voice, 'there are a few things I need, and they should not be too hard to come by, I think.' She explained her requirements, and then selected a piece of paper from the circular table and set about sketching a simple pattern. She recalled her conversation with the raïs about the Prophet's wife Ayesha and her doomed wall hanging. Perhaps it were best she avoid too realistic a representation of the living things of the world; and anyway they seemed to favour more stylized designs. So she made a drawing of repeating ferns, simply suggested, set within a frieze of bands decorated with little cross-stitch flowers.

This met with clapped hands and awe, as if she had somehow performed magic, so she set about another involving stars and crescent moons. This met with rather less approbation. 'That is a Jewish star you have drawn. Here, we make our stars eight-pointed.' The Dutchwoman indicated one of the Fez designs, then showed Cat the same motif incorporated in the wall tiles. 'It represents the seal of Suleiman. Is a sacred symbol.' She folded her hands primly.

Cat was surprised by Leila's solemnity: she had not struck her as a pious woman, nor yet as a Mahometan. She took up another piece of paper and made instead a design involving the eight-pointed stars: a large one set between two smaller stars, and pretty petal patterns running through the friezes above and below. This found universal approval, so that when Habiba returned with the piece of fine cotton, some charcoal crushed to powder and the sharp awl that Cat had requested, they waited impatiently to see what she would do with them.

'Choose the pattern you would like to work,' Cat told them, and was surprised when ten out of the twelve women opted for the stars. She tipped the charcoal into the centre of the square of cotton and tied its corners together. 'This is a pounce bag,' she explained, which gave Leila some trouble in her translation. 'Now see how I transfer my design to your linen.'

She pricked holes along the lines of her paper design and then went from frame to frame, pinning the template to the cloth and dabbing the charcoal bag against the paper. It looked messy – the paper all covered in a dirty grey film – but, when the template was lifted, there was the design as neat as could be underneath. Now they really did think her capable of magic.

'You must choose your colours – try not to choose the same as your neighbour or we will run out of some colours and all the work will look too similar. And choose shades that are complementary. You are lucky – you have so many beautiful colours to choose from. In my country most women are limited to threads that we dye ourselves from onion skins and the like: the colours are rather muted and will fade with time. Only rich women could afford something like this' – she held up a skein of bright masareene blue – 'or this' – a hank of bright scarlet.

They liked this a good deal, the idea that they should be better off than their European counterparts, whom they had long thought wealthier and more privileged than themselves, and chuckled and slapped each other's hands. 'Al-hamdulillah,' said one, and they all followed suit.

Cat smiled, feeling older and wiser than her nineteen short years. 'Together we will make some beautiful things,' she promised them, and watched as her own budding confidence was mirrored in their faces, like flowers upturned to the sun.

That evening she found herself exhausted. She had always thought of embroidery as a relaxing and sedentary pastime, far less taxing than her other chores; but now her shoulders and neck and back ached as if she had done hard physical labour all day. It was perhaps the tension of responsibility, she thought. She had never taught anyone anything before, not unless you counted showing Matty how to lace her gaiters, which had taken far longer than you would expect. But she was content. A good start had been made, and with practice the women would make very fair embroiderers. She knotted her hands behind her head and stretched, feeling her muscles gradually ease.

A shadow fell across her.

In the doorway stood a tall figure, silhouetted by the setting sun. She stared at him, eyes wide, and suddenly her heart began to hammer against her ribs. He stepped into the room.

'Good evening, Cat'rin.'

It was the raïs.

He held her gaze until she looked away, then offered something to her. 'I thought you like this back.'

It was a small object, wrapped in a length of cotton. She unwrapped it, feeling as she did so the contours of the object within. She hardly dared hope, but then suddenly there it was, its calfskin a little scuffed and darkened but otherwise undamaged.

She clasped it to her breast. 'My book.'

'Is a little charred, I fear. Khadija try to burn it.'

'Khadija?'

'My cousin, the amina, she who prepare my female slaves for market. I am sure you have not forgotten her so soon. She has not forgotten you. Unfortunately good djellaba I gave you did not fare so well.'

Now she remembered the amina: the small, imperiously beautiful woman who had stripped them bare and subjected the possible virgins among them to such indignities. Her cheeks flared. She gazed down at her feet. 'I have not forgotten her.'

'She is, I think, jealous of my attentions to you.'

Incredulous, Cat stared at him. 'Jealous? Jealous that you stole me from my home for sale like a common chattel? How could she ever be jealous of me, whom she treated like an animal? No, worse, for no animal is conscious of shame when its naked body is subjected to the scrutiny of strangers!'

He gave her a crooked smile. 'I see that your experiences have not quenched the fire in you, Cat'rin Anne Tregenna.'

'They have not yet served to destroy me, no,' she returned, low-voiced. 'So if that was what you sought, you have not succeeded. In fact, it seems I have been most fortunate, for my new master is a man of considerable sensibility: he has put me to work that I am enjoying greatly, and it has done much to restore to me some self-respect and hope in the world.'

'He must be a fine man, to have achieved so much in so little time.'

'I am sure he is. I have not yet had the pleasure of making his acquaintance.'

'Strange, he should spend so much good coin on you and not even introduce himself,' he mused.

Cat folded her arms and said nothing to this, though she had to admit she thought the same.

'I hope this good master not find you as dangerous as I have found you,' he went on.

'Dangerous?'

'They say God made mankind from clay; He make the djinn from fire. The djinn very dangerous, they have power to possess a man.' He pulled a strand of her red hair loose from the cotton wrap and ran it thoughtfully through his fingers. 'Which are you, Cat'rin: a woman or a djinn?'

She took her hair back from him and stuffed it back inside the headscarf. 'I am a flesh and blood woman,' she said sharply.

'I think maybe that is most dangerous thing of all.'

And with that he swept her a mocking bow and took his leave.

25

We read together, Idriss and I, until the sun started to come up. Its first rays came filtering through the shutters of the salon, making slices of black and white of everything it touched. Where the sunlight hit Idriss's hand on the table, it rendered his skin a pale and radiant gold that was almost white. Mine, by contrast, lay in shadow. But the book was cut in two by it, one half glowing, the other hidden. I wanted to say something about this observation, for it seemed somehow significant, but I was too tired to frame the thought in words, and instead a vast yawn took me in its vice-like grip.

'Why did the raïs sell her to this merchant?' I said, mystified. 'Or is he also Qasem? But then why would he buy her, wasn't she already his property? I don't understand.'

'You need some sleep,' Idriss said firmly. 'Here.' He picked up the book, closed it gently and placed it in my hands. 'When you have slept for two hours, we will finish it together; then we will have breakfast, and later we will go to see Khaled.' He paused. 'And at breakfast you may want to read these too.'

There were three sheets of paper in his hand, rather crumpled-looking. I stared at them, not registering what they were. Frowning, I reached for them, but he stood up and held them out of my reach. 'Not now,' he said.

I realized then with an unpleasant jolt what they were: the note and the photocopies Michael had left for me at the riad. I had folded them into the back of *The Needle-Woman's Glorie* and forgotten all about them. And about Michael. Oh, God, what was I going to do about Michael and his determined pursuit?

'Give them to me!' I cried.

He grinned. 'Now I know something about your Catherine's story that you do not yet know,' he said teasingly, and the sun in his eyes made them as enigmatic as a cat's. 'I had asked myself one question many times, and the doubt it raised made me wonder greatly whether your book was a forgery, for the question was: how, if it was brought on a slave ship that crossed the wide ocean to Salé, did it ever make its way back to England, and eventually into the hands of the extraordinary Miss Julia Lovat?'

'And now you know?'

'I have an idea . . . a theory. And I am more sure than ever that what you have here is a genuine artefact and not a fake.'

'And you know that from the papers you have there?'

'They suggest something . . . remarkable.'

'I wish you would tell me.'

'I do not want to spoil the story for you,' he said, smiling. 'Stories should be told in the right order and at the right time. Did you learn nothing from *One Thousand and One Nights*?'

'This is not a fairytale,' I said frostily. 'And that is my property. What makes you think you have the right to withhold it from me?'

His eyebrows shot up. 'If you are in such a bad temper now, how much worse will it be if you have no sleep? But do not worry, I will keep them safe for you.' And he calmly proceeded to fold the photocopies into quarters and stow them inside his shirt. 'You see, I will sleep with them next to my heart. Besides, there is still a big piece of the puzzle missing, and in order to come by it you – like your Catherine – will have to make a large decision, and large decisions should never be made on a lack of sleep.'

I yawned again, hugely. If I was not careful, my head would be joining the photocopies, and I would be snoring away on Idriss's chest. Would that be such a bad thing, my traitor brain whispered. Yes, it would. I got up abruptly before I could say or do anything really stupid, and went upstairs. Alone.

It was only after I had crept into the little bed and laid my head down on the pillow that I remembered something Idriss had said.

The extraordinary Julia Lovat . . .

He thought I was extraordinary. And with that thought hovering like a protective cloud above me, I fell asleep with a smile on my face.

26

Rob

November 1625

Robert Bolitho had always considered himself a robust man. So it was with some detestation that he found himself weak as a mouse, heaving up a thin yellow bile day after endless day on this, his first sea passage.

' 'Tis just sea-sickness, lad,' the first mate told him, laughing to see such an ox of a man reduced to his piteous state. 'It'll not kill thee.'

But that couldn't be right, Rob thought. His blood was half brine, like that of any Cornishman. There must be some other, more sinister cause.

By the end of the second week at sea, with the vile nausea showing no sign of abating, he was more than ready to cast himself overboard to end the misery. Only the image of Catherine, bruised and beaten by barbarian slave masters, drove him grimly to survive each day. 'She is suffering far worse than I,' he told himself time and again. 'And if she can endure, then so can I.'

Then a day came when he managed to keep down a little stale bread and dried meat, and after that he improved moment upon moment, until one morning he found himself out on deck with the sun on his face and the smell of the salt spray in his nostrils, and the waves spangled with light, and he thought he could be in no finer place in all the world. The wind had whipped the wave tops into peaks and crests, the sails bellied smoothly, and the ship sped along like a great seabird. It had been a fair passage, the first mate told him; he was a lucky man. And then he regaled Rob with tales of storms and broken masts and foundered vessels and the cries of drowning men till Rob felt quite queasy again. 'And that's to say nothing of the pirates,' the man went on, blithely unaware of the effect his reminiscences were having on his listener. 'The waters are infested with 'em. It's a rare vessel makes it through the Strait nowadays without some sea-devil out of Sallee or Argier on its tail. Mate of mine was taken by a renegado just off the Canaries and put to the galleys in the Med. The stories he had to tell would make your balls shrink.'

Rob really didn't want to hear this, but the mariner had got him fair pinned to the gunwale.

'Chained naked to a bench, rowing twenty hours a day, he was, whipped till he was bloody. All they got to keep 'em going was a bit of bread soaked in wine when the officer went round, just to stop the poor wretches from fainting. A round dozen of them died, and then they flogged 'em just to make sure they was dead and not fakin' it, and after that they chucked 'em in the drink. He survived three years of that, then he got bought by another master and put to work building some barracks or such outside of Argier. Not much changed, he said: still got flogged day and night, but at least he got to lie down from time to time on something that wasn't pitchin' and tossin' on the brine. He saw some right fearful sights there. Men beaten on the soles of their feet – bastinadoe, they call it, the brutes – till they was black and bloody and never walked aright again. One who tried to escape, he was brought back and dragged behind horses round and round through thorns and rocks till he expired; another was cut up into little pieces while he was still alive – one joint at a time till he died screaming. For they hates and loathes Christendom, these Mahometans; nothing pleases them better than to see a Christian suffer. Another poor bastard got away but killed one of his guards in the process. When they finally caught up with him, he'd have been better off making a fight of it and having them kill him then and there. Poor bugger, he was cast off the city walls till his body caught fast on one of the cruel spikes they had embedded there for that very purpose, and there he hung, pierced through thigh and groin, unable to move up or down, in agony, while crows picked at him and women came and threw stones at him and laughed when they drew blood.'

He paused to draw breath and was about to go on, when Rob

said quickly, hoping to bring the subject to a close, 'Truly, they sound a most savage people.'

'They are that. For the most part they are barbarous and intemperate, given to violent humours and monstrous appetites.'

Rob turned to find that another man had come to join their conversation and now leaned on the gunwale, cutting off any chance of escape he thought he had had. It was someone he had met, briefly, at the offices of Hardwicke & Buckle, though when this man and Killigrew had begun their more serious discussions Rob had been ushered away into another room. Even in that short time, the man had created an unfavourable impression. Rob couldn't put his finger on it, for the man was bluff and pleasant enough; yet there was something calculating in his regard. His name was William Marshall, and Rob wondered if he were in some distant way related to Killigrew, for they shared the same narrow features and the same chill blue eyes. But Marshall was an older man than the other, although it might just have been that long exposure to sun and sea had hardened his flesh and burned lines into him which his compatriot lacked.

'You have travelled extensively among them, sir?' Rob asked, curious, and keen to draw the conversation along less lurid lines.

'I have made four or five visits to Barbary and swear each shall be my last,' the other said, tugging at a knot in his grey beard. 'The climate is foul and the inhabitants fouler still. But there is money to be made there, and I'd fain make my fortune sooner than later, and have some years left to enjoy it. Aye, even among the scum of Africa, as good Marlowe would have it.'

'Marlowe?'

Marshall exchanged a mocking glance with the mariner. 'Can he really know nothing of Kit Marlowe, the finest playwright that ever graced our shores?'

The mariner shrugged. 'The lad's young,' he said fairly, 'and Marlowe's been dead and buried longer than he's lived.'

Marshall sighed. 'So much for immortality. Give me a pot of gold and the here and now, I say.' He turned back to Rob, an instructive light in his eye. '"The cruel pirates of Argier, that damned train, the scum of Africa" – he had the right of it, did Marlowe. You should make an effort to see one of his pieces when it comes around your way.' He struck a swashbuckling pose and declaimed in ringing tones:

In vain I see men worship Mahomet
My sword hath sent millions of Turks to Hell,
Slew all his priests, his kinsmen, and his friends,
And yet I live untouch'd by Mahomet . . .

And with a flourish he skewered Rob upon the point of his invisible blade. 'Ah, 'twas a fair few seasons past I was on the stage,' he sighed. 'Great times; fine times. Oh, how they cheered when Tamburlaine burned the Mahometans' sacred book and danced upon its ashes!'

'We don't have much opportunity for seeing plays down in Cornwall,' Rob said stiffly. 'And I'd hope we'd have more respect than to burn a sacred text, even if it were not our own.'

'Lord save me from ever being consigned to the provinces! No wonder John spends so much of his time up in town. If the women of Cornwall are as self-righteous as you, there can be nothing down there to keep him entertained.'

'I always heard Will Shakespeare was more favoured than Kit Marlowe,' the mariner said, eager not to be shut out of the conversation.

Marshall pulled a face. 'Old Shake-a-stick was as soft as butter: always conniving with whichever faction was in power, and wordy as the day is long. God, some of those monologues. I could never remember my bloody lines, always made my parts up as I went along and tried to get a laugh or two.'

'There was that there *Titus Andronicus*, though,' the mariner mused. 'I enjoyed that mightily.'

'That was just him trying to catch the general temper of things. He never did it very well,' Marshall said disparagingly. 'No, Kit had the right of it when it came to brutality. There's no touching his

Tamburlaine, or the Jew. Though I'll give Tourneur his due, he had a proper feel for violence; and Kyd had his moments.'

'Aye, I loved that *Spanish Tragedy* of his,' said the mariner with relish. 'But I went to see *The Renegado* last year and left after an hour, it were so dull.'

'That was Massinger, not Kyd,' Marshall chided him with all the world-weariness of the connoisseur.

Rob was beginning to feel ever more at sea, in all senses of the term. But he must try to get along with these new comrades, so, 'I've heard there's a Moor in *Othello*.'

'Aye,' said the mariner cheerfully. 'Black as soot, but he marries a white girl: stands to reason that's against nature. He gets tricked into believing she's made the two-backed beast with another man, so he strangles her.'

'But the poor lass,' cried Rob; 'that hardly seems very fair!'

'Fair?' Marshall clapped him on the shoulder. 'Life's not fair, lad: surely you've learned that much in your – what? Twenty years?'

'Twenty-three,' Rob corrected.

'Aye, you're young enough yet; but old enough too, not to lose your head over a maid.'

Rob's chin came up dangerously. 'What do you mean?'

'John mentioned you have joined our expedition with a mad scheme to save some poor drab taken by the Sallee Rovers?'

'She's no drab,' Rob said hotly.

Now the mariner was agog. 'Tell on, lad,' he cried eagerly, 'for that sounds like a story worth ten of these play-makers' tales.'

Marshall watched Rob go red to the tips of his ears. 'Go about your duties, man,' he told the sailor shortly. 'This is a subject for the attention of gentlemen alone.'

The mariner cast him a knowing squint. 'En't nothing refined about the doings of men and women – *that* much I know. Women are bitches on heat for all their silks and satins; and men but dogs with their pricks up, and there's an end to it. But if my presence makes ye feel less like *gentlemen*, I'll leave ye to it.'

Marshall watched the man retreat, then he leaned in towards Rob. 'I'd give it up, lad, if you've any sense. These Turks have rampant appetites, especially where there's sweet white meat to be had; and they'll take a boy as hungrily as a girl. The wench'll be long ruined, and then where's the point in a gallant gesture? Come along for the ride, that's fair enough, and if we get lucky and catch a Spanish prize on the way home, you'll be entitled to your share of the spoils. We sail under the King's letter of marque: it'll even be legal. Then you can buy yourself no end of fine fillies and go home a hero.'

'She's my fiancée,' Rob said steadily, gritting his teeth with the effort not to smash the man's nose flat. 'I've sworn to bring her back or die in the attempt.'

Marshall shrugged. 'That's the more likely outcome of the two.'

'You will take me with you as Sir John agreed?'

'John has his own reasons, as usual, no doubt in consigning you to me. You can tag along: but don't expect me to risk my neck for you. It'll be hazardous enough without having to nursemaid a simpleton.'

Rob frowned. 'If you're trading with these people, can't we just sail into their port?'

The elder man smiled, but the expression didn't touch his eyes. 'Nay, lad, far too risky. There are too many factions involved, all at each other's throats, and a fine British vessel bearing a valuable cargo is a great temptation to every one of them. Since Mansell's stupid bloody assault on Argier any British ship in these waters is fair game. John Harrison had to put in as far away as Tétouan when he came on his mission earlier this summer and walked five hundred miles across rough country disguised as a Mahometan pilgrim, crazy bastard!'

Rob had no idea who either Mansell or Harrison was, but he nodded as if such things were public knowledge. 'He made it, then, Harrison?'

'Oh, aye. He always does. Neck of the devil, that man. Went with the King's blessing to try to trade free some of the thousand or so English captives held in Sallee, came away, though, with nary a one.'

'A thousand prisoners?'

Marshall looked at him askance. 'The Turks have been stealing the poor bastards off merchant ships and fishing vessels for years, and no one's done a damn thing about it. Not enough money in the Treasury to pay for a decent navy after King James's extravagances, and his son's no better with the purse-strings, and of course now we're at war with Spain again and there's bigger fish to fry. Harrison's a bit of a lone adventurer, in it for the glory, though I dare say he's making a pretty penny on the side with bribes and "fees" and whatnot. But war opens up opportunities for the canny, that's what I always say.' And he winked, then took himself off to the galley for a sup, as he put it.

That night Rob tossed and turned. If the King's agent had been unable to bring the captives away, what chance did he have? It sounded as if he were about to set foot in some region of Hell populated by a legion of monsters and fiends. The prospect frightened him: it was so far removed from his own life at Kenegie, where the worst you were likely to encounter was some poor desperate sheep-thief trying to make off with one of the flock or some travelling mountebank trying to con you out of your wages down at the Dolphin. He had never even learned to wield a sword, though he'd brought one with him; such a skill was rarely called for in rural Cornwall. He could, though, he told himself fiercely, defend himself well enough with fists or a cudgel. And perhaps this man Marshall – who seemed both wily and experienced – might help him to succeed where others had failed. From the little pouch he wore about his neck, Rob took out his grandmother's ring, the one Cat had pressed back into his hand with the instruction to give it to her again at a better time. And what better time might there be than when he had saved her from the pirates? An eternal optimist, Rob closed his hand around the ring and made himself fall asleep on that thought.

The next day they slipped past Salé in the dark and ran some way up the coast till all the lights of human habitation were passed. Then the ship dropped anchor, and Marshall came and shook Rob awake in his berth. 'Rub this on your face, wrap your great, pale head in this turban cloth and keep your sword in its scabbard,' he advised, passing Rob a pot of some acrid-smelling stuff. 'We need no glint of light betraying us. The area we go into is alive with desperadoes. Take only the barest essentials in a pack you can carry on your back: we will move fast and light.'

And with that he was gone, leaving Rob to do as he was told, his stomach tight. The ash paste felt gritty as he rubbed it into his skin, and the length of turban cloth was stubbornly uncooperative in his clumsy hands, but at last he made his way up on to deck. The first mate and another hand awaited them there and accompanied them in the skiff they lowered, rowing as hard as they could towards a long line of surf running on to a flat black shore. Rob could sense their fear at sculling in towards a land full of devils.

Marshall's teeth were white in the moonlight as he grimaced at Rob. 'Putting in is always the worst thing. I hate to get wet.'

The keel crunched on pebbles then, and they were out and running, the water shockingly cold as it penetrated every layer of clothing. Glancing over his shoulder a moment later, Rob saw that the sailors had already turned the skiff hard about and were pulling swiftly away towards the black outline of the ship. There was no going back now. He looked towards the shore of Morocco, a fabled land he had heard of only in the drunken tales of broken-down old sailors in the Penzance inns, who spat and cursed and talked of pirates and heathens.

Marshall was a good distance ahead now, ploughing through the rolling breakers with his head down, his breath soughing as loudly as a pole-axed bull's. Rob ploughed after him through the white water, blundering from thigh-deep to knee-deep, until he hit harmless rills that barely covered his boots. Then he was on dry land and crunching up the pebble beach behind Marshall, every step a loud advertisement to any murderous fiend who might be waiting for them, just out of sight, among the rocks or distant trees.

A long bar of stones gave way suddenly again to water. 'God's body!' Marshall swore. 'They've put us down on the wrong bloody side of the river! This wretched coastline all looks the same from the sea, not that any of those want-wits could read a chart if they tried. Now we're as like to bloody drown inland as if they'd thrown us overboard.'

The lagoon, however, was shallow, and they waded across without further mishap. On the other side it gave way to marsh and reed beds, where a chorus of outraged frogs and a pair of disturbed plovers broke the night silence with a lively racket. Now the Londoner was apoplectic. 'That's right,' he growled, 'tell everyone we're here. Christ's blood, I hate these natural places! Fill 'em up with sand and brick 'em over, I say. What use is God's good land if a man can't even walk upon it without filling his damn boots and having a legion of foul, inedible beasts complain of his presence?'

Rob had spent much of his childhood exploring the reed beds and marshes just outside Market-Jew. He knew there were worse environments – the back alleys of Westminster, for one. He availed himself of a stave of driftwood and, prodding ahead with this makeshift staff, led them through the marsh on to ground that alternated between stinking algae-filled pools with spongy stands of vegetation and reed thickets. Some while later a small, sharp pain announced itself in his calf; minutes later another on the back of his thigh. He knew at once their cause: leeches. He thought longingly of the flint he had so carefully stowed in his pack. They would have to be burned off, but not here in the open. After that with every step he imagined a plague of them fastening their little jaws in his flesh.

For an hour or more they toiled through this hellish landscape, and then stomped across a dreary salt flat, which finally gave way to rock and scrub and a steep incline just as the first rays of dawn lanced red as a burst boil over the sea.

'God's bollocks!' Marshall swore. 'We'd better be in the shelter of those trees before sun-up or we're sitting ducks. Marmora Forest is swarming with outcasts and escaped slaves who'd slit your throat as soon as look at you.'

Uphill they staggered, thighs and calves protesting at this rough treatment after weeks of doing very little on the rolling sea. Rob could feel how his muscles had wasted from lack of nutriment and use in the few short weeks of the passage. Marshall began to pull away from him, and so Rob shut his mind to his pain, to the pack heavy on his back and the unaccustomed sword banging the backs of his legs, and struggled after him, for if he lost Marshall every chance of life – let alone success – was gone. Soon he found a child's verse going round and round in his head, until his feet were pounding the rocks and scrub to its rhythms:

> When I am dead and in my grave
> And all my bones are rotten
> By this may I remembered be
> When I should be forgotten.

Its grim rhymes drove him up the rise. It was only much later, sitting with his back to a tree as Marshall scanned the oil-cloth paper of his rudimentary map, after he had removed his leeches (seven: for luck) and his boots (emptied of water, weed and one crushed frog), that he realized whence the verse had come: a sampler Cat had sewn as a girl, revelling in its macabre tone. It now hung in the dark corridor outside her door in the servants' quarters at Kenegie. How many times had he stood there, gazing blindly at its childish stitching, as he gathered his thoughts before knocking at that door? The scene was so painfully clear in his head that he almost wept.

'Might I ask what our business is with these people?' he asked Marshall at last.

'No,' the other said shortly. 'The details of that matter lie between the company and our trading partners, and have nothing to do with you.'

'Am I not now a part of that company, given that my task is to guard you and the papers you carry?'

'You are neither one thing nor the other, lad. Quite why John thought I needed a lumpen oaf as a bodyguard, I cannot for the life of me imagine. As far as I am concerned, you are here on sufferance, and if you keep on asking me damnfool questions, I will skewer you myself and save the brigands the trouble.'

Rob sat there, watching his boots steam as the sun hit them. At last he could bear it no longer. 'Then perhaps I might ask just one more question: how will we leave Salé, if we ever arrive in one piece?'

Marshall sighed. 'In five days the *Rose* will be off Salé awaiting my sign. Once they receive it they'll sail in as close as they may to take us off.'

And Rob had to be satisfied with this very little piece of information. At last Marshall folded the map away in his sack and told him to get his boots on.

'We'll have to move quietly through this wretched forest. No talking: and watch your feet. There are trips and holes and spikes and all manner of traps for the unwary. Unsavoury folk inhabit this region. Some live here, some take refuge here, and some, like us, are just passing through. But they all have a reason for hiding themselves, and that reason generally has a criminal root: there's no law in the forest, except the law of survival.'

'It seems to me', Rob said, taking this in, 'that we'd still have been better off sailing into the port under full sail and with our guns at the ready, factions or no factions.'

'You are an extremely naive young man, Robert Bolitho. I will spell it out for you. We could not be seen to enter the pirates' nest for a variety of reasons, but the most important reason of all is that if anyone carries word back to England of our dealings – and there are many in that place who come and go as they please and have a host of connections all across Europe – we are all likely to hang. Is that reason enough for you?'

Rob stared at him. 'My God,' he said at last. 'What have I stepped into here?'

'As I have said before, you should have left well alone and stayed at home.'

'Well, I am here now and damned,' Rob said grimly.

27

Well I am heere nowe & damned I sayde to hym, but how damned I was I did not then knowe . . .

'I wonder who he wrote this for,' I said at last, folding the paper and putting it aside among the debris of our breakfast things. We were sitting out on the roof terrace at a rickety old table Idriss had set up there, a huge faded parasol stuck into a concrete block keeping the worst of the mid-morning rays off my pale English skin.

'It's not a journal?'

'It looks more like part of a letter. See how the photocopy shows the ragged edges all the way around? There's no sign of a gutter, or any deformation of the words as there would be if Michael had photocopied a book. Strange. It's on a different sort of paper to the other one too, the letter to Sir Arthur Harris, and the writing looks different, smaller and neater.'

'Maybe he wrote the letter to his employer in a hurry.'

'Or as a young man . . .' I bit my lip. 'So you think Robert Bolitho really came all the way to Morocco to save Catherine from slavery?'

'It was certainly his intention: and he must have succeeded, or the book would never have made it back to England.'

I sighed. 'It's a very romantic story. Perhaps it was a fairytale, after all.'

Idriss made a face. 'If he succeeded, though, I do not know why he thinks he is damned. Perhaps he married her, and she turned out to be a bad wife who made him unhappy. Perhaps she was unfaithful, or cruel, or ran away. There is more to the story than we yet know.'

'Mmm,' I replied non-committally, unwilling to confront the implications of this.

Catherine's journal had come to a sudden end in a rather unsatisfactory manner amid a welter of domestic detail. I read that *everie daie the women of the kasbah come to the howse to sitte with mee & sew. Wee worke in silkes of everie color known to Man. I have never seene such glorious hues except in the flowers of Lady Harrys garden at Kenegy.* She explained how *Hasna has taut mee the makyng of the dish they calle the decorated face*, whatever that might be. I read of a robe she had sewn; how she had prepared her own kohl from a substance bought in the souk, which she spelled 'sook'; how she was learning a few words of their language. All this was fascinating information in terms of a historical document; but to me, I am ashamed to admit, it was deeply frustrating. She sounded, I thought, picking through this minutiae peppered with words I did not recognize, rather to be enjoying her time as a Salé slave, if that was indeed what she was: for teaching embroidery in a rather grand-sounding house with no more onerous duties to perform certainly did not fit my picture of the life I would have foreseen for a woman in her situation. Most annoying of all, it did not relate what had happened when Rob miraculously appeared to whisk her back to Cornwall.

'It seems to me,' Idriss pressed, 'that your Michael holds the other part of this puzzle.'

It seemed that way to me too, and the idea made me feel deeply uncomfortable. The photocopies had been bait: he wanted the book and he was using Rob's letters to lure me to him. I did not want to give him the book, but I did desperately want to know the other side to the story. Even so, I was not yet prepared to face Michael.

Instead, I asked, 'What time do we meet your friend Khaled?'

'He will meet us at two at a café near the station.'

I looked at my watch. It was just coming up to eleven thirty. 'And what shall we do till then?'

'Let me show you the souks Catherine would have visited, and where I grew up.'

*

I put on the dark-blue djellaba he had brought me the evening before over my jeans; but the white headscarf foxed me completely: it simply couldn't contain my abundance of hair. I tried to wear it down my back inside the robe, but whatever I did with my hair, the cloth kept slipping off my head. Eventually I ended up with it screwed up into a knot, and with my hair all over the place.

'Damn!' I grumbled furiously, and turned suddenly to find a stranger in a grey robe and a blue turban leaning up against the door jamb, watching me silently. It took me a good three seconds to realize that this exotic creature was in fact Idriss.

'Here,' he said, taking the scarf from me. 'Let me. With several sisters I have had some practice.'

His fingers brushed my neck, and I couldn't tell whether or not it was accidental; then the soft cotton followed, and moments later the fabric had been wound neatly around my head, and I was wearing the veil.

Thus disguised, we went out into the world.

The medina was bustling with traffic: a bizarre mix of human, animal and machine. Just as you thought you had entered a ped-estrianized area, a man on a scooter would come roaring around the corner, hand pressed exigently to his horn, and everyone would flatten themselves against the narrow walls. Quite how the donkeys coped with such indignities, I had no idea, but they seemed philo-sophical about it, standing patiently in their traces or tethered to their posts while ever greater burdens were added to their carts or backs.

The Moroccans in the souk did not appear to share this pacific philosophy. We passed one woman screeching in fury at a man who had just cut a length of pale-blue cotton from a bolt of fabric. It looked as if she might set about him with the bale, for her hands were flailing everywhere, and he was ducking away from her as if from a physical assault. Idriss caught me staring. 'A disagreement about the price,' he chuckled. 'A classic ploy, to complain about it only when the cloth has been cut and then blame the merchant. My aunt used to do it all the time. Then she'd walk off in a fury, leaving the poor man with his head in his hands, only to return a few minutes later and graciously offer him half the price for it.'

'And he'd let her take it?' I was appalled.

'Of course: he'd already quoted her twice the price he expected to get for it, so they parted satisfied.'

I shook my head. It seemed a very stressful way of doing business, yet it summed up something about the national character: Morocco appeared to be all about social interaction, while Britain was largely about avoiding it. No one was self-conscious about showing their feelings here. I saw men kissing one another in greeting and walking together hand in hand. 'They are good friends,' Idriss explained, 'and not in the euphemistic way Europeans use that phrase. Here, friendship is to be prized, and when people ask how you are they really want to know, not just hear a stock phrase which keeps them at bay.'

I smiled. 'So, how are you today, Idriss el-Kharkouri?'

He stopped still there in the street and turned to look at me. 'Before you ask me a question like that, Julia Lovat, you had better be sure you want to hear the answer.'

Colour flooded my cheeks. I could not help myself: I looked away.

For a while after that, we walked in near silence through the medina, passing stall after stall of produce and kitchen goods, patisseries and cafés. We turned a corner and came upon an old man with his wares spread out on a black sheet in front of him. A crowd of men had gathered to listen to his patter, their faces rapt. I craned for a better view, and one of the men turned, saw me and glared. Several of his companions followed suit, until Idriss drew me away.

'Why did they stare at me like that? They seemed so hostile.'

'They didn't want a woman penetrating their male mysteries.'

'What was he selling?' I demanded angrily. 'I want to know.'

'Impotency cures, aphrodisiacs, substances for prolonging . . . the experience.' He laughed. '*La merde de la baleine.*'

'What?'

'Whale shit. Whales are reputed to have enormous . . . parts. It's sympathetic magic.'

'But how on *earth* would you gather whale shit . . . oh, I see. He's a con artist.'

'It's probably some harmless clay. Anyway, he seemed to be doing a good trade. Good luck to him. *Al-hamdulillah.*'

'Out in the open, in public, too. I thought sex was a taboo subject.'

'You do have some odd ideas. The Qur'an says it is important for a man to satisfy his wife.'

'It does? What an excellent religion.'

After that, we walked in greater ease, with Idriss pointing out unusual items to me: silver hands of Fatima to ward off the evil eye, rose-water sprinklers, musk and ambergris. At one stall he bought me a small dark-blue lump of rock with an odd metallic sheen to it which the old woman wrapped carefully in a piece of torn newspaper. 'It's kohl,' he explained. 'The same as Catherine would have bought here. My sister can show you how to use it.'

He showed me the colourful pottery made at Safi, further down the coast, and exchanged greetings with the ancient, toothless merchant. As we walked away, he told me, 'Every Saturday I came here first thing in the morning before he set up his stall and he let me unwrap the plates.'

'You loved the pottery so much?'

He grinned. 'No: some of them came wrapped in sheets torn out of old comic books – *bandes dessinées* – which my father wouldn't let me have at home. He was a very strict man, my father: only the Qur'an was considered suitable reading material for a boy of six. He certainly wouldn't have approved of the decadent adventures of Rodeo Rick or Pif or Asterix and Obelix. I used to sit at the back of the stall, lost in all these marvellous fragments of story, while my brothers chanted out their verses at home.'

On the Rue des Consuls we found the ubiquitous carpet-sellers, their Aladdin's caves hung with fabulous lanterns and gorgeous colour. I watched one of the merchants flourishing rugs at a pair of tourists who had foolishly stopped to admire the display and were now helplessly trapped. No one had tried to sell me anything. At first I had thought this was because of the forbidding presence of Idriss, though I soon realized it had more to do with the robe and hijab I wore, enabling me to move camouflaged and untargeted through the bazaar. Feeling smug, I watched the two Europeans – she in her expensively cut dress and Prada sandals, he, slightly paunchy in chinos and blue seersucker shirt – wriggle like hooked fish under the carpet-seller's assiduous attentions. Now another man had joined in, flinging carpets dramatically to the floor in front of them. At least a dozen carpets had thus been unfurled: how could they possibly refuse to buy after such a display? One of the carpets came down on top of the woman's foot, and I saw her jump back and steady herself on her husband's arm, her face turned up to him in an expression of dismay.

It was Anna.

Or rather it wasn't. It was Anna *and* Michael, joined together like some symbiotic, two-headed creature, rearing away from attack. Michael had his arm around her, possessive and protective, although he looked just as powerless as she did to ward off the relentless sales pitch.

For a moment I couldn't breathe. Then, instinctively, I caught Idriss's arm, my fingers closing on his hard biceps. 'Quickly, we have to go quickly!'

I turned and dragged him away, past the wrought-iron-sellers and the goatskin lamp stalls, until we were out of the medina and by the side of the ring road with traffic roaring past.

'What's the matter with you?'

I must have looked as if I was about to faint, for he took me by the elbow and ushered me along the road and into an open doorway, which seemed to lead to an unattended reception area for a tiny hotel. Idriss marched to a door at the back, opened it and shouted a name. Seconds later a young man in jeans and a Manchester United shirt appeared, and the pair embraced.

'This is one of my other brothers, Sadiq,' Idriss said, grinning.

'And this is Julia Lovat. She needs tea, plenty of sugar: see what you can do.'

Sadiq gazed at me, awestruck, said something unintelligible to Idriss and promptly disappeared.

'He says you have eyes like Lady Diana,' Idriss told me, steering me around the corner to a dimly lit area of sofas and low tables.

I snorted. 'How ridiculous. He just means they're blue.'

He regarded me solemnly for a moment. 'No,' he said. 'It's your Englishness. It is very . . . exotic.'

Exotic: that was how I thought of him. It was disorientating to realize that the converse might be true. 'Such shameless flattery.' I wagged a finger at him. 'You should be selling snake oil and whale shit alongside that old charlatan in the bazaar.'

His eyes gleamed. 'Another string to my bow.'

Sadiq came with a tray of tea things. I watched Idriss pour out the golden liquid from a deliberately showy height, so that it crashed into the little glass like a miniature waterfall, and then drank it down without complaining about the diabetes-inducing quantity of sugar it contained.

'Now tell me why you ran away.' I must have looked as uncomfortable as I felt, for he paused. 'Oh, I am an idiot. Of course – you saw Michael.'

I bent my head. 'Yes.'

He frowned. 'But I was keeping watch for him – I cannot believe I missed him.'

'He was in one of the carpet-sellers' booths.'

'There was someone, a couple . . . the woman was small, dark, very chic.'

'That was Anna. His wife.' I watched my hands, held loosely in my lap, begin to tremble and told myself the sugar must be having its effect.

Idriss reached across the table and tilted my chin up. 'Julia, I think you had better tell me your story – all of it. It strikes me that there is a lot more to it than the possession of an antique book.'

And so, staring fixedly at the table top, I let it all spill out. My friendship with Anna, my furtive relationship with her husband, my terrors of being discovered, my fear that he would leave me, the way it had shaped the last seven years of my life – a long catalogue of betrayal and moral cowardice. Not once did I raise my head to look him in the eye; I could not. For, suddenly, I realized that it mattered desperately what Idriss thought of me. How and when had that happened? And this first realization was immediately followed by the sickening certainty that by telling him I would ensure that henceforth he would regard me with disgust.

When at last I had finished spewing out my confession, silence fell between us like a thick glass screen. When an eternity of several seconds had clapsed, I risked a glance upwards, but he was not looking at me. His gaze, cool and distant, was fixed on the coloured glass of the window behind me, as if he wished himself out in the hot, clean sea air beyond, rather than here in the stifling gloom with a woman who had betrayed everyone of importance in her life, and in the process had lost everything, including her self-respect. What must he think of me, this man whose life was so simple and straightforward? He had so little, by the standards of the culture that had raised me; but in all the ways that mattered, he had so much.

'I am horribly ashamed of myself,' I said quietly into the stiff silence.

His gaze came back to me slowly. Was I imagining it, or was there cold disdain in those dark eyes now?

'We must go,' he said tonelessly. 'Khaled will be waiting for us.'

He said nothing else to me for the rest of the afternoon.

The café was on the Rue de Baghdad, just behind the central railway station. Khaled turned out to be a rotund little man in his middle fifties with a smooth, unlined face and twinkling, curious eyes. He wore a white gandoura and, incongruously, a green baseball cap bearing the letters ASS across its crown. He caught my hands and shook them warmly. As my eyes strayed back to the cap he laughed delightedly.

'You like my hat? It is my favourite,' he said in excellent, barely accented English. 'I wear it particularly for surprising my American students, who find it hilarious. Stands for *Association Sportive de Salé. C'est rigolant, non?*'

Idriss managed a thin smile, while I nodded, grateful for this break in the tension.

'As I said on the telephone, Julia has a book she wants to show you for your opinion,' Idriss started, as if wishing to complete the task as quickly as possible. He switched to Arabic, talking fast, and Khaled's expression changed to one of shock. A paranoid part of me imagined Idriss telling him that the woman opposite him, looking so innocent in her hijab, was in fact an adulterous infidel, a creature of no morals who had by dubious means come by a treasure she did not merit; that they should relieve her of the book and send her back to the world she came from, where such behaviour was commonplace. I felt my cheeks flushing anew.

'May I see it?' the professor asked at last.

Idriss sat back, his expression closed and remote, and lit up a cigarette.

I reached into my handbag, extricated *The Needle-Woman's Glorie* and passed it to him. At the sight of it, Khaled's eyes grew round and intent. He spread a paper napkin across the melamine table, as if decades of spilled coffee, sugar and ash could by osmosis insinuate their way into its covers to desecrate its contents, and laid Catherine's book down with the reverence of a man handling a religious relic. His fingers brushed the calfskin, caressed the blind bands on the spine. Then, with infinite care, he opened it and began to read.

'*Incroyable.*' The four syllables came separately, the *r* rolled dramatically.

'Is it real?' I asked.

I had sat like a mouse for the best part of two and a half hours, avoiding Idriss's gaze, instead drinking an unpalatably strong coffee and focusing on the professor turning the pages and tilting the book this way and that. At one point he had produced a magnifying glass, at another a small dictionary. He had tutted and hummed and taken his baseball cap off and scratched his head, revealing an unfortunate comb-over, muttered to himself in Arabic, and then in French, and said something to Idriss that he did not translate for my benefit. He had laughed and flicked back a few pages, as if searching for a reference, before reading on. Now he met my concerned look with a vast grin.

'Real?'

'Or is it a clever forgery, a fake?'

'*Ma chère* Julia, it's as real as you or I.'

By this stage, light-headed with hunger and dread, I was feeling so insubstantial as to not be very real at all. 'Sorry, can you explain?'

'There is, as far as I am aware, no other account in any language by a female captive from the early days of the Salé corsairs, even before their independent divan was established; and the fact that it appears to be in her own hand makes it a unique artefact. The Sidi Mohammed al-Ayyachi is a well-documented character, and in the course of my own research I have come across references to a lieutenant of his called Qasem bin Hamed bin Moussa Dib, so to see him featured here is quite fascinating.'

'Who?' I frowned.

'Qasem bin Hamed bin Moussa Dib, known variously in the legends as the Djinn or the Jackal – *dib* means fox or jackal in Arabic – or the man of Andalusia. He appears to have been one of the Hornacheros, Andalusian Moors expelled from Spain by Philip III. According to the stories his family was butchered by the Inquisition, and he returned to Rabat. He supposedly learned his corsair skills under the tutelage of the infamous Dutchman Jan Jansz, otherwise known as Murad Raïs. Qasem was Admiral of the Salé Fleet, after which he was elected a raïs – a captain of the fleet – and fought as an *al-ghuzat*: a holy warrior in the war against the enemies of the Prophet. This tells us things about Qasem no one ever knew: that he was more closely allied to the notorious English pirate John Ward than to Jan Jansz, that he led the fleet to the English coast in 1625, that he was more cultured and more complex than any of the legends infer.'

'You speak about him with far more respect than I'd have thought due to a pirate chief.'

Khaled smiled. 'I might say the same of your Robin Hood or your Francis Drake; and certainly of your Richard the Lionheart. One culture's hero is another culture's villain: it all depends whose side you're on. History is a very malleable thing, usually written by the victors.'

'I always preferred Saladin,' I said softly.

'Another great *al-ghuzat*: and, unlike your Richard, merciful in victory.'

'And all this about the embroidery: can it be true that Catherine taught the local women her skills?'

Khaled spread his hands. 'About that I fear I am no expert.' He leaned forward. 'But it ends very suddenly, this journal. Do you know what happened to her, to this Catherine Tregenna?'

'There is more to her tale.' I showed him the photocopies Michael had left at the riad for me.

He read the sheets, then turned them over, searching for more. 'But where is the rest? You cannot leave me in such suspense. The young man followed her here: was he successful in his ransom bid, did she return to your country with him?'

'I don't know,' I admitted.

'But we must find out! I very much want to read the account of this' – he scanned the first page again – 'this Robert Bolitho.'

'A friend has the letters,' I said uncomfortably.

'Well, then, that's simple enough. Excellent. I shall very much look forward to reading them. Now, in the meantime, Julia, tell me: what are you going to do with your book?'

I hesitated. 'I'm not sure. What do you think I should do with it?'

The professor's eyes gleamed. 'It is a magnificent treasure containing unique insights into the history of my country. It would be a tragedy for it to disappear. I would truly love to do some further research on it, to produce a paper . . . maybe even a book of my own.'

He was candid at least. 'For now,' I said carefully, 'you could have a photocopy. While I decide what I am going to do with it.'

He beamed at me. 'That would be wonderful.'

We found a copy shop around the corner from the Ministry of Justice, and I went outside and sat on the pavement in the late-afternoon sun while Khaled, with the infinite care of a man used to handling old books, made a copy. Idriss came out and leaned up against the door, smoked another cigarette in an agitated fashion, glanced at me once and looked as if he were about to say something, then went back inside without a word.

At last Khaled gave me back Catherine's book, and we shook hands. 'Let me give you my telephone number,' he said. 'So that you can call me when you make your decision, yes?'

I smiled. 'OK.' We both took out our mobiles, and I gave Khaled my number while I turned mine on. Méditel came up on the screen after a few seconds, followed by a powerful beep.

You have seven missed calls

Oh, hell. There were also three messages: two from Michael and one – my heart thudded – from Anna. Avoiding the messages, I keyed Khaled's number into the phone, locked the keypad and stowed it in my bag. 'I will phone you,' I promised the professor, and stood back as he and Idriss embraced and bade each other farewell.

When he had disappeared from view, Idriss turned and looked at me. 'What now?' he asked suddenly.

It was the first time he had addressed me since we had left his brother's place of work. The sun beat down on me, and my head pounded unpleasantly. We had walked to the corner which gave on to the Avenue Mohammed V and were approaching the Gare de la Ville before I could find the words to reply. 'I've really messed everything up,' I said miserably. I felt sick. 'And I know you despise me for it, and I don't blame you. But I'm going to try to put everything right, I am.'

I looked up at him, but the sun was behind him and I couldn't see his face. The next thing I knew, the world spun and I was on the ground, black stars dancing before my eyes.

'Julia!'

He hauled me upright and fairly carried me up the steps and into the shade of the station concourse. Soon I found myself sitting on an orange plastic chair with a huge pastry and a bottle of mineral water in front of me.

'You haven't eaten anything all day,' he said sternly.

'Neither have you.'

'I am used to going without, and to the sun here, which you are not. I thought the hijab would help, but the heat today is unforgiving.'

Much like you, I thought, but did not say.

I bit into the pastry, and little flakes of almond cascaded on to the plate. Over his shoulder I could see on the board that the next train to Casablanca had been announced, leaving in fifteen minutes. Just enough time to buy a ticket and run away again. The thought was tempting: I had my passport and ticket with me, and there was nothing in the bag at Idriss's house I could not live without. I could spend the night in an anonymous hotel in Casa and catch a flight back to London the following day, and bury my head in my new apartment. And then what? And then . . . my future stretched before me like a gaping black void. *Lucky Catherine*, I thought. Someone had loved her enough to cross oceans for her, to risk his life to bring her home to be his bride. Rather than chasing her across continents with his wife in tow in order to take back a gift he had given her to seal the end of their love affair.

'I owe you an apology,' Idriss said suddenly.

'Heatstroke,' I laughed feebly. 'Not your fault.'

'Not that. For today, for not talking to you after you shared your story with me. I should have said something, but I did not know what to say. You brought some painful memories back, and you shamed me by your honesty.'

I thought for a moment his grasp of English had failed him and he meant he was ashamed of me, but, by the time I realized this was not what he had said, he was talking fast and I had to struggle to keep up.

'When Francesca's contract came to an end and she left, I was devastated. I wanted to die. For a while I thought I would, and that would be the best solution to the mess I was in, but somehow I kept living and eating and breathing, and, although I was a lesser man for a long time afterwards, I was still me and still alive and my family stopped me from falling apart completely. We kept in touch for a while after she went back to the States. She told me that she was going to divorce her husband, and asked if I would leave Morocco to be with her. I even went to their consulate to see about a visa, but of course they wouldn't give me one: a single Muslim man from a country which had generated a number of wanted radical Islamists, heading for the US for no apparently good reason just after 9/11? I wouldn't have given me a visa either. And of course I couldn't say anything about my relationship with Francesca: she had been my university tutor, and she was married: our relationship was scandalous on both fronts. They could have imprisoned me for it, and banned her from ever returning. So after that I gave up my studies and worked the taxi full time, every day around the clock, just to forget, and to pay my family back in money what they had given me in support. That was six years ago. So you see, Julia: I do not despise you because I too know what it is to lose my heart, and in the worst of circumstances.'

I didn't know what to say. I wasn't shocked – but I was surprised, for Idriss did not strike me as a man who would give himself over to passion: he had seemed calm and restrained, a man in control of himself, at peace with his world. How deceptive appearances can be. I leaned across the table, forgetting where I was, and put my hand on his arm. He leaped back, as if I had burned him.

People were looking at us now. It was obviously one thing to carry in a heatstruck woman; but quite another for that woman to show even the least physical affection in public.

'You said, before you fainted, "I'm going to try to put everything right." What did you mean by that?'

I took out my phone and laid it on the table between us. 'I can't keep running away. There are things I must face up to, amends I must make, if I can.

Michael's first text message read: *Why did u leave yr hotel? Where r u? Pls call. M*

The second was more frantic: *Need to spk to u urgently. Call me.*

I deleted them both. Anna's message was the third. I didn't much want to read it, but I knew I must. Swallowing hard, I opened her message: *Julia, I know everything, but you are still my friend & I need to see you. There is something I must tell you, & something to show you. Will you call me? Love, Anna.*

Tears sprang to my eyes, and I dashed them away with the back of my hand. *I know everything, but you are still my friend . . . Love, Anna.* She knew it all. She knew Michael was cheating on her, and that it was with me. And yet, after all that I had done to her, she had the grace to say something that touched my heart and reminded me of the girls we had once been. Abruptly I realized that all this time I had been afraid not of losing Michael but of the thought that Anna would discover what I had done to her. Michael and I had tied ourselves together with bonds forged of our guilt; now that what we had done lay exposed to the light, I could see it for the paltry thing it was. A weight seemed to be lifted from me. I was free at last; for all my failings, I understood that I deserved better than a man who could turn a smiling face to his wife every morning, every night, for seven long years, and lie and lie and lie.

There and then, with Idriss looking on, I made a phone call and set up a meeting.

'Anna?'

'Julia? Good grief, is that really you?'

My hand flew up to the hijab. I grinned. 'Yes, it's really me. And this is my friend Idriss.'

I saw her eyes widen as Idriss stepped forward and bent his head to kiss her hand. '*Ravi de faire votre connaissance. Bienvenue à Rabat, madame,*' he said, then turned to me. 'I'll wait for you in the bar, shall I?' And with a flourish of his robe he swept through the modern hotel lobby, exchanging friendly Arabic greetings with the staff, looking for all the world like a medieval camel trader. I shook my head, grinning. Did he know everyone in Rabat?

Anna ordered some tea to be sent up to the room. 'English tea,' she told the man at the front desk firmly. '*Thé anglais* not the mint stuff. Twinings English Breakfast if you've got it.' Then she took me by the arm and led me upstairs. I had half expected to find Michael waiting there, but the room was empty, which was a relief.

'That chap you were with,' Anna said, closing the door. 'Incredibly handsome. Amazing profile – like a male Nefertiti. Wherever did you find him?'

'He found me,' I replied evasively. An awkward silence fell. I forced myself to break it. 'Anna, look, I have to say this. I am so, so sorry. I know it's a completely inadequate thing to say after what I've done, and for all this time, but I do mean it.'

'It's not really something you can say sorry for, is it?'

'No. I've got no excuses, none at all. I know it has destroyed our friendship.'

'To say nothing of my marriage.'

I hung my head.

'Julia, I've been through it all with Michael, and I really don't want to go over it again. It's over now, isn't it?'

I nodded, tight-lipped.

'Then there's very little point in raking over the ashes. I think I knew it, right from the start. In fact, when I married him, I felt weirdly guilty, as if I'd taken him away from you. Left alone, you'd probably have made each other a lot happier than Michael and I have made one another.' She gave a bitter little laugh. 'Which wouldn't be difficult. But in the end I've managed to salvage something positive out of the situation.'

'Fresh start?'

She nodded. 'You could say that. I'm not sure I'd go that far. But after all this time I'm finally pregnant. It's made me wretchedly ill, but I really want this baby, have wanted it for a long time.'

I remembered her now on the platform at Penzance Station looking pale and grim. Pregnant. With Michael's child. And of course he, the eternal coward, had not had the guts to tell me that part of the story. I almost laughed. Michael hated children – the noise, the mess, the endless need for attention. He was obsessive about birth control with me, always checking condoms for defects, and had once marched me to the pharmacist after we'd broken one and demanded a morning-after pill. A wicked little voice inside me whispered, *serves you right*. Anna, with her trademark determination, had got her way in the end.

'Congratulations, Anna. That's wonderful news.' And I actually meant it.

'I'm giving up the job, going freelance. I've got a year's contract from the magazine, and after that who knows? Michael's in a frightful state about it all.'

'Money,' I said succinctly.

She gave a short, humourless laugh. 'To a large extent, yes.'

'So that's why you want the book. I expect it's worth a small fortune if you know the right people.'

'No, no, it's not that –' She was interrupted by a knock at the door and got up to open it. 'Oh . . . it's you.' She sounded surprised. 'Thank you, how very kind . . .'

'It is no trouble,' Idriss said, bringing the tea tray in. He looked across at me. 'I just wanted to be sure everything was all right.'

I smiled at him, so tall and grave in his turban and robe. Under other circumstances I would have hugged him. It was probably just as well Anna was there. 'Everything is fine.'

He set the tray down. 'Lipton's, I'm afraid,' he said to Anna, 'though they'd probably have told you it was Twinings.' He gave me a barely perceptible wink, then bowed and swept out of the room.

Anna watched him go. 'Does he work here?' she asked, puzzled.

'No,' I said, grinning.

'He seems concerned about you.'

'He's a very . . . good man.'

'Do be careful, Julia. You hear dreadful stories about women getting involved with Moroccans who are just after a British passport and their money.'

'It's not always about money, Anna.'

She gave me a quick, nervous smile. 'I know. Sorry. Look, let's allow the tea to steep a little. I want to show you something.'

She got up and crossed the room to where a smart Mulberry carry-on lay on a valise stand against the wall. After opening this, she unzipped an inner compartment and brought out a small parcel wrapped in white tissue paper that she laid upon the bed.

'When Alison told us about the mention of a Tree of Knowledge design in the book Michael gave you, I remembered the family heirloom my great-aunt left me along with the Suffolk house. She said that it had been commissioned for the church at Framlingham, St Michael's, but that it was never finished and never used. Something about the Puritans not favouring figurative art or any kind of decoration that might distract attention during prayer. So I went up to fetch it . . .'

She opened the tissue to reveal a long piece of white linen, yellowing from age, touched here and there with muted autumn colours.

I could not speak. I reached across her and touched it reverently, unfolding the final part until Catherine's Tree of Knowledge lay before us, ancient and incongruous against the bright synthetic of the hotel bedspread. Only part of the embroidery was completed – the intricate border of interwoven leaves and flowers, a rabbit, a couple of doves and an apple, all beautifully and realistically delineated, and above these the tree itself, wreathed in leaves, with the serpent winding down its trunk towards the figure of Eve, her long hair covering her slim white nakedness. Adam was outlined faintly on the other side of her, but his features were blank and blurred, and the rest remained unfinished. Even so, it was magnificent. I sank to my knees, overcome.

'The Countess of Salisbury's altar frontal,' I said at last.

'Is it? Are you sure?'

I dug in my handbag and brought out Catherine's book, turned to the sketch she had made and held it out alongside the cloth.

Anna looked from one to the other, delighted. Her fingers traced the outline of Eve in Cat's sketch, then on the fabric. 'Fantastic. How incredible: it really is, then. The Countess of Salisbury's altar frontal. A genuine seventeenth-century tapestry.'

'It's embroidery, not tapestry,' I corrected her. 'And I can't believe you flew to Morocco with such a valuable thing in your hand luggage!'

She shrugged. 'I knew I had to persuade you to do something for me, and that it would be hard to do that with just a photo: besides, all this has come together through so many bizarre circumstances that I have to believe fate has a hand in it.'

I looked at her. 'What is it you want me to do?'

'You have the book, and that's the proof.'

'Proof?'

'Proof of provenance. For the V&A. It's what Great-Aunt Sappho would have wanted. I have a friend who works in the Publications Department there, and she knows someone in Textiles; they're very keen to see it. I was hoping you'd come with me to show them, and talk about it.'

'I thought you wanted to sell the book,' I said slowly. 'Michael seemed desperate to get his hands on it. He searched my London flat, you know; then he followed me to Cornwall, telling me he'd given it to me in error, then chased me all the way to Morocco and left me a threatening message at my riad –'

'I didn't know. I am sorry, Julia.' She pursed her lips. 'How charming of him. *Given to you in error.* Like himself, no doubt. Michael is under the impression we'll get a lot of money for the altar piece once we can prove what it is, and I haven't disabused him of the idea. In fact, if it's proved to be the real deal I've promised it to the V&A for free as long as they exhibit it with its full family history. Michael will be absolutely furious when he finds out.' She giggled. It occurred to me suddenly that the balance of their relationship had suddenly shifted in her favour, and that she was enjoying every minute of her newfound power.

Something else occurred to me then. I looked at her intently. 'Anna, I've always known your family were quite well off, but, well: the altar cloth, it was given to Lady William Cecil, the Countess of Salisbury . . .'

She laughed. 'Lady William Cecil, née Howard. Mother's a Howard, you see.'

I gaped at her. 'You're one of the Howard family? *The* Howard family, as in Catherine Howard and the Duke of Norfolk and all?'

'Yes, but it's all a bit diluted now. Very grand in our time, but we don't own half of East Anglia any more. All I inherited was Aunt Sappho's Suffolk house, and some funds and the cottage. I do believe the family owned St Michael's Mount for a short time before selling it in the Civil War. Pity: could quite fancy living on an island.'

'So you're rich?'

She shrugged uncomfortably at my crassness. 'Well, I wouldn't go as far as that. Comfortable, maybe.'

'Then why is Michael always so desperate for money?'

She gave me an embarrassed smile. 'It isn't really done to talk about such things in our family. Rather vulgar, I think. Michael doesn't know much about my assets.'

He'd been married to an heiress and fretting all this time. I laughed out loud. 'He said you were short of cash.'

Now it was Anna's turn to laugh. 'Michael's convinced having a baby will bleed us dry.' She shrugged. 'I told him if he was that desperate he could sell the flat in Soho. He was very shocked: he didn't even realize I knew about it. But I've known for years. I saw you together, going in, coming out, a dozen times. At the beginning it made me very miserable and a bit crazy: I used to follow him, spy on him, if you like.'

I closed my eyes, appalled. 'And you never confronted him or me.'

She shook her head.

'You could have left him, married someone else, someone worth having.'

She went very still. 'Yes, he is a bastard, isn't he? But I love him, Julia. I really love him, always have, always will. Can't help it: he's my Achilles heel, and you can't help who you love, can you?'

I smiled. 'No.'

I brushed my hand over Catherine's work again. It was simply beautiful, the more so for being unfinished. It remained an enigma, a mystery: its absences preyed on the mind, and wasn't that what love was all about? Even so, there was still one mystery I had to resolve. I lifted my eyes to Anna again. 'I really need to know what happened to Catherine,' I said.

★

Downstairs in the bar, Anna ordered drinks – white wine for her and for me. Idriss surprised me by asking for a beer.

'Another transgression,' I teased him as she went up to the counter, but he looked pained.

'It *is* Friday. Perhaps I should have water instead –'

Michael chose this moment to stride into the bar. Great patches of sweat had darkened the seersucker shirt; he looked hot and annoyed. His glance slid past the two foreigners seated at the table in front of him and fixed instead on his wife. 'Scotch, and better make it a double!' he demanded, seeing her at the bar, and the bartender – obviously recognizing a man in desperate need – put aside the beer bottle in his hand, grabbed a bottle of whisky and immediately poured out a large measure. 'My feet are killing me. I've been to every bloody hotel in Rabat looking for the damned woman and she's not at any –'

'Hello, Michael.'

He spun around so fast that half the liquid in the tumbler he had just been handed splashed on to his shoes.

'Good for your blisters,' I said childishly, and Anna stifled a laugh.

He stared at me, then at Idriss, and a nasty, knowing look dawned slowly on his face. 'You didn't waste any time going native, did you?' he said unpleasantly.

Idriss rose from his seat, the turban adding inches to his already considerable height.

'Sit down, Michael, and stop making an exhibition,' Anna said severely. I could imagine her talking to a junior employee in such a tone, but it was a surprise to hear her take it with Michael. 'This gentleman is Idriss, an expert on the city and its history.'

'Idriss el-Kharkouri,' Idriss supplied sonorously. '*La bes.*' He inclined his head, then touched his palm to his heart.

Michael regarded him suspiciously, then rudely turned his back on him. 'Where's the book, Julia? I've come a long way to get it.'

'Julia and I have come to an arrangement,' Anna said smoothly. She passed a glass of wine to me and the beer to Idriss, who took it with a *shokran bezef*, playing the Berber guide for all he was worth.

Michael glowered at her. 'What do you mean "an arrangement"?'

'Where are Robert Bolitho's letters, Michael? I can't find them.'

'You didn't think I'd leave them lying around the room for any thieving Arab to nick, did you? They're in the hotel safe with instructions for no one to remove them but me.'

This was a different Michael to the one I had thought I'd known, a nastier, more anxious version. Seeing me with Idriss had certainly stung him, and the thought gave me a certain small and unworthy satisfaction.

'Well, run along and get them,' Anna said, taking his whisky from him and wiping the base of the glass with a napkin as she might dripping milk from a child's bottle. 'Go on.' She waited until he had gone, then leaned across the table to me. 'Here's my promise. I'll give you the letters if you'll let me take the book, for now. Our flight back is tomorrow, but I don't think Michael will set foot on the plane without the book. However, I promise you – and Idriss can be my witness – that it remains your property to do with as you wish, and we'll exchange the letters and the book when you get back, as long as you'll come to the V&A with me to authenticate the altar cloth. Is that a deal?' She held out a hand.

Idriss looked at me warningly, but I gave him a tiny shake of the head. *No, it's OK*. Then I took Anna's hand. 'Deal.'

I was halfway through my wine before I remembered another question I meant to ask her. 'Robert Bolitho's letters – where did you find them?'

'They were in Alison's loft, at the farmhouse at Kenegie. Someone had tucked them inside the cover of the family bible, where they belonged, I suppose.'

'What do you mean?'

'Well, Alison's mother's a Bolitho, isn't she? You should know: she's your cousin. It just always struck me as an odd name. We played that game at college once – you know the one: make your porn star name by taking the name of your first pet and your mother's maiden name? Mine was Silky Pevsner; hers was Candy Bolitho, both rather good, we thought. Anyway, family ties to the place or not, she's moving out; it's a big place if you're on your own.'

I was appalled, and for many reasons. I remembered the chill I had felt while I was there, the depression that settled over me. I had thought at the time I was being superstitious, that I had sensed the presence of Andrew's spirit; but what if there had been something else there? I shivered, unwilling to think about that. 'Where's she going to go, then, Alison?'

'She's going to buy my little cottage in Mousehole; she fell in love with it, and we did a deal: I let her have it cheap and she let me have the letters.' She gave me a wry little smile. 'She's already moved in as a tenant while the conveyancing is done and the alterations are carried out.'

Before I could ask anything else, Michael arrived with an envelope in his hand, looking even more harassed than he had before. 'God, these people don't understand a word of bloody English.'

'That's because they all speak French, darling. Now, then: Julia has agreed to exchange the book we need for the letters you found.'

Michael looked at me, surprised. 'Oh, good.' He hovered over the table, as if suddenly wrong-footed, then sat down, opened the envelope and removed from it several photocopies, plus a sheaf of foxed and spotted foolscap covered in neat ink. Even from a distance I could see it was in Robert Bolitho's small, neat hand. 'The book,' he said, separating the originals from the copies and holding the latter out to me. 'Hand it over, then.'

Anna tutted. She reached across and took the papers from him, dropped the foolscap sheets into the envelope, folded the copies and passed them back to Michael, then gave the envelope to me.

'What the hell do you think you're doing?' Michael roared.

'Fair trade,' Anna said sweetly. 'The book, please, Julia.'

Solemnly, I reached into my bag and withdrew *The Needle-Woman's Glorie*. It felt soft and smooth in my hand. I rubbed my thumb lovingly across the ridges on its spine and the slight discoloration on the back where the corsair captain's cousin had tried to burn it. 'Goodbye, Catherine,' I whispered.

'*Au revoir*,' Anna corrected me gently.

'See you in London,' I told her with a smile. 'I'll be back in a few days. I'll call you.'

Anna's fingers folded over mine. 'Do that, my friend.' Then she drew away, clutching the book against her ribcage like a breastplate.

I got up to leave. Idriss extended a hand to Anna, who smiled up at him. 'It was lovely to meet you, Idriss. I hope to see you again.'

'*Enchanté, madame. À la prochaine, inch'allah.*'

He turned to Michael. 'I hope you have enjoyed your brief stay in my cousin's hotel, and that your visit to Morocco has provided something of an education for you,' he said in his best English. 'Our culture prides itself on the quality of our hospitality and courtesy. And of course we are entitled to demand that the tongue be cut out of anyone who impugns our honour, or that of any member of our family.' The flicker of his smile did not reach his eyes.

It might have been the light, but it seemed to me that Michael went a little green around the gills.

Outside, in the bright sunlight, I squinted up at Idriss. 'Is that really true? About cutting out the tongue, I mean? I know in Saudi with Sharia Law they'll cut your hand off for stealing, and flog people for drinking, and stone women for adultery, and other horrible things, but I thought Morocco was more liberal.'

Idriss drew me into the shadows of an alley, dipped his head and kissed me, very quickly but very thoroughly.

'And that earns me a month in prison,' he said solemnly.

I had no idea whether he was joking or not.

28

Rob

1625

The forest was a strange place. In Cornwall he knew every tree, every plant that grew in the woodlands and hedgerows, their names, their flowers and fruits and seasons. But these trees had a bark that was reddish and rough with long vertical splits and gashes, and their limbs were smooth and round and well spaced. The canopy they made was thick and dark, so the undergrowth grew sparsely, which at least meant there were fewer places from which brigands might ambush them.

They walked in single file, Rob following carefully in the other's steps. Half a day of walking passed without incident. They ate some of the ship's biscuit and dried meat, and drank water from a stream, and walked on without a word. This left Rob's mind free to wander mightily, and he found himself remembering his final conversation with Sir John, which had finished on a bitter note.

'Two, and there's an end to it. Bring any more and I'll sell them into slavery myself!' Killigrew had told him furiously when he had once more argued they should try to bring away as many captives as the ship could carry. Rob had subsided with as good a grace as he could summon. What would folk say when he returned home with only Cat and one other, when so many had been taken? He knew from the ransom letter that Catherine's mother Jane had survived, and duty prompted him that it should be this lady he saved alongside his beloved, but, as he turned it over, the idea sat like lead in his stomach. Rob had never cared greatly for the woman. The lads at home would surely scoff at him for his folly in shipping back such a shrewish mother-in-law to berate and belittle him at every turn. But what if Cat would refuse to come away without her? He had never thought them overly close, but it was said that blood was thicker than water. He had much rather save Matty, now that he thought about it – good, stolid, decent Matty. She was a young woman, and Jane Tregenna old and dried, so surely it was more logical to save Matty, so she might live out a long life in a good Christian country, and bring into the world the children that God intended for her? His mind's eye captured Jane Tregenna's pinched and discontented visage, and compared it unfavourably with Matty's rosy dimples, and his decision was made. He could not stop his imagination from running far ahead: surely Cat would wed him with a whole heart when all this was over, grateful for the mighty effort he had made for her, just like one of the knights in the stories she loved so well. But his conscience pricked at him. It was surely wrong to consider Cat's heart as common payment. If he was making this journey, this quest, with such payment in mind, he was surely being ignoble, for the success of saving her from the heathen ought to be reward enough of itself. Heroic tales took hold of him again: might he not see himself as a Crusader striking a blow for Christendom against the infidel? Yes, that was a finer image to cleave to: if he acted as a godly man on the true path of the Lord, he would earn a reward in Heaven. *But I would rather have my reward on Earth, and in my arms.*

A bird came clattering out of the canopy overhead, cawing a warning, its long tail trailing like a pennant.

A magpie: bird of ill omen, as much here as anywhere.

Marshall turned, grabbed Rob by the shoulder and dragged him down into the lee of a fallen tree trunk. Voices. Through the spindly stalks of a host of foul-smelling fungi which sprouted from the rotten wood, Rob saw shapes moving twenty feet away through the trees. Their striped cloaks made them hard to discern in the slats of light and forest shade, but the animals they led had no such camouflage. Mules, drawing carts piled high with timber.

It was Rob's first view of the natives of this land; at first sight, they did not look like devils or even much like brigands. As they approached, he could tell from their gestures and loud laughter that they exchanged ribaldries like any other working men. Their skin was a few shades darker than his own, but it was not much darker than the skin of the fishermen with whom he supped down in Market-Jew. They seemed to be of slight build. He felt a vague disappointment; if truth be told, he had been expecting fierce black giants dressed outlandishly and with their curved swords flashing, but these were just woodsmen much as you would find anywhere in the world, poor men with a living to make and families to feed.

Six carts rumbled past, accompanied by fifteen men, the final four of whom wore swords and were more watchful than the rest.

Marshall and Rob watched them go. Eventually, the Londoner said heavily, 'That'll be another two pirate ships bound for English shores come the spring. Come on, lad, get up. Let's put some space between them and us.'

By nightfall there was still no sign of an end to the forest. Lying beneath a makeshift shelter of sticks and leaves, Rob dreamed of Cat beaten black and bloody, Cat dead from a dozen causes – from disease, from starvation, from exhaustion, from some mad attempt at escape. Cat lying in a pool of filth; Cat beheaded by a half-naked savage wielding a dripping scimitar; Cat dragged behind a pair of horses till she was unrecognizable; Cat hanging from a spike in a wall, weeping silent tears of blood.

He woke at dawn and trudged behind Marshall through the unending, monotonous trees. At some time in the afternoon the older man held up a hand, then pointed away to the left. Rob followed the line of his finger. In a little clearing two men slept in a pool of sunlight with their cloaks pulled over their heads. Rather than creeping away, Marshall beckoned him to follow. Then he turned, grinned at him and drew a finger across his throat.

With horror, Rob realized his purpose, but before he could protest the Londoner had plunged his weapon into one man, withdrawn it and applied it to the other.

'They like to take a nap in the afternoons,' Marshall declared, pleased. 'Lazy bastards.'

Rob fell to his knees. He had never seen a man killed before, let alone two in cold blood as they slept. Bile filled his mouth, and then he had to turn away to let out a hot wave of vomit.

Marshall wiped his sword on the first man's cloak and resheathed it. Then he started to pull the man's robe up over his head, revealing a pair of scrawny legs and a grizzled scrotum.

Rob stared at him in disgust. 'That was murder.'

'Got no stomach for the work, eh, lad? You'd better toughen up fast. They'd have had no qualms about doing the same to you, and don't you forget it. Now wipe your mouth and help me. We'll take their clothes and anything else we fancy, right?' He regarded the two corpses with his head on one side. 'You'd better take the other one, he's taller. Good thing about these robes: one size fits all, but this one's shoes'll never fit you.'

'I'm not wearing a dead man's clothes,' Rob said obstinately.

'Fair enough: we'll be out of the forest by evening. You'll get maybe a mile if you're lucky, before some band of villagers stone you to death. Your choice.'

So it was that some while later two robed and turbaned figures emerged from the eaves of Marmora Forest into the dreary country-side beyond, each mounted on a dun-coloured mule.

Rob had insisted on wearing his own tunic beneath the robe, and now he was sweltering. He could already feel fleas and lice as they burrowed and bit into his flesh, yet he bore the discomfort with a savage satisfaction. He had stood by and done nothing while two human lives were taken, and he felt filthy inside and out.

He was surprised that no one paid them much attention as they passed, for he could feel his own guilt burning like a beacon, but, other than a group of ragged children who threw olive pits at the mules as they passed through a dusty grove, people barely turned their heads.

'Blasted little urchins,' Marshall grumbled darkly. 'These people breed as easily as rats, then turn their children out into the fields to make mischief without the least threat of discipline. No wonder they grow up into wastrels and thieves. Problem comes from the top down, as is always the case. There is no central authority in this scurvy country: it's a fucking anthill.'

'Sir Henry Marten said there was a sultan, a Moulay something,'

Rob said hesitantly. 'Said he thought King Charles would send an envoy to him to plead the case of the captives.'

Marshall laughed. 'Moulay Zidane: king of nothing but turmoil and trouble, and most of that of his own making. His father was Al-Mansour, called the Victorious because he drove the Portuguese out of Morocco and killed sixty thousand of their army. The son is as nothing compared to the father: he has no morals and earns no respect, not even from his own corsairs. They have stopped paying him his due from the spoils; they mock him at every turn. That is why we do business with the true power here.'

'Do these pirates have a king, then?' Rob asked. 'Someone they have set up in place of the Sultan?'

'The business of pirating is a complex one,' Marshall said, sucking his teeth. 'Morally complex, if you like.'

'I can't see what is morally complex about thieving and slaving.'

'They see it in rather different terms. The Sidi Mohammed al-Ayyachi is a very remarkable man, a respected man to whom all listen, who has managed to draw to himself many like-minded allies. He has forged a formidable fighting force from most diverse quarters – renegade ships' captains from every seafaring nation in Europe, religious fanatics, wealthy Hornacheros, Moriscos thrown out of Andalusia and Grenada by King Philip – just about anyone, in fact, with a grudge to bear against Christendom. He plays a wily game: talks it up as a holy war while encouraging them all to make a fortune. To plunder a Christian ship is to return the wealth of the world to Islam, to the rightful glory of their god; and if in the process that means killing Christians or forcing them to turn Turk, so much the better for the war effort. If we'd had a king like him in England, we'd have conquered half the world by now, for he is a thousand times more charismatic than that fool James or his pompous arse of a son. The old Queen would have appreciated Al-Ayyachi mightily. In many ways they are much alike: they could understand the nature of men and work upon their weaknesses to play them like pawns in the greater game.'

'What manner of being is their god that he demands such offerings of blood and gold?'

Marshall turned to regard him pitifully. 'Why, the same god as our own, lad, the great God Almighty. They have but a different name for him and different practices with which to worship him. Otherwise there is not much to separate our religions except a thousand years of bloodshed!'

This was all too much for Rob, who felt as if his world was tilting end over end. 'But if we all serve the same god, then why are we at war?'

'Why are men ever at war? For power and greed and to enforce their own views on others. Personally, I don't give a toss for any of it: I'd serve the Devil himself if it fit my purpose. But I'll tell you now: when we penetrate this nest of pirates, you'd better keep your head down and show no anger or disrespect, whatever your own views and no matter how you are provoked, or you'll lose both your head and your wench in one fell swoop and there'll be nothing I can do about it.'

As they rode on, the sun beat down, then blessed clouds covered the sky and a light spattering of rain began to fall as they crossed a great fallow waste land dotted with rocks and dusty bushes. After a while they came upon a number of black tents pitched low to the ground. Livestock were hobbled in little groups around the outskirts, including a herd of great, ugly, hump-backed things with long necks and knobbly knees. Beside the tents women sat tending to infants, weaving bright textiles or pounding grain between stones. One of these now saw the travelling pair and came running towards them, her silver bracelets and anklets jangling as she ran. She fit Rob's idea of the exotic he had expected this far-flung place to contain, for she wore any number of colourful wraps of cloth about her head and body bound with great silver brooches and pins. Her eyes were outlined with some thick black cosmetic which made her regard most striking, and there were tattoos on her chin and her forehead, and brown patterns on her hands and feet.

She stretched out one of these patterned hands now in entreaty and gabbled at them. To Rob's surprise, Marshall did not chase her away with angry words but instead dug in his pouch, drew out one of the coins he had robbed from the dead men and placed it in her palm. More extraordinary still, he then exchanged a few words with the woman in a harsh-sounding language, and she chattered back at him.

'Come,' said Marshall, sliding down from his mule. 'Tonight we shall eat and sleep well; and tomorrow we enter Salé.'

'Who are these people?' Rob asked nervously. 'How do you know they won't kill us in the night and leave us for the crows? And what are those horrible beasts they have tethered there?'

Marshall clapped him on the back. 'They're travellers like ourselves: nomads from the desert lands to the south. They travel the ancient caravan routes with their camels and their livestock, trading their produce and whatever trinkets they come by on the way. Did you see how much silver that woman was wearing? No need to worry: their byword is hospitality. Make the most of it: they're the last decent folk you're likely to encounter for a while.'

Rob watched the sun go down in a blaze of gold that left a pillar of violet light reaching high into the darkening sky, while to the south the clouds flushed amber and crimson as if lit by inner fire, which faded to ashes as night fell and the stars came out. His belly was full of a savoury stew he suspected was goat, but was nevertheless as good as any mutton he had ever eaten, served with a soft black fruit that after the first bite was less shocking and increasingly delicious, and flatbreads which had been baked on stones heated by the fire. Listening to the nomads laugh and sing, he felt calm and optimistic for the first time since he had left London. It seemed that not all foreigners were devils. Life could be fine, and, while he and Cat were still alive, there was hope that all would be well.

The next morning four of the nomad herders rode with them on the way to Salé, with their billy-goats trussed up and dumped like sacks over their saddles; others followed at a more leisurely pace with the rest of the livestock and trade goods. Rob got the distinct impression that Marshall had put a few coins their way: a group of nomads riding into the city were hardly likely to attract notice in the same way as two lone travellers, one of whom was unusually tall and possessed of a pair of bright blue eyes.

Within an hour the traffic on the road became noticeably heavier. Peasant women walking with huge baskets of herbs on their backs, their foreheads taking the strain of the handles; farmers with cart-loads of vegetables; girls in black robes balanced precariously upon donkeys, sitting not astride like a man, nor yet sidesaddle like an Englishwoman, but upon a meagre blanket, with both feet bumping against the animal's flank. Occasionally armed men on horses came hammering down the road, shouting for others to get out of the way, and they did so with such alacrity that one cart even toppled into a ditch, spilling its load of turnips and potatoes everywhere. In England, if this had happened, everyone would have made mock of the carter and walked on, laughing; but here men, women and children scurried hither and thither to collect the bouncing vegetables and return them safely to the cart with a smile and a nod to the farmer.

As they approached the city, the nature of the countryside began to change once more from parched waste land – which Marshall referred to as 'the bled', as if indeed the life had all run out of it – to land that was now cultivated and greener, dotted with trees and bushes and strips of crop. Along the roadside women sat amid great pyramids of fruit, the like of which Rob had never seen.

'Pomegranates, lad,' Marshall told him. 'Fruit of life, and Perse-phone's downfall!' Rob was none the wiser on either count.

A nomad peeled off from the group, returning a moment later with one of the fruit. Marshall tossed it to Rob. 'There you go. That'll keep you occupied for a while.'

Biting into it resulted in a mouthful of horrid, bitter pulp and caused the nomads no end of merriment; but at least he could now perceive the fruit within, gleaming like little rubies in the sunlight. Rob dug out a handful and popped them into his mouth. The explosion of sweetness when he bit down on them was so un-expected and so sensual he almost fell off his horse. *Pomegranates*. Would they grow in Cornwall? If they would, he vowed he would never eat another apple.

At last the ochre ramparts of the town rose up before them, and now the traffic became intense and noisy and accompanied by clouds of flies. The road funnelled them towards a huge, arched gateway manned by guards in dusty blue tunics and wide breeches tucked into boots, their turbans so white they hurt the eye. 'Do what I do and keep your head down,' Marshall warned Rob again, 'and say nothing, even if you are addressed.' He wound his own turban about his face so that his eyes were in deep shadow and only a glint of them could be seen, and Rob arranged his own headgear in like fashion.

He glanced up once as they approached, in time to catch a glimpse of an array of huge bronze cannon mounted on the crenellated wall above them, pointing out to sea. Expensive guns, of European design. This was it, then: the pirates' nest, the city to which Catherine had been brought across the wide ocean. He hunched to disguise the breadth of his shoulders and stared fixedly down at the stiff sprouting of dusty hair on the mule's neck as the shadow of the gate fell across him. The nomads chattered like magpies to the guards, then miraculously they were waved through into a great milling chaos of a place, with all manner of unsavoury smells, and a thousand jostling people.

Here, they bade farewell to their nomad escorts. Rob was sorry to see them go, and, as he watched them ride off to sell the goats and barter their wares, he almost envied them.

They abandoned the mules among a hundred other of the beasts, left hobbled to posts near the watering troughs, and joined the mêlée in the winding, reed-roofed pathways, where the sunlight cast lovely, complex spiderwebs of shadow on the ground between the trampling feet. 'The *kissaria*,' Marshall told him. 'The covered market. I've a contact on the other side. Keep close: if you get turned around here and separated from me, you'll be lost in seconds.'

Rob blundered against people, elbowing them out of the way in his need to keep pace with Marshall, who bore through the throng like a bull with his head down. At last he ended by grabbing a handful of the Londoner's robe so that there was a physical bond between them and held on for dear life, like an infant attached to its mother's apron-strings. The market passed in a succession of dreamlike images of whiskered fish and bright spices, crates of chickens and lizards and snakes, bales of silk, sacks of wool, brass and glass and silver, and everywhere the raucous shouting language, not a word of which he could comprehend. He felt dizzy with it all, even nauseous.

At last they dodged leftwards up a side street off the main thoroughfare, and the noise receded. Marshall slowed a little; Rob noticed that he was breathing hard and his sweat was pungent. Fear: it was a smell Rob recognized well enough, and the recognition did not fill him with confidence. 'Now what?' he asked.

'Now we go to the house of the man who knows another who can get us an audience with the marabout Sidi al-Ayyachi. This man and I have done business before; but he will not be happy I've brought another with me, let alone one who stands out in a crowd. If asked, I shall tell him you are my younger addle-witted brother. If made to reveal your face, loll your tongue and cross your eyes. If they perceive you as any kind of threat, they will run you through without a qualm.'

Just as you did those men sleeping in the forest, Rob thought, but said nothing. He nodded and practised crossing his eyes.

Marshall grinned. 'Perfect. You'd pass as an idiot anywhere in the world.'

He knocked on a nail-studded door. After a time a square hatch in the door swung inwards, and Rob caught a glimpse of a brown, wizened face in the shadows on the other side. Marshall said something, then the door swung open and Marshall gave Rob a little push in the back. 'Go on. Quickly.' Rob abruptly found himself inside, with the little foreign man staring up at him. On cue, Rob let fall his turban flap and conjured the most hideous face he could manage, and the man stepped back, making the sign of Fatima's hand to ward off the evil eye. He and Marshall exchanged an explosion of guttural noises, then the Londoner turned to Rob. 'Enough of that: job's done. Follow me.'

They were ushered into a cool inner chamber, where a woman,

dark-eyed and suspicious, brought them tea and ran away before Rob could curse her with his awful face.

Here they sat for what seemed hours. Every time Rob started to say something, Marshall put a finger to his lips and gestured to the door. *Spies*, he mouthed. So Rob covered his face and leaned back against the wall and dozed.

At last voices sounded in the corridor. Marshall got to his feet as another man entered. This one was younger and more dangerous-looking than the first, with lighter skin and a jutting black beard. He carried both sword and dagger at his waist, Rob noticed, and looked as if he knew how to use them. No formal greetings were exchanged: the younger man seemed nervous and distrustful. He prodded Rob with his foot. 'Sit up, Robert,' Marshall told him. 'My poor mad fool of a brother,' he said, turning back to the new arrival and shrugging. 'There was no one I could leave him with.'

The man leaned forward and with a yank ripped the turban away from Rob's head. Rob was so shocked it took him a full two seconds to remember his fool routine; by then it was too late. The man slapped him hard, and Rob stared at him, affronted and dazed by this sudden burst of violence. 'It seems Hassan bin Ouakrim has worked miracle cure,' the man said to Marshall. 'I not think he so mad now.' He drew his dagger – in the dim light of the salon its curving blade glimmered faintly – and held it with its tip towards Rob. 'Who he is and why he here? He no brother you: too pale and white, like filthy pig, eyes blue like Devil. Tell true or I cut him death.'

'His name is Robert Bolitho. He came to save his woman, taken by the raiders from Cornwall in the summer.'

The other laughed. 'Al-Andalusi's triumph, yes! How we laugh see white Christian women sold like cattle in Souk of Gazelle!'

Rob's fists balled so tight he thought the knuckles might spring apart under the pressure. He willed himself not to lose his temper. 'I am able to speak for myself,' he said as evenly as he could. 'One of those captured women is my betrothed, my . . . ah . . . soon-to-be-wife, Catherine Anne Tregenna. She has long hair, red to here' – he indicated his waist – 'the same colour as this' – and now he pointed to the tawny braided belt the other man wore.

At once the dagger whistled down, nicking Rob's hand so that he yelped.

'Keep filthy infidel hands off! Back, like dog, now!'

Seething, Rob complied. Marshall regarded him with a pursed mouth and narrow, furious eyes. 'I beg your pardon for the rudeness of my companion, sir. He is no more than a hot-headed boy who has crossed the seas hoping to make a bargain with your venerable lord for his beloved's release. And I have some private business to share with the Sidi, business which I can assure you will make your lord most happy. Put your dagger up and let us discuss these things like brothers.'

Hassan bin Ouakrim gave him a hard look, then sheathed his blade. 'You lucky is Aziz who came to me: others would have kill you both. I never bother with infidel curs, but I know you made good business with Sidi last spring. Come.'

The Sidi Mohammed al-Ayyachi was not at all what Rob had expected the leader of such fearsome pirates to be; nor was his house grand or showy for that of a man whose followers had stripped the wealth from a thousand foreign ships and sold their crews for a fortune. Rather, it was as old and worn as the man himself, though spotlessly clean. They found him about to sit down to his lunch in a small chamber boasting only a single low table and reed matting on the floor. He wore a robe of cotton as white as his flowing beard, so that the only colour about him was his deeply wrinkled face and hands, and his bright black eyes. He stood up as lithely as a young man when they entered and bowed to them deeply, exchanging pious greetings with Marshall, who bizarrely bent and covered the old man's hands with kisses. More strangely still, the Sidi responded by kissing the former actor's shoulders like a long-lost friend.

'*Salaam*, Sidi Mohammed, and blessings be upon you.'

'May Allah's blessing be upon all those who are for his Prophet. The good Lord be praised that he has brought you safe back to us again, William Marshall. And your young friend here.' He gestured graciously to Rob, who bobbed his head stiffly.

'Tell me,' Sidi Mohammed said, leaning forward and fixing Marshall with those bright, inquisitive eyes, 'what wonders have you brought for me this time? More Christians for our endeavours? It seems to me this young man could pull an oar with the greatest of ease. Why, he is so mighty he could likely row a galley on his own! Is he a part of the goods you bring me, Master Marshall?'

'Alas, no, my lord. The young man who accompanies me is Robert Bolitho from the land of Cornwall, whence your bold captain, Al-Andalusi Raïs, brought away so many Christian captives earlier this year.'

'Ah, our servant Qasem bin Hamed bin Moussa Dib: a fine warrior for the good God, may he live long and prosper so that all may prosper from his righteous deeds, *inch'allah*. Allah be praised. *Al-hamdulillah*.'

'*Allah akbar*,' Marshall agreed, bowing his head. 'Praise be to the Most High, and those who serve him. But we have disturbed your lunch, my lord: pray let us retire for a time so that you may take your ease.'

The old man shook his head impatiently. 'No, William Marshall, no. Sit, eat with me. And young Robert Bolitho, also: sit, please, like brothers: Hassan, please ask Milouda to bring bread for all, and water, that our brothers here may wash.'

A woman brought them a bowl and ewer, and two lengths of cotton on which to dry their hands. The Sidi himself poured the rose-scented water for them. He waited till the woman had taken the bowl away, then returned with bread and olives and a heavy earthenware dish. He lifted the lid so that a great billow of steam from the dish wreathed about his face.

'Ah, chicken with preserved lemon. God is good to me.' He pushed the basket of bread across the table towards Marshall and Rob. 'Eat, please. Are your family in good health, Master Marshall? Your wife, your boys, your mother?'

Rob was astonished. All this time together the man had never once mentioned the existence of a family: for all Rob knew, he might be a bachelor or a widower, and an orphan, to boot.

Marshall answered the marabout at length and then inquired after the old man's health.

'I continue to be hale, *inch'allah*, though I am sure there are many in your country who would wish it were otherwise. I think your Master Harrison was most frustrated by me when he was here. But then' – he spread his hands apologetically – 'he did not bring me what I hoped he would, though I offered him much in return. But maybe the time was not right, and Allah willed it otherwise.'

They ate in silence for a while, then Marshall said, 'You have had a fine trawl of captives this year, I have heard: captives from far and wide.'

The Sidi's black eyes came away from the chicken leg he held. 'Indeed, Allah has been most perceptive in supplying us with fine captains, bold crews and good weather for our ships. Four hundred and twenty-three Christian souls to strengthen our cause,' he said evenly.

Marshall smiled. 'A fine summer's work, Sidi. But perhaps with only four hundred and twenty-one or two, the Lord's work might go equally well?'

'How should it go equally well? Four hundred and twenty-one or two is not four hundred and twenty-three. The scales will not balance: one would fall short of its mark, and that would be most grievous in Allah's eyes.'

'Is it possible that bronze and iron might make up the difference?'

The Sidi paused. 'How may one weigh a soul in base metals, Master Marshall? It would be like weighing feathers and stones.'

'Maybe so. But a ton of feathers is the same as a ton of stones.'

'In weight, perhaps, but not in worth.'

'What if the bronze was of best European origin, and there was enough iron to accompany it to last a year?'

The marabout's lips twitched. He picked up the chicken leg and stripped the last scrap of muscle from it with teeth as sharp and yellow as a rat's. 'It would depend on the quality of the bronze and iron; and on what else was to go into the counter-scale.'

William Marshall thrust a hand into the neck of his robe and withdrew a roll of parchment. This he passed to the marabout, who took it after wiping his fingers carefully on the cloth and muttering his thanks to the Lord. He scanned the contents, his face impassive. 'I know that our culture enshrines haggling at the heart of its trading, but I find it tedious to haggle. This is all most acceptable. Spanish gold we have in plenty; English too, if that would be more . . . practical to your master, but of course we should need proof of their good working order before we strike our deal.'

Marshall inclined his head. 'All shall be as you decree, Sidi.'

'*Inch'allah*. Your ship is . . . where, exactly?'

'Within distance of an agreed sign. She will sail in when I call for her and you can have a boat sent out with trusted men aboard to verify the cargo.'

The marabout looked across the table at Hassan bin Ouakrim and they spoke rapidly in their language for a time. At last the Sidi said, 'Hassan tells me the boy with you has come here to reclaim his wife.'

Rob sat up straighter and tried not to look too hopeful.

Marshall shrugged. 'She is a worthless drudge, not even married to the lad yet, but he has a fancy to wed her nevertheless. I cannot imagine she is of much value to your cause, Sidi. If you could see your way clear to include her in our bargain, it would ease the boy's heart.'

'And Matty too,' Rob said quickly. 'Matty Pengelly.'

Marshall shot him a poisonous look. 'Shut up, Rob.'

The Sidi looked affronted. 'The boy seeks to bargain for souls, does he? You had better tell him that is business best left to the older and wiser among us, and that I trade only with those whom I know well enough to trust. It pains my heart not to be able to grant your request, Master Marshall, but Hassan tells me the girl with hair of fire is already sold to a master who has paid far more for her than you could possibly give him in recompense.'

Rob struggled upright from his place at the table, and at once Hassan shot to his feet, hand on the hilt of his dagger. 'I have money!' Rob cried. He hauled out the pouch of gold he had collected and threw it down on the table where it landed with a resounding clatter.

The marabout stared at it as if Rob had thrown down a dead dog. Then he addressed himself to the Londoner. 'I realize that the boy is young and callow, but you are responsible for his manners, Master Marshall, and they are sorely lacking. I am greatly insulted. Perhaps I should take you both and put you in irons and send Hassan and Al-Andalusi to bring in your ship and its crew of infidels. How many more souls might that add to our cause, I wonder? Sixty, eighty, one hundred? In my time my corsairs and I have consigned to the Devil the souls of seven thousand, six hundred and forty-three Christians, and I should like to make it a round ten thousand before I die. *Al-hamdulillah.*' He paused, then ran the palms of his hands down his face, kissed them and touched them to his heart. 'This house has an exceptionally beautiful courtyard full of symmetry and peace. It is the perfect place in which to turn my attention towards the simplicity of spiritual truths and away from the complexities of the outside world. At the heart of my courtyard I have had a fountain made from a number of Nazarene skulls. I like to contemplate it each day after my morning prayers, to admire the subtle relationship between decoration and form. Water sounds most pretty falling through the eye-sockets of a dead infidel, Master Marshall; it is very pleasing to the ear. Perhaps you would care to join me in my contemplation? I think I might find room for another skull in its centrepiece.'

Marshall had gone several shades paler. 'No, Sidi, I beg you. Forget the captives: they are not an important part of this bargain. The four cannon you shall have, and all the shot and powder you require. They are of the finest quality, as you shall see: you have my word on that. And their provenance is most interesting: I think you will appreciate the irony extremely, for they were founded for the Cornish coast's defence at the Crown's expense, lord. They were destined for the rearming of Pendennis Castle and St Michael's

Mount. Sir John Killigrew commends them to you and says your corsairs are welcome to them and to the wretched Cornish too.'

Sidi Mohammed al-Ayyachi nodded graciously. 'An irony indeed. Sir John has my thanks.' He touched his breast. Then he leaned forward and picked up the pouch Rob had cast on the table and weighed it thoughtfully in his hand. 'This feels to me very like the price of one Christian soul. Let us make our deal, Master Marshall.' He threw the pouch towards the Londoner with the speed and force of a striking cobra.

Surprised, Marshall fumbled the catch: gold spilled out across the room, gleaming in the rays of sun that slanted into the room from its high window.

'Four cannon; all the shot and powder we require; and this fine young man for our galleys.'

Rob felt his bones turn to water. 'What? No!'

He stared at Marshall, his eyes round with horror, but the Londoner was already down on his knees, scrabbling up the coins.

29

Robert Bolitho had never suffered a day's sickness in all his twenty-three years. He had evaded the pox, the plague, the scarlet fever. Years of farm labour had toughened his sinews and rounded out a lanky frame into useful brawn. At six foot five, he towered over other men, and with his sky-blue eyes, fair skin and straw-yellow hair presented as fine a specimen of God's Adam as could ever be imagined.

As a Barbary slave, this boon was soon to prove a curse.

Rob was stripped naked, inspected minutely, even down to the state of his teeth, and given a bundle containing a blanket, a short hooded jacket, a collarless shirt and a pair of wide-legged cotton breeches. A clerk wrote down an approximation of his name and entered it into a register. He was then taken down into one of the slave dungeons, the mazmorra, wherein he found a hundred and more other wretches likewise jammed into dark and stinking close quarters wherein men moaned and whimpered, or crouched wordless and broken on the ground; or cursed and railed in a dozen different languages. In the middle of the night he and the other new prisoners were awoken and taken to have great iron rings fitted about their right legs by a smith who cared not one whit whether he struck iron or bone with his heavy hammer. At this last indignity, one of the men broke into loud and racking sobs: the fetter was the final confirmation of the loss of his humanity.

In the register, did he but know it, Robert Bolitho's name had been written in the section designated for future galley-rowers; but, it not being yet the raiding season, he was meanwhile selected for rock-breaking, the grimmest of ordeals requiring the strongest of the captives. His captors marked him out even as they urged him blinking out into the harsh first light.

'He could last three months, this one,' one of the overseers declared.

'If he does, I'll give you a chicken.'

The first overseer stared at him coldly. 'The Qur'an forbids gambling, Ismael. Watch your step, or you'll be joining them.'

Over four months after Robert Bolitho was set to work in the quarry, hewing out by hand tool and sheer brute force massive stones and hoisting them two miles to the coast via sledge and ropes, he was still alive, against all the odds.

Rob had seen men fail and die by the dozen – dropping from exhaustion and malnutrition, whipped bloody or driven mad by the sun. One man had gone berserk and tried to murder a guard: he had been summarily executed, his head struck without ceremony from his body, which had taken two steps grotesque and headless before collapsing. The head had bounced off down the hill. No one had bothered to retrieve it. Other men had died from contaminated water; others still of shame and despair.

Throughout it all, as the hemp ropes embedded themselves in his flesh, leaving weeping welts, as the iron fetter dug into the infected sores around his ankle, as his back was striped with whip marks, as his muscles wailed in protest as he swung the mallet at the unforgiving rock, as vermin bred in his hair and feasted on his skin, Rob kept on surviving. When he thought he could not go on, he remembered Cat, seated on her ancient throne on Castle an Dinas, her fox-red hair blowing in the wind, and willed himself to live.

There were days when he forgot what the view from Kenegie, which he had loved so dearly, looked like; days when he forgot his own name. But he never forgot the precise shade of Catherine Anne Tregenna's eyes, or the curve of her mouth as she smiled.

30

I was forthwith taken from the howse of the Sidi to a donjon they called a mazmorra which laie beneath the ground into which a small hole gave only a littell raie of light, & there I founde a true picture of miserie & humaine suffering – an hundred poore unfortunates in ragges & squalor, some as thin as wyrms, weak from disease & beatings & lack of repast . . .

I put the letter down, appalled, and looked up at Idriss. 'Were the captives really kept in such atrocious conditions?'

'I expect so. There were so many slaves they probably feared an uprising if they kept them strong and above the ground.'

'Such cruel times; such barbarous people.'

'And of course no one would ever treat prisoners so badly today, contravening their human rights so shockingly. I won't mention Guantánamo Bay. Or the ferocious slaving of Africans by the British, the Spanish, the Portuguese, the Americans . . .' He counted them off one by one on his fingers.

'I take your point,' I said, forcing a smile.

We were sitting in the ante-room of a beautiful courtyard restaurant owned by friends of Idriss, where we had feasted on pigeon pastilla and fish brochettes and been complicit in the sharing of a bottle of fine local rosé – either that, or the contents of the foolscap pages had rendered us both a little tipsy.

'Khaled will just love this,' Idriss said suddenly. 'He's been researching the Sidi al-Ayyachi for years, but I don't think he ever found a source that described him personally or, I suspect, so accurately.'

'He seems like a complete monster.'

'Heroes and villains: they're all monsters really,' Idriss said, smiling. He tapped one of his ubiquitous Marlboros out into his hand, then sat there looking at it. After some seconds of this, he replaced the cigarette, closed the box with a gesture of finality and pushed it away. 'Time to give up one bad habit,' he said.

'Just like that?'

'Just like that.'

'You seem very sure about it.'

'There are some things in life I am very sure about.' He looked at me so intently that I felt dizzy.

Just at that moment one of the waiting staff, who had all evening been both courteous and unobtrusive, knocked over a small vase in the courtyard, and there was a burst of activity as someone saved the scattered roses, someone else mopped up the water, and yet another ran for the dustpan and brush. 'We should go,' I said, looking at my watch. Past eleven, though it felt like three in the morning to my exhausted head.

'Don't you want to finish going through the papers?'

'I'm very tired. We can finish them tomorrow. Or the next day – if you don't mind my staying a little longer.' And I wanted some time to myself, to reflect on what had been a rather extraordinary day. A lot had happened in a very short space of time. Not least the kiss in the alley.

Idriss beamed. 'I was very much hoping you'd say that. Our house is your house for as long as you like.'

We walked back through the deserted medina, the waxing crescent moon casting its silvery light down upon us as we went. Thin cats scurried at the sound of our footsteps. We disturbed a pack of feral dogs worrying at the rubbish left by the day's market; they did not growl at us but simply melted away into the darkness until we had gone. Somewhere a bird sang, its chant hanging plaintive and melancholy in the still air. '*Andaleeb*,' Idriss said. 'I don't know the English name for it, I think it's a sort of lark or something. Our tradition has it that they sing with the voices of lost lovers. If the stars are smiling on them you will hear its mate call back in a moment. Listen.'

So there in the shadow of the ancient Almohad wall we stood

and waited, and seconds passed like an eternity. 'She's not coming,' I joked, but Idriss put a finger to his lips. 'Wait.'

Sure enough the silence gave way to another song, above and to our left.

'She's up on the minaret.' Idriss smiled. 'Now they will be together.'

Alone later in his room, I sat on the edge of the bed and took the envelope out of my bag. Inside lay the truth about two other parted lovers. I had promised Idriss I would not finish reading their story without him, yet I could not help but steal a glance at the pages to come.

Fettered hand & foote in cowlde iron, I read, and *beaten oft & savagelye till wee bledde*. My eye skipped down the page and lighted on *alas, poore Jack Kellynch, so goode a man never deserved so crewel a fate, hys was a verie meane & crewel deth*. Poor Matty Pengelly, I thought then, and wondered what had become of the girl. Had she known what had happened to Jack, or was she already sold to a master who worked her hard in his kitchen or, worse, in his bed? I got up, removed the djellaba and the veil, and brushed out my flattened hair. I took a brief and chilly shower in the little room next door and climbed into my narrow bed. I meant to stow the papers away, I really did, but even as I laid my hand on them my eye scanned *Oure shippe put into Plymouth on the twentie third daie of July 1626 & never was I so gladde to see the shores of England*. So there it was. It had taken Robert Bolitho the best part of a year, but he had, despite all his terrible experiences, finally prevailed and brought his Catherine safely home. I wondered how he had escaped the slave prison and made away with Cat, but I would simply have to wait to find out. I should sleep, I told myself.

But I did not. I tossed and turned and could not get comfortable. I could have sworn I heard an owl hoot outside my window, but that was ridiculous: I was in the heart of an African city and not the wilds of Cornwall. Even so, when I finally fell asleep, it was of Catherine I dreamed.

31

Catherine

1626

To Cat's great surprise, her days passed quickly, and before she knew it a month had gone and the end of the year too. Here, though, no one talked of Christmas. There were no squalls of snow blowing in from the north-west, no holly and ivy wreathed about the fireplace – indeed, there was no fireplace – no hot possets laced with cloves and brandy, no midnight mass at the church at Gulval with everyone stamping their feet to keep warm and surreptitiously blowing on their hands in the middle of the prayers. January gave way to February and the first intimations of spring. Did she miss Kenegie? She tried not to think of her former life, but every so often a memory stole up on her when she was engaged in something else: when the women were bent over their embroidery frames and their chatter sounded just like the chatter of the dairy maids in the cowsheds gossiping about who was taking whom to the village dance; when she walked with Leila up to the gun emplacement at the top of the hill and watched the sea battering against the rocks below, just as it did on the foreshore at Market-Jew; when she peeled a turnip or woke in the morning disorientated and not sure of who she was, or where.

Her life was not at all what she had expected it to be in this foreign place. It was simple but not austere; occasionally hard but never cruel. Although much time was given over to the daily prayers, at least as much was taken by the preparation and serving of tea throughout the day, when the women would break from their work and sit about gossiping in a way that would not have been allowed at Kenegie. Bathing at the hammam was a revelation, and had gone from being a trial to be dreaded to a pleasure to be savoured. Food was never purely filling and functional but inventively spiced and elegantly arranged: as much of a joy to the eye as to the tongue, as Habiba chided her, half in charade, half in words, when she threw her vegetables willy-nilly into a tajine. Hasna showed her how to prepare her own kohl from a stone with a soft-blue metallic sheen like the flash of a magpie's wing that they had bought together in the souk; how to grind it to powder and make a paste; how to fill the pretty bottle with the fine rod of silver attached to its stopper and apply it just so, without making your eyes water so that it fell in runnels down your cheek.

As her facility with the language improved, so did her knowledge of her situation. The man to whom the women referred as the Sidi Qasem bin Hamed bin Moussa Dib was indeed the same man she had known as Al-Andalusi, the captain of the corsair vessel; but the women seemed to regard him not with fear but with respect and affection. He was a great benefactor, a merchant and a righteous man, they told her. That he traded in foreign slaves, including herself, seemed to them entirely normal, as if he traded in horses or prize camels; and after a while even Cat found that her own parameters were shifting. In fact, it was hard to think herself a slave, or even truly a servant, for her master was rarely present, and the few chores she had other than the overseeing of the embroidery workshop were hardly onerous. She also had more time to herself than she had enjoyed in Cornwall, and she found to her surprise that, rather than this chafing at her, she looked forward to the serenity of sweeping the courtyard or tending to its flowers, even though no one had asked her to, and discovered in herself a still, quiet centre she had never suspected to exist.

One day, after Catherine had passed almost seven months in the house of her new master, the raïs appeared unheralded and found her sitting in the courtyard with her eyes closed, her broom at her feet, her face upturned to the sky.

'You look like rose,' he said softly, 'with its petals drinking in the sun.'

Her eyes flew open in shock. She stood up, caught her foot on the broom and almost fell. The corsair caught her neatly and sat her down again. 'Thank you, Sidi Qasem,' she muttered, discomforted.

'Just Qasem is enough.'

'Qasem.' It sounded strange to call him this. She had never called Sir Arthur Harris merely Arthur – the very idea was absurd.

'Why you smile?'

'I was thinking of my last master.'

'Was he like me?'

That made her smile wider. Sir Arthur, stolid, bewhiskered and English to the bone: it was hard to imagine two men less alike. 'Not in any particular!'

It seemed he was not sure how to take this judgement, for now he changed the subject. 'Do you like my courtyard?'

'It is very beautiful, and very . . . serene.'

'I do not know this word "serene".'

'Quiet, tranquil – a good place to sit and think.'

Now his face was transformed, the hard planes softening, the frown lines on his forehead smoothing out. 'Is a *chahar bagh*,' he explained, 'a quartered garden, made in image of celestial garden, the eternal paradise. Human life began in the Garden, and we go back to the Garden when we die. This represents our journey' – he indicated the channels of water running from the central fountain – 'for like water we are always moving, seeking happiness and knowledge and faith. In the Qur'an it say that four rivers ran in the Garden of Eden: rivers of water, milk, honey and wine. But, as you see, here in my little earthly paradise, hidden from rest of the world, I must be content with water alone. And when I am here, I am content.'

He reached up and picked a rose from the bush which climbed the trellis of the arcade. 'Such perfection. God is beauty, and He loves beauty. Today is perhaps the very day for which He designed this bloom. Its petals are not touched by insect or rot; they not yet start to wither. Its scent is scent of Heaven. But tomorrow it start to decay. Better I pick today and cast petals in fountain which is source of its life, so it be remembered in most perfect form.'

He held the rose against Cat's cheek for a moment so that she smelled its aroma and felt its velvet texture brush her skin, and, although no part of him had touched her, she felt something burning in her nerves, as if a great fire had engulfed the pair of them and she could not breathe. Then the raïs crushed the flower in his hand so that its scent filled the air, and walked to the fountain to scatter the petals in its pool.

Cat closed her eyes. When she opened them again, he was gone.

After that whenever she walked in the courtyard she felt his shade there, as if he was watching her from behind the pillars of the arcaded walk, or from the shadows of the pavilion. Sometimes she thought she caught a movement high in the gallery above, but there was never a soul there when she ran to investigate; only the little buntings singing in the jasmine, their ruddy feathers bright against the white blossom.

The women worked hard under her tutelage, excited by their developing skills, and when she was with them and involved in the pattern-making and the stitching Cat thought of nothing else: her mind was given over to simplicity and exactitude, to counting stitches and the careful balance of colours. Too many and the work was garish, too few and it overly resembled the monochrome embroidery of Fez, or the old-fashioned blackwork with which she had been so familiar in England. Now, on the many feast days celebrated in this country, each woman wore something that she had made for herself: a braided belt, a decorated veil or headscarf, kaftans gorgeous with embellishment. Word spread, and soon there were many women calling at the door, wishing to take lessons with the foreign embroiderer so that they too could wear beautiful clothes they could never otherwise afford.

Leila shook her head. 'It is all very well, this pretty sewing of clothing, but it is not the type of work that will bring great riches to your master or to the rest of us.'

Cat looked at her oddly. 'What do you mean?'

The Dutchwoman coloured. Then she shrugged. 'You may as well know. The Sidi Qasem has established a merchant company here and has been so kind as to include me in their number. We will share the profits equally, and each of us will pay one fifth of our share into a common fund for the good of the community. So you see, a child's robe or a bath veil here and there is not going to profit the common good.'

Or your own pocket, Cat thought sourly, but held her tongue. 'What should we make, then?' she asked.

Leila pulled a list from the pocket of her robe. 'Horse trappings and saddle cloths; ceremonial robes; ceremonial hangings, all using plenty of gold and silver thread, tassels and braiding –'

'Rich things for rich men.'

The Dutchwoman's lips flattened into a line. 'If you like. But the more money we take thus from the rich, the more is returned into the common fund, and the more you will be remembered in the prayers of the people here.'

Cat stared at her. 'Why should they pray for me?'

'You are infidel; and, worse, *kafir*. You will go to the sixth level of hell when you die and be forced to eat the thorny fruit of the zaqqum tree, which will intensify your torment while you writhe in eternal flame. The women pray that you will make the *shahada* and join them in their worship.'

'The *shahada?*'

'It is very simple. All you need do is say, "There is no god but Allah and Mohammed is His prophet", and from that moment forth you are accepted into Islam.'

'That is all?'

Leila leaned towards her eagerly, taking her by the arm. 'That is all, and then you are one of us. It is very easy, and would make . . . everyone very happy.'

'I cannot see what worth there would be in such a cheap conversion,' Cat said stiffly.

The Dutchwoman smiled slyly. 'A Muslim cannot be a slave; it would win you your freedom. And it is well known that a Muslim man can take to wife only a Muslim woman.' She paused, measuring her words for effect. 'I hear that the Sidi Qasem's cousin Khadija has commissioned a wedding veil.'

Cat met her questing eye squarely. 'Good for her.'

'Though, of course, relations with a female slave are still

permitted to a Muslim man even when he has taken a wife of his own kind.'

Cat tore the list from the other woman's hand. 'I have work to do. I cannot stand around here gossiping in such a salacious manner.' Her face burned.

For the rest of the day she made error after error in her stitching, and the women shook their heads and clucked their tongues and watched her out of the corners of their eyes. Was she sick? Certainly her colour was high. Perhaps she is in love, Hasna suggested wickedly, and they all laughed.

How Nell Chigwine would chide her for her Jezebel ways, Cat thought as she applied the last touch of her daily kohl and regarded herself in the mirror in her chamber, seeing how her eyes were dramatically outlined to make the blue of them even more arresting, how the silver earrings tinkled in her ears, the sumptuous embroidery at her throat and cuffs enhanced an already striking scarlet kaftan. *A scarlet dress for a scarlet woman . . .*

Then she remembered that Nell was dead and how she had died, and felt ashamed.

Today was an important day. The Sidi Qasem was bringing a group of merchants to the house to discuss his new business venture. All the previous day they had cleaned the best salon, sprinkling its cushions with rose water, beating the carpets, polishing the brass and the wood. More importantly, they had put the finishing touches to a dozen new pieces of work that he might show as samples. The past two months had been filled with stitching and couching with gold and silver thread to produce a number of fine samples for the consortium to show in Meknès and Fez, in Larache and Safi – even as far as Marrakech – in order to gather commissions. To this end they had turned out a fabulous set of trappings for a horse – a saddle cloth fringed with gold tassels and edged with a gorgeous design, a spectacular embroidered saddle cover to be stitched on to the leather, a girth and headpiece replete with gold. In addition to these, there were the usual ceremonial items of clothing, marriage curtains and veils, belts, braid and bed hangings. The raïs had been more involved than usual, visiting often to give advice on the cut and quality of the saddle cloths and harness, and as she worked Cat remembered with the clarity of a true dream the afternoon she had seen him waiting on this side of the Bou Regreg, still and silent, with his finely apparelled mount all in scarlet and gold.

Now she waited, on the pretext of hanging out the linens on the roof terrace, for a glimpse of him. She did not wait long: within minutes a group of men had appeared at the bottom of the hill beneath the house, all robed and swathed against the wind in cloaks and turbans. Her eye was drawn unerringly to the tallest of them, even at this slow pace his gait more of a stalk than a stroll. As they approached, he looked up and met her eye – a lodestone to a magnet – and she ducked her head, frightened by the way her heart fluttered behind her ribs.

Later, it was she who brought the great silver teapot, the tea glasses and the almond biscuits they had baked that morning into the salon where the men lounged, smoking and talking loudly. His regard, so dark and hooded, travelled over her, and, as she watched his eyes widen, she knew she had had her effect. She bowed and left with all modesty, looking neither right nor left; but that evening she waited for his knock at her door, and was not disappointed.

'It seems you are going to make me a great deal of money,' he announced, leaning against the door jamb.

Cat put aside the book she had been studying and looked up. His pupils were dilated from the herb smoke he had taken with his guests. He dangled his prayer beads from one hand, swinging the cord up and catching them in his palm so that the little polished stones clicked against one another.

'The saddle cloth?' she asked, pleased. 'Or the wedding tunics?'

He smiled. 'Hossein Malouda has offered me small fortune. For you.'

She paled. 'For me?'

'He say samples remarkable but that creator of them most remarkable of all. You certainly presented yourself as richly as your work.'

A pulse began to beat at her temple. She had made a foolish error, hoping to win his approval alone. And somehow in all of this she had forgotten that she was a chattel still, a thing to be bought and sold. 'And what did you say?'

He flicked the prayer beads up and down again, then curled them in his hand and sequestered them in his robe. 'I have not yet give him my answer.'

'Why not?' It came out too fast, too anxious. She could feel her neck flushing, the blood beating in her face.

'Because I have not yet decide what to do with you. He is not only one to have offered good price for you.'

'Someone else has tried to buy me from you?'

'Someone came seeking to offer for you some months ago. Unfortunately he not come direct to me but found the Sidi al-Ayyachi instead.'

'Unfortunately?'

'The Sidi decide to make different kind of deal with him.'

'You all seem to think you can buy and sell me like . . . like a camel!'

He laughed then. 'Ah, Cat'rin, in your scarlet robe and your silver: I have never seen a camel so fine. Although' – he rubbed his chin – 'there was one I remember: with great dark eyes and a temper which struck fear into heart of any rider, she spit or bite at least provocation. You remind me of that camel. But she was tamed in the end.'

Cat glared at him. 'You will never tame me: I am not an animal to be broken to your will, or that of any man.'

Red light from the setting sun glinted in his eye so that for a moment he looked as demonic as the djinn the women spoke of. Then he stepped backwards out of the door, and the red light slid away. As he walked out on to the balcony he said softly, 'And that is why I love you, Cat'rin Anne Tregenna.'

But a breeze caught his words and carried them into the twilight sky.

The following morning she and Leila visited the souk to find the woman who made the tasselled braids they needed to trim the headpiece for a horse. Cat enjoyed these excursions considerably. It gave her the chance to view the world in which she now lived, to revel in its sights and scents and pretend that she was a free woman with money in her pocket to spend as she would. In her djellaba and veil she was paid no more attention than the next robed woman, except when someone had reason to glance at her pale hands or into her blue eyes; then most dipped their heads with a smile, though some gave her a stony look, and others refused to touch her. 'Some of the older ones think we're cursed,' Leila said. 'Cursed with skin the colour of a pig's; they think we're tainted, touched by the Devil. But you have blue eyes, and that's a lucky colour. Maybe that'll save you in the end.' She did not explain what she meant by this.

They found the braid-maker at the back of her little stall near the heart of the medina, hunched over her tatting, which was not at all of the quality Cat had expected or been promised. They came away without a deal and without the necessary braid: Cat was not in the best of humours. The stall had been hot and airless, and now she had a headache, so they took a shortcut to the fountain outside the little white *koubba* of one of the local saints, and Cat sat there in the harsh sunlight mopping her face and hands with the end of her wetted veil. She was beginning to feel better when there was a loud cry, and the sound of a whip whistled through the air again and again. In the road ahead a coffle of fettered prisoners was in disarray, with one man on his knees in the dirt and the overseer thrashing at his head and shoulders in a fury.

Cat was so intent on the fallen man that it was several moments before she noticed the captive next to him. She screwed her eyes against the sun. *It could not be . . .*

She leaped to her feet, headache forgotten, but now a crowd had gathered to watch the fallen Christian being beaten, and it was hard to confirm what she thought she had seen. Cat launched herself into the crowd, pushing and shoving with the rest, until someone grabbed her arm and dragged her back.

'What do you think you are doing?'

She had always thought that Leila accompanied her as a translator and guide, but now she realized she had been naive: the Dutchwoman was there as her guard.

Cat fought her arm free. 'I know that man – the tall one, there –'

But now the overseer had the fallen man on his feet again, and the string of captives was on the move once more, offering Cat a glimpse of backs striped with weals and ribs showing through the skin like those of starved donkeys. Then they were gone. She stood there with her hands to her mouth as the crowd dispersed. She must be going mad. She had thought – just for a moment – that she had seen her cousin. But that was impossible, for Robert Bolitho was two thousand miles away in Cornwall.

But what if, a small voice insinuated, *what if the corsairs made another raid?* She said as much to Leila, who laughed. 'No one puts out of Salé at this time of the year: strong winds blow in and make it impossible to re-enter the port. There'll be no more raids till May.'

Even so, Cat could not forget the image of the man who stood just like her cousin stood, with his head held just so, his wide shoulders half a foot higher than those of other men. Although she had not properly seen his face, she grew increasingly convinced of what she had seen. The image of Rob shackled and beaten haunted her nights and her days.

A week later, when the raïs came to the house again, Cat sought him out. 'Might I speak with you?' she asked, keeping her gaze on the floor.

He led her into the salon, and she told him what she had seen in the souk. When he said nothing, she had the sudden impression that he already knew what she was going to say. She looked up to find that his lips were pressed to a hard, flat line, and his eyes were like flint. He looked once more like the man who had ordered a cross branded into Preacher Truran's foot.

'I just wondered if you could find out for me,' she went on quickly before her courage deserted her, 'if there is a captive by the name of Robert Bolitho among the English slaves.'

He was very still. At last he said slowly, 'Why should I do this thing? What is he to you?'

'He is my cousin,' Cat said firmly.

The Sidi Qasem leaned back against the wall, his eyes as slitted as a drowsing cat's. Then he waved his hand, dismissive. 'I do not meddle in affairs of others.' He reached down, took up his chicha pipe, and made a great to-do of cleaning and filling and lighting it.

'Please,' Cat said again. Her heart beat so hard she could hardly get the word out.

He would not even look at her, so at last she turned and left.

Several days passed in a haze of work and chatter, and the raïs did not return. Orders came, brought by one of his slaves from the house on the other side of the river. Cat had the sense the raïs was avoiding her, and was curt with the boy, sending him away again without refreshment. There was a handsome sleeveless tunic to be embellished from neck to floor, a once-gorgeous bed hanging in need of refurbishment and a commission for a wedding veil with instructions that only the finest lawn and silk be used for the purpose. Was it for his cousin Khadija, Cat wondered, and had to fight the memory of Leila's words away.

She set three of her best students to the tunic, gave the bed hanging to Habiba, Latifa and Yasmina, and took the veil herself. Leila went to the souk to seek out a length of soft white lawn, while Cat sat with Hasna and two of the older women and made sketches for the design. 'Pomegranates,' suggested Hasna, her eyes shining. 'Imagine, the gold and red against the white!'

But the widow Latifa clucked her tongue. 'Pomegranates are for the first child: everyone knows that! Do you want the bride to go to her wedding covered in shame?'

Hasna blushed, but everyone laughed uproariously; and it was at that moment that the Sidi Qasem chose to enter the room, followed by another man. Cat had her back to the door, so it was only the sudden hush that fell and the way the women covered themselves with their veils that alerted her to the presence of visitors. She drew her own veil across her face and turned.

Robert Bolitho stared at the scene before him: a dozen native women in the midst of some kind of sewing circle, all with their veils drawn up so that only their shining midnight eyes were visible. Except for one, whose pale hand dropped away to reveal the face he had beheld in his dreams, the face which had compelled him across an ocean, the face he had conjured in his imagination to give himself the strength to survive the travails which had since befallen him. It was *her* face; and yet it was not. Those were her eyes, a pale and startling blue, but they were not the eyes of the girl he had left outside the church in Penzance all those months ago. It was not just the exotic black cosmetic outlining them which made her a stranger to him, but something deeper and more disturbing in their expression. All at once he was more afraid than he had ever been in his life.

Cat gazed at the ragged, bony figure which towered over the Sidi Qasem. The man's face was gaunt and burned brown, his cheeks fallen in on themselves, his nose oddly crooked and his shock of yellow hair gone, leaving only a rough growth like the stubble of a wheatfield once the crop had been taken in. But his eyes were the same cornflower-blue they had always been, wide and guileless, the eyes of the boy around whom she had run such wicked circles in Cornwall.

'Rob, oh, Rob – what have they done to you?' She got to her feet. 'Did they take you too?'

He laughed then, bitterly. 'Aye, you might say that, though it did not happen as you would imagine, for I was taken not there but here. I even raised a bit of money for your redemption – Mistress Harris gave me some, and the Countess bought your altar cloth, I am sorry to have given it to her, Cat, and it unfinished and all, but it was all I could think to do – but they took the money from me, and the ring too –' His voice was cracked from lack of use.

The raïs cut in. 'He speak true, Cat'rin. He made his way here on English ship to bargain for you, but was himself betrayed. The English are a faithless race.' His voice was harsh, toneless, the voice of a man holding his emotions hard in check. He paused, looking between the two of them. 'I found him in slave pens, but he is slave

346

no longer. I have bought him his freedom, and I now make you gift of your own. You are slave – my slave – no more but free, free to leave with him if you wish. You must make choice.'

Cat felt his gaze burning into her, but she could not look at him. It was all too much, too strange. She felt dizzy, displaced, as if she had suddenly been lifted out of herself and was staring down at the tableau from some other part of the room. The great corsair captain, so cruel and confident, reduced to tense silence; the raw-boned Englishman twisting his hands in that old, familiar way; the girl she had once been so cunningly disguised, outlandish in her foreign kaftan and kohl – all three bound together by fate's invisible web.

She was no longer herself, no longer standing in the embroidery workroom, in this merchant's house, in this fortress town, in this foreign country.

The Tree of Knowledge reared up before her then, its roots buried deep in the earth, its vast trunk blocking out the light, its boughs stretching to the heavens, where a crescent moon hung in its branches and constellations wheeled in stately harmony. She could not see them, but she knew that Adam and Eve and the serpent were now part of this tableau, faceless, timeless and infinitely mutable. She felt their presence, enormous and catastrophic, inside her and at the same time beyond her. She sensed in flashes flesh and blood and bark, heat and cold, the vast and the massive, the smooth and the sinuous, and soon she could not tell where she ended and the other began. Was she Eve, or Adam, or the serpent, or the tree? She felt knowledge rising in her like a sap, a great rush of blood that set her heart thudding and her head pounding, and then she crashed to the floor, and the roar of noise inside her was abruptly stilled.

It was the corsair who moved first. He cried out in Arabic, a great oath or exclamation, then bore Cat's prone body up and away. Habiba and Hasna went pattering in his wake, leaving Rob in a sea of babbling women who snatched glances at him with their foreign eyes and laughed behind their veils. He looked away from them. On the floor where it had fallen lay an object he recognized. He bent and picked it up, remembering as he did so how it had felt in his hands the last time he had held it, just before he had given it to Cat on her birthday last year.

He turned to the frontispiece and there, sure as life, was his inscription: *For my cozen Cat, 27th Maie 1625.* Less than a year. It felt as if a century had passed since then. Tears pricked his eyes like hot needles. It must mean something that she had kept it with her through everything that had happened. He turned its pages, amazed to find Cat's writing everywhere, and far neater and smaller than he would ever have expected from his headstrong, difficult cousin. He mused over the diagrams and sketches, turning the book this way and that, and here and there a phrase caught his eye, his name leaping out at him: *Rob has made mee sware to say nothyng of Pyrats . . . trappd for ever here at Kenegy . . .* He skimmed further and found *wed to my dull cozen Robert living in a hovel behynd the cow-sheds, large with childe year after year, rasyng a pack of brattes & dying in obscuritee. I must away from heere . . .* She could not mean it . . . He began to sweat. *My mother ailes, & there is no thyng I can do for her. We have no comforte of light or clene aire . . .* This at least seemed like more familiar ground, similar to his own experiences. He wondered if Jane Tregenna had survived, but found no other reference to her fate in the vicinity of the first quote. Then he came upon: *How I wishe I had took old Annie Badcock's advyse & gone home with Rob to Kenegy . . .* At this his breathing slowed a little. It would be all right after all. Seeking for further reassurance, he flicked back a little, until he came upon: *I lye here in the pyrat captaines cabin . . .*

He shut the book with a snap and stowed it inside his shirt. *No one must see this,* he thought, wild with horror. *When I take her from here we will burn it, or throw it overboard the ship, and we will never speak of it again once we are married.* He strode to the door, thrusting Latifa out of his way as she chattered at him.

'Drink this.'

Cool water touched her mouth. Her eyes fluttered open. There was a face very close to her, features blurred with proximity, but a dark face with eyes as black as coals. Gentle fingers brushed her forehead, patted her cheeks.

'Cat'rin, Cat'rin, come back to me.'

Where had she been? Where was she going? Strange images crowded inside her head, images of a ship at sea bound for a green land, her cousin Rob at the helm. Taking her away . . .

She struggled to sit up, catching at the hand which touched her face, her fingers closing on it galvanically. 'Don't make me go. I don't want to go.' She sounded like her six-year-old self, plaintive and whining, pleading not to be made to visit her aunt and uncle. She did not like the sound of her own voice.

The hand gripped her tight. Someone kissed her fingers.

'Oh.' She turned her head towards the source of the kiss and, before she could form the least rational thought, returned it, lip to lip.

The kiss that followed was not at all like the one that had been forced upon her by Sir John Killigrew, all whiskers and tongue and the stink of tobacco and beer. This kiss tasted of herbs and mint, and she did not want it to stop.

Eventually the raïs pulled away, holding her at arm's length. 'What you saying, Cat'rin? Are you in right mind, or wandering still?'

Back in focus now, he looked anxious. Cat folded her hands in her lap and looked down at them for a while, considering. Silence hung between them like a veil. Thoughts came thick and fast now. She had never willingly kissed a man in all her life. She had not expected it to feel so momentous: it felt as though her skin – her *whole* skin – was alive with his touch. At last, forcing herself to concentrate, she said, 'And I am no longer your slave?'

'I have freed you, you are own woman, and you must make own choice.' He paused. 'In truth, I think I now *your* slave,' he added softly.

She looked down again, trying to suppress a smile. Then she stilled. 'If I stay, must I convert to Islam?'

'If you be my wife, Cat'rin, yes. But you may stay as free woman and live under my roof and continue your work, make own money and I never touch you, if you prefer.'

'You would make me your wife?'

Qasem nodded. 'With all my heart.'

'Your only wife?'

'One is quite sufficient.'

'I thought you were going to marry your cousin Khadija.'

He laughed. 'I think that a story begun by Khadija herself.' He pressed her hand against his chest so that she felt the deep, strong pulse that beat there. 'Will you wed me, Cat'rin Tregenna?'

Her eyes went wide. If she did, she must take his faith and be damned for all time according to the tenets of her own religion; she would become apostate, heretic, infidel. The choice felt unreal. She did not even know if she was a Christian still in her heart, for she had lost something on the voyage and later in the slave pens. She knew that in order to make a considered decision she should take all that had been given to her this day – Rob, her freedom, the heart and hand of this foreign man, a future as a master embroiderer – and spend a long day and night deliberating over the great choice before her.

She knew she should, but she could not: too much thought would drive her mad. She took a deep breath and said, very fast, before the words failed her: 'I will stay here and wed you, Qasem.'

It was at this moment that Robert Bolitho walked into the courtyard. He missed hearing Catherine's words, but the attitude of the two figures kneeling together beside the fountain was unmistakable: he felt himself intruding upon an intimacy he could not bear to witness. The dull pain that spread through him rooted him to the ground; by the time he spoke it seemed the entire world had changed shape.

'Catherine!'

He watched his cousin start away from the corsair captain and turn towards him, and he saw that her eyes were stark and her cheeks flaming, so that she looked like the fallen woman she had become.

'Catherine – let me save you, come home with me. You are not bound to him, whatever he may say.'

Now she was on her feet and the veil had fallen from her hair, which billowed about her like a fire. 'I do not need to be saved, Robert Bolitho. I make my choice freely – so when you return to Kenegie you can tell them all that I *chose* to remain here of my own free will, and for many good reasons that you would never understand.'

'Oh, I understand well enough,' he said bitterly. When he next spoke his voice was loud and uncouth as Cat had never heard it before. 'I do not know whether I shall see Kenegie again, or, if I do, whether I will find I still have a job when I get there. I left without Sir Arthur's permission and took the first passage that was offered me, knowing even as I did it was with rogues who might simply rob me and cast my nameless body overboard into the deeps. They might as well have, for all the good surviving has done me! And with me I brought my grandmother's ring. I told myself that when next I saw you I would place it on your finger, as a promise that no danger would ever befall you again, but' – his voice broke – 'they robbed me of that, just as surely as they robbed me of the money and my freedom. Cat, I have loved you all my life, and I know you love me too. I do not care that you are ruined, I will take you as you are. I will wed you and still cherish you; and if a child comes and it is dark of skin and eye, then it will be our cross and we will bear it. You see, I have thought of everything, and I say it out: I have no pride left to me. No matter what he has done to you, no matter what has happened, I forgive you.'

Cat's hands balled into fists. 'How dare you offer me a charity wedding, Robert Bolitho? I do not need your forgiveness – for anything! I have done nothing that I need be ashamed of. You look at me as if I have betrayed you, but I have never loved you – save as my dear cousin. It is hard to tell you this in such bitter circumstances, Rob, but it is best you know.'

Silence fell between them, heavy with misunderstanding and recrimination. At last, Rob cried, 'How can you stand there without your heart breaking to see me thus? You are as brazen as the temptress Nell called you; and now you have beguiled a richer man than me, and a heathen, to boot. You have lost your mind, Catherine Anne Tregenna, as well as your soul!'

At this the corsair captain sprang to his feet.

'Qasem, no.'

The way she laid a hand on the corsair's arm, and the way the other looked at her and then gave way, was too much for Rob. The anger that had buoyed him up now ebbed away, leaving him unmanned. A great sob welled up and broke from him in a sort of strangled bellow.

Eyes welling, Cat addressed him gently. 'I can see that you think me cruel and heartless, Rob. I know what you have done for me, the enormity of it, the risk, the horror. I am so sorry for what has happened to you. I would never have asked that you come after me. It was immensely brave of you . . .'

He waved a hand at her: he did not want her sympathy.

'It does not matter, I did not do it just for you, there are others to be saved.' A patent lie, the first large falsehood he had deliberately told in his life. 'I hope you will make a good life for yourself here, Catherine,' he said – and that was the second. He watched her face change. Was it surprise he read there, relief or disappointment? She looked nothing at all like the girl he had crossed an ocean to find. That girl was dead to him now. He dragged his gaze from her and fixed it on the man instead.

'Sidi Qasem, I would ask a boon of you.'

'Ask.'

'There is another I would save, if it can be contrived. The gold the Sidi Mohammed took from me should surely cover her ransom.'

The corsair looked surprised. 'Who you wish me to seek?'

'Her name is Matty Pengelly, taken in the same raid on Penzance. She is a simple, decent girl who deserves better than to be a slave in this place.'

Sidi Qasem inclined his head. 'If is possible to do this thing for you, I do it. You have my word. I will also find you place on ship bound for England and write letter that ensure your safety if you have misfortune to fall into hands of other . . . traders. Is anything else you would ask of me?'

It was as if the corsair was glowing from within, Rob thought, as if a sun burned inside him, his triumph was that tangible. He turned away, for it hurt to look upon the man who had taken his dreams from him. 'No,' he said dully. 'There is nothing left in the world worth asking for.'

32

And soe I took you Matty to wyf. A fine wyf you have beene to mee all these yeares, & a fine mother to oure boys. But I have not beene the best husbande to you. I have strayed & beene wyld & angry & fulle of sorrowes that I have too oft tryed to drowne. For alle that I am sorry. Most of all, I am sorry that I did not see the course my life would take in time for me to follow the path alone, rather than dragging you down it with me. Nowe you have a chance to make a new future for yourself. Leave Kenegy. It is a stifling place, full of despair & failure. Get out while you can: save yourself. Finde someone else & do not tie yourself to the lead weight of my life, or my death.

Go, if not with my love, then with my care.

Your erring husbande
Robert Bolitho

Idriss stared from the letter to me. 'Such a sad end to a brave tale.'

We were sitting overlooking the wide mouth of the Bou Regreg in the Café Maure in the Kasbah des Oudaias, where the sun fell brightly through the fretted trellis-work and a breeze off the sea carried the scent of roses to us. I had been watching a small tabby cat chasing a leaf in between the table legs while Idriss read the letter for himself, for I could not bring myself to read it out to him. It felt laden with ill-luck, and I had the sense that if I were to utter Robert Bolitho's final words aloud, disaster would somehow fall on one or both of us.

'Do you believe in ghosts, Idriss?' I asked suddenly.

'Of course. Afrits and evil spirits walk beside us. We don't like to talk about them, it encourages them too much.'

I told him about Andrew Hoskin, about the miasma of despair that had settled itself upon the house, the sense of panic that had engulfed me in the attic, when I had retrieved the family bible for Alison. The family bible in which Robert Bolitho's letters had been hidden.

Then I remembered how I had found that bible: in a box under layers of dust, a box that had clearly not been opened for a very long time. How then, I wondered, had the wording of Andrew's suicide note – Andrew whose sensibility was in no way bookish or archaic – so clearly echoed that of Robert Bolitho? I shuddered, feeling the chill fingers of time on the back of my neck.

'Khamsa oukhmiss.' Idriss touched the wood of the table. What a remarkably universal prophylaxis against bad things that was.

'I am glad I let Anna take the book. I'm beginning to think the story cursed, as if history will just go on trapping people in its toils and squeezing the life out of them. Tregennas, Pengellys, Bolithos – all my Cornish family seem to be caught up in it.'

'Habibi,' he said, taking my hand, 'there are a thousand and one reasons why people take their own lives, just as there are a thousand and one types of people in the world. Patterns may repeat themselves, but we are not entirely fate's slaves. In our culture we believe that every soul is asked of it only what is within its scope to deal with in life.'

'That obviously didn't work for poor Robert Bolitho, or for Andrew either. Such anger, such disappointment.' I sat there with my head in my hands feeling sorrow for them both. After a while I said, 'Do you think the sins of our ancestors are visited upon us?'

Idriss turned my hand over in his and traced the lines on its palm. 'In Islam there is no such thing as original sin. Each soul comes bright and pure to the world, bearing no burden of guilt. There was a Fall, but it was forgiven. Adam and Hawa were sent down from Heaven to the earthly paradise of Jenaa to be its guardians, and it was there that Satan tempted them to taste the forbidden fruit of the Tree; but in the Qur'an the two of them together shared the blame; and when they repented for their transgression, God forgave them both and sent them out into the world as equals, to work the land. Their children carried with them no taint of the parents' failure; no one died to save our souls. The past is past. Things happen, we suffer, and then we move on into the light.'

I blew my nose. 'That's a remarkably humane view.'

'Guilt and blame are corrosive, Julia; they destroy lives. I am sure that it is possible to make fresh starts, to find happiness. I know it to be so.'

That afternoon we left the old city behind us and walked in the wide, sunlit modern boulevards of new Rabat. We visited book stores and cafés and at last a clothes shop, full of vibrantly coloured scarves and kaftans.

'You should have something to take back to London with you,' Idriss said. 'To remind you of Morocco.'

I touched one of the scarves. It was woven silk, all blues and greens and golds, like a summer sea. 'Very pretty,' I said appreciatively.

He held it up against me. 'Very.'

It was ridiculously cheap, but even so Idriss spent a long time haggling furiously with the poor woman who owned the shop until they both looked exhausted. At last, she wrapped it in paper and held it out to me, and I paid, and thanked her and turned to leave.

Idriss caught my arm. 'No, no: there is something else.' He exchanged a smile with the woman behind the counter: they looked wickedly complicit.

'What?' I asked, frowning.

'Imane will show you.'

The woman ushered me into a curtained area at the back of the shop and left me stranded there with the fluorescent light shining down on me in front of a vast, unforgiving mirror. In it I looked washed out and ghostly, my skin and hair white-pale, my eyes as dark as pits. It was a relief to have something else to look at when she returned a minute later with a bundle of turquoise fabric in her arms.

She shook it out. It was a silk kaftan in traditional style, floor length and with long, wide sleeves. Buttons ran from neck to hem, each worked into a perfect Turkish knot which fitted into a corresponding chain-stitched loop. The facings on either side were hand-embroidered with crescent moons and stars in gold and silver thread; more stars and moons adorned the cuffs and hem.

I gasped. 'It's beautiful. *Fabuleuse.*'

Imane smiled and helped me into it. Then we stood there together, admiring the transformation in the mirror.

'*Ça vous vraiment convient, madame. C'est votre couleur. Allez montrer votre mari!*'

'He's not –' I started. But really, what was the point of making a complicated and clumsy explanation? I grinned. 'OK.'

Idriss was standing by the door, looking very much like a man who wanted a cigarette. When he heard the curtain rings rattling, he turned, and his eyes widened.

He had, it transpired, already paid for it; hence the haggling.

'I want you to wear it and think of Morocco.'

'How could I ever forget Morocco?'

It was a generous gesture, and it made me uncomfortable: I didn't know what to say to him. There was already something unspoken in the air between us, an edge of tension that clouded our afternoon. I was flying back to London the next evening. In some ways I did not want to go – but I also needed space to myself, to weigh up my choices and make some decisions.

We walked through some pretty ornamental gardens where men played chess at little tables outside a café and children played on the pavement beside them, some complicated game involving bottle tops and stones. I watched the café owner come out and put down a bowl, and three rangy cats immediately detached themselves from the shade in which they had been lying and ringed the dish, making a swift end to the scraps of chicken with silent, focused greed.

'It is said the Prophet once sat in contemplation in his garden,' Idriss told me, while we watched them eat, 'but when it came time for him to leave to attend his prayers, he found his cat Muezza had fallen asleep on his sleeve. Now this was the very cat that had once saved him from a serpent, so, instead of disturbing it, he cut off the sleeve of his garment and went about his business.'

I smiled, watching the three cats finish licking out the bowl and wander away, tails high. It was a very charming tale. How nice to be a cat and confident that the world would always provide.

At that moment Idriss's mobile sounded. He opened it and spoke loudly into it, laughing and gleeful. When he finished, his eyes were shining. 'Jeddah is back from the mountains. She is waiting to meet you.'

I don't know what I expected Idriss's grandmother to be like, but when I first saw her standing there in the salon I thought she was some other visitor to the family home. But Idriss told me proudly, 'This is Lalla Mariam,' and then exchanged an embrace with her and a great rush of Berber in which I heard 'Julia' twice, isolated like islands in a sea of incomprehensible sound.

The next thing I knew I was enfolded in her arms. No frail old lady, this, I thought, feeling corded muscle and strong bones press against me. She bade me welcome – *marhaban, marhaban* – and there followed a torrent of Berber of which I understood not a word. Then she flew off across the room, and I heard her footsteps on the tiling of the stairs clatter as swiftly and as surely as the hooves of a mountain goat.

I stared at Idriss. 'She's a force of nature, your grandmother! How old is she?'

He shrugged. 'No one knows, it's not something we speak of much; and they didn't have birth certificates or documentation where she was born. Even Jeddah probably has no idea how old she is. We don't count away our days the way you Westerners do.'

'How old is your mother, then? She is your mother's mother?' I persisted.

He nodded; but he had to think about that for a while too. While I waited, I thought what a very different culture this was to mine, in which every newspaper article would identify the age of its subject alongside the name no matter how irrelevant such a detail might be.

'I . . . think, sixty-three.'

'And how many brothers and sisters does your mother have?'

He counted them off on his fingers. 'Twelve. Malika was the seventh.'

I made a rough calculation. I had read that women in the mountain regions often married very young, but even given that and any possible gaps between births that made her . . . 'Good grief. Eighty-five, at least!'

'She's remarkable, isn't she? Come upstairs – she's brought the thing I wanted you to see.' He held his hand out to me and together we went up the stairs.

At the top of the house, on the other side of the stairs from Idriss's room, the door was ajar, and inside someone was singing. I stopped on the landing to listen, not wanting to interrupt. A moment later Idriss joined in without any hint of self-consciousness, surprising me by raising a melodious light tenor as a counterpoint to the old woman's shriller notes. I thought of the birds we had heard in the medina, singing across the ancient walls to one another.

'Tell me the words,' I begged when he finished.

> 'God divided beauty and gave it to the ten:
> Henna, soap and silk – those are the first three.
> The plough, the livestock and the hives of bees –
> That makes six.
> The sun when it rises over the mountains –
> That makes seven.
> The crescent moon, as thin as a Christian's blade –
> That makes eight.
> With horses and with books we come to ten.'

He raised my hand to his lips. 'You shall be loaded up with beauty before leaving us for your grey old city,' he promised, pushing the door open. 'You have your silk, Jeddah has brought argan soap from the south, and my cousin Hasna will henna your hands for you later.'

I hardly heard what he was saying. The light from the unshuttered window fell upon Lalla Mariam, who stood there, straight as a reed, examining a length of shining cloth. But it was not the item in her hands which caught my attention, but her face as she looked out at me. Downstairs in the semi-gloom of the salon I had formed an impression of a stately old woman with silver hair framing long bones and smooth, dark planes. Now the sun fell squarely upon her, and I caught my breath.

'Yes, it's beautiful, isn't it?' Idriss was saying. 'I knew you'd love it, it's so craftily made. Jeddah is very proud of it, she loves to show it off to people.'

I tore my gaze from his grandmother's face and looked down at the thing she had brought from the mountains. It was a great swathe of brocaded white silk, and along all its yards of selvedge, both top and bottom, someone had embroidered the most exquisite design. Hundreds of ferns and stylized curls of bracken fronds uncoiling towards an unseen sun, adorned here and there by tiny pink blossoms and rich golden flowers. The ferns and fronds were orderly, almost geometric in the exactitude of their execution: they formed a framework through which the rambling roses twined. But it was the tiny golden flowers on their spiky stems which made my knees go to water.

'It's gorse,' I said, remembering the crown Robert Bolitho had made for the girl he had loved. The buds and blossoms were embroidered with such unusual realism that I could almost smell their rich confectionery aroma – like warm marzipan – unfurling from the cloth.

'Gorse?'

'This flower here. It grows all over the hills and cliffs of Cornwall. It's a wild and thorny thing: a very unlikely flower to find depicted in embroidery.'

Idriss translated this for his grandmother, who through it all stood there calmly watching me with her unblinking bright regard. Then she started to speak quickly and Idriss answered her, then asked a question, to which she responded, and then the flow of words went back and forth like the chatter of magpies.

At last he turned to me. 'Jeddah says three things. First, that this flower – this bush – is also found here on the Atlantic coast. Secondly that this veil – it's a bridal veil – has been in the family for generations, but no one knows where it came from or who made it, though there have always been handy women in our family, expert with a needle. Thirdly: that the style of the piece is known as *aleuj*. It is a mélange of traditional Berber skills – very dense and precise and geometric – with a more fluid and realistic European style. *Aleuj* in classical Arabic means "alien" or "foreign", or even "foreigner": but it can also mean "one who has converted to Islam". And the earliest known examples are from the seventeenth century.'

The old woman added something very distinctly then, repeating it three times so that Idriss understood.

'She says that here in Rabat there was once a woman who was a master embroiderer, and she was known as Zahrat Chamal.'

I looked at him blankly.

'It's a given name, not a born name,' he said. 'It means Flower from the North.'

Had Catherine become Zahrat when she converted and married her raïs? Did 'Chamal' mean from the north of Morocco or from further beyond? Was Zahrat Chamal the Muslim name she had adopted when she changed her faith, like Will Martin becoming Ashab Ibrahim? Perhaps the gypsy fortune-teller had told true, that she would never be married as Catherine, after all. I looked at the stitching on the bridal veil: fine and precise, a delicate slanting satin stitch, just like the one on the Countess of Salisbury's altar frontal. Not that that was any proof: everyone used satin stitch, even me. I pictured Cat wound from head to toe in this lovely veil, like the women in the pictures I had seen, with a silver Berber crown set on her head, its jewelled teardrops framing her pale face, her fiery hair hidden beneath a coloured scarf, her blue eyes blazing proudly out at a man clad from head to foot in scarlet and gold. And I saw him take her by the hand and lead her to the throne beneath the spectacular bridal curtains the women of the embroidery class had

361

made as their gift to Sidi Qasem bin Hamed bin Moussa Dib and his foreign wife.

And when I looked back at Lalla Mariam I found that she, like me, had tears glittering in her blue eyes.

33

Alison turned my hands over in hers, the better to examine my palms. 'And this?' she asked.

'A rose, I think – an old variety, like a rambling rose – one of the flat-petalled roses. But the plant on the left hand – I don't know what it is.'

She traced the pattern of leaves like a chain of hearts that ran from the palm to the tip of my forefinger. 'So pretty. And what about this – did you buy it in Rabat?' She touched the antique ring I wore on the third finger of my right hand, where Idriss had placed it when he said goodbye to me outside the airport. 'It belongs to Jeddah,' he had told me solemnly. 'She says it's a loan, and she wanted me to give it to you because it will bring you back to Morocco.' Then he closed my fingers over it and kissed me gravely and thoroughly, hidden from prying official eyes by the sun curtains of his taxi. My knees had still felt weak by the time I reached the security gate. Since then we had spoken every night on the phone, so that a holiday romance had turned into a charming and old-fashioned courtship. In that time we had discussed everything from French poetry to the failings of our respective national football teams, and now I felt I knew more about him than I had ever known about Michael.

'How long will it last?'

I looked up, startled. 'Pardon?'

'The tattoo, dope: how long will it last?'

Already the henna had faded and was no longer the fiery burnt orange that had surprised me when the dried paste came away under the shower on the morning of my departure. Now it was the same shade of brown as my freckles, and, like them, it felt a part of me. I did not want it to fade. 'Idriss said about a month.'

'He's marked you as his property, this Idriss,' she teased.

'He has not! It's traditional: women wear henna tattoos as a form of protection against evil influences,' I said hotly, and at that we both fell silent.

I had returned from Morocco two weeks before, and the time had passed in a whirl of activity. There were three offers on my flat waiting for me as well as a new and potentially lucrative commission. The neatness and speed with which all this came together had rather astonished me: as if fate were pushing me in a specific direction. And I had spent a lot of time with Anna. Together we had visited her friend in the Publications Department at the V&A – an elegantly turned-out and smartly spoken woman in her late fifties, who in turn had taken us to meet someone in English Textiles. Seeing their unalloyed delight at Cat's work and their gasps of excitement as they viewed the sketches she had made in *The Needle-Woman's Glorie* was almost reward enough in itself. They asked – of course – whether they might have the book to display alongside the altar frontal, and I told them honestly that I had not yet decided what I was going to do with it. Their faces fell, but soon they were discussing how to make fine facsimile copies and perhaps having the book on loan for a time, and we all parted in good spirits.

Anna looked radiant, and I told her so. 'I am just so very happy to be able to do this for the family and, well, posterity, if that doesn't sound too pompous.' I assured her it did not. 'And, thank God, I've stopped throwing up, and I'm past the dangerous stage, and the scan was normal.'

'Boy or girl?'

'I didn't ask. Better not to second-guess fate, I think. I am learning to take life as it comes.'

I smiled. Anna was changing. Perhaps we all were.

★

'Ready?' said Alison, breaking into my thoughts.

'As ready as I'll ever be.' I picked up a small flat stone from where I had been sitting and sent it skimming out across the sea towards St Clement's Island. It touched the surface six times before sinking beneath the waves. 'Damn,' I said. 'I was aiming for seven.'

'Six for gold,' Alison laughed. 'I don't think that's too bad.'

'What, like the magpie verse?'

'It's what we always used to say. Though there's a different version Andrew used to quote, which came from the Scottish side of his family: one for sorrow, two for mirth, three for a wedding, four for a birth, five for Heaven, six for Hell, seven you'll see the De'ill himsell . . . Oh, dear.'

'Oh, great: Hell,' I said, subdued. 'Perhaps this isn't a very good idea.'

'Well, you certainly don't have to do it for me,' Alison said firmly. 'I'm never setting foot in the place again. Those letters freaked me out completely. Are you quite sure you want to do this?'

'I have to. I feel . . . responsible, somehow, though I know that sounds mad.'

Fifteen minutes later we were standing outside the farmhouse at Kenegie just as the sun was starting to go down.

'Have you got everything?'

I had: torch, lighter, candle, bread, salt, water. And Robert Bolitho's letters, tied with a band of fine embroidery Lalla Mariam had given to me. The letters were the originals: when I had explained to Anna what I intended to do, she had laughed at me, but waived her deal. 'Keep copies for me – good ones,' she made me promise. 'It'll only annoy Michael all the more.' The piece of embroidery was surely by the same hand as the bridal veil: it bore Catherine's trademark theme. 'It was something she would have used to tie back her hair at the hammam,' the old lady had explained to me via Idriss. In poor exchange for this generosity, I had given her my own peacock-feathered embroidered headsquare, and had promised to complete the fourth corner for her with whatever motif she chose for it.

Leaving Alison sitting on the bonnet of the car, I went into the house, my footsteps echoing through the empty rooms. I switched on every light switch as I went up. At the foot of the stairs to the attic, I paused.

Then gritted my teeth and climbed the stairs.

The attic light, absolutely typically, was the only one in the house that did not work. I lit the candle and placed it on Andrew's desk. In its trembling golden circle of light I laid out the bread, a little pile of salt and a flask of holy water from the font at Gulval Church. Heat and water and sustenance: all the things the dead missed, lacked and craved, as my mother used to tell me in her ghost stories on All-Hallows Eve. Then I placed Rob's letters down beside them.

Taking a deep breath, I said, 'Robert Bolitho, if you are here I hope you will hear me. My name is Julia Lovat: you and I may be very distantly related, I don't know. That's probably not very important. What is important is that I've brought your letters back. I'm sorry that you've been disturbed, and I'm sorry we took your letters away. I know you asked in the postscript that Matty burn them, but I'm afraid she didn't. I understand that: women like to hold on to things, even things that are painful to them. It was wrong of her to leave them to be read by others, but you cannot really blame her, or us for reading them. I read your letters, Robert, so I know that you are a decent, brave man. Even so, you should not have done what you did to Andrew Hoskin, and perhaps there were others here too, others I don't know about. Maybe you hurt so much you didn't care who else you caught in your despair. You did a very courageous thing by following your heart and risking your life to try to save Catherine Tregenna –'

Out of nowhere there came a chill draught, and the candle suddenly guttered, sending long, jagged shadows shooting out across the room. I hugged my arms around myself and watched the reflection of the flame play across the etched silver of the ring Idriss had placed on my hand and tried to still the hammering of my pulse.

'There is nothing so painful in the world as love that has been wasted on someone who doesn't love you back. But Catherine's decision to stay in Morocco wasn't just about not wanting to marry you, and it wasn't only for love of the corsair captain either.' I laid my hand on the fragment of embroidery which lay across the letters so that the silver threads of the roses and ferns and gorse, her eternal theme, caught the light. 'Do you see this, Robert? It is very fine work: your cousin had a true gift, a rare gift – see these wild roses, this gorse? Do you remember the crown you made for her? She did. She carried Cornwall in her heart all the time she was there; but if she had stayed here in Cornwall, that gift would have been wasted. In Morocco she became what she had always dreamed of becoming: a master embroiderer. Do you really begrudge her that dream, Rob?'

I paused. 'I don't know why I'm rambling on like this. It's probably pointless. I'm either talking to myself, or you don't care about anything but your own pain. But I wanted to try to say these things: that I understand, a little, at least, and that what you went through must have been terrible. But, Rob, don't you see? You saved Matty Pengelly – dear, lovely Matty – who must have thought herself lost for ever in that strange country. You saved her and you made a life together, you had sons: it is an extraordinary thing that you did, and I am very proud of you.'

I ran out of words and sat there in the darkness, waiting for I don't know what, and feeling a fool. Through the Velux window I could just glimpse a strip of reddening sky: soon it would be full dark.

'I am going to leave now. I've had my say. I just wanted to bring your letters back and pay my respects,' I said softly, and stood up to go.

I am sure – quite sure – that I did not nudge the desk as I rose. But at that moment the candle fell over and rolled – as if pushed, or by the forces of gravity – until it came to rest against the letters, which caught the flame in an instant and went up with a whoosh. I cried out then and dropped the torch. I watched the fire burn deep red, then orange, then a pale bright gold that was almost white. Two thoughts tugged at me: I should save Catherine's embroidery; and that the entire attic, and me in it, was likely to go up in flames. But in the same instant that these thoughts crossed my mind, the fire extinguished itself as quickly as it had caught, and I found myself standing in pitch darkness.

With a shaking hand I bent to search for the torch, expecting at any moment to feel the chill of some unearthly hand on the back of my neck. But nothing happened. Nothing at all. The air was still, and seemed warmer, and at last my fingers closed around the torch and I flicked it on and trained it on the desk, fearing to see the damage that had been done.

The letters were gone, every scrap of them, leaving just a pile of cool, grey ash. In the midst of the ashes Catherine's embroidered band lay gleaming and unburned. I picked it up gingerly, but, despite the metallic threads running through it, it was not even warm. How could that be? My rational mind told me that it was probably a good deal more durable than paper – especially 400-year-old paper – but even so . . . Trembling now, I sprinkled the flask of water around and stood the candle up again. Then I did my mother proud by throwing a pinch of salt over my left shoulder to keep the Devil at bay.

By the time I got back down outside my teeth were chattering and I was shaking with adrenalin. Alison took one look at me, took off her jacket and draped it around my shoulders. 'Job done?' she asked.

'I think so.' I smiled wanly. Who could say?

In the garden, with my cousin's arm around me, I gazed out at the distant sea, striped now by the last dull red streaks of the setting sun. St Michael's Mount stood in stark romantic silhouette in the bay, just as it had that fateful July day in 1625 when – flying their Salé pavilions of crescent moons and crossed bones, Al-Andalusi's fleet had slipped past its inadequate defences.

I closed my eyes, remembering. At last I smiled.

In just under three weeks' time, just as my henna faded to a ghost of itself, I too would be going back to Morocco, the Island in the West.

Inch'allah.

Author's Note

Crossed Bones is a work of fiction, though it is based on historical fact.

Seventeenth- and eighteenth-century Barbary corsair raids on the south coasts of England have been increasingly well documented over the past few years, although when I grew up in Cornwall they were never mentioned, and most people are still ignorant of this particular bloody chapter in England's history. The corsairs of Salé, known in England as the Sallee Rovers, have a particularly fascinating history. Driven by religious fervour, they plundered far and wide to the extent that one corsair fleet was able to raise its skull-and-crossbones flag over Lundy Island in the Bristol Channel in the early summer of 1625, from which they launched innumerable raids on south-west shipping and coastal towns.

The historical document prefacing this novel, that is, the letter from the Mayor of Plymouth to the new King's Privy Council in the spring of 1625, warning of the likelihood not only of corsair raids (which had become a regular summer threat to shipping) but for the first time of attacks on coastal settlements, does not, in the usual bureaucratic fashion, appear to have resulted in raised security.

The attack I have described on the church in Penzance is based on a reference in the state papers to an event in July 1625 when 'sixtie men, women and children were taken from the church of *Munnigesca* in Mounts Bay' (my italics). No one to this day is sure what 'Munnigesca' refers to. Some have speculated that it is the church on St Michael's Mount, but I cannot believe that to be true, since it would have meant that Sir Arthur Harris, who was the Master of the Mount at the time, and his family would have been among those sixty captives, and they never suffered such a fate. Sir Arthur died at home in 1628 at Kenegie Manor; his last will and testament is included in the local parish papers. The only two large-enough settlements likely to generate such a congregation at the time, according to Carew and Leland, would have been Marazion, then known as Market-Jew (a corruption of Marghasewe), or Penzance. I decided on the church at Penzance, which would have stood where St Mary's does today – on a promontory overlooking the bay. It would have been clearly seen from sea, thus presenting an attractive target for attack. It is curious that the Mount did not see and fire upon the corsairs (there is no mention in the CSP of any attempted defence); but Sir Arthur Harris had indeed been lobbying for funds to rearm the Mount for several years.

The smuggling, however, of four cannon destined for the rearmament of Pendennis and St Michael's Mount by Sir John Killigrew to the Sidi al-Ayyachi is my own invention.

I am no great expert on embroidery; however, I have researched the methods and styles of the time as well as I can, and am greatly indebted to the works of Caroline Stone, who knows a great deal more about the embroidery of North Africa, and specifically Morocco, than I ever shall.

It was a great disappointment to me to discover that no records of the captives taken by the Sallee Rovers in 1625 remain in Morocco. A number of first-hand accounts of English captives' misfortunes and experiences have, however, survived; although few from as early as 1625 and none by a woman of that time. I have read many of these accounts and borrowed details here and there for authenticity; though taken with a healthy pinch of salt, since the temptation for captives to embellish their hardships with lurid detail was great, commercial pressures in the seventeenth century being all too similar to those of the twenty-first.

I have listed below some of the key texts that proved invaluable to me in my research. I must also thank a number of individuals, without whom I could never have written this novel. First, my mother, for reminding me of this long-buried family legend; secondly, my climbing partner Bruce Kerry, who accompanied me on my first and crucial research visit to Morocco; thirdly, Emma Coode, friend and colleague, who read the text chapter by chapter as I wrote and provided me with both encouragement and the perfect audience. I must also thank my wonderful agents Danny Baror and Russell Galen for their passionate encouragement, my publishers Venetia Butterfield and Allison McCabe for their invaluable support and suggestions, and Jenny Dean and Donna Poppy for their meticulous help in honing and polishing the text. Finally, and most importantly, I want to thank my husband, Abdellatif Bakrim, who has been the most extraordinary source of Berber, Arabic and Moroccan history, culture and language; he has helped me with the translation of foreign texts and provided me with a sounding board for all the Moroccan material. He was also, before I knew him well, the inspiration for the raïs. Since I have come to know him, I cannot imagine him making a ruthless corsair captain or zealot; and for that I am profoundly grateful.

A Short History of Piracy:
The Barbary Corsairs in Context

I don't pretend to be a historian, and so my research for this novel has had to be rather more thorough than if I were already an expert. I spent over two years researching the historical background to *Crossed Bones* before starting to write the story, and it proved to be a fascinating and eye-opening task. I will attempt to skim a little of the cream off the top of that research here, in order to place the Barbary corsairs in some sort of context, but if you are interested in further detail then please come and visit the *Crossed Bones* website, www.crossedbones.co.uk.

Ever since men took to the sea in ships there has been piracy. Sea robbers menaced the trade routes of ancient Greece more than two thousand years ago. Phoenician traders armed themselves against pirates; Roman ships were robbed of their cargoes of olive oil, wine and grain. The Vikings perfected the art, pillaging both sea lanes and coastal settlements. Piracy flourished throughout the medieval period, as well as throughout the fifteenth and sixteenth centuries, finally peaking in the 'golden age' of the seventeenth and eighteenth centuries. Wherever there were trade routes and goods and gold to be plundered, there were pirates. Buccaneers were the scourge of Spanish shipping in the Caribbean; and privateers were granted letters of marque by their governments, that turned them into official state pirates. The coffers of Queen Elizabeth I were regularly swelled by the predations upon Spanish treasure ships of such privateers as Sir Francis Drake.

However, not all piracy was motivated purely by human greed, either personal or royal. For many, piracy was vindicated by religion, and its practitioners were termed 'corsairs', rather than pirates, a word that etymologically derives from the Italian word *corso*, meaning 'chase', a corsair being 'one who gives chase'. Maltese corsairs were granted licence to attack the ships of the Muslim

Turks by the Christian Knights Templar, the Knights of St John. And, conversely, the Barbary corsairs, operating out of the North African states of Algiers, Tunis, Tripoli and Morocco, were in turn authorized by their rulers to attack the ships of Christian countries, to kill the infidels and render their goods unto Islam. Barbary corsairs, therefore, were seen as religious warriors and defenders of their faith; they were referred to as *al-ghuzat*, which was the term used to denote those who had fought beside the Prophet Mohammad.

The predations of the corsairs operating out of Rabat-Salé, in northern Morocco, were further fuelled by revenge.

The Moors – originally Berbers from Morocco – had occupied Spain since their general, Tariq ibn-Ziyad, conquered the Iberian peninsula in AD 711. Over the centuries they had become concentrated in Granada (leaving behind them such exquisite creations as the Alhambra palace and hundreds of mosques and public baths). But the rising tide of Catholicism in the sixteenth century resulted in a steady exodus of Moors back to their native North Africa, largely as a result of religious persecution. The crux of this pogrom occurred around 1609, when the Catholic King of Spain, Philip III, decided to expel definitively all those of Moorish extraction from Spanish soil, no matter how long they had been established there, no matter whether they had at any stage converted from Islam to Catholicism. The expulsion was both abrupt and violent, involving the worst brutalities of the Spanish Inquisition.

Over one million Moors were expelled, with many fetching up on the bleak northern coast of North Africa and in the ruined city of Rabat, a desolate place previously abandoned on account of 'wild beasts'. Some were now reduced to penury; but some had anticipated the expulsion decrees and managed to smuggle their worldly wealth out of Spain with them. These latter were the Hornacheros – from Hornachos in Estremadura – and they also brought with them a fighting spirit, a ruthless instinct for independence and a determination to re-establish their fortunes and wreak vengeance on those who had insulted and maltreated them.

They refortified the ruined city of Salé (including the beautiful and now-tranquil Kasbah des Oudaias, which bewitched me on my research trips to Rabat), vowing revenge on Christendom, and specifically on Spain. From their new base, they forged alliances with the pirates of Algiers and Tunis, who had been preying on Christian shipping in the Mediterranean for over a century. All manner of brigands and cut-throats – many of them Europeans turned Turk (having expeditiously converted to Islam) – converged upon New Salé to train the Hornacheros and other expelled Moors in the art of piracy. The refugees learned fast, driven by righteous indignation and jihadi fury. In 1617 a Dutch captain wrote 'a year ago the Moors didn't have a single vessel; now they own a quarter of the sea: they will become extremely powerful if we do not take care.' How prescient he was.

The Salé corsairs ranged far and wide, their ambitions limited only by their technology. Galleys and xebecs, the small, shallow-drafted vessels used to raid shipping in the calmer seas of the Mediterranean, soon gave way to the big square-riggers, mastery of which enabled the corsairs to raid along the Atlantic coasts of Spain, Portugal, France and England, and further to Newfoundland, Ireland and Iceland. At first it was only cargoes that were plundered; from 1620 to 1630 Cornwall and Devon lost a fifth of their shipping to corsair attacks. But it was soon realized that the taking of slaves was a far more lucrative option, and during that same period more than a thousand Christians were taken captive. The raid on the church in Mount's Bay, which forms the basis for *Crossed Bones*, was the first recorded attack in which captives were taken from English shores.

From 1627 to 1641 the Salé corsairs had absolute independence, paying neither tithes nor taxes to the Sultan and ploughing all their riches back into what was rapidly becoming a significant business. Their audacity was extraordinary: they established a base of operations on Lundy Island in the Bristol Channel, raising the pirate skull and crossbones over the island and launching raids on the West Country coast. In a single day in 1636 they were to raid two hundred slaves from Plymouth; soon more than three thousand Christian sailors were held in the prisons of Salé. Fewer than a quarter of captives returned home. Many died in transit or in the *mazmorras* or on war-galleys, from disease or other hard treatment. Others turned Turk and stayed to make their fortunes, often adding their expertise to pirate crews.

The European maritime nations had no answer to such rapaciousness: the corsairs were swift, ruthless and expert. The West's attitude to the corsairs, however, could be duplicitous. In public, the predations of the corsairs were loudly deplored, and action was called for in terms that echo modern calls for a war on terror. In private, it was conceded that the larger European powers gained considerable commercial advantage from the corsairs' actions, since the maritime interests of smaller nations were significantly damaged by such attacks. At one time or another England, France and Holland all made treaties with the Barbary states to gain immunity for their own merchant fleets in their waters. It was a shameful period for England in particular, which until this time had boasted of ruling the seas – a period soon to be conveniently forgotten when history books were written.

From such a synopsis one might suppose the North African slave trade to be an especially vicious anomaly; but it is worth remembering that the institution of slavery extends back before recorded history and that most of the world's civilizations had their foundations sunk deep in such human misery. Slavery was well established in Homer's Greece; the Roman Empire thrived on its slave trade; references to slavery appear in the ancient Babylonian Code of Hammurabi; and slave labour was used in Egypt to build temples and pyramids.

Slavery went through a particularly savage revolution in the fifteenth and sixteenth centuries. Explorations of the African coast by Portuguese navigators resulted in the taking of thousands upon thousands of African slaves, and for nearly five centuries the predations of slave raiders along the coasts of Africa generated a lucrative and important business carried out with terrible brutality. Yet it was not in Europe that African slavery was eventually to render up the greatest profit but in the Americas. The British, Dutch, French, Spanish and Portuguese all engaged in this trade. Indeed, British 'heroes' John Hawkins and his cousin Francis Drake made three trips to Guinea and Sierra Leone, enslaving between them 1,200 and 1,400 Africans. Hawkins (later to be knighted following the defeat of the Spanish Armada) made such a huge profit from selling slaves that Queen Elizabeth 1 granted him a special coat of arms bearing the image of a bound African slave.

Which all goes to show that history is a morally murky business. I have tried to be fair-minded in my portrayal of events and characters in *Crossed Bones* and as faithful as I can be to what pass for historical facts; but four hundred years away from those times, who can know where the real truth lies? In the end we are always left with more questions than answers, and in the gaps between knowledge and ignorance lies plenty of space in which a storyteller may weave a lively tale.

Source Material and Further Reading

The Tragicall Life and Death of Muley Abdala Melek, John Harrison (Delph, 1633)

The Crescent and the Rose, Samuel C. Chew (New York, 1937)

Les Corsaires de Salé, Roger Coindreau (Paris, 1948)

The Lands of Barbary, Geoffrey Furlong (London, 1966)

The Barbary Slaves, Stephen Clissold (London, 1977)

The Embroideries of North Africa, Caroline Stone (London, 1985)

Corsari nel Mediterraneo, Salvatore Bono (Milan, 1993)

Nine Parts of Desire, Geraldine Brooks (London, 1994)

The Berbers, Michael Brett and Elizabeth Fentress (Oxford, 1996)

Islam in Britain, Nabil Matar (Cambridge, 1998)

Piracy, Slavery and Redemption, ed. Daniel J. Vitkus, intro. Nabil Matar (New York, 2001)

Captives, Linda Colley (London, 2002)

The Pirate Wars, Peter Earle (London, 2003)

'Ward the Pirate', Abdal-Hakim Murad (internet article, 2003)

Infidels, Andrew Wheatcroft (London, 2003)

White Gold, Giles Milton (London, 2004)

The Sermons of Christopher Love (internet sources)